CAROLE MORTIMER

Masking Her Secrets

Two classic historical stories

CONTENTS

THE DUKE'S
CINDERELLA BRIDE

Chapter One

1816, St Claire House, London

'I have no immediate plans to marry, Hawk. Least of all some chit barely out of the schoolroom that you have deigned to pick out for for me!'

Hawk St Claire, the tenth Duke of Stourbridge, viewed his youngest brother's angrily flushed face across the width of the leather-topped desk that dominated the library in the St Claire townhouse, his mouth twisting slightly as he noted the glitter of rebellion in Sebastian's dark brown gaze. 'I was merely suggesting that it is past time you thought of taking a wife.'

Lord Sebastian St Claire felt the flush deepen in his cheeks under the steely gaze of his eldest brother. But this awareness of Hawk's displeasure in no way lessened his own determination not to be coerced into a marriage he neither sought nor wanted.

Although it was a little difficult to maintain that stand,

Sebastian acknowledged inwardly, in the face of his brother's piercingly intense gaze. A chilling gaze from eyes the colour of gold and ringed by a much darker brown, and one that had been known to almost reduce the Duke's valet to tears on occasion, and to cause lesser peers of the realm to quake in their highly polished boots when Hawk took his place in the House.

'Do not take that insufferably condescending tone with me, Hawk, because it won't wash!' Sebastian threw himself into the carved chair, facing his brother across the desk. 'Or is it only that you have decided to turn your attentions to me because Arabella failed to secure a suitable match during her first Season?' he added slyly, knowing that his eighteen-year-old sibling had stubbornly resisted accepting any of the marriage proposals she had received in the last few months.

He was also completely aware that Hawk had hated his role as occasional escort for their younger sister. It had resulted in the marriage-minded debutantes and their ambitious mamas seeing the unusual occurrence of the Duke of Stourbridge's presence at balls and parties as an open invitation to pursue him!

Until, that was, Hawk had made it known, in his chillingly high-handed manner, that none of those young women met the exacting standards he set for his future Duchess!

Hawk's mouth tightened. 'We were not discussing a match for Arabella.'

'Then perhaps we should have been. Or possibly Lucian?' Sebastian mentioned their brother. 'Although it really should be you, Hawk,' he continued tauntingly. 'After all, you are the Duke, and of the four of us surely the one most in need of an heir?'

At one and thirty, and over six feet tall, his brother Hawk had powerful shoulders and an athletic body that was the pride and joy of his tailor. Today he wore a black jacket which fit snugly across wide shoulders, a pale grey waistcoat and paler grey breeches above highly polished Hessians. His thick dark hair, streaked with gold, was styled with casual elegance, and beneath a wide, intelligent brow were intense golden eyes, the straight slash of a nose between high cheekbones, and a thin, uncompromising mouth above a square jaw. All spoke of his arrogant and determined character.

Even without his title, Hawk was undoubtedly a force to be reckoned with. As the powerful Duke of Stourbridge he was formidable.

Hawk looked completely bored by this particular argument. 'I believe I have made it more than plain these last months that I have yet to meet any woman who is up to the arduous task of becoming the Duchess of Stourbridge. Besides,' he continued, as Sebastian would have argued further, 'I already have two obvious heirs in my younger brothers. Although, going on your more recent behaviour, I would not be happy to see either you or Lucian becoming the next Duke of Stourbridge.' He gave Sebastian a silencing glower.

A glance Sebastian totally ignored. 'If either Lucian or I *were* to become the next Duke of Stourbridge, you can depend on it that you would not be around to see it, Hawk!'

'Very amusing, Sebastian.' The Duke's dismissal was absolute. 'But following the…events of last month, I realise I have been somewhat remiss in not settling your own and Lucian's future.'

'Last month? What did Lucian and I do last month that

was so different from—? Ah.' The light finally dawned. 'Can you possibly be referring to the delectable and recently widowed Countess of Morefield?' he challenged unabashedly.

'A gentleman does not discuss a lady by name, Sebastian.' Hawk eyed his brother disapprovingly. 'But now that you have brought the incident to my attention...' he steepled slender fingers '... I could indeed be referring to your reprehensible behaviour concerning a certain lady of our mutual acquaintance.' His voice was icy.

Sebastian grinned unapologetically. 'I can assure you that no one, least of all the Countess, took our interest seriously.'

Hawk looked down the long length of his nose. 'Nevertheless, the lady's name was bandied about at several clubs—my own included. Many of your friends were making wagers, I believe, on which one of you would be the first to oust the Earl of Whitney from the Coun—from the lady's bedchamber.'

Sebastian looked unrepentant. 'Only because they were all aware that we were both totally in ignorance of the other's interest in the lady. Of course, if you had cared to confide in either of us that *you* intended taking up residence in that particular bedchamber, then Lucian and I would simply have backed off and left you and Whitney to decide the outcome!' He eyed Hawk challengingly.

Hawk's wince was pained. 'Sebastian, I have already had occasion to warn you of the...indelicacy of your conversation!'

'So all this talk of the parson's mousetrap is because Lucian and I inadvertently stepped on your toes last month?' Sebastian could barely restrain his humour. 'Or possibly it was another part of your anatomy we intruded upon? Although I do believe,' he continued, as Hawk looked in danger of delivering another of his icy setdowns, 'that you have also now tired of the lady's…charms…?'

The slight flaring of the Duke's nostrils was the only outward sign of his increasing displeasure with the trend of the conversation. 'After the attention you and Lucian brought to that unfortunate lady I deemed it necessary to withdraw my attentions so as not to add further speculation to the impending scandal.'

'If you were not so damned secretive about your mistresses the whole incident could have been avoided.' Sebastian shrugged dismissively. 'But I do assure you, Hawk, I am not about to marry just to appease your outraged sensibilities!'

'You are being utterly ridiculous, Sebastian—'

'No, Hawk.' Sebastian's humour faded. 'I believe if you were to give this subject more thought, you would realise that *you* are the one who is being ridiculous in trying to choose my wife for me.'

'On the contrary, Sebastian. It is my belief that I am only acting in your best interests. In fact, I have already accepted an invitation on our behalf from Sir Barnaby and Lady Sulby.'

'I take it they are the parents of my intended bride?'

Hawk's mouth tightened. 'Olivia Sulby is the daughter of Sir Barnaby and Lady Sulby, yes.'

Sebastian gave a derisive shake of his head as he stood up. 'I am afraid that whatever invitation you have accepted on my behalf you will just have to unaccept.' He moved to the library door.

'What are you doing?' The Duke frowned at him darkly.

'Leaving.' Sebastian gave him a pitying look. 'But before I go I have a proposition of my own to set before you, Hawk...' He paused in the open doorway.

'A proposition...?' Hawk found himself so deeply disturbed by his brother's stubbornness that—unusually—he could barely hold his temper in check.

Sebastian nodded. 'Once you are married—happily so, of course—I promise I will give serious consideration to the parson's mousetrap for myself!' His step was jaunty as he closed the library door softly behind him.

Hawk sat back heavily in his chair as he contemplated the closed door for several long seconds before reaching for the decanter of brandy that stood on his desktop and pouring a large measure.

Damn.

Damn, damn, *damn*.

He made a point of never attending house parties in the country once the Season had ended and the House had dispersed for the summer. He had only committed himself to spending a week in Norfolk with the Sulbys for the sole purpose of introducing Sebastian to the young woman he had hoped would become his brother's future bride.

His own acquaintance was with Sir Barnaby Sulby—the two of them having dined together at their club several times. There had been no opportunity for Hawk to meet the other gentleman's wife and daughter during the Season, the Sulby family not having received an invitation to the three balls at which Hawk had been Arabella's escort, but Hawk knew from his enquiries that on her father's death Olivia Sulby would inherit Markham Park and its surrounding thousand acres of farmland. As the younger brother of a duke such a match could be considered perfect for Sebastian.

Except Sebastian had now told Hawk—all too succinctly!—that he had no intention of even considering taking a wife until Hawk had done so himself. Leaving Hawk committed to spending a week in Norfolk—a county of flat fenland so totally unlike his own beloved Gloucestershire.

It had all the appeal of a walk to the gallows!

'There you are, Jane. Do stop your dawdling on the stairs, girl.' Lady Gwendoline Sulby, a faded beauty in her mid-forties, glared her impatience as the object of her attention came to a halt neither up nor down the wide staircase. 'No, do not come down. Proceed back up to my bedroom and collect my shawl for me before our guests start to arrive. The silk one with the yellow rosebuds. I do believe the weather might be changing, Sulby.' She turned worriedly to her portly husband as he stood beside her in the spacious hallway in anticipation of the arrival of their guests.

Jane knew that Sir Barnaby was twenty years older than his wife, and he was looking most uncomfortable in his high-necked shirt and tightly tied necktie. His yellow waistcoat stretched almost impossibly across his rounded stomach, and his brown jacket and cream breeches were doing little to hide that strain.

Poor Sir Barnaby, Jane mused as she turned obediently back up the stairs to collect the requested shawl. She knew her guardian would so much rather have been out on the estate somewhere with his manager, wearing comfortable old clothes, than standing in the draughty hallway of Markham Park, awaiting the first dozen or so house guests who would shortly arrive for the start of a week's entertainments and gentile frivolity.

'Bring down my white parasol, too, Jane.' Olivia frowned up at her, a young replica of her mother's earlier beauty, with her fashionably rounded figure, big blue eyes, and golden ringlets arranged enticingly about the dewy beauty of her face.

'Do not shout in that unladylike manner, Olivia.' Lady Gwendoline looked scandalised by her daughter's behaviour. 'Whatever would the Duke think if he were to hear you?' She gave an agitated wave of her fan.

'But *you* shouted, Mama.' Olivia pouted her displeasure at the rebuke.

'I am the mistress of this house. I am allowed to shout.'

Jane smiled slightly as she continued on her way back up the stairs, knowing that the illogical bickering between mother and daughter was likely to continue for several more minutes. The arguments had been constant and sometimes heated during the last week as the household prepared for the arrival of the Sulbys' house guests, and most of them had the phrases 'the Duke' or 'His Grace' in their content.

For the Duke of Stourbridge was to be the Sulby's guest of honour this week—as every member of the overworked household had been constantly made aware, as they cleaned and scrubbed and polished Markham Park in preparation for 'His Grace, the Duke's' arrival.

Not that Jane expected to be included in any of the planned entertainments, or even to meet the illustrious Duke in person. She was only a poor relation. Jane Smith. A distant relation that the Sulbys had taken pity on and charitably offered a home to for the last twelve of her two and twenty years.

Markham Park had seemed rather grand and alien to Jane when Sir Barnaby and Lady Gwendoline had first brought her here, her childhood having been spent in a tiny south coast vicarage, being lovingly cared for by her widowed father and Bessie, his elderly but motherly house-keeper.

But Jane had consoled herself with the fact that at least Markham Park was within walking distance of the sea—allowing her, during the brief times she was able to escape the seemingly ever-watchful gaze of Lady Sulby, to go down to the rugged shoreline and enjoy its wild, untamed beauty.

Jane had quickly discovered that she liked Norfolk winters the best—when the sea would seem to rage and fight against the very restrictions of nature as an inner part of her longed to fight against the ever-increasing social strictures that were placed upon her. For, after she had shared the nursery and schoolroom with Olivia, until she reached the age of sixteen, she had stopped being treated as Olivia's equal and had become more maid and companion to the spoilt and pampered daughter of the house.

Jane paused as she passed the cheval mirror in Lady Sulby's bedroom, studying her reflection critically and knowing as she did so that she was everything that was not fashionable. She was tall, for one thing, with long legs and a slender willowy figure. She wished she could say that her hair was an interesting auburn, but instead it was a bright, gleaming red. And, although her complexion was creamy, she did have that unattractive sprinkling of freckles across the bridge of her tiny nose. Plus, her eyes were green.

None of this was complemented in the least by the gowns Lady Sulby had made up for her. They were always of a pastel shade that did nothing for Jane's vibrant colouring. Her present one, of the palest pink, was so totally unflattering with the red of her hair.

Of course it was very doubtful that Jane would ever meet anyone who would want to marry her. Unless the local vicar took pity on her and made an offer. And as he was a middle-aged widower, with four unruly young children all under the age of eight, Jane did so hope that he would not.

She gave a weary sigh as she collected the requested silk shawl from Lady Sulby's dressing table, noticing as she did so that Lady Sulby's jewellery box had not been returned to its proper place in the top drawer.

But Jane's attention was diverted from the jewellery box as she heard the sound of a carriage outside, travelling down the yew-lined gravel driveway to Markham Park.

The Duke and his brother Lord Sebastian St Claire at last? Or one of the Sulbys' other guests?

Curiosity impelled Jane to move quickly to the window to look outside. A huge, magnificent black carriage, pulled by four of the most beautiful black horses Jane had ever seen, was being driven down the driveway by a black-liveried groom. Two other servants dressed in black perched upon the back, and a ducal crest was visible on the door.

It was indeed the Duke, then.

He did seem to like black, didn't he? Jane mused, even as she gave in to further temptation and gently moved the brocade curtain to one side, the better to be able to see the Duke himself when he stepped down from the carriage.

A groom had hopped nimbly down from the back to hold the door open for him, and for some inexplicable reason Jane's heart seemed to have increased in tempo. In fact it was beating quite erratically, she noted frowningly. Just

in anticipation of the sight of a Duke? Was her life really
so dull?

She gave a rueful smile as she acknowledged that it
would indeed be exciting to at last see the much-talked of
Duke of Stourbridge.

Her breath caught in the slenderness of her throat as first
a booted foot descended onto the lowered step, quickly followed by the ducking of a head as the Duke of Stourbridge
stepped completely out of the carriage and then down onto
the gravel driveway, straightening to take his hat from the
waiting servant before lifting his haughty head to take in
his surroundings.

Goodness, he was tall, was Jane's first breathless realisation. Quickly followed by the acknowledgement that, with
hair the colour of mahogany shot through with streaks of
gold, and those powerfully wide shoulders and athletically
moulded body, he was also the most handsome man she
had ever set eyes on. His features were severe, of course,
as befitted a duke who looked to be in his thirtieth year at
least, but there was such hard male beauty in that austerity
that just to look at him took Jane's breath away.

In fact she did not seem able to stop looking at him.

There was intelligence as well as arrogance in that wide
brow, though the precise colour of his eyes was something
of a mystery as he viewed his surroundings with unmistakable disdain, looking down his nose at the scene before him. The sculptured mouth had narrowed, and dark
brows were rising in haughty surprise as he turned to see
his hostess hurriedly descending the steps towards him,
rather than waiting inside Markham Park for him to be
formally announced.

'Your Grace!' Lady Sulby swept him a low curtsey and

received a haughtily measured inclination of that arrogant head in return. 'Such an honour,' she fluttered. 'I—But where is your brother, Lord St Claire, Your Grace?' Lady Sulby's voice had sharpened to an unbecoming shrill as she realised there was no one else inside the Duke's carriage.

Jane could not discern the Duke's reply—could only hear the deep rumble of his voice as he obviously made his hostess some sort of explanation for his solitary state.

Oh, dear. Everything did not appear to be going to plan. Lady Sulby's plan, that was. And an already thwarted Lady Sulby was not to be displeased further by the delay of the delivery of the shawl she had requested Jane to bring to her almost ten minutes ago.

Jane moved quickly down the hallway to Olivia's room to collect the parasol before hurrying to the wide staircase with the required items, aware of the rumble of voices below as Sir Barnaby engaged his guest in conversation.

Lady Sulby had previously expressed high hopes of Olivia making a favourable impression on the Duke's youngest brother, Lord Sebastian St Claire, and now that the young lord had failed to arrive Lady Sulby would no doubt be in one of the spiteful moods that usually had the servants running downstairs to the sanctuary of the kitchen at the first opportunity. Jane knew she wouldn't be allowed the same privilege until after she had helped Olivia change into her dress for dinner and styled her hair.

When the family were at home Jane was usually allowed to dine with them in the evenings, but Lady Sulby had informed her only that morning that once their guests had arrived she would be expected to take her meals downstairs with the other servants.

Which would not be any hardship at all, when Jane considered the few dresses she had in her wardrobe. None of them was in the least suitable for dining with a duke, she acknowledged ruefully as she hurried to the staircase. And if she could deliver the shawl and parasol while the Duke still engaged the attention of his host and hostess, then she would perhaps manage to avoid the rebuke Lady Sulby was otherwise sure to make concerning her tardiness.

Jane could never afterwards explain how it happened. Why it happened. She was only aware that the staircase was no longer firm beneath her slippered feet, and that instead of hurrying down the staircase she instead found herself tumbling forwards.

Or at least she would have tumbled if a pair of strong hands hadn't reached out and grasped her upper arms to halt her.

She found herself instead falling forward into a hard, immovable object. A man's chest, Jane quickly realised, as she found her nose buried in the delicate folds of an impeccably tied, pristinely white necktie, her senses at once assailed by the smell of cologne and clean male flesh, both mingling with the faint smell of a cigar.

The Duke of Stourbridge's clean, male chest. The Duke of Stourbridge's perfectly tied cravat too, Jane discovered seconds later, as she struggled to right herself and looked up into that aristocratically austere face and discovered that his eyes—those eyes whose colour she had been unable to discern earlier, as she had looked down at him from the window of Lady Sulby's bedroom—were of the strangest, most intense shade of gold. Not brown, not hazel, but pure, piercing gold, rimmed with a much darker brown that somehow gave him the appearance of a large bird of prey. The mesmerising appearance of a large, dangerous bird of prey...

Hawk's mouth tightened at the unexpectedness of this physical assault. Having spent the last two days confined to his carriage, the comfort of which had nevertheless not been enough to prevent him from being rocked and bumped about on the sadly uneven roads, he wished only to be shown to his rooms and provided with hot water for a bath before he had to present himself downstairs, in order that he might be introduced to his fellow guests before they dined.

The hostelries at which he had dined along the way, and the inn he had had perforce to stop at the previous night, had been far beneath his usual exacting standard. And minutes ago his hostess, until then a woman totally unknown to him, had shown such want of breeding as to almost accost him as he alighted from his carriage.

Hawk had reflected long and hard as to the advisability of coming to Markham Park at all during the two days preceding his departure from London, as well as during the long, interminable hours it had taken to arrive here, and this latest incident of having one of the Sulby household servants actually throw herself into his arms only served to prove how correct had been his misgivings.

'I am so sorry, Your Grace.' The maid's voice was slightly breathless, her expression stricken as she glanced warily down into the hallway, where Sir Barnaby and Lady Sulby could still be seen and heard engaged in conversation with Lord and Lady Tillton. The other couple had arrived with their son Simon just as Hawk was being taken up to view his suite of rooms by the footman, who had now fallen discreetly back from this unexpected exchange.

Hawk's gaze narrowed and his mouth tightened as he

detected a look of apprehension in the shadowed green eyes the maid turned back to him. He certainly wasn't accustomed to having anyone, least of all a servant, accost him in this way, but he realised now that the girl must have tripped—that as he had ascended the stairs he had merely been standing in the way of her tumbling unchecked to the hallway below. Certainly there was no need for her to look quite so apprehensive on his account.

Although that glance down at Sir Barnaby and Lady Sulby seemed to imply that it was not his own displeasure this young girl feared...

Hawk's mouth thinned even more at the realisation. He had always found Sir Barnaby to be a pleasant, even jovial companion on the few occasions they had dined together, so he could only assume that it was from Lady Sulby that the maid feared retribution for her ill-timed actions.

'I really am sorry, Your Grace.' The young girl moved to pick something up from the stairs that she seemed to have dropped when they collided. 'I—Oh, I am so sorry, Your Grace!' The girl gasped her dismay as she poked him in the stomach with the parasol she had just retrieved from the stair.

Hawk drew in a sharp breath at this second unexpected attack, and wondered incredulously if the last few minutes were going to be indicative of this week's stay in what he had discovered on the drive here was indeed a flat, uninteresting fenland, with little to recommend it.

Including the delivery of letters. His own missive explaining that his brother Sebastian would be unable to attend after all had clearly not arrived, resulting in Hawk having to make Sebastian's excuses verbally to his host and hostess.

In light of the ill-bred behaviour of Lady Sulby on his arrival, and the fact that Olivia Sulby, when introduced, had all the indications of being exactly the type of simpering miss Hawk found irritatingly exhausting, he could not help but frown as he wondered if perhaps Sebastian had been privy to some insight about the Sulby household that he had not.

Jane gave an inward groan as she saw the visible signs of the Duke's displeasure, sure that such an illustrious person was completely unaccustomed to being physically accosted in this way.

Not only had she almost knocked him down the stairs, but now she had actually poked him in that flat, manly stomach with a parasol.

None of which Lady Sulby or Olivia seemed to have witnessed, thank goodness, as they still conversed with the Tilltons in the hallway below. But it could only be a matter of time before one or both of them looked up and became aware of the debacle taking place on the staircase above them.

Jane gave the patiently waiting footman a desperate look of pleading as he stood silent witness to the encounter—although she had to look hastily away again when she thought she detected a glint of laughter in John's otherwise deadpan expression.

'If you would come this way, Your Grace? I will show you to your rooms.' John stepped sideways to allow the Duke to move around the obviously mortified Jane and so precede him up the wide staircase.

Some of Jane's tension eased, and she gave John a grateful smile as the Duke did exactly that—only to once again find herself the focus of those all-seeing gold-coloured eyes as the Duke paused briefly and gave her one last narrow-eyed frowning glance.

Her smile faded, and she clutched the parasol and shawl to her bosom as she found herself held mesmerised by that penetrating gaze for several long, heart-stopping seconds. He took in her appearance from red hair to slippered feet, before those thin, chiselled lips tightened once more and the Duke turned to continue his gracefully elegant way up the stairs.

Jane breathed shakily as she found herself continuing to watch him, her breasts quickly rising and falling, her cheeks feeling uncomfortably hot, and her pulse racing as she stared at the broadness of the Duke's shoulders in that perfectly tailored jacket, admired the slight curl in the darkness of his fashionably styled hair…

'For goodness' sake, Jane. I said my shawl embroidered with the pink roses, not the yellow.' Lady Sulby finally seemed to have seen her on the staircase. 'Really!' She turned confidingly back to the Tilltons. 'I declare the girl does not understand even the simplest of instructions.'

Jane knew, as she turned to go back up the stairs and saw Olivia's expression of derision, that she had under-stood Lady Sulby's instruction perfectly—that it was Lady Sulby who was being deliberately awkward. But it would serve no purpose to contradict Lady Sulby. Especially not in front of her guests.

The blush intensified in Jane's cheeks as she reached the top of the stairs and saw that the Duke had once again paused on his way to his rooms, on the gallery overlook-ing the hallway this time. His top lip was now curled back in cold disdain as he stood witness to Lady Sulby's wasp-ish set down.

'Your Grace.' Jane gave a polite inclination of her head as she approached, and then hurried past him down the hallway, knowing that the blush on her cheeks would clash horribly with her red curls, and that the unattractive freckles on her nose would be rendered more visible by her high colour.

Not that it particularly mattered what the Duke of Stourbridge made of *her*. He was far, far above her precarious social station, and as such would have no further reason to even notice her existence.

If, that was, for the rest of his stay Jane desisted from falling down the staircase into his arms or attacking him with a parasol!

How could she have been so ungainly, so inelegant, so utterly without grace? Jane wondered as she sat down shakily on the side of Lady Sulby's four-poster bed, dropping the shawl and parasol on the bedcover beside her as she put both her hands against her hot and flustered cheeks. The Duke, as had been obvious from that last disdainful glance in her direction, had obviously been wondering the very same thing.

Oh, this was dreadful. Too horrible for words. She just wanted to curl up in a ball of misery in the windowseat in her bedroom and not appear again until that beautiful black carriage, with its ducal crest and its illustrious guest inside, had rolled back down the driveway and disappeared to London, whence it came.

'Whatever are you doing, Jane?' A stunned Lady Sulby came to an abrupt halt in the doorway to her bedchamber, and a guilt-stricken Jane rose from her sitting position on the side of her silk-covered bed.

The older woman's gaze moved critically about the room,

a frown marring her brow as she saw the jewellery box on the dressing table. Jane had earlier intended returning it to the still open top drawer, but had totally forgotten to do in the excitement of the Duke's arrival.

'Have you been looking at my things?' Lady Sulby's demand was sharp as she swiftly crossed the room to lift the lid of the jewellery box and check its contents.

'No, of course I have not.' Jane was incredulous at the accusation.

'Are you sure?' Lady Sulby glared.

'Perfectly sure.' Jane nodded, stunned by her guardian's suspicions. 'Clara must have left the box out earlier.'

Lady Sulby gave her another searching glare before replacing the jewellery box in the drawer and closing it abruptly. 'Where is my shawl, girl? And you have failed to bring Olivia's parasol down to her,' she added accusingly.

'Which I need if I am to accompany Lady Tillton and Simon Tillton into the rose garden.' Olivia smiled smugly as she stood in the open doorway.

Jane had not even noticed the younger girl until that moment, and avoided meeting Olivia's triumphant gaze as she hurriedly handed her the parasol, her own thoughts still preoccupied with Lady Sulby's earlier sharpness concerning the jewellery box.

Why would Lady Sulby even suspect her of doing such a thing? As far as Jane was aware the box contained only the few costly jewels owned by the Sulby family and several private papers, none of which was of the least interest to Jane.

'It really is too bad of Lord St Claire not to have accompanied His Grace after all,' Lady Sulby murmured distractedly once Olivia had departed for her walk in the garden.

'Especially as it has caused me to rearrange all my dinner arrangements for this evening. Still, the influenza is the influenza. And I do believe that the Duke was rather taken with Olivia himself,' she added with relish. 'Now, would *that* not be an advantageous match?'

Jane was sure that she was not expected to make any reply to this statement—that Lady Sulby was merely thinking out loud while she plotted and planned inside her calculating head.

But Jane's silence on the subject did not mean that she had no thoughts of her own on an imagined match between Olivia and the Duke of Stourbridge. Her main one being that it was ludicrous to even think that a man as haughtily arrogant as the Duke would ever be attracted to, let alone enticed into marriage with, the pretty but self-centred Olivia.

'Why are you still standing there, Jane?' Lady Sulby demanded waspishly as she finally seemed to notice her again. 'Can you not see that my nerves are agitated? I shall probably have one of my headaches and be unable to attend my guests at all this evening!'

'Would you like me to send for Clara?' Jane offered lightly, knowing that Lady Sulby's maid, a middle-aged woman who had accompanied Gwendoline Simmons from her father's home in Great Yarmouth when she had married Sir Barnaby twenty-five years ago, was the only one who could capably deal with Lady Sulby when she was beset by 'one of her headaches'.

A regular occurrence, as it happened, but usually relieved by a glass or two of Sir Barnaby's best brandy. For medicinal purposes only, of course, Jane acknowledged with a rueful grimace.

'I do not know what you can possibly find to smile about, Jane.' Lady Sulby threw herself down onto the chaise, her hand raised dramatically to her brow as the sun shone in through the window. 'You would be much better served returning to your room and changing for dinner. You know I cannot abide tardiness, Jane.'

Lady Sulby's comment on Jane changing for dinner caused her to frown. 'Did you not tell me earlier that I was to dine belowstairs this evening—?'

'Have you not been listening to a word I said, girl?' Lady Sulby's voice had once again risen shrilly, and she glared across at Jane, not even her faded beauty visible in her displeasure. 'The Duke has arrived without his brother, leaving me with only thirteen to sit down to dinner. A possibility I cannot even contemplate.' She shuddered. 'So you will have to join us. Which will make an imbalance of men to ladies. It will not do, of course, but it will have to suffice until our other guests arrive tomorrow.'

Jane's own face had lost all colour as the full import of Lady Sulby's complaints became clear. 'You are saying, ma'am, that because Lord St Claire is indisposed you wish me to make up the numbers for dinner this evening?'

'Yes, yes—of course I am saying that.' The older woman glared at her frowningly. 'Whatever is the matter with you, girl?'

Jane swallowed hard at the mere thought of finding herself seated at the same dinner table as the formidable Duke of Stourbridge, sure that after their disastrous meeting on the stairs earlier it was probably his fervent wish never to set eyes on her again!

As Lady Sulby had already remarked, it really would not do.

'I am sure I do not have anything suitable to wear—'

'Nonsense, girl.' A flush coloured Lady Sulby's plump and powdered cheeks as she bristled at this continued resistance to her new arrangements. 'What of that yellow gown of mine that Clara altered to fit you? That will do perfectly well, I am sure,' Lady Sulby announced imperiously.

Jane's heart sank as she thought of the deep yellow gown that Lady Gwendoline had decided did not suit her after all, and which had been altered to fit Jane instead.

'I really would not feel comfortable amongst your titled guests '

'I am not concerned with *your* comfort!' Lady Sulby's face became even more flushed as her agitatation rose. 'You will do as you are told, Jane, and join us downstairs for dinner. Is that understood?'

'Yes, Lady Sulby.' Jane felt nauseous.

'Good. Now, send Clara to me.' Lady Sulby lowered herself down onto the cushions once again, her eyes closing. 'And tell her I am in need of one of her physics,' she added weakly, as Jane moved obediently to the door.

Jane waited until she was outside in the hallway before giving in to the despair she felt just at the thought of going down to dinner wearing that horrible yellow gown. Of the arrogantly disdainful but devastatingly handsome Duke of Stourbridge seeing her in that bilious yellow gown.

Chapter Two

'Is this some new sort of party game? Or is it just that you are contemplating what singular delights you might have in store for me later this evening?' Hawk mused derisively to the woman standing—hiding?—behind the potted plant at his side. 'Perhaps you intend spilling a glass of wine over me during dinner? Or maybe hot tea later in the evening would be more to your liking? Yes, I am sure that hot tea would cause much more discomfort than a mere glass of wine. That potted plant really is an insufficient hiding place, you know,' Hawk added, when his quarry made no response to any of his mocking barbs.

His humour had not been improved when he'd come downstairs to the drawing room some minutes ago, to meet and mingle with his fellow house guests before dinner. His bath water had been hot, but of insufficient quantity for his needs, and his valet, Dolton, was no happier with his present location than Hawk. In his agitation he had actually caused the Duke's chin to bleed whilst shaving him, an event that had never happened before in all his long service.

But Hawk had found his darkly brooding mood lightening somewhat a few minutes later when, while in polite conversation with Lady Ambridge, an elderly if outspoken lady he was long acquainted with, he had spotted what appeared to be an almost ghostly yellow being flitting from behind one oversized plant pot to another. He had assumed it was in an effort not to be noticed, but it had actually achieved the opposite.

It was testament to how bored Hawk already was by the conversation of his fellow guests that he had actually excused himself from Lady Ambridge's company to stroll across the room and stand beside the plant at that moment hiding the elusive creature.

A single glance behind the terracotta pot had shown her to be the earlier perpetrator of the painful bump in his chest followed by the even more painful dig in his stomach with a parasol. Hawk's surprise that she was not a maid after all but was obviously a fellow guest was completely overshadowed by the strangeness of her behaviour since entering the drawing room.

He was also, Hawk realised with not a little surprise, more than curious to know the reason for it. 'You may as well come out from behind there, you know,' he advised, even as he continued to gaze disdainfully out at the room rather than at her, impeccable in his black evening clothes.

This time, at least, he did receive an agitated reply. 'I really would rather not!'

Hawk felt compelled to point out the obvious. 'You are only drawing attention to yourself by not doing so.'

'I believe you are the one drawing attention to us both by talking to me!' Her voice was sharp with indignation.

He probably was, Hawk acknowledged ruefully. The fact that he was the highest-ranking person in the room, and so obviously the biggest feather in Lady Gwendoline Sulby's social cap, also meant that he was attracting many sidelong glances from his fellow guests while they pretended to be in conversation with each other.

As the Duke of Stourbridge, he was used to such attention, of course, and had learnt over the years to ignore it. Obviously his quarry did not have that social advantage.

'Perhaps if you were to explain to me why it is you feel the need to hide behind a succession of inadequate potted plants...?'

'Would you just go away and leave me alone? If you please, Your Grace,' she added with guilty breathlessness, as she obviously remembered exactly who she was talking to, and in what way.

For some inexplicable reason Hawk had the sudden urge to laugh.

And, as he rarely found occasion to smile nowadays, let alone laugh with a woman, he noted it with surprise. Women, those most predatory of beasts, as he had found during the ten years since he had inherited the title of Duke following the death of both his parents in a carriage accident, were no laughing matter.

He sighed. 'You really cannot hide away all evening, you know.'

'I can try!'

'Why would you want to?' His curiosity was definitely piqued.

'How can you possibly ask that?'

His brows rose. 'Perhaps because it seems a reasonable question in the circumstances?'

'The gown,' she answered tragically. 'Surely you have noticed the gown?'

Well, yes, it would be difficult *not* to notice such a violent yellow creation, when all the older ladies present were wearing pastels and Miss Olivia Sulby virginal white. The colour really was most unbecoming with the vivid red of this girl's hair, but…

'Please do go away, Your Grace!'

'I am afraid I really cannot.'

'Why not?'

Hawk, having no intention of admitting to an interest he himself found unprecedented, chanced another glance at her. That gown was most unattractive against the red of her hair and the current flush to her cheeks, and the matching yellow ribbon threaded through those vibrant locks only added to the jarring discord.

'Did your modiste not tell you how ill yellow would suit your—er—particular colouring when you ordered the gown?'

'It was not I who ordered the gown but Lady Sulby.' She sounded irritated that he had not realised as much. 'I am sure that any modiste worthy of that name would have the good sense never to dress any of her red-haired patrons in yellow, giving the poor woman the appearance of a huge piece of fruit. Unappetising fruit, at that!'

This time Hawk was totally unable to contain his short bark of laughter, causing the heads of those fellow guests closest to him to turn even more curious glances his way.

Jane, aware of the curious glances of the other Sulby guests, really did wish that the Duke would go away.

The gown, when she had put it on, had looked even worse than she had imagined it would, and the yellow ribbon Lady Sulby had provided to dress her hair only added to the calamity.

But Jane had known that Lady Sulby would only make her life more unbearable than usual if she did not go down to dinner as instructed, and so she really had had no choice but to don the hated gown and ribbon and enter the drawing room—before trying to make herself as inconspicuous as possible by moving from the shelter of one potted plant to another, hoping that when she actually sat down at the dinner table the gown would not be as visible.

But she hadn't taken into account the unwanted curiosity and attention of the Duke of Stourbridge. And his laughter, at her expense, was doubly cruel in the circumstances.

'You really should come out, you know,' he drawled. 'I am sure that there cannot now be a person present who has not taken note of my conversation with a very colourful potted plant!'

Jane's mouth firmed as she accepted the truth of the Duke's words, knowing he had been the focus of all eyes for the last five minutes or so as he apparently engaged in conversation—and laughter—with a huge pot of foliage. But it really was too bad of him to have drawn attention to her in this way when she had so wanted to just fade into the woodwork. Not an easy task, admittedly, when wearing this bilious-coloured gown, but she might just have succeeded until it was actually time to go in to dinner if not for the obvious attentions of the Duke of Stourbridge.

In the circumstances she had little choice but to acknowledge and comply with his advice, stepping out from behind the potted plant and then feeling indignant all over again as the Duke made no effort to hide the wince that appeared on his arrogantly handsome face as he slowly took in her appearance—from the yellow ribbon adorning her red hair to the lacy frill draping over her slippers.

'Dear, dear, it is worse even than I thought.' He grimaced.

'You are being most unkind, Your Grace.' Her cheeks had become even redder in her indignation.

He gave an arrogant inclination of his head. 'I am afraid that I am.'

Jane's eyes widened at the admission. 'You do not even apologise for being so?'

'What would be the point?' He shrugged those powerful shoulders in the black, expertly tailored evening jacket that somehow emphasised the width of his shoulders and the lean power of his body. 'I am afraid you also have me at something of a disadvantage…?'

Jane drew in an agitated breath. 'On the contrary, Your Grace. I am sure that any disadvantage must be mine!'

Hawk's gaze was drawn briefly to the swelling of creamy breasts against the low bodice of her gown—enticingly full breasts, considering her otherwise slender appearance—before his narrowed gaze returned to her face. Like her colouring and her figure, it was not fashionably pretty. But the deep green of her eyes, surrounded by thick, dark lashes, was nonetheless arresting. Her nose was small, and covered lightly with the freckles that might be expected with such vibrant colouring, and her mouth was perhaps a little too wide—although the lips were full and sensuous above a pointedly determined chin.

No, he acknowledged, she did not possess the sweetly blonde beauty that was currently fashionable—the same sweetly blonde beauty he found so unappealing in Olivia Sulby!—but this young lady's colouring and bone structure were such that she would remain beautiful even in much older years.

All of which Hawk noted in a matter of seconds, which was surprising in itself.

Women, to the Duke of Stourbridge, had become merely a convenience—something to be enjoyed during the few hours of leisure that he allowed himself away from his ducal duties.

His alliance with the Countess of Morefield had been brief and physically unsatisfactory, and had only served to convince Hawk that the demands a mistress made on his time were invariably unworthy of the effort expended in acquiring that mistress.

Surprisingly, Hawk recognised that this young woman— for she was much younger than the women he usually took as mistress—if dressed and coiffured properly, could, in the right circumstances, be worthy of his attention.

Except that he still had no idea who or what she was. She was several years older than those 'simpering misses' of which Olivia Sulby was such a prime example. But, from the way Lady Sulby had spoken to her earlier, she did appear to be part of the Sulby household. Although in what capacity Hawk could not guess. Olivia Sulby, as he already knew, was an only child, so this interestingly forthright creature could not be Sir Barnaby's daughter.

Perhaps Lady Sulby's daughter from a previous marriage? His hostess had certainly spoken to her sharply enough for such a relationship to exist, although Hawk could see absolutely no resemblance between the plump, faded beauty of Lady Sulby and the strikingly beautiful redhead standing before him.

But if she was a young, unmarried lady of quality Hawk knew he could not take her as mistress—no matter what his unexpected interest. That he had even been thinking of doing so was reason enough for him to maintain a distance between them. And sooner rather than later.

Before he could effect a gracious withdrawal, a flustered and obviously disapproving Lady Sulby bustled over to join them. 'I see you have met my husband's ward, Jane Smith, Your Grace. Dear Jane came to us from a distant relative of Sir Barnaby's. An impoverished parson of a country parish,' she added dismissively, shooting a censorious glance at the object of her monologue, a hard glitter in her eyes. 'You look very well in that gown, Jane.'

Hawk's brows rose at the insincerity behind the compliment even as he shared a look of sceptisism with the young lady he now knew as Jane Smith. Jane Smith? The blandness of the name did not suit this vibrant young woman in the least.

'Miss Smith.' He bowed formally. 'Might I be permitted to escort Sir Barnaby's ward in to dinner, Lady Sulby?' he offered, as the dinner bell sounded.

As hostess, Lady Sulby naturally would have expected this privilege to be her own, for some inexplicable reason—despite his earlier decision to distance himself from Jane Smith—Hawk now felt a need to thwart his hostess.

Maybe because she had—deliberately?—drawn attention to the gown that was making Jane so unhappy. Or maybe because of the way she had spoken so condescendingly of Jane's impoverished father. Whatever the reason, Hawk found himself unwilling to suffer Lady Sulby's singularly ingratiating attentions even for the short time it would take to escort her to the dining room.

Although the stricken look on Jane Smith's face as she became the open focus of the angrily hard glitter of Lady Sulby's gaze told him that it had perhaps been unwise on his part to show such a preference.

A realisation that was immediately confirmed by Jane Smith. 'Really, Your Grace, you must not.'

Hawk gave her a hard, searching glance, noting the slight pallor to her cheeks and the look almost of desperation now in those deep green eyes. Jane Smith, unlike almost every other woman of Hawk's acquaintance, most definitely did *not* want the Duke of Stourbridge to single her out for such attention. In fact, those green eyes were silently pleading with him not to do so.

'In that case... Lady Sulby?' He held out his arm, the polite smile on his lips not reaching the icy hardness of his eyes.

His hostess seemed almost to have to drag her attention away from Jane Smith before turning an ingratiating smile in his general direction. 'Certainly, Your Grace.' She placed her possessively grasping hand on his arm before sweeping regally through the room ahead of her other guests.

Jane stood back and watched them, her heart beating erratically in her chest, having easily recognised the look of promised retribution in Lady Sulby's gaze before she had turned and graciously accepted the Duke's arm.

Why had the Duke offered to escort Jane in to dinner? He of all people had to know that as the Sulbys' principal titled guest, etiquette demanded that he escort Lady Sulby. To do anything else would cause something of a sensation.

But, oh, how Jane wished she could have accepted.

How—despite the cruelty of his laughter at her expense—she would have loved to be the one who was swept regally from the room on the arm of the aristocratic Duke of Stourbridge. He was so haughtily attractive, so powerfully immediate, that Jane had no doubt those austere and yet mesmerising features would appear in her dreams later tonight.

'What do you mean by making such a spectacle of yourself, Jane?' Olivia had appeared at her side, her fan raised so that her acerbic tone and disdainful expression could not to be observed by the other guests as they prepared to follow Lady Sulby and the Duke through to the dining room. 'Mama is going to be absolutely furious with you for deliberately attracting the Duke's attention in that way.'

Jane gasped at the unfairness of the accusation. 'But I did nothing to—'

'Do not lie, Jane. We all saw you making a fool of yourself by openly flirting with the man in that shameless way.' Olivia glared, the tightness of her mouth giving her a look very much like her mother's at that moment. 'Mama is going to be very angry if your behaviour has caused the Duke any embarassment,' she told Jane warningly. 'That gown looks absolutely horrid on you, by the way,' she added cuttingly, before walking away to smilingly take the arm of the waiting Anthony Ambridge, the elegible grandson of Lady Ambridge.

Dinner was, as Jane could have predicted, an absolutely miserable time for her. Lord Tillton sat to the left of her, and constantly tried to put his hand on her thigh until she put a stop to it by digging her nails into his wrist, and a deaf and elderly woman sat the to her right, talking in a monologue that thankfully required no response on Jane's part—because she was sure she would not have heard her even if she had attempted a reply.

To make matters worse, the Duke, on Lady Sulby's right, with Olivia seated next to him—two blonde sentinels guarding a much valued prize—proceeded to ignore Jane completely and so succeeded in increasing her misery.

By the time Lady Sulby signalled for the ladies to retire and leave the men to their brandy Jane's head was pounding. She longed for nothing more than to escape to her room, where she might at last take the pins from her hair before bathing her heated brow and hopefully alleviating the painful throbbing at her temples. After Olivia's earlier comments it would merely be postponing the inevitable confrontation with Lady Sulby, of course, but Jane hoped that even a short delay might be advantageous.

'I think you are being very wise, Jane.' Lady Sulby, talking to Lady Tillton in the drawing room, paused and gave a terse inclination of her head when Jane asked to be excused because of a headache. 'In fact, I think it would be beneficial to everyone if you were to keep to your room until we can be sure that you are not the carrier of anything infectious.'

Jane's face whitened at the deliberate insult—did it promise retribution?—before turning to lift the hem of her gown and almost run from the room.

'*That you are not the carrier of anything infectious.*'

Lady Sulby could not have told Jane any more clearly that she considered Jane's very presence to be a dangerous source of infection to her guests—but no doubt especially where the Duke of Stourbridge was concerned!

* * *

Hawk was sure he had never spent an evening of such boredom in his entire life, knowing after only two minutes in the company of Lady Sulby and the vacuously self-centred Olivia that the older lady was everything he disliked, in that she was a gossipy small-minded, social-climbing woman, with not a kind word to say for anyone or anything, and that in twenty years or so—if not sooner!—her daughter would be exactly like her.

But the dinner fare, unlike the company he had been forced to endure, had been surprisingly excellent, with each course seeming to outdo the last, to such a degree that Hawk had wondered if, before taking his leave at the end of the week, he might not be able to persuade the Sulbys' cook into joining one of his own households.

And of course there had been that strangely memorable incident with Jane Smith earlier. Although, with hindsight, Hawk had decided that even there he had been unwise— that the eligible Duke of Stourbridge should not have engaged a young unmarried lady to whom he had not even been formally introduced at the time in conversation of any kind. The fact that she was, despite Lady Gwendoline's obvious sharpness to her, Sir Barnaby's ward, meant that no doubt she had ambitions of her own concerning advantageous marriage.

His wariness had been confirmed when he had observed her from between narrowed lids for several minutes at the start of dinner. She had proceded to flirt outrageously with James Tillton—a man Hawk knew to keep two mistresses already, in different areas of London—constantly turning in his direction whilst completely ignoring the poor woman seated at her other side, as she'd gallantly attempted to engage her in conversation.

'What do you think, Stourbridge?'

He turned his attention to the other gentlemen seated around the table, partaking of the surprisingly excellent brandy. 'I agree with you entirely, Ambridge.' He answered the elderly gentleman—he believed was the matter of horseflesh—before moving languidly to his feet, carrying his glass of brandy with him. 'If you will excuse me, gentlemen? I believe I will partake of some of this brisk Norfolk air our hostess was in such raptures about earlier.' He strolled across the room to open one of the French doors before stepping outside onto the moonlit terrace, relieved to step out of the room and away from the banality of the conversation.

How was he possibly to stand another six days of this? Hawk asked himself wearily. Perhaps he could arrange for Sebastian to have a 'relapse', and so excuse himself on the pretext of brotherly concern? Such a course presented the problem of arranging to have a letter delivered to himself, of course, but surely that was preferable to the prospect of dying of boredom before the week was out?

Although there really was something to be said for the bracing Norfolk air, he discovered, as he drew in a deep breath and felt his head immediately begin to clear. Perhaps he would consider an estate in Norfolk, after all. Just not this one.

Having now met and spent time in the company of Olivia Sulby, his marital plans regarding that young lady and his brother Sebastian were definitely cancelled. For one thing he loved his youngest brother far too much to inflict that simpering chit on Sebastian and the rest of the St Claire family, let alone her social-climbing mother. It really—

Hawk's attention had been caught, and held, by a movement to the left of the moon-dappled garden—a slight deviation in the shadows beside the tall hedge that told him he was no longer alone in his enjoyment of the bracing air. He had been joined by a fox, perhaps. Or maybe a badger.

But, no, the moving shadow was too tall to be either of those nocturnal animals. The intruder into his solitude was definitely of the two-legged variety, and it moved purposefully along the hedge towards the gate that Dolton, a dedicated city-dweller, had shudderingly informed his employer earlier led down to a beach and the open sea.

It was a man, then. Or perhaps a woman. On her way to some romantic tryst, maybe? Or could it be something slightly more serious, such as smuggling? Hawk believed that it was still as rife here in Norfolk as it was reputed to be in Cornwall.

While actively fulfilling his role as a justice of the peace in Gloucestershire, Hawk did not consider it any of his business—but his attention sharpened as the breeze gusted strongly, lifting the dark shielding cloak that encompassed the prowler and revealing something much lighter in colour worn beneath.

Such as a gown of vivid yellow...?

Could that possibly be Jane Smith moving stealthily away from the house in the direction of the beach? And, if so, for what purpose?

Hawk told himself again that it was none of his business what Jane Smith did. She was the unmarried ward of Sir Barnaby, and Hawk would be well advised to keep well away from her for the remainder of his visit here, or risk

finding himself manoeuvred into the parson's mousetrap—
a fate he had no intention of succumbing to until he had
seen all of his siblings happily settled, and certainly not
with the impoverished ward of a minor peer. When the time
came Hawk fully intended marrying a woman of suitable
breeding—one who would quietly and efficiently provide
the heirs necessary for the Duke of Stourbridge but would
make no other demands upon his time or his emotions.

To deliberately seek out Jane Smith, a young woman who
had already caused him to act completely out of character
earlier this evening, would be decidedly unwise. He would
be better served by rejoining the other gentlemen and forgetting even the existence of Jane Smith.

But the impulse—madness?—which had afflicted him
earlier, when his curiosity had first been piqued enough to
engage Jane Smith in conversation, did not seem to have
dissipated, and rather than rejoining the gentlemen inside
the house Hawk instead found himself placing his brandy
glass down on the balustrade and moving down the steps
into the garden, with the sole intention of following to see
exactly where Jane Smith was going alone so late at night.

And why.

Chapter Three

'Are your tears because your lover has failed to arrive for your tryst, or because as yet there is no lover?'

Jane stiffened as she easily recognised the Duke of Stourbridge's deep, slightly bored voice coming from above and behind her as she sat among the dunes. Her chin was resting on her drawn-up knees, the hood of her cloak having fallen back to reveal the wildness of her hair, now free of the confines of its pins, as she stared out at the wildly beating waves upon the shore, tears falling unchecked down her cheeks.

She pulled her cloak more firmly about her before answering him. 'The reason for my tears is not your concern, Your Grace.'

'And if I choose to make it my concern?'

'Then I wish you would not. In fact, I would prefer it if you left me.' She was too miserable at that moment to even attempt to be polite. Even—especially?—to the exalted Duke of Stourbridge. Though polite was not a word she would have used to describe any of their encounters to date!

'You are ordering me to leave, Jane? Again?' he mocked lightly.

Jane was dimly aware of his having now moved to stand beside her in the shelter of the dune, probably ruining his evening slippers in the process. But she did not care. She was too unhappy, too desperately low, to consider the Duke's discomfort at that moment. After all, she had made no invitation for him to join her here.

'I am, Your Grace.' She nodded tersely.

'I am afraid that will not be possible, Jane.' He gave a sigh as, completely careless of his expensively tailored clothing, he lowered his considerable length to sit down on the dune at her side. 'It would be most ungentlemanly of me, having discovered a lady in such distress, to simply walk away and leave her here, where anyone might come along and, discovering that she is alone, attempt to take advantage of the situation.'

Jane glanced at him frowningly in the darkness. 'Even if she has asked you to do so? Even if she is not a lady?' She turned her face away so that he wouldn't see the anger that was quickly replacing her tears.

'Is this about the gown, Jane?' Impatience edged his voice now, and he continued with disdain. 'Because if it is then you only have to look at Lady Sulby, to engage her in a moment's conversation, to know that a fine gown does not make a lady.'

Jane made a choked sound, caught somewhere between a sob and a laugh. 'That remark is certainly not that of a gentleman, Your Grace!'

The Duke gave another sigh. 'I am finding it increasingly difficult to behave like a gentleman since arriving here in Norfolk.'

Jane gave him another sideways glance. The moonlight was throwing into stark relief the sharp edges of his aristocratic profile, his high cheekbones, his strong and determined jaw.

He was dressed meticulously in black again this evening, with a high-collared white shirt and his cravat tied neatly at his throat, a pale grey satin waistcoat beneath his jacket. But the force of the wind had ruffled the dark thickness of his hair into disarray, giving him a somewhat piratical appearance and, strangely, making him appear less like the haughty and unapproachable Duke of Stourbridge who had arrived at Markham Park earlier this afternoon.

But she must not forget that was exactly who he was, Jane reminded herself firmly, and that no matter how disconsolate she might feel, however much he might appear in sympathy with her plight at this moment, at the end of his week's stay he would leave to return to his privileged life in London—while she would still be here under the tyrannical rule of Lady Sulby.

Just the thought of that was enough to cause the now angry tears to fall anew.

'Come now, Jane.' The Duke turned to her. 'Whatever is wrong? It really cannot be so bad—'

'And how can you possibly know that, Your Grace?' Misery and, yes, a certain despair gave her the courage to lift her head and glare at him. 'You are not the one who has been made to feel unwanted and less than you know yourself to be!'

Hawk stared at her. The moonlight chose that moment to come out from behind a cloud, clearly illuminating the tangled wildness of her hair, the deep sparkling green of her eyes, and the full sensuality of those pouting lips.

Dear God, he wanted to kiss those lips!

He did not just want to kiss them, he wanted to devour them!

Such an uncontrolled longing shocked Hawk intensely, as he had not felt it once since assuming the title of the Duke of Stourbridge ten years ago, all of his actions and words since that time had been measured and well thought out as he thoroughly considered and weighed any possible repercussions.

But at this moment Hawk found he could not think of anything else but kissing the lush ripeness of Jane Smith's inviting lips, of crushing the slenderness of her body to his, under his, as his mouth plundered hers and his hands became entangled in the thick fire of her unconfined hair before he explored the creamy swell of her full breasts, that slender waist and curvaceously welcoming thighs. Hawk realised with even more shocking clarity that, to him, Jane Smith was neither unwanted nor less than she knew herself to be. In fact, he could not remember ever wanting any woman as hotly, as immediately, as he now wanted the inadequately named Jane Smith!

Instead of acting on that impulse, and shocked at the intensity of his sudden desire to taste and hold Jane Smith, he moved abruptly to his feet and stepped away from her. 'I will leave you to your solitude, then, Jane.'

'I hope I have not offended you, Your Grace...?' She grimaced as she too rose to her feet, her cloak falling back further to reveal that she did indeed still wear the detested yellow gown. The gusting wind moulded its thin material to that slender waist, and the long, shapely length of her legs.

'I am not in the least offended.' Hawk stood rigidly, a nerve pulsing in his tightly clenched jaw as he kept his gaze averted from the temptation she represented to his normally rigid control. 'I am merely acknowledging my intrusion—'

'I did not—'

'Do not come any closer, Jane!' Hawk found himself warning her from between clenched teeth as she reached out a hand towards him, the heat in his body, the throbbing of his loins, telling him just how dangerous this situation had become.

Had he been so long without the warm comfort of a woman—that brief, physically unsatisfying liaison with the Countess of Morefield excluded—that he was in danger of forcing his attentions upon a vulnerable and unprotected young girl? Was this what years of restraint and enforced solitude as Duke of Stourbridge had brought him to? If so, it was intolerable, and Hawk made a vow to see to the tiresome business of taking a mistress as soon as he returned to London.

Jane had come to a stricken halt as she heeded the Duke's warning, staring up at him in the darkness. Did he too think that because she was only the orphaned daughter of an impoverished country parson she was unworthy of his notice? That she was beneath even the politeness of the high and mighty Duke of Stourbridge?

'Go then, Your Grace.' She faced him proudly, her head back defiantly. 'And I will endeavour to ensure that you are not bothered any further by my unwelcome presence for the remainder of your stay at Markham Park!'

'Jane, you misunderstand me—'

'I do not think so, Your Grace.'

'Jane, you will cease "Your Gracing" me in that contemptuous tone.'

'I most certainly will not!' She was beyond reason, beyond caution, wanting only to hurt as she was being hurt.

'Jane, you are playing with fire,' the Duke warned harshly, his hands now clenched at his sides.

'Fire, Your Grace?' Jane echoed tauntingly. She was tired, so very tired. For the last twelve years she'd always been meek and submissive, never being allowed to have a mind or will of her own. 'What would *you* know of fire? You, who are cold and haughty and look down your disdainful nose at everyone. What are you doing, Your Grace?' She gasped incredulously as the Duke moved to grasp her arms and began to pull her forcefully towards him.

'Hawk, Jane.' His face was only inches away from hers now, his breath warm against her cheek, those haughty features hard and predatory in the moonlight. 'My name is Hawk,' he explained harshly.

She looked up at him questioningly.

Hawk?

The Duke of Stourbridge had been named for a bird of prey?

A dangerous bird of prey. Jane dazedly recalled her assessment of him earlier today even as she stared up at him in shocked fascination.

'A fanciful notion of my mother's.' His tone was grim as he held Jane easily against the hard strength of his body.

Jane didn't care at that moment how he had come by his unusual name. She was only concerned with the fact that the Duke of Stourbridge—the haughty and arrogantly aloof Duke of Stourbridge—was holding her tightly in his arms as he moulded the softness of her curves against his much harder ones and his gaze became fixated on her mouth.

In fact, everything about the high and mighty Duke of Stourbridge gave every indication that he was about to kiss her!

It was unthinkable.

Unimaginable...

And yet Jane found she *could* imagine it. Could already feel the hardness of those perfectly moulded lips on hers as his mouth plundered and claimed. Possessed. For surely any woman the Duke of Stourbridge chose to kiss would know the full force of the ardour he was normally at such pains to hide from his fellow beings, but which Jane could now see so clearly in the fierce glitter of his eyes? Just as clearly she could feel the tense hardness of his body as it pressed intimately against her own...

'You should not have come here alone, Jane.' The Duke's gaze, that fiercely golden gaze, moved searchingly, hungrily, over the pallor of her face. 'You should not, Jane!' He began to lower his head towards hers.

Jane was held in motionless fascination for several long seconds as her lips parted instinctively to receive his.

A kiss.

One kiss.

Her first ever kiss.

Surely it was not too much to ask? To take for her own? After twelve long years of being denied the touch, the warmth, of another human being?

But a deeper, more knowledgeable instinct told her that Hawk St Claire, the powerful and forceful Duke of Stourbridge, would not stop at one kiss. His years and experience would demand he take more, much more. He was a man who would take and take again, while giving nothing of himself in return.

'No!' She turned her head away to avoid his kiss and at the same time pushed against his restraint, fighting to escape the steely band of his arms, but only succeeding in pressing herself more intimately against him. 'No!' Again she protested, fearing the desire that she could clearly see still held him in its grip. 'You must not! Please, Hawk, you must not…!'

Her pleas pierced the fierce desire that raged through Hawk's body, causing him to pause, to blink dazedly as he stared down at her in stunned disbelief.

This woman—this girl—was the ward of his host. The *unmarried* ward of his host.

He released her abruptly to step back, jaw tight, eyes gleaming a glittering, inflexible gold. 'You should not have come here alone, Jane,' he repeated harshly.

Her throat moved convulsively in the moonlight. 'No, I should not. But I had not expected anyone to follow me—'

'No, Jane?' Hawk's voice was hard, inflexible. 'Are you sure that your present indignation is not due to the fact that it was the wrong man who responded to your invitation?'

She looked bewildered by his accusation. 'The wrong man? I do not understand—'

'Was it not James Tillton who was supposed to attend you here tonight rather than myself?' Hawk had realised belatedly, as he remembered the flirtation he had witnessed during dinner, that this must be the case—that Jane's dismay when he had joined her here had really been due to the fact that her lover—James Tillton?—had not arrived for their arranged tryst.

'Lord Tillton?' Jane gasped at his accusation. 'I detest

Lord Tillton! He behaved most disgracefully towards me during dinner—to such a degree that in the end I had to pierce his wrist with my fingernails in order to stop his pawing of me beneath the table. Besides which, he is a married man!' she added frowningly.

Hawk's mouth twisted scathingly. 'Summer house parties like this one are notorious for the night-time assignations of people who are indeed married—but not to each other.'

'Indeed, Your Grace?' Her voice was icily cold. 'And which female guest's bed have you chosen to grace with your *own* illustrious presence tonight?'

Even now, in her pride and anger, Hawk could appreciate how beautiful, how tempting the inaptly named Miss Jane Smith truly was. Admittedly, her years spent under the guardianship of the forceful Lady Sulby seemed to have cowed the more spirited parts of her nature, but they were still there nonetheless—in the way that Jane challenged him, in the way that she never flinched from contradicting him. Two things that rarely, if ever, happened to the Duke of Stourbridge.

Jane Smith was unusual in that she did not seem to see him as just a duke. She saw past his title to the man beneath, and it was to that man that she spoke during her moments of rebellion. It was to that man that her beauty appealed. To such a degree that Hawk had briefly forgotten all the caution that had served him so well these last ten years.

It would not—it *must* not!—happen again.

'I have no interest in bedding any of the ladies now residing at Markham Park,' he said disdainfully, knowing by the way Jane stiffened that she had heard his intended rejection of her own charms in that carefully worded dismissal. 'Now, if you will excuse me, I believe I will make my excuses to the Sulbys before retiring to my bedchamber for the night.' He bowed abruptly before turning to leave.

'Not without first making me an apology, Your Grace!'

Hawk turned slowly back to her, his narrowed gaze taking in the taut lines of her body and the challenge in her defiantly raised chin.

'For almost kissing you...?'

She gave him a contemptuous glare. 'For wrongly accusing me of encouraging Lord Tillton!'

Was it possible Hawk had mistaken the events he had witnessed earlier at the dinner table? Had Jane not been encouraging Tillton after all, but rather, as she claimed, fighting off the other man's unwanted attentions? Attention towards a young woman about whom it was obvious her guardians did not care, let alone offer protection to?

'If I was mistaken—'

'You were!'

'If I was mistaken then I apologise.' Hawk nodded abruptly. 'But in future I would advise you not to come here alone. You might find yourself in much graver danger another time than you have this evening.'

'Until now these dunes have always been my place of refuge!'

Until Hawk had intruded.

Until he had held her in his arms and attempted to kiss her.

But that was a temptation she had not demanded apology for...

She was magnificent. Hawk could acknowledge that even with his inner determination not to initiate any fur-

ther intimacy between them. Her unconfined hair blew
in the wind, a thick curtain of flame, her eyes were wide
and challenging, and those perfectly pouting lips were set
defiantly.

All of those things told Hawk that she would be a formidable lover. That this woman was more than capable
of matching the depths of his own passion, which he was
always at such pains to hide from others and which Jane,
instinctively, was able to touch and ignite.

Jane Smith, he decided determinedly, was a definite danger to the icy reserve of the Duke of Stourbridge.

Jane Smith was even more of a danger to the inner man
that was still, at heart, the sensual Hawk St Claire.

'They obviously no longer offer such refuge,' he pointed
out coldly, unpityingly. 'I will bid you goodnight, Miss
Smith.' He turned away, and this time he did not look
back, did not hesitate as he strode purposefully back to
Markham Park.

Jane watched him go—a tall, forbidding shape that
finally disappeared into the darkness—knowing that it
wasn't only the refuge of the dunes that the Duke of Stourbridge had invaded this evening. When he had touched
her, when he had looked in danger of kissing her, he had
awakened a hunger deep inside her, a desire she had never
known before, which had caused her breasts to swell and
harden, and which had ignited a fiery warmth between her
thighs that had made her want to forget all caution as she
met and matched the passion she had been sure would be
in his kiss. At that moment Jane knew she had wanted to
lie down with him amongst the sand dunes, to strip away
every vestige of the haughty coldness of the Duke of Stour-

bridge even as they stripped away their clothing, to explore, to kiss, to caress—

There Jane's heated thoughts came to an abrupt halt. Because she had no idea what came after the kissing and caressing!

She did remember Lady Sulby's cautions to Olivia at the start of her Season concerning her behaviour with the more roguish members of the ton—the main one being, 'A lady may take as many lovers as she wishes after she is married, but not a single one before she has the wedding ring upon her finger.'

Did Jane's wanton longings concerning the Duke of Stourbridge mean that she was not, after all, the lady she had always thought herself to be...?

'You sent for me, Lady Sulby?' Jane stood obediently in front of the other woman the following morning as Lady Sulby sat at the table in her private parlour, reading through the correspondence strewn across the table in front of her.

The blue gaze was ice-cold as Lady Sulby swept her a disparaging glance before answering. 'You are completely recovered this morning from your headache, Jane?'

Her tone and demeanour were surprisingly mild. Instantly increasing Jane's wariness. She had been expecting further retribution for what Olivia had warned her Lady Sulby perceived as Jane's 'flirtatious behaviour' with the Duke of Stourbridge the evening before. The mildness of the older woman's tone now did not in the least deceive her into dropping her guard.

'I am quite recovered, thank you, Lady Sulby.'

The older woman gave a gracious inclination of her head. 'You slept well?'

'Fitfully.' As expected, Jane had found her dreams full of images—not of the Duke of Stourbridge, but of the man who had held her in his arms and ordered her to call him Hawk. Those images had been so erotically arousing that she had awoken suddenly in the darkness, gasping, her body shaking, her nipples hard and aching to the touch, and an unaccustomed dampness between her thighs.

'Indeed?' Lady Sulby sat back in her chair, the once beautiful face hard and unyielding as she looked at Jane from between narrowed lids. 'Could that possibly be because you failed to sleep alone…?'

Jane gasped at the accusation even as she felt the colour drain from her cheeks. Surely Lady Sulby had not misunderstood Jane's response to Lord Tillton's advances towards her the evening before in the same way the Duke had?

Or could Lady Sulby possibly be referring to the Duke himself…?

Coming so soon after the memory of Jane's erotic dreams about him, the thought made her cheeks now suffuse with colour.

'Do not trouble yourself to answer, Jane,' Lady Sulby snapped, before Jane had recovered sufficiently to refute the accusation. 'It will serve no purpose for me to hear any of the sordid details—'

Jane's shocked gasp interrupted her. 'But there *are* no sordid details—'

'I said I did not wish to hear!' The older woman looked at her with unguarded dislike. 'It is enough that, despite all our efforts, all the guidance and care that Sulby and I have so generously given you these last twelve years, you have still grown into a woman exactly like your wantonly disgraceful mother!'

Every drop of blood seemed to drain from Jane's head and she felt herself sway dizzily. 'My—my mother...?'

Lady Sulby's top lip curled back disgustedly. 'Your mother, Jane. A woman much like yourself. That is, completely lacking in morals and—'

'How dare you?' Jane had known when the maid had informed her that Lady Sulby wished to see her that she was about to bear the brunt of that lady's displeasure, but she had been in no way prepared for the vitriol of this attack on her mother and herself. 'My mother was good and kind—'

'And who told you *that*, Jane?' The other woman eyed her with scorn. 'That fool of a parson who married her?' She shook her head contemptuously. 'Joseph Smith—like every other red-blooded man, it seems!—never could see any fault in his beautiful Janette. But I knew. I always knew that she was nothing but a shameless wanton.' Her eyes glittered fanatically. 'And in the end was I not proved correct about her immoral character?' Lady Sulby surged to her feet, her face twisted and ugly in her fury.

Jane staggered back from the attack, all the time shaking her head in denial of the dreadful things Lady Sulby was saying about the woman who had died shortly after giving birth to her. 'My mother was sweet and beautiful—'

'Your mother was a harlot! A temptress and a whore!'

'No...!' Jane recoiled as if from a physical blow.

'Oh yes.' Lady Gwendoline glared at her contemptuously. 'And you are exactly like her, Jane. I warned Sulby when he insisted we take you into our household. I told him what would happen—that you would only disgrace us as Janette disgraced us. And last night I was proved correct in my misgivings.'

'But I did nothing last night of which I am ashamed!'

Jane attempted to defend herself, totally stunned at the things Lady Sulby was saying to her, and shocked to the core by the raw hatred she could clearly see in the other woman's face.

'Janette was not ashamed, either.' Lady Sulby shook with rage, that wild glitter in her eyes intensifying. 'She did not even apologise for being three months with child when she married her gullible parson!'

Jane really felt as if she were going to faint dead away at this last accusation. Her mother had been with child when she had married her father? With Jane herself?

But that did not make her mother a harlot or a whore. It only meant that, like many couples before them, her parents had precipitated their marriage vows. Jane was far from the first child to be born only six months after the wedding...

She shook her head. 'The only person that should concern is me, and I—'

'You *would* think that.' Lady Sulby glared at her. 'You who are just like her. With never a thought for the disgrace you bring on this family with your wanton actions.'

'But I have done nothing—'

'You have most certainly done *something*!' Lady Sulby's hands were clenched at her sides. 'The Duke's valet has informed Brown, the butler, that they are leaving this morning, and—'

'The Duke is leaving...?' Jane repeated hollowly, surprised at how much this knowledge managed to distress her when the rest of her world appeared to be falling apart—when she already felt as if she were in the middle of a nightmare without end.

'Do not pretend innocence with me, Jane Smith,' Lady Sulby told her sneeringly. 'We all witnessed the way in which you deliberately set out to attract the Duke yesterday evening—to tempt him to your bed, no doubt with the intention of trapping him into marriage. But if that was your hope then his hasty departure this morning must tell you that it was a wasted effort. The Duke is not a man to be trapped into anything—least of all marriage to a wanton chit like you. Oh, you are a wicked, hateful girl, Jane Smith!' Lady Sulby's voice rose hysterically. 'A veritable viper in our midst! But I see from your rebellious expression that it bothers you not at all that you have totally ruined any chance of Olivia becoming the Duchess of Stourbridge!'

Jane very much doubted, after the Duke's comments yesterday evening concerning Lady Sulby, that there had ever been the remotest possibility of Olivia finding herself married to the Duke, and was sure that any hope that Olivia would do so had only ever been Lady Sulby's own misguided fantasy after Lord Sebastian St Claire had failed to arrive.

'I want you out of this house today, Jane,' Lady Sulby told her shrilly. 'Today—do you hear?'

'I have every intention of going.' After this conversation, and the things Lady Sulby had said about her mother, Jane knew that she could not stay here a day, an hour, a moment longer than absolutely necessary.

'And do not imagine you can come crawling back here if, like your mother, you find yourself with child!' Lady Sulby scorned. 'There is no convenient parson here for you to marry, Jane. No besotted fool you can beguile into marrying you in order to give your bastard a name!'

Jane became very still, all the pain she had felt at the unfairness of Lady Sulby's accusations concerning the Duke fading, all emotion leaving her as she stared at the other woman as if down a long grey tunnel.

Lady Sulby's eyes narrowed with spite as she saw the shocked disbelief Jane was too stunned to even attempt to hide. 'You did not know?' She trilled her triumph at having shaken Jane's composure at last. 'Even after she died giving birth to you Joseph Smith could not bear to sully the memory of his beloved Janette by telling you he was not your real father!'

'He *was* my father!' Jane's hands had clenched at her sides. 'He was...' Tears of anger blurred her vision at the terrible things this dreadful woman was saying about her mother and father.

She had never known her mother, but her father had been everything that was gentle and kind. Jane did not believe he could have been that way with her if he had not been her real father.

Could he...?

'He most certainly was not.' The older woman looked at her with triumphant pity. 'Your mother seduced your real father, a rich and titled gentleman, into her bed, hoping that he would become so besotted with her he would discard the woman who was already his wife. Something he refused to do even when Janette found herself with child!'

'I do not believe you!' Jane shook her head in desperate denial. 'You are simply trying to hurt me—'

'And *am* I hurting you, Jane? I hope that I am,' Lady Sulby crowed triumphantly. 'You look very like Janette, you know. She had that same wild beauty. That same untameable spirit.'

And suddenly Jane saw with sickening clarity that Lady Sulby had spent these last twelve years trying to break that spirit in Janette's daughter. She had belittled the physical likeness she perceived to Janette by dressing Jane in gowns that did absolutely nothing to complement her. Lady Sulby hated Jane as fiercely as she had hated her mother before her...

'Janette was spoilt and wilful,' Jane's nemesis continued coldly. 'She had the ability to twist any man around her little finger in order to persuade him into doing her bidding. But she made a terrible mistake in judgement in her choice of lover,' Lady Sulby sneered. 'A mistake immediately brought home to her when he did not hesitate to dismiss her from his life when she told him of the child she was expecting. You, Jane.'

'You are lying!' Jane repeated forcefully. 'I have no idea why, not what Janette was to you, but I do know that you are lying!'

'Am I?' Lady Sulby eyed her derisively even as she reached out a hand to her desk and plucked up one of the sheets of paper lying there. 'Perhaps you should read this, Jane?' She held up the page temptingly. 'Then you will see exactly who and what your mother really was!'

'What is that?' Jane eyed the letter warily. Who could be writing to Lady Sulby now, twenty-two years after Janette's death?

'A letter written twenty-three years ago by Janette to her lover. Never sent, of course. How could she send it when her lover was already married?' Lady Sulby sniffed disgustedly.

'How do you come to have her letter?' Jane shook her head dazedly.

Lady Sulby gave a taunting laugh. 'Think back to twelve years ago, Jane. Surely you remember that I came with

Sulby when he came to collect you after Joseph Smith died...? Of course you remember,' she scorned, as Jane flinched at the memory. 'Just as I remember going through Janette's things and finding letters she had written to her lover but never sent. Vile, disgusting letters—'

'There was more than one letter?' Jane felt numb, disorientated.

'There are four of them.' Lady Sulby snorted. 'And in each one Janette talks to her lover of the child they have created together in sin—'

'Give that to me!' Jane snapped warningly, snatching the letter from Lady Sulby's pudgy hand to hold it fiercely against her breast. 'You had no right to read my mother's letters. No right! Where are the others?' She moved to the desk, sifting agitatedly through the papers there, easily finding the other three letters written in the same hand as the one she already held. Letters which Lady Sulby had obviously been reading when Jane came into the room. 'Does Sir Barnaby know about these letters...?'

'Of course he does not.' Lady Sulby sniffed scornfully. 'I have kept them hidden from him these last twelve years. Why do you think I was so concerned when I saw you with my jewellery box yesterday?'

Because the letters had been hidden there!

'How dare you?' Jane turned fiercely on the other woman, cheeks flushed, her eyes glittering deeply green. 'You are not fit to even touch my mother's things, let alone read her private letters!'

Lady Sulby recoiled from that fiery anger, her hand held protectively against her swelling breasts. 'Stay away from me, you wicked, wicked girl.'

'I have no intention of coming anywhere near you.' Jane

faced the older woman unflinchingly. 'I would not want to soil my hands by so much as touching you. I have tried so hard to like you but never could. Only Sir Barnaby has ever been kind to me here. Now I can only feel pity for him, kind and loving man that he is, in having such a vicious and vindictive woman as his wife.'

'Get away from me, you horrible girl!'

'Oh, I am going—never fear.' Jane's head was up as she walked to the door, her spine proudly straight. 'Let me assure you that I shall leave here as soon as I have packed the few things that truly belong to me.' Including her mother's letters!

Jane knew, as she hurried down the hallway to her tiny bedroom at the back of the house, that she was glad—relieved!—to at last have reason to leave Markham Park.

No matter what the future held for her—where she went, what she had to do in order to survive—Jane knew it could never be as awful as the years she had spent at Markham Park under the knowing and cruel hatred of Lady Sulby.

Chapter Four

Hawk luxuriated in the heat of his bath, relaxing back in water that today was pleasurably hot and shoulder-deep—compliments of the fastidious Dolton, he felt sure.

Hawk had risen early and dressed before going down to the stables to mount the horse he had instructed Dolton to have saddled for him, surprisingly enjoying the ride across the sandy beach, his mood lightening as the salty breeze whipped through his hair and drove the cobwebs from his brain.

He had even allowed himself, briefly, to think of Jane Smith. The early-morning light had helped to put their encounter late the previous evening into perspective, thus making a nonsense of it—and of the sudden desire Hawk had felt for her. He had been bored—extremely so—and not a little irritated, and Jane, with her curvaceous body and sharp tongue, had presented a diversion from that boredom and irritation. Not necessarily a welcome one, he had acknowledged with a frown, but a diversion nonetheless.

Hawk's mood had been further lightened when he had returned from his ride to Markham Park and read the letter that had been delivered in his absence. It was only a weekly missive forwarded from his man of business in London, Andrew Windham, but the Sulbys could not know that. Without knowing the contents of the letter they had readily accepted Hawk's explanation that they necessitated he leave immediately.

Or at least as soon as he had bathed, Hawk acknowledged with a satisfied sigh as he sat forward to pick up the jug beside the bath and tip its hot contents over his hair, before washing it, musing as he did so on the fact that he would be away from Markham Park within the hour. The arrival of Andrew's letter—a letter Hawk had so wanted to arrange himself—could not have been more fortuitous.

He could be at Mulberry Hall by tomorrow. Back in Gloucestershire. In control of his surroundings and the people who inhabited them.

And safely removed from that brief lapse of control he had known last night with Jane Smith...

Hawk banned Jane Smith and her bewitching green eyes firmly from his thoughts as he stepped out of the bath to wrap a towel about his waist and use another to dry his hair. He would ring for Dolton so that he might help him dress and shave before being on his way. He would not even delay his own departure until Dolton had packed his belongings into the second coach, preferring to be away from here, from the Sulbys—from the temptation of Jane Smith?—as soon as was possible.

It was not cowardice on his part but self-defence that made him so determined not to see or speak to Jane Smith again before he left. Desire was something one felt for a mistress, not a young, unmarried woman—in this particular case the orphaned daughter of an impoverished country parson, who would surely have marriage rather than bedding in mind.

A bedding was definitely what he was in need of, Hawk mused as he strolled through to his bedroom. A good, satisfying tumble in bed with a woman of experience who would expect nothing from him in return but a few expensive baubles. Yes, that would dispel any lingering thoughts of Jane Smith firmly from—

He turned incredulously in the direction of the bedchamber door as, after the briefest of knocks, it was flung open. The subject of his thoughts came hurtling through the doorway, her face flushed, her eyes over-bright, and that glorious red hair dishevelled, with wisps trailing loosely against her cheeks and down her creamy throat.

'Oh!' Jane Smith came to an abrupt halt, the colour deepening in her cheeks as she obviously took in Hawk's state of undress.

His first instinct was to pick up and quickly don the robe that lay waiting on a bedroom chair. His second instinct was to ask why should he? He was in the privacy of his bedchamber—a privacy Jane had rudely intruded upon—so why should he concern himself with her obvious embarrassment at his semi-nakedness?

He raised one disdainful brow. 'I trust you have good reason for interrupting my ablutions in this abrupt manner?'

Jane stared at him. *Did* she have good reason? She couldn't think—had no idea why she was even here. And Hawk—most definitely not the Duke of Stourbridge!—was standing there looking so—so—

His shoulders had appeared wide and powerful in those superbly tailored jackets, but the naked flesh was so much more immediate. His arms were muscled, a dark smattering of hair grew on his tanned chest, and down below the towel wrapped about his tapered waist...

Her startled gaze returned to his face, and just as instantly became aware of the disarray of his recently washed hair as it curled, as yet ungroomed, across his brow, taking away much of his austerity and giving him a youthfully rakish appearance.

Minutes ago it had seemed vitally important that Jane speak to the Duke before he left. Now she could not even remember what she had wanted to speak to him about!

That dark brow rose even higher. 'Jane?'

She swallowed, frowning as she tried to remember.

'I wish you to take me with you when you leave today, Your Grace!' The words tumbled from Jane unchecked as she finally remembered her purpose for being here.

She had gone back to her bedroom after leaving Lady Sulby in order to read her mother's letters. Not 'disgusting and sinful' letters at all, but those of a woman pouring out her heart to her lover as she told him of the child she carried—the child they had created in love—assuring him that she loved their child as she still loved him. Whoever he was. Because all four of the letters had begun simply, 'My dearest love', and ended with, 'Ever yours, Janette'.

Jane had sat and cried after reading them. For Janette. For Joseph Smith, whom her mother had obviously felt a deep affection for but had never loved in the way she had her married lover. For the real father Jane had never known...

But once the tears had ceased Jane had remembered her

vow to leave here today. And that there was someone else leaving Markham Park this morning who, if asked, might take her with him.

The Duke of Stourbridge.

Except this morning he did not look anything like the Duke of Stourbridge, with his hair still damp and dishevelled after bathing, and only a towel draped about those powerful thighs!

'You wish me to take you with me when I leave…?' He spoke softly, incredulously, those sharply etched features revealing nothing of his inner thoughts at her request.

Jane nodded. 'If you would not mind, Your Grace.'

If he would not mind!

This girl burst into his bedchamber, unannounced and with complete disregard for his privacy, and then proceeded to ask if she could accompany him when he left here today!

With what purpose in mind?

Yes, Hawk accepted that he had behaved with reckless impulsiveness the previous evening, when he had taken Jane into his arms and attempted to kiss her. But that really did not give her the right to think he might possibly want to pursue a relationship with her. Certainly not to assume he would want to take her with him when he left today!

His mouth twisted derisively. 'Jane, can you be under the delusion that I wish to make you my mistress?'

'No, of course not!' She recoiled at the suggestion, her face paling, her eyes turning a deep, appealing green.

They had an appeal that, even in his wariness over her exact intentions, Hawk found he was not immune to. Irritatingly.

He lifted the towel from his shoulders to absently dry his hair. 'Then what do you want from me, Jane?'

She blinked. 'Merely to ride in your carriage with you when you leave here today. I have a small amount of money saved, if you require payment—'

'No, I do not require payment, Jane! Not of any kind.' Ice edged his voice. 'Because you will not be coming with me.' He threw the towel impatiently down on a chair before donning his robe after all, a dark scowl creasing his brow. 'How old are you, Jane?' he demanded as he tied the belt tightly about his waist.

She looked dazed by the question. 'How—? I am two and twenty, Your Grace.'

'Indeed?' Hawk nodded abruptly. 'Old enough by far to know that you do not burst unannounced into a gentleman's bedchamber and then, finding him in a state of undress, proceed to ask him to take you away with him!'

Put like that, perhaps his assumption that she wished to become his mistress was understandable, Jane acknowledged ruefully. If completely wrong. She simply wanted to leave here as quietly and as speedily as possible.

She grimaced. 'I do not wish you to take me away with you, Your Grace. I merely wish to share your coach with you when you leave.' She also wished she'd had the forethought to wait until he had invited her to enter before bursting into his bedchamber in this way. She would certainly have saved them both embarrassment if she had done so.

Although the Duke didn't exactly *look* embarrassed as he began to pace the room restlessly. Even dressed only in the black silk robe, he was still possessed of that supreme self-confidence that seemed such a natural part of him it surely had to be inborn.

Deservedly so, Jane acknowledged as she found herself remembering the lean strength of his body. Muscles rippled in those long legs even now as he walked, and the defined muscles in the chest she had viewed earlier were something she dared any woman to resist. And especially a woman who had already found herself dreaming about him quite shamelessly the night before.

Jane felt her nipples swell and harden against the softness of her drab-muslin gown, her breasts rising and falling beneath the bodice. She suddenly found it difficult to breathe, and that strange warmth was back between her thighs.

She did not believe the accusations Lady Sulby had made about her's mother wantonness. Those letters she had read seemed to confirm that her mother had loved only one man: her married lover, Jane's natural father. But as Jane looked at the Duke of Stourbridge—at Hawk—she could not help wondering if she might not herself be a wanton. She had dreamt of this man last night. Hot, erotic dreams. And she was so physically aware of him now that she once again felt an unaccustomed ache low in her stomach.

'You have no idea what you are asking, Jane!'

She raised her eyes to meet the Duke's glittering golden gaze as he glared at her. 'I assure you I would try not to be any trouble—'

Hawk interrupted with a humourless laugh. 'Believe me, Jane, you do not have to try!' He could not spend hours, days, confined in his coach with a woman he had already physically responded to so uncharacteristically.

Damn it, he might respond in that way again, once alone in his coach with her, and take her on one of the seats!

'Why the urgency, Jane? What has happened since yesterday evening to make you so determined to leave here?'

She turned away so that he could no longer read the emotions in her eyes. 'I have decided I can no longer reside under the same roof as Lady Sulby. That is all.'

No, damn it. It was not all. What had that witch done to Jane to create the desperation he sensed in her? What could Lady Gwendoline possibly have said or done to Jane this morning to precipitate her immediate flight from Markham Park?

It was none of his business, Hawk reminded himself sternly. He did not like Lady Sulby, and had found her to be a pretentious and spiteful woman, but she was nevertheless the wife of Jane's legal guardian, and as such Hawk knew he had no right to interfere.

No matter how disturbed he was by the haunted look he had perceived in Jane's eyes a few minutes ago. Even if the thought of leaving her here to the continued coldness of Lady Sulby brought the bile rising to the back of his throat.

If Jane left her guardian's home with the Duke of Stourbridge—a single gentleman—then without a doubt the Duke of Stourbridge would be forced into marrying her.

Something Hawk did not intend to happen!

He turned away from the renewed appeal in those expressive green eyes. 'No, Jane. I am afraid it will not be possible for you to travel in my coach with me today. Whatever disagreement you have had with Lady Sulby, you must face it and deal with it. Running away from your problems solves nothing.' Hawk knew that what he was advising was the correct and only course in the circumstances, but inwardly he could not help but feel appalled as he listened to his own pomposity.

What other choice did he have? None that he could see. But he could have wished that Jane did not look at him so disappointed before she turned her head away and her slender shoulders slumped defeatedly.

He drew in a sharp breath. 'Perhaps if you were to tell me exactly what has occurred to cause this distress—'

'Thank you, no, Your Grace.' Her shoulders were tensed proudly now. 'It only remains for me to wish you a safe journey.' She walked towards the door.

'Jane!'

'Goodbye, Your Grace.' The quiet dignity of her voice cut through him like a knife.

Hawk crossed the room in long, forceful strides to press his hand against the closed door. 'Jane, surely you must see how unsuitable it would be for you to travel anywhere alone with me?'

'I understand completely, Your Grace—'

'Jane, I have warned you about "Your Gracing" me in that dismissive way!' Hawk reached out to grasp her shoulders with both hands. 'I can see that you are upset, Jane.' His voice gentled. 'But can you not see it is an upset that will quickly pass? Lady Sulby does not mean to be cruel, I am sure—'

'You know nothing of the sort!' The defeated air had completely left Jane as she glared up at the Duke, her hands clenching at her sides. 'She is a bitter, hateful woman, full of viciousness for those she considers beneath her. I do not believe you would treat even one of your dogs in the cruel way that she has dealt with me!'

She wrenched out of the Duke's restraining grasp before turning to leave, aware of his golden gaze following her frowningly as she let herself out of the his apartments to hurry back down the hallway to her own room.

The Duke might have refused her passage in his coach,

but that made little difference to her decision to leave. In fact, she refused to remain here for even another day!

If she could only get to London she could then take a public coach to Somerset—could find Bessie, her father's old housekeeper, who she believed now resided with her married son in a village only two miles from where they had all used to live.

Bessie had known both her mother and her father before Jane was born. And household servants, as Jane well knew from her position as neither a family member nor quite a servant in the Sulby household, often knew more about their employers than those employers might have wished.

Bessie would perhaps know more about Janette's lover than Lady Sulby, in her vindictive prying into Janette's personal letters, had ever been able to learn.

Once Jane's tears had stopped after she had read her mother's achingly emotional letters—letters that had never been sent to her married lover—she had come to a decision. Her real father might never have wanted her, might have callously cast off his lover once he knew she carried his child, but that did not mean that child could not now come back to claim *him*.

As a married man, it might not be comfortable for him to suddenly be presented with a daughter of two and twenty— but how much care had he given for Janette's comfort when he had denied both her and their unborn child?

None, as far as Jane could see.

Yes, the Duke might have refused to allow Jane to accompany him when he left later this morning. But her resolve was now such that Jane knew she would walk to London if she had to!

* * *

'More wine, Your Grace?' The serving girl at the inn in which Hawk had decided to spend the night hovered expectantly beside the table, holding up a jug of wine.

Hawk nodded distractedly, having touched little of the food that had been served to him along with the wine in this private dining room. Not because there was anything wrong with the food, but because wine alone served him better in his darkly brooding mood.

He had left Markham Park shortly after that unsatisfactory conversation with Jane, any relief he had expected to feel at his release from the Sulbys' oppressive company—Lady Sulby especially—completely overshadowed by that last haunted look in Jane's eyes as she had turned away from him. As the distance between the ducal coach and Markham Park had increased Hawk had found those inner shadows deepening. Until now, ten hours later, he was beset with such feelings of guilt at leaving Jane to her fate that he could think of little else.

But to have brought Jane away with him would have compromised her as well as himself. Totally.

Perhaps that was what she had wanted?

Somehow he did not think so. Her despair this morning had been too intense, too overwhelming to be anything but genuine in her desire to get as far away from Lady Sulby's viciousness as was possible.

That he was partly to blame for that viciousness Hawk did not doubt, having been totally aware of his hostess's fury the evening before, when he'd singled Jane out for his attentions. And that lady's ambitions concerning her daughter and himself had become apparent during the long, tortuous dinner, when he'd had Lady Sulby seated on one side of him and the fair Olivia on the other.

As if that had ever been even a remote possibility!

But Hawk was haunted by the accusations he had himself hurled at Jane the previous evening, concerning her behaviour at dinner with Lord Tillton. Accusations he now knew to be unfounded.

Having failed to see James Tillton again before retiring yesterday evening, Hawk had deliberately sought him out this morning, when taking leave of his fellow guests, and had noted grimly the half-crescent indentations in the older man's wrist. Indentations very like the piercing of neatly trimmed fingernails. *Jane's* neatly trimmed fingernails.

There had also been nothing of the siren about Jane when she had appeared so suddenly in Hawk's bedchamber that morning—none of the beguiling seductress using her persuasive skills in order to entice him into taking her away with him. There had been only the paleness of her cheeks and that haunting look of desperation in her eyes.

Damn it, there was nothing he could have done!

And yet that he had done nothing at all did not sit well with Hawk, either...

'Can I get you anything else, Your Grace...?'

He looked up at the frowning serving girl, realising by the uncertainty of her expression that she had taken his scowl of frustration as a personal comment on the inn's fare.

'No.' He sighed, nodding as she offered to remove his almost untouched plate of food from the table. 'Except perhaps another jug of wine. Also...' He halted her at the door. 'Send my manservant to me here as soon as he arrives, will you?'

Much to Hawk's added displeasure, his own departure from Markham Hall had been so precipitate that Dolton had not yet arrived at the inn with the second coach conveying Hawk's clothes.

What was keeping the man? He might have news of Jane—might be able to report that when he'd left she had been smiling and happy...

No, he would not. Hawk instantly rebuked himself heavily. Any more than Dolton would be able to tell him that Lady Sulby had suddenly become a lady of grace and beauty! By even hoping Dolton would be able to tell him of anything pleasant left behind at Markham Park. Hawk was merely trying to appease his own conscience, for abandoning Jane in the way that he had after she had asked for his help.

What would Jane do now? Would she still go ahead with her decision to leave the only home she had known for the last twelve years? If so, where would she go? And to whom?

'Your Grace?'

Hawk had been so deep in thought that he had totally missed Dolton's arrival. He smiled at the sight of a friendly face before Dolton's look of surprise made him realise that he was not usually so familiar with his valet. 'Dolton.' He sobered. 'I trust you had an uneventful journey?'

'Er—not exactly, Your Grace.' The other man frowned uncomfortably. He was a small, slender man of middle years, his blond hair slightly thinning, his eyes a watery blue. Eyes that at this moment seemed to be evading his employer's.

'No?' Hawk arched surprised brows. His question had been a politeness only. He expected that any problems Dolton might have encountered along the way would have been dealt with without the necessity of informing his employer of them.

Dolton still avoided meeting Hawk's piercingly questioning gaze. 'No, Your Grace. I—perhaps we could discuss this upstairs in your room, Your Grace?' he added awkwardly, as the serving girl bustled back into the parlour with the second jug of wine Hawk had requested.

Hawk's brows rose even higher at the strangeness of Dolton's behaviour. 'As you can see, I have not yet finished dining.'

'No, Your Grace.' Dolton chewed on his bottom lip. 'It's just that I really would like to talk to you in private. If you please, Your Grace?' He shrugged uncomfortably.

'Leave us, please.' Hawk dismissed the serving girl as she still hovered, probably with the intention of seeing to Dolton's dinner requirements. 'Now,' he turned musingly to the other man once they were alone, 'kindly tell me what has thrown you into such confusion, Dolton?'

His manservant drew in a deep breath before grimacing. 'I would much rather show you, Your Grace.'

'What can possibly have happened to disturb you so, Dolton?'

Hawk shook his head bemusedly as he stood up. 'Have you discovered a stain on one of my jackets you cannot remove? Or perhaps a scuff on one of my best boots?' It had been known for Dolton to be thrown into a paroxysm over just such an occurrence.

'Nothing so simple, I am afraid, Your Grace.' Dolton shook his head mournfully before opening the door for the Duke to precede him out of the room.

'A wheel has fallen off the coach, perhaps?' Hawk continued to dryly ridicule the man as he ascended the narrow stairway that led to the bedchambers above.

This inn was no better than the one Hawk had stayed at on his journey to Markham Park, but he had consoled himself with the realisation that at least this time he was on his way to his own home, rather than facing the unpleasant prospect of a week spent amongst virtual strangers.

'No, Your Grace.' His valet sighed as he mounted the stairs behind him.

'For God's sake, man—will you stop shilly-shallying and tell me what all this is about—?'

Hawk had opened the door to the bedroom allocated to him but came to an abrupt halt in the doorway to stare uncomprehendingly at the bonneted and cloaked figure that stood so demurely in the centre of the sparsely furnished room.

Jane Smith raised her lashes to look at him with green eyes that were far from demure.

'What is the meaning of this?' Hawk breathed chillingly, unable to remember when he had last felt so angry. If ever.

'I only left the coach unattended for a minute or so, Your Grace. When I went to collect the picnic lunch the cook had prepared for our journey.' Dolton launched into defensive speech as he stepped around the Duke to enter the room, his expression imploring as he looked up at his employer. 'She must have slipped inside the coach while I was in the house. As you know, Your Grace, I always travel outside, with Taylor, so we were unaware of Miss Smith's presence inside the coach until an hour ago, when it became rather cold and I had the coach stopped so that I could get my cloak. I discovered Miss Smith hiding amongst your trunks, Your Grace,' he concluded unhappily.

Hawk did indeed know of Dolton's preference for sitting up with the coachman. His valet suffered from motion sickness if confined inside the coach for any length of time.

None of which altered the fact that Jane Smith should not be here.

At the inn.

Once again in his bedchamber.

'You seem to be making a habit of this, Miss Smith.' His tone was icy.

'So I do, Your Grace.' She met his gaze unflinchingly.

Hawk drew in a sharply angry breath as he easily recognised her challenging look of defiance. 'I should have you beaten and taken back to Markham Place immediately!'

Jane's chin rose. 'I invite you to try, Your Grace.'

His mouth thinned. 'I was not intending to apply the beating myself, Jane.' He gave his valet a steely glare from beneath ominously lowered brows.

Jane tried, and failed, to suppress her laughter as she saw the look of obvious dismay on Mr Dolton's face at the thought of his employer ordering him to beat her.

'It really is too cruel to tease Mr Dolton in that way, Your Grace.' She shook her head, the heavy weight of Lady Sulby's hatred having lifted as each mile passed, taking her farther away from Markham Park. In fact, apart from the obvious precariousness of her future, Jane was feeling more light-hearted than she had done for some years.

'And what makes you think I was teasing?' The Duke raised haughty brows.

'The fact that I am perhaps two inches taller than Mr Dolton—and possibly stronger, too?' The laughter still gleamed challengingly in her eyes as she easily met the Duke's forbidding gaze.

Not that she did not sympathise with the frustrated anger he must be feeling. Having left Markham Park, he must have assumed he had seen the last of her.

The glittering gold gaze swept over her from head to foot before the Duke turned to spear his still-quaking valet with it. 'Miss Smith will not be staying,' he said ominously.

'Miss Smith most certainly *will* be staying.' As if to prove the point, Jane reached up and untied her bonnet, before removing it completely and placing it on a chair, then turned her attention to her cloak. 'Perhaps not in this exact room,' she allowed, with a mocking inclination of her head. 'But I am sure that the innkeeper will have another room in which I might spend the night.' Her cloak joined the bonnet on the bedside chair.

'And then what?' The Duke glared at her stonily. 'Is it your intention to walk the rest of the way to your destination?'

'If necessary, yes.' Jane perched herself daringly on the edge of the four-poster bed to look up at him with cool deliberation.

His mouth tightened. 'You are without doubt the most irresponsible, stubborn—'

'I think you may excuse yourself from the Duke's displeasure now, Mr Dolton.' Jane turned to smile warmly at the nervously hovering man.

It had perhaps been unfair of her to involve the Duke's valet in her escape from Markham Park and the Sulby family, but the opportunity to slip inside the unattended coach this morning had been too tempting to resist. And the fact that Mr Dolton had then elected to sit up with the driver meant she had managed to remain undetected for hours.

Far too many hours for the valet—or the Duke—to consider returning her to Markham Park tonight.

Neither did Jane intend being bullied into returning there tomorrow by the obviously infuriated Duke of Stourbridge.

'Yes, you may leave us, Dolton.' The Duke coldly echoed her instruction. 'For now,' he added gratingly.

'Please go down and have some dinner, Mr Dolton.' Jane gave the valet another encouraging smile. 'I shall join you shortly.' It had been a long day—a day without any food or water—and Jane felt very much in need of both. But not, of course, until she had finished her conversation with the Duke of Stourbridge.

'I do not believe I gave you leave to issue instructions to members of my staff.'

Jane turned her attention back to the Duke now that Mr Dolton had left the room and closed the door softly behind him. 'You were simply tormenting the poor man—'

'Miss Smith!'

She quirked auburn brows. 'Your Grace?'

Hawk found that his anger had not abated in the least since he had walked into the room and seen her standing there so unexpectedly. In fact, he would have dearly loved to pull her to her feet and give her a good shaking.

Except that he did not trust himself to touch Jane at this moment. He had no idea, if he did, whether he would shake her or kiss her!

He had spent hours tormenting himself with thoughts of having left Jane to the untender mercies of Lady Sulby, only to find that she was no longer at Markham Park after all, but cosily ensconced in his second-best coach as it travelled along some distance behind his own.

His gaze narrowed as he saw her smile. 'I suppose you

are congratulating yourself on managing to defy my instructions so effectively?'

Jane was not sure that 'congratulating' herself exactly described it, but she was feeling rather pleased with herself for having so successfully removed herself from Markham Park.

'I am not sure that your instructions came into my thinking when I climbed inside your coach this morning—'

'I am certain they did not!' He glared coldly.

'However,' Jane continued undaunted, 'I cannot deny I am pleased to be away from the Sulby household.'

The Duke's mouth thinned. 'You do realise that your disappearance, and the coincidence of my own departure this morning, will be noticed? That Sir Barnaby will send someone after you?'

She thought of Lady Sulby's deliberate viciousness this morning—of the fact that she had ordered Jane to leave. 'Somehow I do not think so, Your Grace.' She gave a firm shake of her head.

'Jane, do you not see how reckless your behaviour is?' The Duke crossed the bedroom to stand beside her, looking directly into her face. 'You are a young woman alone—an unmarried woman. If anyone should find you at this inn with me—'

'Do not concern yourself, Your Grace.' Jane stood up abruptly to move away, slightly disconcerted by his close proximity. 'If it became necessary I am sure that Mr Dolton could be persuaded into claiming me as a relative.'

He scowled. 'Just how long did you and Dolton spend together inside the coach?'

Jane turned to look at him, suspecting yet another accusation of flirtation but instead finding only grudging humour lurking in the depths of those mesmerising gold eyes.

Some of the tension left her shoulders. 'Only an hour or so. But I believe he likes me well enough to claim me as his niece if anyone should ask.'

'I am sure that he does.' Hawk straightened, finding his temper somewhat abated. He was under no illusion whatsoever that Dolton would voice his protest most strongly if his employer should attempt to cast Jane out into the night.

As the Duke of Stourbridge, he knew that he should demand that Jane return to her guardians immediately—that not to insist on that was madness on his part. But he could not deny that Jane's desperation earlier today to escape those guardians, and his own refusal to help her, had been haunting him all day. Too much so for him to now demand that she return to them.

Instead he sighed wearily. 'Are you hungry, Jane?'

'Ravenous!' she acknowledged ruefully.

'Very well, Jane.' He gave a terse inclination of his head. 'We will have dinner—'

'Oh, thank you, Your Grace.' She stood up to cross the room and clasp both his hands in hers. She looked up at him with glowing green eyes. 'Thank you. *Thank you*!' She punctuated her words with kisses placed upon his hands, finally laying her cheek against one of them with warm gratitude.

Hawk had stiffened at her first touch, needing all of his will-power at that moment not to snatch his hands from the soft feel of her skin against his as she pressed his hand to her cheek. It was such a creamy softness. A sensual softness.

His thumb seemed to move of its own volition in order to

stroke that silky warmth, and Hawk hesitated only slightly before he allowed his thumb to touch the rosy pout of her lips. Lips that parted slightly at his touch. The warmth of her breath against his skin was a caress in itself as she looked up at him with those trusting green eyes.

What Hawk would do next hung finely in the balance. His gaze remained on those softly parted lips, a nerve pulsing in his tightly clenched jaw as he fought the need he felt to taste those lips. To taste all of her. From her creamy brow to her dainty feet. He was sure that at this moment, being her reluctant saviour, Jane would deny him nothing.

But if he were to take advantage of her gratitude what would that make him? Beneath contempt—and in his own eyes no better than the people she was so desperately trying to escape!

'Stop it, Jane!' His voice was harsh as he pulled his hands from hers, turning sharply away from the hurt that now shadowed those expressive green eyes. 'I suggest that you wait here while I go in search of Dolton and instruct him to arrange overnight accomodation for my ward—'

'Your ward, Your Grace...?' Jane echoed faintly, sure that she could not have heard him correctly.

His mouth thinned disapprovingly. 'I can think of no other explanation for the presence of a young and single lady, travelling alone in the company of the Duke of Stourbridge. I am sure that Dolton, with his new penchant for subterfuge, will have no trouble at all in thinking of an excuse for your lack of maid,' he continued dryly. 'Perhaps he could invent an unexpected illness that has prevented her immediately accompanying us to Gloucestershire?'

'Gloucestershire?' Jane said dazed, suddenly very still.

'But I thought—You are not returning to London, Your Grace?' she prompted sharply.

'No, Jane, I am not,' he confirmed mockingly. 'Mulberry Hall, principle seat of the Duke of Stourbridge, is in Gloucestershire. My plan had always been to go there for the rest of the summer. As I have no intention of allowing you to travel anywhere unchaperoned, you will obviously have to accompany me there.'

Jane stared at the Duke disbelievingly, too shocked at that moment to argue.

She had believed the Duke of Stourbridge to be returning to London from where she would be able to buy passage on a public coach to Somerset. And to the warm, comforting bosom of Bessie.

Instead, it seemed Jane now found herself forced to accompany the Duke—a man who had already induced the most erotic longings inside her—to his estate in Gloucestershire...

Chapter Five

'You are very quiet this morning, Your Grace.'

There was no response to Jane's soft observation except the sound of grinding teeth. The Duke's teeth.

It was a sound she had heard several times during the two hours they had shared the ducal coach as it travelled to the Duke's family seat in Gloucestershire. It was rather irritating coming from a man who normally displayed such an air of control and good breeding. Perhaps it was a habit he was unaware of...?

The silence that had beset him since the two of them had parted the previous evening, following a shared dinner downstairs in the inn's parlour, was also unsettling.

They had disagreed throughout most of the meal, of course, as Jane had continued to protest vehemently at the Duke's assertion that she would accompany him to Gloucestershire. The Duke had remained equally adamant, especially in view of her refusal to share her future plans with him, that he would not even consider leaving her at a coaching inn along the way, so that she might make her own way to London.

Jane had thought the awkwardness between them at least partially resolved when she had been forced to back down in the face of the only alternative the Duke would consider to his own plans, which Jane liked the sound of even less than accompanying him to his estate in Gloucestershire—that of being returned to Markham Park and her guardians forthwith!

Admittedly, their goodnights to each other had been a little frosty, but Jane had felt slightly mollified when she'd found that, along with a second bedchamber for the Duke's 'ward', Mr Dolton had also engaged the services of the daughter of the innkeeper to act as Jane's temporary maid, and a steaming hot bath had been there for her enjoyment.

After a good night's rest, Jane had risen from her bed this morning, determined to make the best of her situation. After all, although the Duke was completely unaware of it, Gloucestershire was in fact much closer to her real destination of Somerset than London...

Mary, the innkeeper's daughter, had returned to Jane's room shortly after she had completed her ablutions, carrying a breakfast tray. So Jane had no occasion to see or speak to the Duke again before joining him inside the ducal coach to resume their journey.

As expected, the coach was as magnificent inside as out, with seats upholstered in such a way as to afford them the maximum comfort. Even the sun had come out mid-morning to cheer her. In fact, it would have been a very pleasant journey indeed if not for the noticeable silence of the Duke.

And the grinding of his teeth, of course...!

Now Jane risked a glance at the Duke from beneath her

lashes, at once seeing the reason for those grinding teeth: his jaw was clenched so tightly the bones there looked in danger of actually snapping beneath the pressure.

She had tried several times to engage him in conversation these last two hours. She had remarked on the weather as she removed her cloak, and her increasing nervousness at his continued silence had caused her to explain that the green gown she wore today—a particular favourite of hers—had been a birthday gift from Sir Barnaby the previous year. On both occasions she had received only a scowl and a grunt in reply, and she had not felt brave enough since to attempt further conversation.

She sat forward slightly now. 'Have I done something to disturb you this morning, Your Grace?'

'Have I not told you—repeatedly—to stop "Your Gracing" me with every other word?' He glared darkly.

Jane blinked at the fierceness of his expression. 'I do not know what else to call you, Your—sir...' she amended hastily, as he breathed so heavily down his nose it sounded almost like an unbecoming snort.

'Have I not invited you to call me Hawk?' His scowl darkened.

'You have,' Jane confirmed softly, her cheeks feeling slightly warm as she remembered the occasion on which he had done so. 'But while that may do when we are alone, it will hardly suffice when we are in the company of others.'

'It cannot have escaped your notice, Jane, that we are not at this moment in the company of others!' he bit out tautly.

He was being boorish, Hawk knew. But he could not seem to stop himself. As he had already surmised the previous day, when Jane had first asked to accompany him and he had refused, travelling alone with her in the confines of his coach was pure torture!

For one thing she looked so damned happy this morning. Totally unlike the cowed creature he had met for the first time two days ago on the stairs at Markham Park. Was it really only two days since this young woman had literally launched herself into his presence? It seemed much longer! Her eyes shone with excitement today, her cheeks were flushed, and her lips seemed to be curved into a constant smile of contentment.

To Hawk's way of thinking Jane had no right to look so happy when she had thrown his own normally peaceful existence into such disarray!

Her earlier remark about the weather being warm had been accompanied by the removal of her travelling cloak. A move that had revealed she wore a pale green gown beneath that lent her skin a creamy hue while at the same time intensifying the colour of the fiery red curls piled upon her head. Her explanation that the gown had been a gift from Sir Barnaby had at least restored Hawk's faith in his own judgement of the older man; it seemed that Sir Barnaby's only lapse in good taste had occurred twenty-five years ago, when it had come to the choosing of his wife!

But as Jane sat opposite Hawk, looking so relaxed and beautiful, it was impossible for him not to notice that the gown also revealed the bare expanse of her breasts. That creamy swell moved enticingly every time his coach ran over a rut in the road, causing Hawk to shift uncomfortably in his seat as his body hardened in awareness.

Hawk knew that his tailor in London took great delight in fitting his clothes precisely to the muscled width of his shoulders, his tapered waist and powerful thighs—but at this particular moment Hawk could have wished that the man had allowed him a little more room for manoeuvre in the cut of his breeches!

Jane, still an innocent despite her claim of being two and twenty, remained completely oblivious as to the reason for his discomfort.

Hawk scowled anew. 'You dare to rebuke me for my silence, Jane?'

The colour warmed Jane's cheeks as she guessed the reason for his accusation. The Duke had tried repeatedly during dinner yesterday evening to encourage Jane to tell him of her reasons for leaving Markham Park so abruptly had been, and of exactly what she intended doing once she reached London. It had been encouragement Jane had very firmly resisted.

For how could she possibly tell the Duke of Stourbridge—a man who no doubt knew each and every one of his antecedents, reaching back several centuries at least—that her only reason for going to London had been to find further transport to Somerset, all with the intention of discovering who her real father might be?

Jane simply could not tell him that. Not only would the Duke question the wisdom of even associating with one such as her, but it would also be disloyal to the mother Jane had never known, who had married a man she did not love in order to give her daughter a name.

And so, much to the Duke's obvious chagrin, Jane had remained stubbornly silent concerning her reasons for travelling to London.

It was a silence that obviously still displeased him.

'I did not rebuke you, Your Grace.' Jane chose to ignore

his impatient snort. 'I merely remarked upon the fact that you seem unusually uncommunicative this morning.'

'Unlike some people, Jane, I do not feel the need to spend my every waking moment prattling on about innocuous or—even worse—irrelevant subjects.'

She drew in a sharp breath at his deliberately insulting tone. 'In that case, Your Grace, I will allow you to return to your solitude.' She turned away from him to stare sightlessly out of the window beside her, blinking back unexpected tears as she did so.

Was she wrong not to confide in him?

If he had been just Hawk St Claire, the man Jane had talked to amongst the sand dunes two evenings ago, perhaps she might have felt able to talk to him about such a personal matter. But it was impossible to forget he was also the Duke of Stourbridge, a rich and powerful peer of the realm, a man Jane simply could not tell of her mother's relationship with a married man which had resulted in her own birth.

No matter how much it displeased the Duke, she simply could not!

Hawk's heart clenched in his chest as he saw Jane blink back the tears obviously caused by his impatient anger.

Since the death of his mother ten years ago the only female to have been a constant in his life had been his young sister, Arabella. As a child, Arabella had been engagingly charming, but during the last few months spent at her first London Season she had shown herself to be as wilfully determined to have her own way as her two older brothers, causing Lady Hammond, their amenable aunt and Arabella's patroness, to pronounce her completely unmanageable. Which meant that Arabella was currently unchaperoned, his aunt having taken to her bed in her London home to recover from the rigours of chaperoning a young girl through the Season.

Jane, as Hawk knew from the fact that she was here in his coach with him at all, could be equally stubborn when the occasion warranted. She just went about achieving her objective without his sibling's penchant for confrontation. No doubt her years of being subjugated at every turn by the sharp-tongued Lady Sulby were responsible for her more restrained defiance. At best she had been treated as a poor relation in the Sulby household. At worst—as Hawk had disapprovingly witnessed for himself on the day he'd arrived at Markham Park—as little more than a servant.

He sighed heavily. 'I believe I owe you an apology, Jane.'

She turned to give him a surprised look, those suppressed tears giving an extra sheen of brightness to the green of her eyes. 'An apology, Your Grace?'

He chose to ignore her formal address this time. 'My mood is—churlish.' He nodded. 'But I really should not take out my bad temper on you.'

Jane gave him a rueful smile. 'Not even if I am the reason for that bad temper?'

'But you are not. At least, not completely,' he allowed derisively, as he saw a teasing look of sceptisism enter her eyes. 'You do not have any siblings of your own, do you, Jane?'

'I do not, Your Grace,' she confirmed huskily.

What had he said to make Jane suddenly lower her lashes and clench her hands so tightly together in her lap? He had talked only of siblings, something Jane obviously did not have, and yet curiously the mention had caused her previous air of contentment to fade.

Much as Hawk found it irksome that Jane stubbornly refused to discuss with him her last interview with Lady Sulby, he also found himself most unhappy at being the one to cause her further distress.

He shook his head. 'Jane, you have no idea how lucky you are to be an only child.' He watched intently this time for Jane's reaction—if any—to his remark.

But in the few seconds during which Hawk had noted and questioned her earlier response Jane had somehow drawn upon hidden reserves, and her expression was one of cool interest now. 'Lucky, Your Grace?'

He grimaced. 'I have two younger brothers and an even younger sister—all of whom, it seems, are trying to age me before my time!'

Jane smiled at the image his words projected. 'In what way, Your Grace?'

'In every way!' He gave an impatient grimace.

At that moment he had such a look of a man weighed down by his family responsibilities—an expression so at odds with the arrogantly imperious Duke of Stourbridge— that Jane could not help smiling. 'Tell me about them,' she invited softly.

He sat back on the seat. 'Lucian is eight and twenty, and morose and unapproachable since he resigned his commission in the army following Bonaparte's defeat. Sebastian is six and twenty. He enjoys nothing more than involving himself in every scandal you could think of and some I would rather you could not.' He grimaced with distaste. 'As for Arabella…! My sister is eight and ten in years, and recently attended her first London Season.'

There was such a wealth of feeling in his last statement

that Jane had no doubt that Lady Arabella's first Season had not been the success the Duke had hoped it would be.

'She is still very young, Your Grace. There will be plenty more opportuny, I am sure, to receive the required marriage proposal.' Jane attempted to placate him, sure that, as the sister of the Duke of Stourbridge, Lady Arabella St Claire must be a very eligible young lady indeed.

The Duke's mouth twisted ruefully. 'You misunderstand me, Jane,' he drawled. 'My sister has received numerous offers of marriage in the past few months—she has steadfastly refused to accept any of them!' he added hardly.

The fact that the Duke had allowed his sister to do so was very telling indeed, and indicated an indulgence for his younger siblings that had not been apparent in his initial comment about them.

Jane shrugged. 'Perhaps Lady Arabella felt unable to love any of those men—'

'Love, Jane?' he interrupted scornfully. 'What does love have to do with marriage?'

'Oh, but—' Jane broke off her exclamation to bite her bottom lip as she recalled that even her own mother had not married for love but to give her unborn child a name.

Was that really all marriage amounted to? Merely a necessary requirement for the sake of having children, made out of duty rather than love?

Was that what the Duke of Stourbridge would require in his own marriage? A woman to bear him legitimate children, necessary heirs to the dukedom, while he no doubt supported a mistress in town and continued to live his life as he chose?

Was that what all men of the ton required in marriage? If so, then Jane was glad she had no part of it.

She had already spent too much of her two and twenty years knowing what it was like to be unloved to ever contemplate deliberately committing the rest of her life to such an emotionless state. Better to remain an old maid than to be merely suffered in a loveless marriage.

Besides, who would ever want to marry her now anyway? The daughter of a single woman abandoned in her pregnancy by her married lover!

'Jane…?'

She had allowed her guard to drop, her thoughts to wander, Jane realized as she looked across at the Duke with a guilty start. And the illustrious Duke of Stourbridge was too astute a man, those strange gold-coloured eyes of his too all-seeing to allow such a lapse to pass unnoticed.

He did look so handsome this morning, in a jacket of royal blue, his shirt a snowy white, his waistcoat of pale blue satin and cream breeches worn above highly polished Hessians. But it really would not do, when Jane had just reasoned for herself how small were her own marriage prospects, for her to notice how strikingly handsome the Duke of Stourbridge looked today!

Jane forced a dismissive smile to her lips before answering him. 'Your brothers and sister do not sound so bad, Your Grace.'

He grimaced. 'That is because you do not know them.'

Hawk, although unaware of the reason for it, had been completely aware of the shadows that had briefly claimed Jane's expressive green eyes. That she was hiding something more from him than a disagreement with Lady Sulby he did not doubt. That Jane intended to keep hiding it from him was also not in doubt; he knew, even on such a brief acquaintance, that Jane was possessed of a stubborn need for privacy that almost, but not quite, matched his own.

He eyed her speculatively. 'But you will. At least you will have occasion to meet Arabella,' he added with a frown, not sure that he at all liked the prospect of Jane being introduced to the handsomely brooding Lucian or the mischievous Sebastian.

Despite what Sebastian might have assumed to the contrary during their conversation the previous week, Hawk was in fact very fond of his younger brothers. But he also knew their natures much better than they would perhaps have wished. And the thought of either of those handsome scoundrels taking a fancy to the innocently beautiful Jane was not a comfortable one.

She gave a puzzled frown at his comment. 'How so, Your Grace…?'

Hawk was still scowling at the thought of Jane becoming the object of either of his brothers' romantic interest. 'Now that the Season has ended for the summer my sister Arabella has returned to Mulberry Hall, of course.'

Jane's eyes widened. Lady Arabella St Claire would be in residence at Mulberry Hall when they arrived? Was already there eagerly awaiting her eldest brother's arrival?

Well…no. From the little Hawk had said of his strong-minded young sister, Jane did not think the other girl would be waiting in the hallway of Mulberry Hall eager-eyed and breathless in anticipation of the Duke's arrival!

But eager-eyed or not, Lady Arabella would be at Mulberry Hall when the Duke arrived there with Jane at his side. How did he intend to explain the presence of Jane, a young lady completely unknown to Lady Arabella, who had obviously accompanied the Duke completely unchaperoned on the long coach journey to his Gloucestershire home?

'Of course,' Jane acknowledged quietly, her lashes lowered onto creamy cheeks. 'I...' She paused to moisten suddenly dry lips. 'What explanation do you intend giving Lady Arabella for my presence, Your Grace?' She looked across at him anxiously. 'After all, she will know that I am not your ward.'

He quirked dark brows. 'Why not simply tell her the truth, Jane? That you begged to be allowed to come away with me.'

Jane gaped at him.

She had given little thought to what explanation the Duke would give his staff for her having accompanied him to his home. If she had thought of it at all, she had assumed that none of the staff employed on the Stourbridge estate would dare to question the Duke concerning his actions. But she doubted a young and headstrong sister would as readily accept Jane's unaccompanied presence.

Ah—at last he seemed to have shaken Jane from the cool reserve she had assumed minutes ago, which had so irritated him, Hawk noted with satisfaction. Although it was highly insulting to realise, from the consternation he could now see in Jane's expression, that she now wondered at his motive for allowing her to travel to Mulberry Hall with him. That she believed his young sister might make assumptions about that motive also!

Before inheriting the title of Duke of Stourbridge, Hawk had been as much of a rakehell as Sebastian now was— had for years enjoyed the same carousing and wenching with his own reckless friends. But the last ten years had necessarily seen a change in Hawk's life. His nature had become outwardly coolly reserved, and, as Sebastian had complained only days ago, any relationships of an intimate nature kept discreetly hidden away from public scrutiny. That Jane could even suspect him of being thought to take a mistress to Mulberry Hall—to the St Claire family's principal seat, the home where his sister was also in residence—was unacceptable. So unacceptable that Hawk could not repress his instinct to make Jane suffer a little for even entertaining such a suspicion.

'Do not look so concerned, Jane,' he taunted as he lounged back on the seat. 'No one, not even my sister Arabella, would dare to question what position I intend you to occupy in my household.'

And what position was that? Jane wondered dazedly. Had she misunderstood the Duke the previous evening when he had been so insistent she would travel under his protection? Despite what he had said to the contrary, was he now saying he expected her to become his mistress as payment for that protection?

'Come, Jane.' He sat forward to take both her tightly clenched hands in one of his. 'When we were together in the dunes two evenings ago you did not give the impression that you found my…attentions repulsive.'

In truth, Jane did not find anything about the Duke of Stourbridge repulsive. In fact, just having him touch her hands in this way had reawakened those feelings of longing that had so disturbed her that night amongst the sand dunes. An experience she had found herself dreaming of repeating ever since.

More than repeating!

This man—Hawk—had awakened longings inside her that she had not even known existed, and even now she could feel herself being drawn towards him, found herself held captive by the intensity of that golden gaze.

He should stop this right now, Hawk knew. Should release Jane's hands, distance himself from her, before explaining exactly what role he intended her to take up at Mulberry Hall.

And yet as he gazed upon the temptation of her softly parted lips, felt the silkiness of her skin beneath his fingertips, he was aware of a desire to reach out and take her fully into his arms and taste her. The hard throb of his body echoed that need. It was a need that Hawk had firmly resisted two evenings ago, but which he now succumbed to as. His gaze hooded, he effortlessly pulled her across the small distance that separated them to settle her light weight comfortably on his knee as his arms moved about her and his mouth claimed hers.

Her lips felt as soft and silky beneath his as Hawk had imagined they would, and the smooth skin of her bare arms was like satin to his touch. He moved his hand to curve about her nape and pull her deeper into the kiss.

Fire blazed through him, deep and hot, his mouth hardening against hers before he parted her lips with his tongue and sought the moist heat within.

Her skin exuded the exotic perfume of flowers mixed with that of sexual arousal, telling Hawk that Jane was not averse to his attentions at all—that in fact she more than returned the desire that raged through him.

He groaned low in his throat, his lips devouring hers as he sipped and tasted the nectar to be found there. One of his hands caressed restlessly down the slender length of her spine before moving to curve possessively about a thrusting breast.

Jane felt drugged from Hawk's kisses. Then, as if she had died and gone to heaven, she felt his hand cup her breast—one of those same breasts that seconds ago had seemed to swell and harden as he kissed her. Her breath caught in her throat as he touched the hardened tip, sending that now familiar heat spiralling between her thighs.

Jane had no idea what took place between a man and woman once they were in bed together—knew only from Lady Sulby's advice to Olivia concerning any future marriage that it was something she would just have to lie back and suffer on the occasions her husband demanded it of her. But this—being in Hawk's arms, having him kiss and touch her in this intimate way—did not feel like suffering. In fact, she felt weak with wanting!

Did that mean that Jane was really not destined for the marriage bed? Her mother's letters to her lover had indicated that she had enjoyed their intimate relationship. Was Jane also one of those wanton women who actually *enjoyed* having a man make love to her?

No, it could not be!

Jane was not any of the things Lady Sulby had accused her of being. She was not!

Even as desire clouded Hawk's mind, and the heated throb of his body made him ache to lie Jane on the seat and ravish her totally, he sensed—knew—the moment Jane was no longer a willing recipient of his attentions.

At the same time he also knew that if he were to uphold any authority as the Duke of Stourbridge, as well as being Jane's proxy guardian, he must be the one to put an end to this. And in such a way that there would be no danger of it happening again.

His mouth had a deliberately cruel twist to it as he raised

his head to look down at her, his gaze hard and mocking as she lay limply in his arms. 'Do you see, Jane, how true was my warning of the danger you put yourself in when you chose to travel alone in a gentleman's carriage with him?' he taunted scornfully, even as he lifted her bodily and placed her back on the seat opposite his own.

Her face had become very pale, her eyes wide with shock. 'You—you kissed me only in order to teach me a lesson, Your Grace?'

Hawk steeled himself not to show how the hurt in her eyes and the trembling of her slightly swollen lips affected him. 'Partly,' he confirmed coldly. 'But I also wished you to know, no matter what you may have been thinking to the contrary—' his tone hardened icily '—that the Duke of Stourbridge has no need to use blackmail in order to seduce comely wenches fresh from the country into his bed. I have no need to bother with such persuasion when such women obviously fall into my bed all too willingly!' he added with scathing scorn.

Jane gasped at the accusation even as she knew that the Duke only spoke the truth. She *was* fresh from the country, and she had—momentarily—been all too willing a recipient of his lovemaking.

'That is what you thought I was about, was it not, Jane?'

If anything his voice had become even icier. At that moment he looked every inch the arrogantly self-assured Duke of Stourbridge of their first meeting—his eyes narrowed with ominous intent, those sculptured lips thinned to cruel mockery.

That his accusations had some merit caused Jane to straighten proudly, and she met his gaze unflinchingly, already knowing the Duke well enough to realise that he showed nothing but contempt for people who lacked the courage to stand up to his dictatorial arrogance.

'I was not about to succumb to your bed, Your Grace.'

'All evidence to the contrary, Jane!'

Her brows rose coolly. 'I am not a liar, Your Grace.'

The Duke gave a mocking shake of his head. 'Did no one tell you that self-deception is a form of lying, Jane?'

At that moment Jane's fingers itched to wipe the arrogant smile of satisfaction from the sneeringly curved lips that only minutes ago had so capably devoured her own!

'I would not advise it, Jane.' The Duke's voice had softened warningly as he obviously observed that instinct in the clenching of Jane's hand. 'You have already presented enough of an inconvenience to my peaceful existence without adding striking me to your list of offences!'

She was breathing hard in her agitation. 'Might I remind Your Grace that it was your decision, not mine, that I accompany you to Gloucestershire!'

'So it was.' He nodded dourly. 'A decision I have already come to regret, I do assure you!'

Jane bristled indignantly. 'The remedy to the inconvenience of my company can be easily found, Your Grace.'

His mouth tightened. 'If you are once again suggesting that I allow you continue on to London alone—'

'I am.'

'Then I advise you to put such a thought completely from your mind, Jane,' Hawk continued frostily over her interruption. 'The only people left in London during the summer are rakehells and dissolutes who would find themselves totally bored if removed to the country. Such men,' he added hardly, 'would see you as nothing more than an innocent tasty morsel to be quickly devoured and as speedily discarded!'

Jane's breasts quickly rose and fell. 'Do you speak from experience, Your Grace?' There was challenge in her tone.

Hawk eyed her with chilling derision. 'If I did, Jane, then you can be assured you would not now be sitting across this carriage from me with your innocence still intact!'

'You are arrogant, sir!'

'I am honest, Jane,' he came back tersely, having no doubt whatsoever that Jane would not last a day in London without some well-practised reprobate—his brothers Sebastian and Lucian, for example!—trying to seduce her into his bed.

Jane dearly wanted to deny the Duke's accusations. But how could she do so when she was aware of the way she still inwardly trembled from the effect of his kisses and the feel of his caressing hands against her breasts...?

That arrogant mouth twisted knowingly. 'Nothing to add to that particular argument, Jane?' he taunted. 'In that case,' he continued grimly, 'before we reach Mulberry Hall I would have your promise that you will not make any attempt to go to London until I am free to accompany you there.'

Her eyes widened incredulously. 'It is your intention to accompany me to London, Your Grace?'

'It is,' he confirmed impatiently. 'I have several estate matters that require my attention for the next few days, but after that I should be available to take you to London. In other words, Jane, I will not hear of you even *thinking* of continuing your journey alone!'

Jane frowned. Had the Duke guessed? Could she have somehow given away thoughts of that being her intent?

'I will have your promise, Jane!' The Duke reached out to firmly grasp her wrist between strong fingers, his narrowed gaze intent upon her face.

Jane's thoughts raced. If she made such a promise then she would have to keep to it. Had she not just assured him that she was not a liar? But it had never been her intention to remain in London, and the Duke of Stourbridge, albeit unknowingly, was now bringing her within a carriage ride of her real destination…

Would it still be lying to make him such a promise when London had never been her ultimate goal?

Possibly.

But not actually.

Pure semantics, Jane knew. But the Duke was really leaving her little choice in the matter.

Because it was not her intention for the Duke of Stourbridge to accompany her *anywhere*!

Her business in Somerset, her need to talk to Bessie, was completely personal to herself and certainly not in need of any witnesses. Least of all the aloofly superior Duke of Stourbridge!

She gave a cool inclination of her head. 'I give you my promise, Your Grace.'

His gaze narrowed. 'What do you promise, Jane?'

She gave a humourless smile at his obvious suspicion concerning her easy acquiescence. 'I promise that I will not attempt to travel to London until you are able to accompany me there.'

Hawk's gaze narrowed as he looked across at her searchingly. There was something about Jane's promise that did not quite ring true.

He just had no idea what it was.

Yet.

Chapter Six

'Before introducing me to Lady Arabella as her new companion, you might have first taken the trouble to confide that fact to me, Your Grace!'

Hawk couldn't help but wonder why he was surprised at the interruption as he looked across to where the door to his library had been thrown back on its hinges. Jane Smith entered and strode imperiously across the room to stand before the wide desk behind which he sat.

Hawk had believed, when he'd excused himself from the ladies' company a short time ago, leaving the two of them to enjoy their afternoon tea together, that it would allow the two women time in which to become better acquainted with each other. And at the same time, now that the introductions were over, allow him the opportunity of escaping to the relative sanctuary of his library!

Its walls lined with leather-bound volumes, two comfortable armchairs placed on either side of the fireplace, along with a decanter of brandy within his easy reach, the room was normally beneficial in that it afforded him a few hours' solitude when he might deal with estate business.

Obviously no one had told Jane Smith that the Duke was never to be disturbed when ensconced in the library. Or, as was more likely to be the case, Jane had been given that information but had chosen to ignore it!

'Do you have nothing to say in your defence, Your Grace?' she demanded accusingly now, the colour high in her cheeks.

Hawk had plenty of things he might like to say on that subject and several others—but he doubted that any of them were suitable for Jane's delicate ears!

'It might interest you to know, Jane—' Hawk's tone was deceptively mild as he sat back in his chair to look at her from beneath narrowed lids '—that you are the only person of my acquaintance who actually dares to speak to me in this disrespectful manner.' His voice hardened glacially over the last few words.

'Really, Your Grace?' The increased flush to Jane's cheeks indicated that she was not as unchastened as her tone would have Hawk believe. 'You surprise me!'

'Do I?' Hawk rose languidly to his feet to move lightly around the desk, a hard smile of satisfaction curving his lips as Jane instinctively took two steps back. 'I think that once again you are choosing to deceive yourself, Jane,' he drawled mockingly.

Was she? Jane wondered, slightly breathlessly. Perhaps so. But she had found herself completely overwhelmed a short time ago, when the carriage had entered through imposing iron gates that had preceded a fifteen-minute carriage ride to where Mulberry Hall itself reposed. Deer and cattle had grazed undisturbed amongst rolling parkland as the carriage had proceeded on its leisurely way along a driveway edged with hundreds of yew trees, before reaching a wide courtyard that had revealed Mulberry Hall bathed in late-afternoon sunshine.

Jane had gazed up as if hypnotised at the Hall's magnificence. As the Duke had helped her alight from the coach. The house was built of mellow sandstone, with seemingly a hundred windows on its frontage, and a wide balcony over huge oak doors.

One of those doors had opened wide the moment the Duke had put one of his highly polished boots upon the first stone step leading up to the entrance, an elderly butler greeting his employer with solicitous warmth as he enquired as to the comfort of his journey. Jane had continued to gaze wide-eyed at her surroundings, sure that the whole of Markham Park would have nestled snugly into the cavernous entry hall of Mulberry Hall!

The bedroom she had been allocated had been yet another pleasant surprise after the almost cupboard-like space she had occupied at Markham Park for the last twelve years, with its highly polished floor, sunnily bright yellow walls, a four-poster bed draped with the same gold-coloured damask that adorned the two windows which, she discovered, looked out over the rolling parkland.

Jane had been happily enchanted with her new surroundings when she had returned downstairs and a footman had shown her into the drawing room where the Duke and his sister were about to take tea.

Only to have the Duke spoil it all by making the announcement to his sister that, as Lady Hammond had been indisposed since their sojourn in London—whoever Lady Hammond was—Jane was now here to act as her new companion. A companion that the Lady Arabella, once the Duke had excused himself and left the two women alone, had immediately informed Jane she had absolutely no need of!

It had been obvious from the first that Lady Arabella and the Duke of Stourbridge were closely related. That lady was several inches taller than Jane, and the aristocratic features that were so hard and unyielding on the Duke were softened to a striking beauty in the much younger Arabella. Her eyes were a dark brown, and she had hair of gold shot through with streaks of deeper honey, where the Duke's was dark with those golden streaks.

A single minute alone in Lady Arabella's company had shown Jane that that young lady had also inherited her brother's arrogantly imperious manner!

Jane's mouth tightened as she recalled the awkwardness of their conversation. She addressed the Duke once more. 'I am very sorry if you take offence at my tone, Your Grace—'

'Oh, I do, Jane. I do,' he assured her softly. 'And must I point out—yet again—that we are not in the company of others...?'

He might point out that fact as often as the occasion arose, but since arriving at the Duke's ancestral home, and seeing the deference with which his household staff treated him, Jane had become even more aware of the differences in their social stations.

In a very different way she was also aware of being alone with him now, here in the privacy of his study... Even more so since he had risen to his feet and moved to stand in front of the huge mahogany desk.

Because once he had stood up it had become obvious that

the Duke had not expected to be interrupted. For he had removed the royal blue coat and waistcoat that Jane had so admired earlier, and loosened his neckcloth. Following so closely on that incident in the carriage, Jane found his less than impeccable appearance more than a little disturbing!

Hawk narrowed his gaze as he saw the flush that suddenly brightened Jane's cheeks. 'Is something troubling you, Jane…?'

'Something other than your not informing me that I was to be your sister's companion?' Her tone was waspish.

Deliberately so, Hawk surmised knowingly, allowing a mocking smile to curve his lips as he crossed his arms over his chest. He had the satisfaction of seeing Jane quickly avert her gaze. 'As I recall, Jane, our earlier conversation concerning what was to be your place here at Mulberry Hall was…interrupted…'

He was rewarded by a deepening of that blush. 'That is all very well, Your Grace,' Jane dismissed briskly. 'But my purported role here is obviously as much of a surprise to Lady Arabella as it has been to me!'

Hawk's smile immediately faded. 'My sister has said something to upset you?'

Jane looked up frowningly as she heard the sharpness that had entered his tone, inwardly relieved that she could now see only the Duke of Stourbridge in the angular handsomeness of his face, rather than the more disturbing Hawk St Claire.

But as the Duke, she had come to realise, he expected his simplest instruction to be carried out without question…

Jane chose her next words carefully. 'Lady Arabella is quite rightly displeased at having a person she is totally unacquainted with suddenly thrust upon her in this high-handed way—'

'How displeased?'

Jane blinked at what she knew—from the cold glitter that had entered his eyes and the sudden hardness to the set of his jaw—to be the Duke's deceptively mild tone. Both of which boded ill for someone. In this case Lady Arabella.

'Come, Jane,' he encouraged in that softly disconcerting tone. 'In what way exactly has my sister expressed her displeasure to you?'

Now that she was actually here in the Duke's presence—in his disturbing presence!—Jane found herself loath to pursue the subject. In truth, she dearly wished that she had waited until her own temper had cooled before even broaching this subject with him.

But it was too late for such caution now. The Duke was waiting, compelling her to answer, those dark brows raised in deceptively lazy expectation.

Her chin rose challengingly. 'I do not believe I said that Lady Arabella had given voice to her displeasure. It is merely that I believe—although Lady Arabella did not actually say so—that your sister sees me more in the role of—well, of spy for you, Your Grace,' she finished lamely.

Hawk drew himself up to his full considerable height and looked down his nose at her. 'A spy, Jane?' he repeated hardly. 'And why would my sister suppose that I would want to set a spy on her? Unless—' He broke off, his expression darkening as he glanced towards the open door. 'Damn it, what has that girl been up to now?'

'Your Grace...?'

Hawk glared, his hands clenching into fists at his sides before he turned sharply on his heel to move and stare sightlessly out of the window. 'You will leave me now, Jane. Return to the drawing room and tell Lady Arabella that I wish to see her. Now. Immediately. Did you hear me, Jane?' He turned to scowl at her darkly when he heard no movement to show she was about to do his bidding.

'I—For what purpose, Your Grace?'

Hawk became very still as he looked at the pointed angle of Jane's chin, at the stubborn set of her mouth and the challenging sparkle that now lit those deep green eyes as she steadily met his gaze.

He had doubted the wisdom of his visit to Norfolk even before his arrival there. The ill-bred behaviour of his hostess and her obvious matchmaking attempts between himself and her daughter had only confirmed those doubts, so hastening his desire to leave Markham Park at the earliest opportunity.

In the normal course of events that would have been the end of the matter, enabling Hawk to put the whole unpleasant experience behind him. Unfortunately the main irritation of his stay—and the main amusement, he inwardly admitted—was now standing before him!

With open challenge in her sparkling green gaze…

It really was a novel experience for him, Hawk acknowledged ruefully. He had become even more aware since his return to Mulberry Hall, where even his slightest need seemed to be fulfilled before he had expressed it, of how unusual it was for anyone to oppose him in the way Jane constantly did.

As a novel experience it had caused him amusement on several occasions, but it was surely not to be tolerated when it came to his dealings with his young sister!

He arched dark, arrogant brows. 'The purpose of my summons is none of your concern, Jane.'

'It is if it is something I have said that has instigated that summons!' Jane refuted impatiently. 'I cannot in all conscience—' she gave a firm shake of her head '—give Lady Arabella such an instruction if, when she arrives, you intend to inflict some sort of unjustified rebuke or cruelty upon her—' She broke off abruptly, alarmed by the way in which the Duke's face had darkened ominously.

Her breath actually halted in her throat as he strode back to the dark and rested his clenched fists on its top, to lean so far forward that his face was now only inches from her own, his eyes glittering dangerously, nostrils flared, his mouth thinned to an uncompromising line.

'I have no idea, Jane—no idea at all,' he repeated in an icily soft voice, 'what I could possibly have done in our so far brief acquaintance to give you the belief, even the idea, that I might—what was it you called it exactly?—Ah, yes, that I might intend inflicting "unjustified rebuke or cruelty" upon my sister. They were your exact words, were they not—'

'Stop it, Your Grace!' Jane cried her agitation as he once again spoke to her in that deceptively mild tone.

Because there was nothing in the least mild about the Duke's emotions at that moment. In fact, he appeared so full of suppressed fury that it might cause him to explode at any moment!

'If you wish to shout at me, Your Grace, then I would much rather you did so and got it over with. But do not, for goodness' sake, play with me like a cat tormenting a mouse—' She broke off, frowning, as the Duke gave a hard bark of laughter. 'Did I say something to amuse you, Your Grace?' she prompted, slightly indignantly.

Hawk gave an incredulous shake of his head. Anyone less like a mouse than Jane Smith he could not imagine!

This young woman challenged him, reviled him, defied him—and yet still something stopped him from telling her to go to the devil, to absent herself from his company and never show her face to him ever again.

The proudness of her carriage, perhaps? The sharpness of her spirit? The creamy turn of her cheek? The unfathomable depths of those enticing green eyes? Or maybe the fullness of her lips? Those lips that could be curved with amusement one moment and then turned down with such disapproval the next...

As they had been twisted with disapproval constantly since entering Mulberry Park an hour ago!

'Leave me, Jane,' Hawk instructed wearily, as he straightened before resuming his seat behind the desk. 'Just go now—before I cease to be amused by anything about you!'

Jane hesitated, continuing to look at him uncertainly even though she knew herself to be well and truly dismissed.

She had meant to soothe Lady Arabella's obviously ruffled feathers by talking to the Duke about the wisdom of his announcement, but instead she seemed only to have succeeded in annoying the Duke even further.

'Still here, Jane?' His tone was bitingly dismissive as he looked up at her coldly.

Jane caught her bottom lip between her teeth and turned slowly to walk to the door, dearly wishing there was something she could do or say that might somehow soften a situation that she was aware was partly of her own making—although she was not naïve enough to believe that the self-possessed Lady Arabella would have kept her opinions on the subject of Jane's presence in the house to herself the next time she saw her brother!

Nevertheless, Jane was conscious of the fact that she had been the first to broach the subject, so causing the Duke to be more angry with his sister than he might otherwise have been.

'Your Grace...?' She hesitated in the doorway, looking back at him. His head was bent, his hands at his temples, fingers threaded through the dark thickness of his hair.

He gave a weary sigh as he slowly looked up at her. 'Yes, Jane?'

Her throat moved convulsively as she swallowed. 'Perhaps—perhaps if you were to assure Lady Arabella that I will not be staying long...?'

His mouth firmed. 'But we have no idea *how* long you will be staying, do we, Jane? I have your promise concerning your future travel arrangements, remember?'

Yes, the Duke had her promise, Jane acknowledged with a slow nod of her head, before leaving the room to close the door behind her much more quietly than she had opened it.

But the promise she had made him only applied in regard to her attempting to travel to *London*...

'Please sit down, Arabella,' Hawk invited, with an abrupt gesture towards the chair in front of his desk as his sister swept into the room some ten minutes later.

Long enough, Hawk guessed, to show him in what contempt she held his summons. An opinion supported by the fact that, instead of sitting in the chair he had indicated, his sister chose to make herself comfortable in one of the armchairs beside the empty fireplace.

What had he ever done, Hawk wondered impatiently as he stood up to join her, to deserve two such stubborn women in his life at the same time? One openly rebellious, the other less obviously so but nevertheless just as determined to go her own way?

Arabella regarded him with cool brown eyes as he sat in the chair opposite hers. 'I cannot help but question your reasons for bringing Miss Smith here, Hawk.'

He had been expecting his sister's attack—if not actually prepared for the subject of it!—having already taken warning at the rebellion darkening the beauty of Arabella's eyes.

Arabella had grown so quickly from child to young woman, it seemed now to Hawk as he looked at her, that for once he was not quite sure how to proceed with the interview. He was certainly in no mood for cajolery, but to openly forbid a continuation of what he saw as Arabella's wilfulness might only result in her doing something totally reckless.

He quirked dark brows as he decided to ignore—for the moment—the slight she had cast upon Jane's character. And his own... 'You do not like Miss Smith?'

Arabella met his gaze unblinkingly. 'I did not say that. I merely wondered as to the propriety—'

'I advise you not to proceed any further along this line of conversation, Arabella!' Hawk cut in with harsh warning. 'Suffice to say that Jane's presence here is one of complete innocence.'

Arabella's eyes—those brown eyes that could look at a man and melt his very soul—yes, even those of her three elder brothers!—met his own with hardened scorn. 'I am supposed to believe that Miss Smith is here for my amusement only?'

His mouth tightened. 'Those are the facts, yes!'

'They are…?'

The turn this conversation had taken was highly insulting to Jane—as well as echoing Jane's own concerns of earlier—and yet even so a part of Hawk could not help but appreciate, even secretly admire, his young sister's refusal to be cowed by him.

Although that admiration in no way deflected Hawk's own determination not to be dictated to by a girl of only eight and ten. 'I did not ask you here to talk about Jane Smith, Arabella,' he said quietly.

'I very much doubt that you *asked* at all!' Arabella's tone was sharply resentful. 'Despite Miss Smith's attempt to make it seem as if you did,' she added tauntingly.

Hawk shook his head. 'We will return to the subject of Jane later. For the moment I wish only to talk about you, Arabella. You have been on your own since your return to Mulberry Hall almost two weeks ago. I wonder how you have managed to fill your time during those two weeks?'

'You forget that Lucian remained for several days after accompanying us here,' Arabella dismissed. 'Talking of Lucian—'

'Which we were not,' Hawk cut in hardly.

'Then perhaps we should have been,' his sister came back tartly. 'Have you seen or spoken to Lucian recently…?'

Hawk frowned. 'Not for several weeks, no. Why?'

Arabella sighed. 'He seems—changed. Hardened. Even cynical.'

'War does that to people, Arabella,' Hawk dismissed impatiently. 'I am sure that is only a temporary—aberration. We were talking of you, Arabella...' he reminded her firmly.

Arabella met his gaze coolly for several long seconds before turning away with a dismissive shrug. 'I have been forced to fall back upon reading and embroidery for my amusement.'

He nodded. 'And I understand from Jenkins that you have also been out riding on the estate every day, have you not? Without your groom?'

'What of it?' Arabella challenged sharply.

She loved and admired all her older brothers. Loved Sebastian perhaps the most, as he was nearest to her in age. Lucian, more taciturn and private now following his years in the army, had always been her steadfast protector—the one who had always been there to pick her up if she should fall. But Hawk—so tall and broad-shouldered, always so busy about the St Claire estates and so toplofty when it came to his rare and infrequent appearances in Society—was the brother whose approval Arabella had always sought, the brother she most wanted to please.

And she knew that she had not pleased him during the weeks of her first Season...

But Hawk was the Duke of Stourbridge, a man looked up to and respected wherever he went, and Arabella was well aware that it was because of who her brother was, because of his title, that she had received at least half the marriage proposals that had been forthcoming during those weeks in London. The other suitors perhaps had genuinely believed themselves to be in love with her, but Arabella, determined to marry a man she admired and loved as much as her brothers, had felt unable to return the feelings of any of those men.

For the first time in her young life Arabella knew she had genuinely displeased her eldest brother. It was something that she had felt, still felt, dearly. But she had hoped to talk to Hawk once he returned to Mulberry Hall—to perhaps explain the reason for her refusals. And now, instead of being alone at Mulberry Hall with her eldest brother, Arabella found him accompanied by a single woman of quite breathtaking beauty!

Miss Jane Smith.

What was she, Arabella, supposed to make of such a strange occurrence? What was she supposed to make of Miss Jane Smith?

To Arabella's way of thinking, Hawk had only added insult to injury by announcing that he had brought the other woman here to act as her companion!

Her brother raised a languid hand. 'I am merely attempting to make conversation with you, Arabella—' He broke off to look at her frowningly as she gave a hard laugh. 'Have I said something to amuse you…?'

The hard glitter in his eyes told Arabella that he, at least, was not in the least amused!

She stood up impatiently. 'I am sure that you recognise scorn when you hear it, Hawk. We are both aware that you never merely "make conversation"!' She began to pace the hearth. 'Whatever it is you wish to say to me, Hawk, please say it and stop prevaricating in this tortuous way!'

Hawk watched her from behind guarded lids, appreciating how much like their mother she looked at that moment, with the colour flaring in her cheeks and that sparkle in her eyes. The pale lemon-yellow gown she wore—not that garish yellow so unsuitable for Jane!—with its touches of cream lace, suited Arabella's golden colouring perfectly, its becoming style proof once again, if he should need it, that Arabella was no longer a little girl to be cossetted and spoilt.

'Very well, Arabella,' he drawled hardly. 'What I really want to know is did you arrange to meet anyone while you were out?'

'Arrange to meet anyone?' She frowned her puzzlement. 'What—? Ah.' A knowing smile curved her lips. 'What you are really asking is if I happened to meet any single gentlemen whilst out alone and unchaperoned?'

Hawk pursed his lips consideringly. 'It is a possibility that has occurred to me.'

'Hawk, if you suspect me of having taken a lover then why do you not just say so?'

He could hear the slight trembling in his sister's voice even as she issued the challenge, realising as he did so that he had pushed Arabella almost to the point of tears. He did not have to look far for the perpetrator of this new sensitivity within him to a woman's emotions—Jane Smith had stormed his male defences in just this way too. More than once.

He sighed. 'I am not making any such accusation, Arabella—'

'Are you not?'

Hawk's mouth firmed at her scornful tone. Damn it, he was the Duke of Stourbridge, with all the power and influence that went along with that title, and as such he would not suffer this lack of respect a moment longer!

'No, Arabella, I am not,' he bit out forcefully, standing up to look down at her censoriously. 'However, I do forbid you to go out riding on your own again.'

'You *forbid* me, Hawk?' she echoed incredulously.

'I forbid you,' he repeated tersely. 'In future, if you wish to go out riding without the protection of a groom, perhaps Miss Smith might accompany you—'

'To the devil with your Miss Smith!' Arabella stamped her slipper-clad foot in temper.

'She is not *my* Miss Smith, Arabella,' Hawk reproved frostily.

'Well, she is certainly not mine—nor ever will be!'

Hawk drew in a deeply controlling breath before speaking again. 'It is my wish that you will be kind to Miss Smith, Arabella—'

'You may wish all you like, Hawk—but unfortunately wishes are not always granted, are they?'

Hawk frowned at the acerbic comment. His mouth tightened. 'I advise you to put your own feelings aside in this matter, Arabella, and do all that you can to ensure Miss Smith is made to feel a welcome guest during her stay here with us.'

Arabella raised mocking brows. 'I thought you said she was to be an employee...?'

Hawk eyed her coldly. 'She is to be your companion, yes. But she is first and formost a guest of the Duke of Stourbridge!'

His sister looked as if she might have liked to say more on that subject—and had thought better of it when she saw the warning in his icily glittering gaze. 'Very well, Hawk.' She gave a cool inclination of her head. 'Oh, I almost forgot...' She paused in the doorway, much as Jane had done such a short time ago.

'Yes?' As then, Hawk did not think he was going to like what Arabella was about to say to him!

Arabella's smile was almost triumphant. 'I have arranged

a small dinner party for three days hence, to be followed by dancing in the small ballroom.'

The 'small' ballroom would hold thirty people comfortably, at least…

Hawk grimaced. 'How small is this dinner party to be, Arabella?'

Arabella's smile widened. 'About twenty-five people, I believe—no, twenty-seven now that you and Miss Smith have arrived.' She turned to leave and then suddenly paused once again. 'Oh…and Lady Pamela Croft sent word this morning that her brother has arrived for a visit. So that will make us twenty-eight.'

Hawk had stiffened at the mention of their nearest neighbour's brother. 'Can you possibly be referring to the Earl of Whitney?'

'I believe Lady Pamela has only the one brother.' Arabella nodded with a questioning raise of her brows.

Hawk knew that she had. And he also remembered that the last time he and the Earl of Whitney had had occasion to meet had been shortly after Hawk had usurped the other man's place in the Countess of Morefield's bedchamber! A fact both men, never the easiest of acquaintances, were both very much aware of.

Was Arabella, like Sebastian, and possibly Lucian too, also aware of it…? Her almost triumphant air seemed to imply that it was a distinct possibility!

'There is just one more thing, Hawk—'

'For God's sake, Arabella,' he cut in icily, 'either leave or stay. But most certainly cease dithering about in the doorway in that unbecoming manner!'

'I take it you are not interested, then, in the fact that while we were talking I chanced to see Miss Smith passing by the library window? Ah, perhaps you *are* interested, after all?' his sister mused tauntingly as Hawk stood up abruptly to turn and look searchingly out of the window. 'Perhaps, after all, it is I who should act as chaperon to Miss Smith...?'

Hawk shoulders stiffened as he exerted every effort of his considerable will over his own temper in order to prevent himself from responding to Arabella's deliberately provocative taunt.

Knowing that he was responsible for leaving himself open to such comments in having brought Jane here at all in no way lessened the impatient anger he was feeling.

Why had Jane left the house?

Where could she have been going?

As far as he was aware, Jane was completely unfamiliar with her surroundings—so why would she have gone outside at all so soon after her arrival?

Chapter Seven

Jane arched mocking brows as she stared down the length of the dining table at her host. 'Do I take it that your interview with Lady Arabella did not go well this afternoon, Your Grace?' There had been no opportunity for Jane to speak to him since his conversation with his sister, although she had seen him in conversation with the butler earlier, when she'd returned from her walk outside.

Still, her observation concerning his sister was a fairly accurate one to have made, considering the two of them were seated alone at the table in what Jenkins had informed Jane was 'the family dining room'. Lady Arabella, and the Duke's aunt, Lady Hammond, had both sent down their apologies.

That Jane and the Duke were seated at either end of a table that could have seated twelve only added to the feeling of distance that had been stretching further and further between the two of them since their arrival at Mulberry Hall earlier today.

The Duke looked as immaculate as ever tonight, in black evening clothes and snowy white linen, but the impeccable formality of his dress only made Jane more aware of the inadequacy of the muslin gown she had worn on the day she'd left Markham Park, which was all she had to change into for dinner.

'My conversation with Arabella, as you so rightly guess, Jane, did not go well,' the Duke confirmed impatiently. 'Were you ever such a contrary miss, Jane?' he added with languid weariness.

Jane was very aware, even if the Duke was not, of the presence of the stiffly unreadable demeanour of Jenkins, as he quietly attended them by removing their empty fish plates from the table. She was also aware that this was definitely not one of those occasions when they were 'not in the presence of others'—which meant that the Duke was being far too familiar with a woman he had supposedly engaged as companion to his young sister. Especially as that sister had not even had the good manners to join them!

'Such behaviour would have been seen as self-indulgence, Your Grace,' she answered him, somewhat distantly.

'I suppose that it would,' Hawk acknowledged ruefully, and he realised how ridiculous had been his question after the way in which Jane had been treated by her guardians. At the same time he could see, from Jane's awkward glance in Jenkins' direction, that she was not happy conducting this conversation in front of his butler.

'That will be all, thank you, Jenkins.' He dismissed the elderly man once the roast beef and vegetables had been served to them. 'I will ring for you when we are in need of you again.'

If the butler saw anything unusual about this turn of

events he did not show it by so much as a flicker of an eyebrow as he bowed formally before leaving the room.

Hawk sighed. 'The unfortunate situation developing between Arabella and myself has shown me how little experience I have in dealing with the capriciousness of young ladies, Jane.'

'You surprise me, Your Grace.'

Hawk could not fail to notice the mocking glint in her eyes. 'Young ladies that are related to me, Jane!'

'Of course, Your Grace.' She nodded coolly. 'But if that truly is the case, perhaps the answer might be to forget that Lady Arabella is related to you...?'

Hawk had far from forgotten Jane's disappearance outside earlier this evening. Or the fact that she had returned to the house while he was in the process of questioning Jenkins as to whether or not he knew of her whereabouts—which he had not. No, Hawk certainly had not forgotten. He was simply awaiting the appropriate moment in which to introduce the subject...

He shook his head now. 'I am not sure that I understand you, Jane. Arabella may not like me very much at this moment, but there is no doubting the fact that she is my sister!'

'Assuredly not, Your Grace,' Jane answered dryly.

He raised dark brows. 'Now, why do I sense some sort of rebuke in that remark, Jane...?'

'I have no idea, Your Grace,' she came back innocently. 'But from what I have observed of Lady Arabella I believe that at the age of eighteen she wishes to be treated as an adult rather than as a child. As a child in need of a companion, for instance...'

Hawk's mouth tightened at the rebuke. 'Arabella *is* still

a child, Jane, and at the moment she is behaving like a spoilt, wilful one.'

'Was it a child who received several marriage proposals only weeks ago? Was it for a child that you would have approved of her accepting one of those marriage proposals?'

'You insult me if you think I would have been happy for her to accept a proposal of marriage just for the sake of it, Jane,' Hawk defended coldly.

'The nature of any marriage proposal and the suitability of the man involved are both irrelevant to this conversation, Your Grace,' Jane reasoned softly. 'What is pertinant is that you cannot expect Lady Arabella to receive proposals of marriage one day and be treated like a child again the next. Moreover, a child who is to be told what she may or may not do, and when she may do it.'

Hawk drew in a sharp breath as he bit back his icy retort. A part of him knew that he had invited Jane's criticism by confiding in her in this way, and another part of him was surprised that he had done so...

In the years since he had assumed his role as head of the St Claire family, Hawk had expected his siblings to respect his wishes. That he did not appear to have achieved this as well as he might have wanted had been brought home to him not once but twice in recent weeks. First in Sebastian's absolute refusal to contemplate the idea of any marriage—let alone one suggested by Hawk—and yet again today by Arabella's stubbornness when it came to acceding to any of his demands.

He did not, however, appreciate having Jane, of all people, point out these failings to him! He looked down his nose at her. 'I refuse to believe I have ever been guilty of such arrogance with any of my siblings, Jane.'

'Really?' She gave an acknowledging inclination of her head. 'Then I must assume it is only where "nuisances who disrupt your peaceful existence" are concerned...?'

Hawk picked up his glass of claret and took a much-needed drink, his gaze narrowing as he looked down the length of the highly polished table at the woman who had disrupted his peaceful existence from the moment they had first met.

Jane was looking particularly lovely this evening. Her gleaming red hair was arranged in an abundance of ringlets upon her crown, with several enticing tendrils brushing her nape and brow, her creamy throat was once again bare of any adornment—possibly because Jane had no jewellery with which to adorn it?—and the simple cut of her gown succeeding only in emphasising the curvaceous perfection of her body.

A warmly seductive body that Hawk could not deny he was totally aware of. 'I believe you malign me in saying I have ever told you what you may do, Jane.' His voice was harsh.

Her mouth thinned. 'Only what I may not do, sir!'

'You are referring, I presume, to the fact that I refused to allow you to run off to London in a reckless manner?'

'I am referring, Your Grace, to the fact that at two and twenty I am perfectly old enough to make my own decisions!' Her eyes glittered warningly.

It was a warning Hawk had no intention of heeding. 'Even if those decisions are wrong?'

'Even then!'

He eyed her consideringly. 'Tell me, Jane, did you accompany the Sulbys when they came to London for the Season?'

'I did...yes,' she answered, almost warily.

'And did you meet someone whilst you were there? A young man, perhaps?' He frowned. 'Maybe that is why you are so set on returning there? In order that you might seek him out...?'

Jane gave him a pitying look. 'I met no one whilst in London, Your Grace. My only excursions during that time were to the shops, and then simply so that I might carry Olivia's purchases for her!'

Once again Hawk was reminded that Jane had been more servant than ward in the Sulby household. Her presence at the Sulbys' dining table two nights ago had been the exception rather than the rule.

He sipped his wine. 'Where did you go earlier this evening, Jane, when you decided to go outside?'

Jane stiffened. 'I trust I am at liberty to walk in the grounds, at least, Your Grace?'

She was being overly defensive, Jane knew. Probably because she had *not* simply gone for a walk in the grounds of Mulberry Hall earlier, but had in fact made her way deliberately to the stables, with the intention of enquiring of one of the grooms exactly how far it was—and how long it would take—to get to her true destination of Somerset!

Which she had done—and in such a way, Jane hoped, that she had not aroused the groom's suspicions as to the true purpose of her enquiries.

Although that might not be the case if the Duke of Stourbridge were to question the other man!

'Did I say otherwise?' the Duke prompted softly now.

'You implied it!' she snapped agitatedly.

Hawk looked at her wordlessly for several long seconds as the anger inside him grew. This situation, with both a wilfully defiant Arabella and a stubbornly determined Jane, was not only trying his impatience in the extreme, it was becoming unendurable!

'Do you find my concern for you so unacceptable, then, Jane?' The icy softness of his tone was in no way indicative of his inner frustration at this situation.

'Yes!'

Hawk drew in a sharp breath before rising to his feet. 'Then I must give you leave to put yourself in the path of danger at any time you so choose! Just so long as you accept that I will no longer be in a position to save you from your own reckless folly!' He picked up the decanter of brandy and a glass from the dresser before turning sharply on his heel to stride forcefully towards the door, very much aware that if he did not leave now he would resort to either kissing her or spanking her!

'Hawk…?'

He would not—could not—allow himself to be deterred from his resolve, his immediate need to get as far away from Jane as was possible. Neither by the uncertainty to be heard in her tone nor the fact that she had at last once again called him by his first name. He was very aware that if he did not leave this room now—right now!—he was definitely going to do something Jane would find even more unacceptable than the arrogance she complained of so bitterly.

He paused only long enough in the doorway to turn and inform her, 'I have forgotten to tell you of the dinner party my sister has arranged for three evenings hence, Jane.' His mouth twisted derisively as he added, 'The same sister with whom, according to you, I have the seemingly annoying habit of saying what she may do and when she may do it!'

Jane swallowed convulsively, never having seen the

Duke in quite such a towering rage as this, and knowing, although Arabella had obviously caused him some irritation earlier, that it was *she* who had provoked this chilling anger.

She moistened dry lips. 'I—'

'I will inform that same sister,' the Duke continued icily, 'that you are in need of a new gown for the evening. And I implore you, Jane, do not say another word to contradict me!' The fierceness of his warning came through gritted teeth.

'But—'

'Will you not, just for once in our acquaintance, accept that I am doing this for your comfort rather than my own?' His mouth had thinned ominously.

Her chin rose determinedly. 'That is the argument of all dictators, I believe.'

Hawk's gaze flared, and then glittered coldly. 'One day, Jane—one day you will go too far!' he finally managed to grind out. 'And I give you fair warning that on that day you will discover exactly what I am capable of!'

He turned and left the room before he could no longer control the urge he had to commence teaching Jane that lesson forthwith.

Leaving Jane with the uncomfortable knowledge that her plans to make her way to Somerset at the first opportunity, would probably arrive rather sooner than the Duke could ever have imagined...

'Is it the horses you are so fond of visiting, Jane, or do you have some other reason for haunting my stables in this way...?'

Jane gave a guilty start at the sound of the Duke's voice behind her, turning so sharply to face him that her slippered foot lost its purchase on the thick layer of straw that covered the floor, causing her to lose her balance completely.

She barely had time to register how handsome the Duke looked in his work clothes—a tight-fitting brown jacket and thigh-hugging breeches above highly polished brown boots—before the world tilted on its axis and she toppled over backwards.

Luckily the stall she was in had been cleaned earlier that morning and laid with fresh straw, and this sweet-smelling mattress cushioned Jane's fall. She lay sprawled on her back, slightly winded, as she stared up at the dumbfounded Duke of Stourbridge.

He did not stay dumb for long, however. 'Are you making me an invitation, Jane? Or is it that you suddenly felt a need to lie down?' He moved farther into the confines of the stall to look down at her, heavy lids lowered to shield the expression in his eyes.

So giving Jane no idea whether the Duke was just being his normally mocking self, or if he actually meant her to take his first question seriously…

Considering the impatient manner in which he had deserted the dinner table the previous evening, Jane decided that he was being his normal mocking self!

Her own eyes glittered with impatience as she sat up. 'I would not have lost my balance at all if you had not crept up behind me in that sly fashion!' she said waspishly.

'Please do not get up, Jane,' Hawk drawled derisively as she began to do so. 'After the dampness of the dune which we once shared, the stables are a much cosier place for us to converse,' he assured her dryly, before dropping down onto the clean straw at her side.

Hawk grimaced inwardly, knowing that if any of his

grooms had seen him do so they would probably seriously question the Duke of Stourbridge's state of mind. And quite rightly so!

'Converse, Your Grace?' Jane echoed guardedly, as she made a show of picking stalks of straw from the sleeve of her gown.

Several more tufts had attached themselves endearingly in the brightness of her hair, but Hawk decided that now was perhaps not the right time to point them out to her. Nor, indeed, to attempt to remove them himself...

He was aware that, apart from the slight movement and snorting of a horse in one of the other stalls, the stables were very private and quiet at this time of day, his grooms having moved on to other chores about the estate after completing the exercising of the horses and the cleaning of the stalls earlier this morning.

Meaning that he and Jane were completely alone here, with little chance of interruption.

He felt a reawakening of the same desire to take Jane in his arms and kiss her that he had known the previous evening. A desire Hawk had resisted yesterday evening by leaving her so abruptly but which he was not sure he would be able to a second time...!

Perhaps, in the circumstances, it had been unwise on his part to suggest they remain here.

He would not have sought her out at all had Jenkins not informed him that, 'Miss Smith left the house half an hour since and walked in the direction of the stables.' It transpired from his groom that she had already done so yesterday, instantly arousing Hawk's curiosity as to why it was she had felt the need to visit his stables twice in as many days.

Unfortunately, as he looked now at a slightly dishevelled Jane, her face flushed, the soft pout of her lips slightly parted, Hawk knew that it was no longer just his curiosity that was aroused.

'Your Grace...?'

He frowned down at her darkly. 'Jane...?'

She looked at him quizzically. 'You said you wished to talk to me.'

'Did I?' Hawk blinked, but the movement did absolutely nothing to dispel the tempting vision of Jane's moistly parted lips.

Jane felt a frisson of alarm course through her as she saw the direction of the Duke's gaze, quickly followed by a wave of heated awareness as that gaze moved down to the creamy swell of her breasts above her simply styled muslin gown.

She could hear him breathing now, feel the softness of that breath move over her skin as he suddenly seemed much nearer. Had he moved? She had not been aware that he had, and yet he was definitely much closer than he had been a moment ago.

Jane stared up at him in mesmerised fascination, held in thrall by the deepening gold of his eyes as he moved even closer, her lids dropping, lips parting, as he raised one of his hands to cup her cheek. The soft pad of his thumb caressed those parted lips with an eroticism that made her gasp as she raised her lids to look up at him with darkened green eyes.

He stared long and hard into those emerald depths before he groaned achingly, 'Dear God, Jane...!' His mouth claimed hers, his arms moving about her as he drew her close against the hard strength of his body.

His gloriously male body that only days ago Jane so clearly remembered viewing in all its almost naked glory. Inexperienced as she was, she had still been able to appreciate the broadness of his shoulders and chest, the stomach muscles clearly defined, his hips lean and powerful...!

And those firm lips—lips that could so often be thinned in disapproval or quirked in mocking humour—now moved against hers searchingly, devouring, causing Jane's pulse to leap wildly and heat to course wantonly throughout her whole body as she arched closer against him in urgent need.

He should never have been tempted into kissing her, Hawk admonished himself impatiently, even as he began to press Jane back onto the warm cushion of straw. But the warmth of her body, her own enticing perfume, both acted as a heady temptation it was impossible for him to resist.

He lay half across her as he deepened the kiss, knowing by the way Jane's body arched against his, by the fact of her hands now beneath his jacket as she restlessly caressed the length of his back through the thin material of his shirt, that Jane was as aroused as he was—even if her inexperience gave her no idea how to deal with that arousal.

Neither did Hawk know quite where this was taking them. He was aware only of the need he had to touch her, to taste her. His lips left hers to travel the length of the arched column of her throat, down to the creamy swell of her breasts, his fingers dealing deftly, quickly, with the buttons of her gown as he lowered the material to reveal pouting breasts covered only by the thin material of her chemise.

His fascinated gaze fastened on the rosy hardness of her nipples, clearly visible through that material, and lightly caressing fingers moved across those aroused tips, causing Jane to gasp before arching her back in breathless supplication.

It was too much. Jane was too much tempation for Hawk to be able to deny her. His glittering gaze briefly held hers before he lowered his head to draw one of those rosy tips into the heated cavern of his mouth, his tongue rasping across the already aroused nipple as he suckled her deeper into his moist warmth—harder, fiercer. He heard her groans of pleasure and felt her fingers curl convulsively into the hardness of his back, nails scraping as she held him tightly against her.

Hawk's hand moved to cup her other breast, and he felt it swell beneath his touch, her nipple a tight bud as he ran the pad of his thumb across it in the same rhythm with which he suckled its twin.

His thighs were rigid with arousal, with the need to claim her fully, to slide into the heat that awaited him inside her before giving them both the release they craved.

He should stop now—should pull away from her before that need overwhelmed them both. But he was powerless to resist as he felt Jane's hands unfastening the buttons of his waistcoat and shirt to push the material aside. She sought to touch his naked flesh, her hands echoing his own caress, and his groan was one of aching defeat as her tiny fingers touched his own hardened nubs.

No woman had ever touched Hawk so innocently, so erotically before. Jane's lack of experience in physical intimacy gave her no boundaries, no set of rules to follow, and her fingers touched, caressed, her nails gently raking his hardness, causing his thighs to pulse wildly as he grew more swollen still, his arousal almost painful.

He wanted her. Now. Here amongst the sweet-smelling straw. He was filled with such an urgent need for posession, that his senses were fully awakened by the pleasure-ache of her caresses, the sweet, drugging sensation of her womanly perfume.

Jane had known herself lost to reason, to caution, at Hawk's first touch, and she was totally unable to deny him now, as she felt his hand move from her breast to push the material of her gown up to her waist. He caressed the length of her leg from her knee to the aching heat that had pooled between her thighs. Her hips arched invitingly against him as he placed that hand against her most intimate place, cupping, pressing, those caressing fingers igniting a pleasure that Jane could never have imagined even in the nightly dreams she had of this man.

She gasped, falling back weakly against the straw, as Hawk's lips, mouth and tongue continued to minister to her aching breast and his fingers began to stroke against her. Her head moved restlessly from side to side as she felt the pressure building inside her, her legs parting in heady expectation as the heat between her thighs became hot and urgent.

'I told him that, no, I hadn't seen the Duke out and about at all this morning. How about you, Tom? Have you seen him anywhere on the estate?'

Reality, like the icy shock of a bucket of cold water, penetrated Hawk's desire-befuddled brain the moment he heard the voice of his head groom talking of 'the Duke'. He raised his head sharply. The look of dazed shock on Jane's face as she stared up at him told him that she was also aware they were no longer alone.

Hawk's gaze darkened as he stared down at her—as

he acknowledged the rumpled dishevelment of her gown, its skirt pushed up almost to her thighs, its bodice unbuttoned. Her chemise was clinging damply to her breasts, their nipples still hard and aroused from the ministrations of his lips, tongue and hands.

He gave a low groan of self-disgust as he fell back onto the straw beside her to stare up at the wooden ceiling above.

Dear God! Seconds ago, before this timely interruption, he knew his intention had been to make love to Jane fully. To take her here in the stables as if she were some willing serving wench, enjoying a tumble with her wealthy patron. As if he were some untried youth unable to keep his arousal in his breeches.

Forget his employees questioning his state of mind— Hawk now questioned it himself!

'Hawk—'

'Silence, Jane!' he hissed fiercely, even as he moved to place his fingers against her lips. His head tilted as he listened intently and waited to see if his head groom and Tom, one of the grooms Hawk had brought with him from London, would venture farther into the stables in their search for him.

'Nah. We'd see 'im if he was in 'ere,' Tom dismissed. 'Better go an' tell Mr Jenkins that we don't know where 'e is neither.'

The sound of their boots retreating could clearly be heard before the stable door closed noisily behind them.

Hawk's breath left him in a shaky sigh of relief as he heard their departure. But nevertheless he continued to keep his hand gently over Jane's lips for several more seconds, just in case either Jack or Tom should change their minds and decide to give the stables a more thorough search for him.

At the same time he was aware that his precaution was not being taken entirely so that Jane should not do or say anything that would reveal their whereabouts. No, the fierce accusation in those green eyes as she stared up at him from behind that restraining hand was enough to warn Hawk that when Jane *did* next speak it was likely to blister his eardrums!

Deservedly so.

Damn it—not only was Jane a young lady without experience of physical intimacy, but the reason she was here at Mulberry Park at all was in order that he might protect her from such unwanted attentions.

He slowly removed his hand before standing up and moving as far away from her as was possible in the confines of the stall. 'This was a mistake, Jane. A regrettable mistake.' He ran an agitated hand through the dark thickness of his hair. 'I should not—'

'No, you most certainly should not!' Jane acknowledged breathlessly as she scrambled hastily to her feet, her gaping gown clutched in front of her.

She stared across at him for several seconds before turning suddenly on her heel and running from the stables.

And him...

Chapter Eight

'You look wonderful, Jane!' Arabella's face was flushed with excitement two evenings later, as she looked with pleasure at Jane's transformed appearance in the new gown she was to wear for the dinner party this evening.

To Jane's heartfelt relief she had not seen much of the Duke of Stourbridge in the days that had followed that embarrassing incident in the stables, his time having been occupied with estate business.

Everything about that time together was an embarassment to Jane. The wantonness of her response. The evidence of that response when she had seen that she had actually ripped off one of the buttons on the Duke's fine linen shirt in her desperation to touch his flesh. Even worse had been the moment when she had looked down and seen her own state of undress, and realised just how intimately she had allowed the Duke to touch her.

Jane had been so stricken by that realisation, so mortified by what she had encouraged to happen between them, that at that moment she had only been capable of gathering together her dishevelled clothing before fleeing the stables as if the devil himself pursued her.

Not the Duke. *He* was not the devil who pursued her. It was the evidence of her own wanton behaviour that did that.

That the Duke was just as shocked by what had occurred between them had become equally apparent when he had avoided even taking his meals with the ladies of the house over the next two days.

Jane had caught the occasional glimpse of him from her bedroom window as he walked the parkland with seemingly tireless energy, checking the livestock, or the crops in the ploughed fields with his estate manager, with little apparent concern for the state of his clothes and boots. Or for Dolton's tearful state when he saw them. This was an occurrence Jane had had occasion to witness for herself one evening, when Dolton had trailed unhappily from the Duke's apartments with dirt-spattered clothes and boots in his hands.

Fortunately Lady Arabella, realising from the Duke's lengthy absences from the house that Jane was no more in his confidence than she was herself, had first grudgingly and then more readily begun to spend time in Jane's company. The only negative aspect of this was that Jane, filled with a new urgency to escape Markham Park, now had very little opportunity in which to find a way to further her travel arrangements to Somerset.

It had occurred to her to wonder at one point whether Lady Arabella was deliberately preventing her from having time alone in which to achieve that goal—possibly at her brother's instigation, following the suspicions he had voiced concerning Jane's visits to his stables. But as Arabella's demeanour became distinctly frosty whenever the Duke's name was so much as mentioned, Jane decided that was not the case.

Arabella had, however, thrown herself wholeheartedly upon her brother's instruction that Jane would need a new gown for the dinner party—resulting in the two women having taken a carriage ride into the nearest town, and then making a second journey on the following morning so that the gown might be fitted and have last-minute alterations made.

Obviously there were some advantages to being the sister of a Duke. Her gown had been made to fit perfectly in just twenty-four hours!

'Did I not tell you that the pale cream silk with the slightly paler lace would be perfect on you?' Arabella prompted now with satisfaction.

Yes, Arabella had assured her of that. And as Jane's experience of choosing material and style for a new gown was non-existent, she had been only too happy to allow the other woman to take charge.

One glance in the mirror showed Jane that she looked transformed. High-waisted and styled off-the-shoulder, with tiny puffed sleeves and a low neckline, the cream silk dress seemed to drape round her shapely curves rather than cling to them, and her hair had been styled into fashionable curls and escaping ringlets this evening by Arabella's own maid.

It was difficult to imagine, as Jane looked at this pleasing image, that she was the same young lady who had been forced to wear that unbecoming yellow gown only days ago.

'I wonder what Hawk will make of your appearance?' Arabella mused gleefully.

Jane had been wondering the same thing—although probably not for the same reason!

Tonight she looked elegant—pretty, even—the gown giving her poise and style, and a maturity she had hitherto lacked. Completely unlike that yellow gown, which she believed had made her look like a huge piece of unbecoming fruit!

Jane could not deny, however, that her pleasure in her changed appearance was marred a little by the fact that, much against her protests, the Duke was to receive the bill for her new gown.

But how could it be otherwise when Jane had so very little money of her own? Sir Barnaby had given her a small allowance, and Jane had managed to save some of it, but she was not even sure it would be enough to pay for her passage to Somerset, let alone purchase a new gown and gloves.

Arabella's assurances that the Duke would not even notice one new gown amongst her own costly purchases had done very little to allay Jane's feelings of discomfort at having to accept such largesse from a man who could have nothing but the worst opinion of her.

'Oh, what could I possibly have said to bring that frown to your brow?' Arabella clasped Jane's hands in her own as she looked down at her searchingly. 'Does the mere mention of my autocratic brother make you unhappy, Jane?'

'In all probability, the answer to that is yes, Arabella.' The Duke spoke abruptly from behind them before Jane could make any reply, causing both women to turn—Arabella with some surprise, Jane with reluctance. 'Well, well, well,' he drawled as he stood languidly in the doorway. 'I am not sure Mulberry Hall or its guests this evening will be able to accommodate two such lovely ladies.'

Jane felt the blush that warmed her cheeks and heated her body as that unfathomable golden gaze moved over her with slow deliberation. She was relieved that Arabella forestalled the need for her to respond to the Duke's mockery as she moved to her brother's side and smiled up at him triumphantly.

'Have I not done well, Hawk?' She beamed. 'Does Jane not look beautiful?'

'You have done very well, Arabella,' Hawk confirmed dryly.

In truth, he was more than a little stunned by how ravishingly beautiful Jane looked in her new finery. The cream gown with its delicate lace adornment adding a lustre to the smooth perfection of her skin, her eyes were a clear, translucent green in her heart-shaped face, and a cream ribbon threaded amongst her red curls added to their fiery depth of colour.

He was aware that Jane had avoided being in his company at all these last two days, quietly leaving the room if he should enter it, her gaze averted as she did so.

Not that he did not deserve to be treated with such coldness after almost making love to her—in such a way, and in such a place, that she could not help but be insulted by it.

Oh, yes, Hawk knew he completely deserved Jane's newly felt aversion to him. Knew it, and aided that aversion by retreating to his library when he was not working about the estate.

Unfortunately for him Jane looked every inch a beautiful and confident young lady tonight. So much so that Hawk was having trouble keeping his gaze from her.

'I came to bring Jane these,' he bit out abruptly, and he held up the pearl necklace and earbobs he had brought with him in the hopes of them becoming a possible truce-offering between them.

It seemed that Arabella had been far too busy these last days, organising her dinner party and ministering to Jane's need for a new gown, to notice the coldness that now existed between himself and Jane. But Hawk did not doubt that once this evening was over his sister would not be able to help but become aware of the strain between them.

His mouth twisted ruefully. 'But I cannot help but wonder, now that I have seen how lovely she looks already, if it would not be gilding the lily...?'

'Oh, no, Hawk. I think the pearls are a perfect choice!' His sister beamed her approval, herself a vision of loveliness in a glowing-pink gown. 'Do you not agree, Jane?' she prompted warmly.

Jane could only stand and stare at the necklace and earbobs that looked so delicately lovely in the Duke's large but elegant hands, totally stunned, after days of silence, by his making such a gesture.

She wondered where the pearl jewellery could have come from. Surely the Duke had not purposely purchased them for her...? If so, then no matter how enchanted Jane might be at the idea of his having done such a thing on her behalf, it would be the height of impropriety for her to accept.

'Of all Mother's jewels, these will certainly suit Jane the best,' Arabella approved delightedly.

Jane's startled gaze rose from the pearls to the Duke's now unreadable expression. The necklace and earbobs had belonged to his mother? The former Duchess of Stourbridge?

Somehow that knowledge made his offer that Jane should

wear them this evening an even more intimate gesture than if the Duke *had* gone out and purchased them for her.

She gave a firm shake of her head. 'I am sure your offer is a kind one, Your Grace, but I really could not even think of wearing something of such a—a personal nature to your family.'

Hawk looked at her searchingly. Those green eyes were now huge in the otherwise paleness of Jane's face. Was Jane refusing to wear the jewellery because it had belonged to another woman? Or because it was he who suggested she should do so? Was Jane so angry with him, so disgusted with him, that she would not even accept this gesture of apology on his part?

Despite Jane's avoidance of his company since the episode in the stables, Hawk had been pleased to note the two young women were much together, and he was grateful to Jane for taking such an interest in his young sister. Remembering that Jane had no jewellery of her own to wear tonight, he had impulsively decided to bring her the pearls.

But one glance at Jane's slightly stricken expression and he knew he had once again acted in error. Could he do nothing right where this young woman was concerned...?

'Come now, Jane—they are only on loan to you,' he assured her irritably as he stepped farther into a bedroom that, apart from the gown she had recently taken off, which now lay draped over a chair, showed little sign of Jane's occupation. But then, from the little luggage she had brought away with her from Markham Park, Jane did not *have* many personal possessions with which to adorn it. 'Turn around, Jane, so that I might put the necklace on,' he instructed with impatient briskness, his inner anger directed at his own behaviour towards Jane as much as at the guardians who had treated Jane with such neglect.

Hawk did not doubt that Jane had been warm, clothed and fed during the years she had lived at Markham Park, but when those things had been so grudgingly given he felt that Jane might have been better served going to people less wealthy who might have loved her. Now that he knew Jane better—perhaps too well...?—Hawk was sure that the Sulbys' emotional dereliction had been more cruel to someone of Jane's temperament than any deprivation of food or warmth could ever have been.

He had followed Jane to the stables that day with the intention of telling her of his plans to make enquiries on her behalf concerning other, more kindly relatives that she might have. He had failed to do so, and her frosty manner since he had made love to her had certainly not invited confidences of any nature.

Hawk had not yet received any word back from his enquiries, but the moment he did he knew he would no longer be able to delay discussing Jane's future with her. And whether Jane believed him or not—and no doubt she would not!—he had acted only out of concern for her.

But those enquiries had become all the more urgent, he acknowledged grimly, since making love to her!

Jane looked up at the Duke guardedly, where he stood before her expectantly, not knowing quite how to respond to his instruction. If she refused absolutely to wear the pearl jewellery then she knew she would upset Arabella as much as the Duke. She had come to value the other girl's friendship these last few days, and did not doubt that to refuse to wear the jewellery of Arabella's dead mother would put that intimacy in jeopardy.

It was a dilemma the Duke made no allowances for as he took Jane firmly by the bareness of her shoulders to turn her so that her back was towards him.

Jane tensed expectantly. She knew that in a few seconds the Duke's fingers would once again brush against her nape as he secured the clasp of the necklace.

Her breath caught as his arms moved about her, so that he might drape the necklace about her throat. The slightest touch of those long, elegant fingers seemed to sear the bareness of Jane's flesh, causing her to quiver involuntarily, quickly followed by an uncontrollable trembling as he smoothed the ringlets from her nape.

If the two of them had been alone then Jane would have lost no time in turning to confront him, to firmly assure him that she was perfectly capable of securing the necklace herself. But they were not alone. Arabella was standing as silent witness to any exchange between them.

Jane could only hope that the Duke did not intend to attach the earbobs himself...

No matter that it was two days since the Duke had kissed her, nor that they had rarely exchanged a word since then, Jane knew that her insides would melt entirely if the Duke did not soon stop touching her so intimately.

How could it be that his slightest touch made her feel this way? The touch of a man who, when he was not making love to her, provoked her to such feelings of antagonism at his arrogance that she argued with him constantly?

Jane did not have the worldly experience to answer these questions herself. Neither did she have someone to whom she could voice these questions—no one in whom she could confide. She certainly could not tell Arabella of the unimaginable longings that surged up inside her whenever the Duke—Arabella's own brother—touched her!

It did not help that he seemed to be taking an age—or possibly it just seemed that way to her sensitised flesh?— to secure the clasp. Jane was starting to feel slightly light-headed, and she found it difficult to breathe...

This had not been one of his better ideas, Hawk ac-knowledged with self-disgust as the gentle arch of Jane's nape, the soft perfume of her hair, her very closeness, all seemed to cause him more physical discomfort than he would have wished.

'There,' he rasped dismissively, as the catch finally caught and he could step back from Jane's disturbing prox-imity.

'Oh, they really are perfect on you, Jane!' Arabella moved forward to clasp Jane's hands in her own as she looked at her admiringly. 'You have exquisite taste, Hawk,' his sister added, with what Hawk realised was the first gen-uine smile she had directed at him in some time.

Even so, it was a smile that Hawk had no chance to re-spond to, because Jane turned to face him and all of his attention became transfixed on her.

The delicate cream-coloured pearls nestled softly against the swell of her breasts, visible above the low neckline of her new gown. Breasts which gently rose and fell as she breathed, causing Hawk's jaw to clench and his mouth to tighten. He could not seem to take his gaze from her rounded softness.

The Duke looked so grim, Jane noted regretfully, as she moved one of her hands to touch the pearls at her throat. 'Perhaps...' she began, her voice husky. 'Perhaps now that you have seen the pearls again, Your Grace, you would prefer it if I was not to wear them?'

They were his mother's pearls, after all, and had once adorned the no doubt delicate throat of the Duchess of Stourbridge. As such it must surely seem like something of an insult to her memory for them now to be worn by a young woman whose irritating presence had been forced upon him.

A young woman who, although the Duke was not aware of it, did not even know the identity of her real father...

'I hope you realise, Jane, just how insulting it is to even suggest that might be either Arabella's feeling or my own!' he rasped impatiently. 'As Arabella has already assured you, the pearls complement your gown perfectly,' he added with haughty dismissal, before turning away. 'Come, Arabella.' He held out his arm to his sister. 'It is time we went downstairs to await the arrival of your guests.'

Even as Jane inwardly acknowledged how well brother and sister looked together, both so tall and elegant, she could not help but feel disappointed—contrarily so!—that the Duke had made no particular comment on her own appearance. His only compliment had been upon how beautiful the new gown was, and how well the pearls looked with that gown. A gown that he himself had instructed to be chosen and which, in time, he would also pay for.

Despite Jane's inner turmoil of emotion over the last few days, whenever she had recalled the way the Duke had kissed and caressed her, she had found Arabella's excitement about her dinner party infectious. Had even found herself looking forward to the occasion almost as much as the young hostess.

But now Jane had been reminded of the fact that the

gown she wore was not really hers—that the pearl jewellery was only on loan to her for the evening. She was, in effect, merely a cuckoo in borrowed plumage.

She bowed her head. 'I will join you both downstairs shortly. I—I have the earbobs to put on yet,' she excused lightly, when she saw that Arabella was about to protest her need for delay. 'I assure you that I will not be long, Arabella,' she said warmly.

'See that you are not, Jane.' The Duke was the one to answer her stiffly as he escorted his sister to the door.

Jane waited until the two had left her bedchamber before moving to sit down in front of the mirrored dressing table.

The pearls *did* look well with the gown and Jane's newly styled hair, but as she looked at her reflection she could find no pleasure in them. Could only look at herself and berate herself for a fool.

For she had made a great discovery about herself when the Duke had touched her and the warmth of his breath had softly caressed her nape. Had realised in the last few minutes, when her main emotion when she'd turned to face him had been deep hurt as he had looked and spoken to her with such coldness, that she was falling in love with the Duke of Stourbridge.

A man even more unsuitable for Jane to fall in love with—if that was possible!—than Jane's real and married father had been for her mother...

Chapter Nine

Hawk was aware of Jane—as were several other pairs of male eyes—from the moment she stood, slightly hesitant, at the top of the sweeping staircase to stare down at the guests who had already arrived and were now milling about the entrance hall, chatting and laughing with friends they had not seen for several weeks or months.

For a few seconds Jane looked slightly overwhelmed by the prospect of meeting so many people, and then Hawk saw her bare shoulders straighten and her chin rise determinedly, before she held her head regally high and began her slow descent of the staircase.

She really did look magnificent this evening. The simplicity and colour of her gown gave her skin the creamy texture of velvet, and the deep red of her hair made her stand out from the other women in the room like a beautiful, exotic butterfly amidst less colourful moths.

Hawk was not even aware of making excuses to his guests as he began to cross the room to Jane's side, barely acknowledging the remarks addressed to him as he did so, the intensity of his gaze fixed firmly on Jane as she reached the bottom of the staircase.

But his gaze narrowed, his mouth thinning disapprovingly, when he realised, despite his own promptness, that another man had already stepped forward to take Jane's hand in his own and raise it to his lips.

Justin Long, Earl of Whitney. The very last man Hawk would wish anywhere near a young woman under his protection!

A man who, the last time the two men had met, had made known his displeasure at being asked to relinquish his place in the Countess of Morefield's bedchamber to Hawk.

It was so typical of Whitney that he had seen and at once sought out the only young lady present not already known to him! A young lady who surely could not help but be drawn to and flattered by the attentions of a man such as the rakishly handsome Earl of Whitney.

Would Jane be flattered and attracted…?

The older man certainly had much to recommend him—and not only to the matchmaking mamas of Society. Oh, the Whitney estates were very wealthy ones, but it was Justin Long himself that the women of the ton seemed to find so fascinating. His blond good looks and rakish exploits seemed to challenge the interest of both old and young women alike.

Whitney had been a widower since his wife and young son had died of influenza twenty years ago, and since that time had displayed absolutely no inclination to repeat the marital experience. Neither did the man show the slightest hesitation when it came to taking advantage of his boyish good looks, his ruthlessness where women were concerned was legendary.

And Jane did look very desirable this evening…

Hawk's mouth tightened grimly as he moved forward to join them. 'Whitney.' His greeting was deliberately cool.

Whitney turned to look at him with amused blue eyes. 'Stourbridge.'

Hawk bristled at his amusement. 'The Countess has not accompanied you this evening?' he challenged hardly, immediately knowing from the light of challenge that entered the other man's gaze that he should not have done so. It had been extremely indiscreet on his part to so much as mention in front of Jane the woman who had been mistress to both men.

That he had done so Hawk knew was due solely to the fact that he was disturbed enough by Whitney's interest in Jane to feel goaded into the challenge.

'I believe that is now *your* privilege…?' the Earl taunted.

Hawk eyed the older man coldly. 'I have not seen the Countess for several months. I was not aware that you had been introduced to my ward, Miss Jane Smith…' he added tersely.

'Your ward?' The older man raised his brows in surprise before returning his speculative blue gaze to Jane. 'In that case perhaps you would care to make the introductions now, Stourbridge?' he prompted dryly, as he continued to look at Jane.

Far too familiar for Hawk's liking. But in his role of host this evening he had little choice but to comply. 'Jane—may I present Justin Long, Earl of Whitney?' he bit out harshly. 'Whitney—my ward, Miss Jane Smith.'

'My Lord.' Jane inclined her head politely. 'What a pity

that your Countess was unable to accompany you this evening,' she added lightly.

The Earl's eyes glinted wickedly. 'You misunderstood, my dear,' he drawled. 'It was not *my* Countess to whom Stourbridge alluded.'

'Oh...' Jane looked even more confused.

As well she might, Hawk acknowledged, as his narrowed gaze dared the older man to explain exactly whose Countess she was—or indeed had been!

Whitney ignored the challenge and instead bestowed his most charming smile on Jane. 'I hope you will forgive any offence I may have caused earlier by speaking to you so impulsively, Miss Smith? I had thought this to be an evening spent amongst old friends and acquaintances, with none of the stuffy formality that invariably makes an evening with the ton so incredibly tedious.'

In truth, Jane had been slightly surprised, but not in the least offended, when this handsomely distinguished man had approached and spoken to her. In view of the nervousness she had felt as she descended the stairs, Jane's principal emotion had been relief at having someone speak to her at all!

But she knew from just one glance at the Duke, as he looked so contemptuously down his arrogant nose at the older man, that he, at least, did not like or approve of at least one of his sister's guests this evening.

And who exactly *was* the Countess the two men referred to so challengingly...?

'I have taken no offence, My Lord,' she assured the older man coolly, as she gently but firmly released the fingers he still held in his own. 'And, never having spent an evening with the ton, I have no idea if their company be tedious or otherwise.'

'No?' The Earl's eyes widened. 'Where can you have been hiding Miss Smith until now, Stourbridge?' he taunted the other man softly.

The Duke stiffened. 'Miss Smith resided with relatives in the country until very recently.'

'Really?' The Earl still mocked the younger man. 'And which part of the country would that have been, Miss Smith?' His narrowed blue gaze returned to Jane.

'It is surely of little consequence where Miss Smith once resided, Whitney, when it must be obvious she now resides here in Gloucestershire with my family,' the Duke cut in harshly.

Jane was finding the intensity of the Earl's gaze upon her more than a little disconcerting. The shrewdness in those blue eyes was a complete contradiction to the lazily mocking drawl he affected when speaking.

'Of course,' the Earl answered the other man dryly. 'I was merely showing polite curiosity, that is all.' He shrugged dismissively.

Despite the fact that the other man's estates seemed to prosper, and his business interests to thrive, Hawk had always considered Whitney something of a wastrel—a man who spent his time in London, when not at the gambling tables, occupying the bed of one bored wife or another of his fellow peers.

He was certainly not a man Hawk could ever approve showing an interest in an innocent such as Jane!

Hawk reached out to lift Jane's hand and place it firmly upon his arm. 'I believe it is time for us to go in to dinner.' He nodded his cool dismissal of the other man before turning away, the firmness of his hand over Jane's leaving her no choice but to accompany him.

'You will stay away from the Earl of Whitney for the remainder of the evening, Jane,' he rasped grimly, once they had moved out of the Earl's hearing. 'Besides being far too old for you, the man is an obvious rake who is only interested in bedding a woman rather than wedding her!'

Jane gasped—both at the Duke's arrogance in once again telling her what she should do, and at the indelicacy of his warning about the Earl. He almost made it sound as if she had deliberately set out to engage the other man's interest.

Well, she might be inexperienced in the ways of men, but that did not mean Jane did not recognise a consummate flirt when she met one. Although, strangely, the Earl's behaviour had not been in the least flirtatious with her until the Duke had appeared at her side...? But after days of not knowing exactly how she should behave towards the Duke since he had made love to her, she now found herself consumed with anger at the return of his high-handedness.

She also recognised that the apparent intensity of her conversation with the Duke was now attracting attention from Arabella's other guests...

'Surely you are mistaken, Your Grace?' she said evenly, her expression deliberately serene in acknowledgement of those curious glances. 'I thought it was the case that *all* titled gentlemen needed to marry and produce an heir?'

The Duke turned to scowl down the sharp blade of his arrogant nose at her. 'It may have escaped your notice, Jane, but *I* have not yet chosen to do so.'

'I am sure that is only because you have so far been too busy.'

'My estates—'

'I was not referring to work on your estates, Your Grace.'

His dark brows rose. 'Then to what were you referring, Jane…?'

Her lips curved into a smile even as her eyes glowed with challenge. 'I had assumed that the reason you are still unmarried at the age of…thirty…?'

'One and thirty,' Hawk supplied cautiously, sensing from Jane's too-innocent demeanour that he was about to receive another one of her infamous setdowns.

'Exactly.' Jane nodded coolly. 'I had assumed that the reason you are still unmarried at such an advanced age must be because you are far too busy interfering in other people's lives to have time to attend to your own…'

For what had to be the second time in Jane's company—or possibly the third?—Hawk found himself unable to repress the hard bark of laughter provoked by this woman's wicked sense of humour.

At his own expense this time!

The unexpected laughter also served to dispel the tension he had been feeling since he first saw her in Whitney's company.

'Touché, Jane,' he drawled dryly.

'You are more than welcome, Your Grace,' she returned pertly.

'I never doubted for a moment that would be the case.' He nodded, still smiling, relieved that after days of awkwardness Jane at last seemed to be showing signs of returning to her more forthright self. 'Perhaps you will now allow me the honour of escorting you in to dinner, Jane?'

Her brows rose. 'Is there not some other, worthier lady present this evening, who is eagerly awaiting the Duke of Stourbridge's attentions?'

Yes, Hawk knew that Lady Pamela Croft, the most highly raved lady in the room, and Whitney's older sister, would be expecting him to escort her into dinner.

But, unlike that evening at Markham Park almost a week ago, when Hawk's offer to take Jane in to dinner had been thwarted by Jane herself, Hawk felt no more inclined to bow to Society's dictates than Whitney. At an evening 'spent amongst old friends' he could ignore rules of etiquette for once.

'Perhaps,' he dismissed arrogantly. 'But none that I would rather have on my arm,' he added distractedly, as his attention was drawn to the fact that a blushingly pretty Arabella had accepted being escorted into the dining room by a smugly triumphant-looking Earl of Whitney.

Damn the man.

First Jane. Now Arabella.

Surely he would not have to spend the entire evening fending off the other man's attentions from one or the other?

'If you are sure, Your Grace?' Jane answered him huskily.

'I am very sure, Jane,' Hawk confirmed tersely, and he turned his gaze reluctantly away from Arabella and Whitney.

Jane's hand trembled slightly as it rested on the Duke's arm, and her face felt flushed as the other guests turned to watch the formidably arrogant Duke of Stourbridge escorting her, a young woman with whom none of them were as yet acquainted, through to the formal dining room.

Neither could she help but notice the narrowed blue gaze of the Earl of Whitney as he too turned to watch the two of them. It was an intense blue gaze that was fixed firmly on Jane. And, unless she was mistaken, not in the least rakishly.

She was aware of his shrewd gaze several times during dinner, but deliberately ignored it. The Earl even smiled at her in a frankly conspiratorial manner on one occasion, as if encouraging her to share with him the joke of such pompous formality. Jane did not so much as acknowledge the smile as she turned her attention to Lord Croft, where he sat to the left of her at the table.

The Duke presided over the head of the table, of course, with Arabella, as his hostess, seated at the other end. Arabella had placed Jane between Lord Croft and his son Jeremy. Both men were charming and affable as they easily put her at her ease. The younger man was especially attentive after learning that Jane had spent her early years in Somerset, proceeding to talk knowledgeably about the area from memories of his own visits there as a child.

But still Jane could not help but be aware of the intensity of the Earl of Whitney's interest as he sat across the table from her, listening intently to her conversation rather than taking any part in it...

Hawk found his attention wandering constantly from the dry wit of Lady Pamela's conversation. Instead he watched Jane with a brooding intensity. The fact that several other men were looking at her as intently, the Earl of Whitney and Jeremy Croft but two of them, caused his brows to draw together darkly.

'Miss Jane Smith has become quite the darling of the evening, has she not?' Lady Pamela commented dryly.

'What?' Hawk turned to bark tersely.

His friend and neighbour arched teasing brows at his obvious irritation. 'I was commenting on the fact that Miss

Smith seems to hold my husband entranced, my son be-guiled, my brother amused and the Duke of Stourbridge mesmerised,' Lady Pamela drawled.

Hawk frowned at her. 'You are imagining things, Pa-mela.'

'I do not think so.' She shook her head slowly. 'Can it be possible that the elusive Duke of Stourbridge has at last settled on his choice of bride...?'

Bride?

Could Pamela possibly be referring to Jane...?

'Do not be ridiculous, Pamela.' He snapped his impa-tience at the absurdity of her suggestion that he could se-riously be contemplating making Jane his Duchess. 'Jane Smith is my ward, not my future bride.'

'Really?' Pamela drawled derisively. 'In that case, Hawk, and unless you wish others to make the same assumption I did, I would advise you not to spend quite so much of your time staring at her in that hungrily devouring way.'

'Now you are being deliberately provoking, Pamela,' Hawk bit out harshly, before emptying his wine glass and motioning for it to be refilled.

'And you are drinking far more wine than usual this eve-ning, too, Hawk.' As a friend of his mother, and his closest neighbour these last thirty years, Lady Pamela felt no hes-itation in speaking her mind to him whenever she chose.

Hawk bared his teeth in a humourless smile. 'When I wish for your advice, Pamela, be assured I will ask for it!'

She gave a softly indulgent laugh. 'Be assured, Hawk, you will receive it whether it is asked for or not!'

Hawk gave a rueful shake of his head, knowing that there was no point in arguing with Pamela—that since the death of his own mother Pamela had chosen to take on that role for herself.

Could there possibly be some basis for her observation concerning the way in which he had been watching Jane? *Had* his gaze been 'mesmerised' and 'hungrily devouring'...?

Surely not?

Admittedly, he had not liked Whitney's attentions to her earlier, and nor did he particularly care for the way that Pamela's own son was paying Jane such marked attention, but surely that was no reason for Pamela to imply that his own interest was any more personal than any guardian for his charge?

No, of course it was not, he assured himself determinedly. He was merely concerned for Jane, that was all. Because she was young and innocent, and could have no idea of the danger a man with Whitney's reputation represented to that innocence.

It was an ignorance Hawk had every intention of correcting as he made his way immediatately to Jane's side once dinner was over, when she and all the other guests were making their way to the small ballroom where dancing was due to commence.

Unfortunately for Jane, an hour of watching as both Jeremy Croft and the Earl of Whitney seemed to become more and more captivated by her every word had not diminished the force of Hawk's temper in the slightest.

'I think it might be as well, Jane, if for the remainder of the evening you were to refrain from flirting with every man in the room under the age of sixty!' Hawk bit out harshly as he glared down at her.

Jane gave a gasp, her face paling at the unexpectedness

of the Duke's attack. In fact she had been quietly congratulating herself on having successfully negotiated the intricacies of social behaviour, and now the Duke was accusing her of doing the opposite.

She returned his glare unblinkingly. 'I have not yet had the opportunity to flirt with *you*, Your Grace!'

'Neither will you, if you know what is good for you!' Those gold eyes glittered warningly.

Jane looked up at him challengingly. 'Could you possibly be threatening me, Your Grace?'

His jaw was clamped tightly together. 'I am trying to assist you, Jane—'

'By insulting me?'

'By advising you.'

'I was mistaken, then, Your Grace. For your advice sounded distinctly like an insult to me!' Jane breathed indignantly.

Hawk's nostrils flared angrily. 'You—'

'Sorry to interrupt your little *tête-à-tête* with your ward, Stourbridge, but perhaps I might have your permission to invite Miss Smith to dance?' the Earl of Whitney interrupted smoothly.

Hawk turned a quelling glance on the older man, having every intention of telling Whitney that he most certainly did not have his permission to dance with Jane. Or indeed to do anything else with her!

'I do not need the Duke's permission to dance, My Lord.'

Jane was the one to answer before Hawk had a chance to do so, not sparing Hawk so much as a second glance as she took the other man's arm and allowed herself to be taken onto the dance floor.

Leaving Hawk no choice but to stand impotently by and

watch as the rakish Earl of Whitney took a hold of Jane's hand and led her confidently into the dance.

An unpleasant image that was reflected back at Hawk many times over from the mirrors that adorned the walls of the small ballroom at Mulberry Mall.

'I am so pleased to see that Jane is enjoying herself.' Arabella spoke softly beside Hawk.

Hawk turned to scowl at his young sister—who, as hostess, should have been on the dance floor herself. 'Whitney is hardly a suitable companion for her to be enjoying herself with!'

Arabella looked up at him steadily for several seconds, before allowing a knowing smile to curve her lips. 'So, Lady Pamela was right in her assertion that you are far too interested in your young ward,' she murmured with satisfaction.

'I—'

'I must admit I was a little taken aback when Lady Pamela described Jane as such,' Arabella continued lightly. 'I had not realised. Exactly *when* did Jane become your ward, Hawk?' She arched blonde brows.

'You are being deliberately obtuse, Arabella,' he snapped dismissively.

'I do not think so.' Arabella shook her head.

Hawk gave an impatiently snort. 'Obviously I made that distinction for Jane's sake. It simply would not do for our friends and neighbours—for the ton—to realise that an unmarried young lady with no family connection to us is staying here at Mulberry Mall under the protection of the Duke of Stourbridge.'

'Perhaps you should have given some thought to that possibility before bringing Jane here...?'

'Given a choice, I would not have brought Jane here—' Hawk broke off as he realised he had been provoked into being indiscreet for the second time this evening. Something that, as the haughty Duke of Stourbridge, he never was. Or at least he never had been before Jane came crashing into his life.

'If you had been "given a choice", Hawk?' Arabella echoed curiously. 'You never have fully explained to me how you came to be acquainted with Jane, or your reasons for bringing her here. Perhaps—'

'I do not think now is the right time for us to discuss this, Arabella.'

'Will there ever be a right time?'

Hawk's mouth thinned. 'No.'

'I did not think so.' Arabella shrugged. 'But you must admit that captivating the Earl of Whitney would be a marvellous feather in Jane's social cap...'

'I admit nothing of the sort!'

Arabella turned towards the dancing couples. 'They do look very well together, do they not...?'

Hawk turned to follow the direction of his sister's gaze, his own eyes narrowing ominously as once again he found himself looking at Jane as she danced assuredly with the Earl of Whitney.

Arabella was quite right in her assertion: Jane and Whitney did look well together. The two were of a similar height, one so blond while the other a fiery redhead, and their movements were both light and graceful. And when the dance allowed, their conversation was softly exclusive.

Hawk frowned darkly as he wondered what subject two such mismatched people could possibly have found to talk about so earnestly...

Chapter Ten

'Have you been Stourbridge's...ward for very long, Miss Smith?'

Jane had been lost in the enchantment of the 'small' ballroom, as Arabella called it. Dozens of candles illuminated the room, and the dancing couples were reflected in the ornate mirrors that covered the walls. A warm breeze came in through the open doors that led out into the garden beyond.

Now she looked up frowningly at the Earl. 'Why do you ask, My Lord?'

He raised mocking blond brows. 'Possibly because Lady Arabella describes you as her companion, and the Duke as his ward. I wondered which of them spoke in error...?'

Jane stumbled slightly in the dance—a slip the Earl deftly masked as he matched his steps to her own. 'Perhaps neither of them, My Lord,' she finally dismissed smoothly. 'There is surely no reason why I cannot be both ward to the Duke and companion to Arabella?'

'None at all,' the Earl conceded. 'But neither description tells me who you really are.' All humour had now left that handsome face, and he stared down at her with that same intentness of purpose that Jane had found so disconcerting during dinner.

Jane withstood the intensity of that gaze as she gave a rueful smile. 'I am nobody, My Lord. Absolutely nobody.'

'One thing Lady Arabella and the Duke do seem in agreement on is your name... Jane Smith...?'

For all that the Duke had warned her the Earl was reputed to be a charmer and a seducer, Jane was finding his persistence in asking her personal questions irritating in the extreme.

The Earl shook his head. 'I am sorry to disagree, Jane, but I really cannot accept any loving mother with the surname of Smith baptising her child Jane.'

'Then perhaps she did not love me!' Jane snapped, still trying to come to terms with her emotions towards her mother after discovering that Janette had married a man who was not the father of her baby. 'She died on the day I was born,' Jane explained flatly, as the Earl continued to look down at her speculatively.

His expression instantly changed to one of frowning regret. 'Please forgive me if I have caused offence, Jane.' He sighed. 'My own wife and child died many years ago, too,' he added, with a grimace.

It was an explanation that at once touched Jane's tender heart, and perhaps explained many things about this man's rakish reputation... 'You did not cause any offence, My Lord,' she assured him huskily.

'You may call me Justin, Jane,' he drawled.

'I would rather not, My Lord,' she came back firmly.

The Earl gave a rueful shake of his head. 'You do not seem to be part of the artifice that makes up the world of the ton, Jane…?'

Perhaps that was because Jane did not belong to this world. She was merely an intruder, there on sufferance only because the Duke of Stourbridge had decided it should be so!

She gave him a sharp look. 'That is the second time this evening that you have spoken so disparagingly of your peers, My Lord.'

He gave a humourless smile. 'Perhaps because for the main part that is how I choose to think of them…'

'Why?'

The Earl shrugged his broad shoulders. 'I doubt you would understand the reason for my cynicism, Jane.'

'Perhaps if you were to explain your reasons to me…?'

His gaze became quizzical at the earnestness of her expression. 'Talking about one's past does not make it any less painful, Jane. Nor does it make it possible for the ton to forgive those past indiscretions,' he added harshly.

'Not even if one is genuinely repentant?'

'Ah, but there lies the problem, Jane. For, you see, I remain totally unrepentant.'

'Then you cannot expect forgiveness.'

The Earl gave a rueful shake of his head. 'Have things always been so black and white to you, Jane?'

She nodded. 'My father—a parson—brought me up to be honest, I hope.'

'He did indeed.' The Earl gave a hard smile of acknowledgment.

'But a lack of artifice and guile is unusual in any woman, I have found, Jane, let alone one so young as you,' he added.

'Indeed, My Lord?' she said dryly.

'Oh, yes.' His smile became derisive. 'But perhaps your own honesty is due in part to the fact that you have no interest in becoming my Countess...'

Her eyes widened. 'I certainly do not, sir!'

The Earl gave an appreciative chuckle. 'And so you intrigue me even further, Jane!'

'I can assure you it was not my intention to do so,' Jane told him primly.

'Perhaps it is for that very reason I find you so interesting, Jane,' he murmured tauntingly.

Jane moved back slightly to look up at him. 'Are you flirting with me, My Lord?'

'As it happens...no, Jane. I am not,' he assured her hardly. 'Strangely, you bring out a protective element in me that I have not felt since—' He broke off abruptly, his frown dark. 'Why is that, do you think, Jane?'

'I have no idea, My Lord.' Jane was tired of this enigmatic conversation, but she was even more annoyed with the way the Duke stood at the side of the room, glaring at her so disapprovingly. As if he feared that at any moment she might do or say something to embarrass him or one of his guests. She curtseyed to the Earl as the dance ended. 'If you will excuse me, My Lord? I believe I would like go outside for some air.' She turned in the direction of the open French doors.

'An excellent suggestion.' He fell into step beside her.

Jane turned to frown at him. 'My suggestion was not an invitation for you to join me, My Lord.'

'I am well aware of that, Jane,' he acknowledged unconcernedly.

She gave a tight smile. 'But you choose to accompany me anyway?'

'I do, indeed.' He gave an inclination of his head as he took a light hold of her arm. 'I am not yet ready to relinquish my...interest, you see, Jane.'

'But I am not trying to interest you, My Lord!'

'Now you are starting to repeat yourself, Jane, and I really would prefer that you not become as boringly predictable as all the other ladies of my acquaintance.' He grimaced.

It was much cooler outside on the terrace, the sun having set, leaving the surrounding gardens dappled in the half-light between night and day.

But Jane wasted no time on appreciating the beauty of her surroundings as she turned to face the Earl, her chin determinedly high. 'I do not care, one way or the other, My Lord, in whether you find my company boring or intriguing.'

He shrugged stiffly. 'I have not conversed for this length of time with a lady so young as you for a very long time, or so frankly,' he repeated frowningly. 'Where do you come from, Jane? Who are your family?'

'I have already told you that I am nobody—'

'But I do not believe you, Jane. There are Smiths in the Lakes, Kent and Bedfordshire. Can you be related to any of them...? I warn you, Jane,' he added softly, 'you will only deepen my interest further by your determination to remain a mystery...'

Jane frowned her consternation; having yet another person curious about her was the very last thing that she wanted or needed. 'Release me, sir.' She was breathing heavily in her agitation.

The Earl's narrowed gaze studied her face searchingly for several long seconds, before his handsome features relaxed into a wolfish smile. 'I have already told you, I am not ready to do that, Jane.'

Her eyes widened as his fingers tightened about her arm, that single movement enough to make her aware of how alone they were out here on the deserted terrace.

She had been foolish in allowing the Earl to accompany her outside, Jane realised belatedly. Not that he had really given her any choice in the matter, but even so…

'Do not look so concerned, Jane,' he taunted softly. 'You really are far too young for me to be genuinely enamoured of you. But perhaps it is you who explected a light dalliance in the moonlight—'

'Whether that is Jane's wish or not, it most certainly is not mine!' An icily furious voice—the Duke of Stourbridge's icily furious voice!—cut in at the same instant Jane felt herself being pulled from the Earl's grasp and back against the hard strength of the Duke's chest.

The Earl's pale gaze glittered challengingly in the moonlight. 'Is it your intention to spoil *all* Jane's fun this evening, Stourbridge?' he taunted mockingly.

Fun? Until Hawk's appearance, this man's conversation had been far from light or flirtatious!

Did the Duke believe otherwise?

One glance over her shoulder at the chilling expression on Hawk's face and Jane knew that was exactly what he believed!

Hawk drew in a harsh breath as he glared coldly at the older man. 'I have not given you leave to call her by her first name!'

'Perhaps the lady herself has allowed me that liberty?' the Earl taunted derisively.

Hawk's mouth tightened. 'As was explained to you earlier, Miss Smith is unfamiliar with the ways of the ton. She is especially naïve, Whitney, when it comes to men like you,' he added insultingly.

Jane felt as light as thistledown as Hawk held her firmly against him, as slender as a nymph, with the softness of her bright curls brushing against his chin. But as Hawk's most recent memory of that slenderness was of Jane standing far too close to the Earl of Whitney, he found he was in no mood at this moment to appreciate any of her womanly charms.

'A man like me?' the Earl repeated softly. 'I will have you know, Stourbridge, that I have called men out for lesser insults!'

Hawk was well aware of the other man's reputation for duelling, even though it was no longer approved of—either by the ton or the Crown.

Hawk, a master swordsman an an excellent shot, had never been involved in such idiocy himself, but he would be willing to make an exception where the Earl of Whitney was concerned!

'Yes?' he challenged hardly, even as he put Jane firmly out of harm's way.

The Earl thrust his face close to Hawk's, his eyes glittering coldly. 'If you would care to name a time and a place I will have my seconds call upon yours—'

'Now, really!' An indignant Jane interrupted impatiently. 'You cannot seriously intend to challenge each other to a duel over such a trifling matter?' She looked incredulous.

Having been sure that Whitney was about to take Jane into his arms, no doubt with the intention of kissing her, was no 'trifling matter' as far as Hawk was concerned. In fact, it had made him feel more than a little murderous.

'And how else would you suggest we settle this, Jane?' Hawk demanded scathingly, even as his gaze remained unwavering on the older man.

'Settle what?' she gasped incredulously. 'You are both behaving like children rather than two titled gentlemen who should know better!'

'My dear Jane, this is exactly how two titled gentlemen settle their differences,' the Earl told her dryly.

'I have warned you against calling her by her first name!' Hawk reminded him chillingly.

The Earl quirked mocking brows. 'You reserve that privilege, for yourself, eh, Stourbridge?'

Hawk's hand clenched into fists at his sides. 'Explain that remark, if you please!'

'Do not explain that remark—or indeed any other!' Jane instructed impatiently, and she put out her hands and rested one on either man's chest, her face flushed with anger, green eyes glittering warningly as she glared at them both. 'Really, I have never encountered such nonsense in my life,' she continued fiercely, keeping her hands on the men's chests in order to hold them at bay. 'You will *not* name a time and a place,' she told the Duke disgustedly. 'And you, My Lord—' she turned impatiently to Whitney ' you will not challenge the Duke to a duel for mentioning a reputation that I have absolutely no doubt you took great delight in acquiring and which you have long enjoyed!'

Whitney gave an appreciative grin. 'How well you have come to know me in such a short time, dear Jane. But nevertheless...' He sobered as the Duke gave a warning snort of impatience '—it simply is not done for a gentleman to cast aspersions upon another's reputation—'

'I do not believe they can be called aspersions when they are the truth,' Jane cut in disgustedly.

'From a lady they might be considered the truth,' the Earl conceded. 'From another gentleman they are an insult,' he assured her. 'In Stourbridge's case deliberately so, I am sure.' He looked at Hawk from between narrowed lids.

'Nevertheless,' Jane said determinedly, 'I absolutely forbid either of you to continue with this foolishness.'

Hawk looked down at her as she stood between himself and Whitney, a hand still on each of their chests. A completely ineffective gesture when both men were inches taller than she, with powerfully muscled chests and arms that could easily have put her tiny form to one side before they continued with their argument.

That neither man chose to do so was due in part, Hawk knew, to the fact that Jane looked so magnificent in her outrage. The red vibrancy of her hair seemed almost to crackle like flame, her eyes glittered like emeralds, her normally full lips were thinned to a disapproving line, and those creamy breasts were quickly rising and falling in her agitation.

A glance across at Whitney showed the indulgent laughter lurking in the other man's eyes, as he too looked at the spitting little vixen Jane resembled in her outrage.

She really did think that she was stopping the two men from fighting with a paltry hand on their chests. And she 'absolutely' forbade them from duelling.

It was too much to endure. For either man.

Jane looked at the two men incredulously as first the Duke and then the Earl burst into deep-throated laughter.

Laughing? After the last few fraught minutes the two men were now actually *laughing* together?

Seconds ago she had been literally terrified—either that the Duke was going to be killed or else put in prison for killing the Earl of Whitney. Both prospects had filled her with dread.

And now, instead of duelling the two men were laughing together. Her own indignant expression seemed only to increase their humour. The Earl was actually bent double, his hands braced on his knees, as he laughed so long and heartily he could barely catch his breath. The Duke fared little better, almost seeming to have tears in his eyes as he openly guffawed.

Jane stood, hands on hips, bristling with indignation at this unwarranted humour. 'Perhaps when you two gentlemen have ceased this hysteria, one or both of you might care to tell me the source of your amusement?'

'I am afraid you are, dear Jane.' The Earl was the first to regain some sort of decorum as he straightened to take a handkerchief from his pocket and dab the moisture from his eyes. 'Just now, as you stood so bravely between the two of us, you gave every appearance of a bantam hen rebuking her chicks!' He gave a rueful shake of his head.

'You were laughing at *me*?' Jane breathed disbelievingly, her eyes wide as she glared first at the Duke and then the Earl.

'Unforgivable, I know, Jane. But nonetheless true,' the Earl confirmed, a smile still curving his lips.

Not a good move, as Hawk could have warned the other man—but he chose not to, and two bright spots of temper appeared in Jane's cheeks.

'You were laughing at *me*?' she repeated softly. 'Do you have any idea how ridiculous the two of *you* looked a few minutes ago? How absolutely—'

'That is enough, Jane,' Hawk cut in sternly.

'After your most recent—your absolutely childish behaviour just now, you will not even attempt to tell me what to do, Your Grace!' She turned on him fierily.

'She is priceless, Stourbridge,' Whitney remarked admiringly. 'Absolutely delicious!'

Hawk's humour had faded as suddenly as it had occurred, but he sobered completely as he realised he did not care for the other man's last comment. 'Now, listen here, Whitney—'

'Not again!' Jane burst out exasperatedly, her tiny hands now clenched into fists at her sides. 'I wish I had let the two of you duel. I wish you had pierced each other through the heart with your swords. I wish—Oh, never mind what I wish!' she concluded disgustedly. 'If you two gentlemen will excuse me?' She turned sharply on her heel—not in the direction of the ballroom, but towards the steps leading down into the moon-shadowed garden.

Hawk's hand snaked out to grasp her wrist. 'Where do you think you are going?'

'I do not *think* I am going anywhere—I *am* going into the garden!' Her eyes glittered up at him in challenge.

Hawk refused to release her arm. 'I cannot stand by and let you walk off into the darkness, Jane—'

'I do not advise you to try and stop me, Your Grace!'

Green eyes battled with gold for several seconds, before Jane lifted her slippered foot and brought the heel down forcefully on top of Hawk's instep. The unexpectedness of the attack caused him to move sharply backwards and so loosen his grip on her wrist. A lapse in concentration that Jane took full advantage of as, with one last sweeping look of disgust, she turned and marched away.

In the direction of the garden—as she had said she would!

'Magnificent!' the Earl murmured wonderingly as he stared after her. 'Truly magnificent.'

Despite—or because of—the pain in his foot, Hawk bristled angrily. 'You will stay away from her, Whitney!'

The other man turned to look at him with amused eyes. 'Will I?'

'Yes, you damn well will—'

'Surely that is for the lady to decide?' Whitney taunted. 'Unless, as I suggested earlier, you have a prior claim…?'

Hawk drew in a sharp breath. 'Jane is my ward—'

'So you have said.' The other man nodded. 'But from what I have just witnessed I would say the young lady has a definite mind of her own.'

Hawk could not deny that. Nor could he deny that, if anything, he admired that trait in Jane even more than Whitney did.

He *knew* her to be priceless. And delicious. And magnificent…!

'Yes, she does,' he confirmed tightly. 'But I can assure you that she is also one hundred per cent of sound mind!'

The Earl quirked blond brows. 'I trust, Stroubridge, that you are not implying that she would have to be *out* of her mind to be attracted to me?'

'And if I were?'

The older man shrugged. 'I have already told you I will be more than happy to meet you at a time and place of your choosing…'

Yes, he had. But Hawk knew, despite what Jane had said minutes ago, that she would never forgive him if he should enter into a duel with the Earl of Whitney with her at the centre of it.

That he was even thinking of doing so told Hawk just how ludicrous this situation had become.

He was the Duke of Stourbridge. The formidably correct Duke of Stourbridge. A man with a deliberately spotless reputation. A man he had heard his peers hold up to their children as an example of one of the finest members of the aristocracy, for them to emulate.

And yet here he was, on the terrace of his own family seat, contemplating challenging another man to a duel over a young woman who had already told him how much she deplored such behaviour.

'I do not believe Jane would approve,' he said flatly.

The Earl arched mocking brows. 'And that concerns you?'

'That surprises you?' Hawk grated.

Whitney gave a derisive smile. 'You know, Hawk, I still remember you when you were the disreputable Marquis of Mulberry. Before you became every inch the superior Duke of Stourbridge.'

Hawk stiffened. 'Meaning?'

The older man shrugged. 'Meaning you might do well to remember it too sometimes.'

Hawk shook his head. 'I have no idea what you are talking about.'

But he did know.

Life had been much simpler ten years ago. Hawk had been a different person then. As Marquis of Mulberry he had only been *heir* to the Dukedom, and as such able to be as riotously devil-may-care as he knew Sebastian now was.

But that had been in a different life. And he a different man. He was the Duke of Stourbridge now, with all the responsibility that title implied. He could no longer do what he wanted without thought to the consequences.

'In my opinion, your Jane Smith is unique, Stourbridge.' The Earl nodded towards the direction Jane had taken when she had left them so abruptly.

'A young woman to be priced above—I believe Jane is wearing pearls this evening, Stourbridge? Your mother's pearls, are they not…?' he taunted softly.

Hawk stiffened. 'What if they are?'

'Idle curiosity on my part. That is all.' The Earl shrugged uninterestedly. 'But be assured, Hawk, that if you do not care to claim Jane for your own, then some other lucky man soon will.'

Hawk's jaw clenched. 'Not you!'

The Earl gave a humourless smile. 'No, not me,' he conceded wryly. 'Although I am sure that not even the estimable Jane would dismiss the idea of becoming the Countess of Whitney.'

Hawk eyed the other man scornfully. 'And we all know how devoted you were to your last Countess!'

'Have a care, Stourbridge,' Whitney grated harshly, all humour gone as his eyes glittered dangerously in the darkness. 'Just because I did not love my wife, it does not mean that I am incapable of understanding the emotion—'

'Understanding it, perhaps,' Hawk conceded derisively. 'But feeling it? Somehow I do not think so.'

'I have loved, Stourbridge,' the other man bit out coldly. 'Too much to ever feel the emotion for another woman! I—'

'Ah, there you are, Hawk,' Arabella greeted him brightly as she came out onto the terrace. 'And the Earl of Whitney, too,' she recognised happily. 'The absence of two such eligible gentlemen has left some of the ladies in desperate need of dancing partners for the next set,' she added, with a playful tap of her fan on the Earl's arm.

The last thing Hawk felt like doing at the moment was playing the polite host to Arabella guests—male or female. In fact, he had never felt less polite in his life!

'As long as you will promise to be my partner, I will indeed return to the ballroom, Lady Arabella,' the Earl drawled in reply to her rebuke.

'Hawk...?'

'Oh, I believe your brother has...some urgent business about the estate he has to take care of before he is free to rejoin us,' the Earl dismissed lightly as he drew Arabella's hand into the crook of his arm. 'Is that not so, Stourbridge?' he added, with a challenging glance in Hawk's direction.

Hawk met the other man's gaze in a silent battle of wills, knowing Jane to be the 'urgent business' Whitney referred to.

'Hawk...?' Arabella said uncertainly as the silence stretched between the two men. 'Surely whatever it is it can wait until morning...?'

'Doubtful, hmm, Stourbridge?' the Earl drawled mockingly.

Hawk gave the other man one last narrow-eyed glance before turning to his sister. 'I will rejoin you as soon as I am free to do so, Arabella.' He could not, after all, simply return to the ballroom when he knew Jane was alone somewhere out in the garden.

'Oh, very well,' his sister accepted, with an impatient flick of her fan.

'Our dance, I believe, Lady Arabella?' the Earl prompted smilingly, as the sound of the quartet of musicians hired for the evening could be heard once more.

Hawk waited until his sister and the Earl had returned to the ballroom before turning his narrowed gaze in the direction of the garden. But he could detect no sign of movement either on the lawns or along the hedges to indicate Jane's presence.

Where could Jane have disappeared to so completely? The stables once again? Or somewhere else?

Chapter Eleven

Jane sensed rather than heard the Duke's presence behind her in the darkness of the summerhouse to which she had fled so angrily such a short time ago.

Angrily? She had been more than angry; she had been incensed.

'Have you come to once again laugh at my fears?' she demanded, without turning.

'Fears, Jane...?' he echoed softly.

Jane had not lit the lamps when she entered the summerhouse, preferring to hide her blushing cheeks in the darkness as she acknowledged how close she had come to revealing her feelings for the Duke—both to Hawk himself and to cynical the Earl of Whitney.

She turned now, her chin stubbornly high as she stared across the distance that separated her from the Duke as he stood silhouetted in the doorway.

Arabella had shown Jane the summerhouse yesterday afternoon, and the two women had lingered to enjoy a glass of lemonade on the veranda surrounding it in the heat of the afternoon.

But the single room that had seemed so bright and airy during the day was full of shadows this evening, and the Duke appeared very tall and imposing in the darkness, the haughty arrogance of his face all sharply etched angles.

Jane made a brief movement of her shoulders. 'I would not like to see you imprisoned, or more likely hanged, for killing another man.'

His teeth glinted white in the gloom as he drawled. 'That is always supposing, Jane, that it was not I who was killed.'

That had been her real fear, of course. The fear Jane had almost revealed, and along with it her newly discovered love for this man. The same fear she dared not reveal now, for that very same reason.

'Was that ever a possibility?'

He shrugged. 'Whitney has something of a reputation as a swordsman.'

Jane repressed the shiver than ran through her. 'Then you were doubly foolish to have challenged him in that way.' She snapped her impatience with his recklessness.

'Was I, Jane?' He moved farther into the summerhouse to close the door softly behind him.

Jane resisted the impulse to take a step backwards, determined that she would not reveal how much being alone here with him like this disturbed her. Even if it did. Very much so. 'Very foolish, indeed, Your Grace.' She nodded abruptly.

'Are you not cold in here, Jane?' he prompted huskily, instead of responding to her rebuke.

'Perhaps a little,' she acknowledged frowningly. 'But it was not my intention to remain here for long...' Her voice dwindled off as the Duke went down on his haunches by the fireplace and put a flame to the kindling already laid there. The yellow-orange flames that instantly flared into life illuminated his sharply etched profile.

'There.' He rose slowly back to his feet before turning to look at her. 'Is that not better, Jane?'

It was certainly warmer. Cosier. More intimate. None of which was in the least 'better' after what had happened the last time she and the Duke had been so alone together.

'Jane?' he prompted huskily, those gold-coloured eyes warmly searching on her upraised face.

The warm flames now crackling in the hearth were as nothing compared to the flames leaping inside Jane as she stared up at the Duke. Her pulse was beating erratically. Her heart thumping so loudly she thought he must hear it. Her palms were slightly damp. Her breathing shallow.

She nodded abruptly. 'Much better, Your Grace.'

Hawk watched the movement of her tiny pink tongue as it moved moistly across her lips, her throat moving convulsively as she swallowed, and the soft swell of her breasts slowly rising and falling as she breathed softly.

It had taken him several long, anxious minutes to locate Jane here in the darkness of the summerhouse, but now that he had found her he questioned the wisdom of being alone with her like this.

The summerhouse was situated in a copse of trees at the far end of the spacious gardens that surrounded Mulberry Hall, well away from the main house, and was the place that he and his siblings had disappeared to as children, when they had wanted to escape the restraining company of adults.

As he and Jane had now escaped the restraining company of other adults...

A move, he now realised, not without its own dangers.

'Did it not excite you earlier, Jane, to have two men challenging each other to a duel over you?' he prompted huskily.

She arched auburn brows. 'Over me, Your Grace?'

Hawk frowned darkly. 'Who else, Jane?'

She gave a derisive shake of her head. 'Perhaps some other lady of your mutual acquaintance? This Countess, for example?'

Hawk's eyes widened at the directness of her attack. Although he should perhaps have expected nothing less from a young woman who was never less than forthright.

She gave a knowing smile. 'Ah, I note by your scowling silence that my surmise is possibly the correct one. The Countess was your mistress as well as the Earl's?'

Hawk stiffened. 'I do not believe this to be a suitable subject for discussion between us, Jane—'

'Why?' Her eyes were curiously wide. 'Or is it that the Countess is a married lady?'

He frowned darkly. 'She is widowed.'

Jane frowned her puzzlement. 'The Earl has informed me he is also widowed. And you are a single gentleman.' She shrugged. 'I do not see where the problem lies...?'

Hawk looked at her in exasperation. 'The problem lies, Jane, with the fact that a single young lady such as yourself does not discuss a man's mistress—ex-mistress!—with him.'

'Why not?'

'Because it simply is not *done*, Jane!'

She gave a derisive smile. 'Perhaps in the polite company that you keep, Your Grace, for which the Earl voices such contempt.' She nodded. 'But, young as I was, for lack of anyone else in whom to confide my father occasionally discussed such matters with me when it involved one of his parishioners.'

'I am not one of your father's parishioners, Jane!' Hawk muttered irritably.

Inwardly, he was wishing that he had never met the Countess of Morefield—let alone so briefly and, as it had transpired, so unsatisfactorily shared her bed!

He had no doubt that it was because of that brief dalliance that Whitney was behaving so provokingly this evening, in monopolising the company of both Jane and Arabella. The other man had made it obvious at the time that he had taken exception to Hawk's interest in the Countess, which had resulted in her changing from sharing her bed with an Earl to a Duke.

'No, you are not,' Jane acknowledged ruefully, staring into the flames of the fire as she wondered what her father would have made of a man such as Hawk St Claire, the forceful Duke of Stourbridge.

Her father—her adopted father—had not been a man of the world, but a simple country parson. Nevertheless, in the boundaries of his parish there had existed avarice, jealousy, incest, adultery and even murder. Perhaps not, as the Duke had said, subjects for a young girl's ears, but in the absence of a wife to share his worries Jane's father had sometimes talked to her about such matters.

'What manner of man was your father, Jane?'

She looked up sharply at the softly spoken query. 'He was a good man,' she stated defensively. 'A good, kind and loving man.'

The Duke's mouth twisted derisively. 'All things I am sure you believe me not to be!'

'Untrue, Your Grace!' Jane gasped.

He looked grim. 'Was it a kind man who refused to let you continue on your journey as you wished and instead brought you here, Jane? Was it a kind or loving man who only days ago took advantage of your lack of a protector?' He shook his head self-disgustedly. 'In the six days of our acquaintance, Jane, it seems to me I have shown you I am not any of the things you so admired in your father!'

They were two very different men, yes. But these last three days, as Jane had watched the Duke work so tirelessly about his estate, he had shown himself to be just as good a master to the people who lived on his estate as her father had been minister to his parishioners.

Besides, her feelings towards the Duke—the wild, soaring love she felt just looking into that aristocratically handsome face—bore absolutely no resemblance to the sweet, uncomplicated love she'd had for her adopted father!

She shook her head. 'I do not think of you in that way, Your Grace.'

Hawk looked down at her searchingly. 'Then how *do* you think of me, Jane…?'

That pink tongue ran once more over the softness of her parted lips. 'I—I see you as a man. A strong, arrogant, forceful man who expects—demands—to be obeyed without question.'

Hawk smiled ruefully at her description. '*You* do not obey me, Jane.'

She gave the ghost of a smile. 'Perhaps that is why you are here with me rather than with the Countess…?'

Hawk found his breath catching in his throat. That was

exactly the reason he was here with Jane rather than any other woman. Jane challenged him. Thwarted him. Disobeyed him. Aroused him.

As he gazed into the beauty of Jane's face, as he looked at her softly parted lips and into the unfathomable depths of her eyes, as he felt the fierce desire that ripped through him, he knew that it had been a mistake to follow her here. That being alone here with Jane like this, desiring her as he did, was the last thing he should have allowed to happen.

'Jane...' He was not aware of having made a step towards her, or of her making one towards him, but knew that he—that she—must have done so. His arms moved about her and he drew her fiercely against him as his mouth claimed hers.

She was all softness and the sweet perfume that was uniquely Jane, her lips parting willingly beneath his as Hawk deepened the kiss, feeling his desire raging hotly out of control as her slender fingers threaded into his hair and her ample breasts and slender hips curved invitingly against his own chest and thighs.

Hawk had never known such fierce desire. The need to possess. To own. His thighs pulsed with that need, and the hardness of his arousal moved restlessly against her as he strained to draw Jane even closer.

There were too many clothes between them. Too many layers of fabric between Jane's body and his own. Between the feel, the sensation, of her silken nakedness pressed against his.

Hawk groaned low in his throat as her own actions seemed to echo his need, her hands trailing down his throat to splay against his chest as her fingers dealt deftly, quickly, with the buttons of his waistcoat and shirt before she touched his burning flesh and those fingers became entangled in the silky hair beneath.

Her touch was too much. Jane was too much. Hawk deepened the kiss hungrily, devouringly, drinking in her sweetness as his tongue plunged hotly, ravenously, into the heat of her mouth.

Seeking. Capturing. Claiming her for his own.

For Jane was his.

His.

She belonged to this man, Jane acknowledged feverishly, clinging to his shoulders. Hawk was continuing to kiss her even as he swung her up into his arms to carry her across to a chaise, laying her gently down upon it before quickly joining her there, the hard length of his body pressing her down amongst the cushions as his lips and tongue continued to plunder her own.

At that moment Jane cared for nothing else—needed nothing else but Hawk's lips and hands upon her. She arched her back as he reached to release the fastening of her gown and slide it down the length of her body. She was wearing only her stockings and chemise now, and closed her eyes in ecstasy as she felt the caress of his tongue across her silk-covered breast before he suckled her deep inside his mouth, drawing on her greedily, hungrily, even as his tongue continued that wild caress across the hardened tip.

But she wanted—needed—to touch him too, and slid the jacket from his shoulders, the waistcoat quickly following, then his shirt, until Jane knew the sheer pleasure of touching his naked flesh. Her fingers were caressing as they glided over the hardness of his muscled chest, tangling in the silky hair that covered him, before she touched him, her nails scraping accidentally against one of the hardened nubs that nestled there.

His sharply indrawn breath was enough to tell Jane that the caress gave Hawk pleasure too, making her bolder still as she touched him deliberately now, and felt him quiver, shudder in uncontrollable response.

Before Hawk, she had never caressed a man's naked body before, but now, as she began to experiment with what gave Hawk pleasure, Jane felt a sense of her own power over the flesh that hardened and quivered at her slightest touch.

Hawk fell back with a gasp as he felt Jane's hands upon him, his groan one of aching longing as he lay on his back and felt the lap of her tongue against him. Her hands were running the length of his chest now, his muscles quivering, tensing at her slightest touch. A touch that was all the more arousing because of her lack of experience or artifice.

Hawk looked down at her in the firelight, at the play of flames against her hair as it fell free of its confining pins onto his bared chest. His hand shook slightly as he raised it to touch that brightness, his fingers tangling convulsively in its silkiness as her kisses followed the line of hair that moved from his chest down to his navel.

He sucked in a sharp breath as he felt the experimental dip of her tongue into that sensitised well, that shy plundering sending him very close to losing complete control.

Jane raised her head to look at him, eyes dark with her own arousal. 'Did I hurt you...?'

His short bark of laughter was self-derisive as he moved so that she now lay beneath him. 'Jane, if you "hurt" me any more in that particular way I am not sure I will be answerable for the consequences!'

She looked up at him quizzically. 'You liked my touching you so intimately...?'

Hawk grimaced. 'I liked it too much, Jane, to let you continue.'

'I do not understand...?'

How could she? How could Jane know that just to look at her as she lay there, with her long hair spread on the cushion beneath her, her lips swollen from his kisses, wearing only her stockings and chemise, her nipples hard and pouting beneath the silky material, her curving hips and thighs turned invitingly towards him, was more than enough temptation without the added arousal of her lips and hands upon his own body?

'Let me show you, Jane,' he groaned throatily, as he slipped the slender straps of her chemise from her shoulders to bare her breasts completely and gaze down hungrily at those rosy aureoles of pleasure. 'How do you feel when I do this, Jane?' He bent his head to run his tongue lightly across the sensitised nipple, instantly feeling her quivering response. 'And this?' He bestowed the same caress upon its twin, and again felt Jane tremble. 'And perhaps this...?' He moved his hand to push up her chemise and bare her thighs to his slow caress, as first touching the silken curls there before moving lower.

Her lids closed at Hawk's first touch of her silken folds, her flesh already swollen and moist with arousal as her thighs parted to his caressing fingers.

Hawk stroked her slowly, purposefully, circling the hardened nub but never quite touching as he allowed her to become accustomed to the intimacy of his touch, waiting until Jane arched instinctively against his hand before deepening the caress. The soft pad of his thumb then sought and found the swollen centre of her arousal before moving rhythmically against her.

Jane, having been lost in a wondrous sea of pleasure only seconds earlier, now opened wide, incredulous eyes to look up into Hawk's fiercely concentrating face as her pleasure intensified to fever pitch—burning, scorching, flooding her.

She could feel her own slickness as Hawk probed gently against her with one experimental finger, felt as it entered her slowly, questioningly, before he withdrew. Only to repeat the caress, again and again, the pad of his thumb a constant caress against her, fiercely and then more gently.

Fierce and gentle. Fierce and gentle.

Each time Jane imagined she was about to discover that there was more—much more!—as Hawk gentled his caress and withdrew, and the ache between her thighs, at the tips of her breasts, became unbearable.

'Please…' she finally groaned achingly, wildly. 'Please, Hawk!' She sat up slightly against the cushions, offering her breasts in silent plea. 'I want—I need—'

'I know exactly what you need, Jane!' he growled triumphantly, before his head swooped and his mouth claimed one aching nipple, drawing it deeply into his mouth as he suckled, tongue stroking, teeth biting. The caress of his hand was no longer in the least gentle as he thrust rhythmically inside her and felt the first of her pleasurable convulsions.

'Hawk…' Jane gasped mindlessly as pleasure both burned and filled her. 'Hawk…!' She fell back, her hands clenching on the chaise, as wave after wave of pleasure claimed her, beginning as a fire that raged between her thighs and spreading like an ever-increasing flame to her every extremity—licking, throbbing, consuming all in its path.

'Yes, Jane. Yes!' he groaned fiercely, before transferring his attentions to her other breast, drawing it deep into the hot cavern of his mouth as he continued to stroke her swollen flesh until Jane had experienced every last moment of wondrous pleasure.

Incredible. Amazing. Miraculous pleasure.

Jane fell back weakly against the cushions, never having known that such pleasure existed. Never having known that this was what happened between a man and a woman. Never guessing at the shared intimacy that resulted in such ecstasy.

Was it always this way between a man and a woman? Had it been this way between her mother and her lover? If so, Jane could perhaps at last understand how Janette had succumbed to his seduction. As Jane had just succumbed to Hawk's...!

Did that make her the things Lady Sulby had accused her of being? Was she indeed a harlot and a whore?

'What is it, Jane?' Hawk demanded as he saw the shadows racing across her face—a face that seconds ago had been lit from within as she reached the climax of her pleasure. But now it was shadowed with—with what? With embarrassment at her own lack of control? Or with regret for what had transpired...?

Neither of which was acceptable to Hawk.

His hands moved to cradle each of her cheeks as he tilted her face towards him. 'Look at me, Jane,' he ordered firmly, when she kept her lids determinedly closed. 'Jane!' he rasped impatiently as she did not immediately comply.

Jane bit down painfully on the trembling of her bottom

lip as she resolutely kept her lids closed. 'I think it would be best if you left me now, Your Grace—'

'How dare you attempt to put a distance between us by addressing me in that cold, distant way?' he cut in fiercely. 'Jane, you *will* look at me now!' His hands moved to her shoulders, digging into the softness of her flesh as he shook her.

How could she possibly look at him ever again? How could she bear to look into his face—the hard, arrogant face that she loved—and see the disappointment, the disgust that must be written there as he recalled her wanton writhings as she pleaded with him to pleasure her?

'Look at me, Jane!' Hawk demanded again harshly, as he sensed that inwardly she was withdrawing even further away from him.

Minutes ago he would have sworn that Jane had wanted his attentions, his caresses, but now he doubted that certainty. Jane could not even bear look at him—as if the very sight of him repulsed her.

Had Jane merely acquiesced to his kisses, the intimacy of his caresses, because she had not been strong enough to deny him? Or, worse, because she felt beholden to him for aiding her escape when she could no longer tolerate Lady Sulby's cruelty?

The thought that that might be the case filled Hawk himself with revulsion.

He released her abruptly to sit up on the chaise, his face turned away as he stared sightlessly into the flames of the fire which minutes ago had bathed Jane's nakedness so seductively.

Had he forced his attentions on Jane? Had Jane surrendered to the Duke of Stourbridge because she'd felt she had to, rather than to Hawk the man because she desired him as fiercely as he desired her?

Oh, yes, Jane challenged, thwarted and disobeyed him when it suited her, but had she felt unable to do so just now? The very force of his desire having alarmed her into submission?

He was sure that had to be the case when he recalled how distantly she had addressed him as 'Your Grace', immediately after his caressing hands had brought her to a climax it must now shock and revolt her to recall.

His expression was grim as he stood up abruptly to pull on his rumpled shirt, his back towards Jane as he refastened the buttons with fingers that were not quite steady. 'I believe it best if I leave you, after all, Jane,' he rasped harshly.

Jane had taken advantage of Hawk's distraction to pull her chemise back into some sort of order, wincing slightly as the material brushed against breasts that were still achingly sensitised from his ministrations, between her thighs was even more so.

She stared up at the rigid implacability of Hawk's back, at the silkiness of his dark, gold-shot hair brushing the collar of his shirt in unaccustomed disarray—a fact he seemed aware of too, as he pushed impatient fingers through the mahogany darkness before pulling on his waistcoat and jacket and turning to face her.

Jane almost recoiled from the fierceness of his expression. His mouth was a thin, uncompromising line above his clenched jaw, and those golden eyes glittered coldly as he looked down his long, arrogant nose at her. Every trace of the indulgently attentive lover had now disappeared from his harshly etched features.

But she refused to allow herself to show weakness. Her

nature was such that she refused to be cowed by anyone—least of all the arrogant Duke of Stourbridge. 'By all means return to your sister's guests, Your Grace,' she told him lightly as she swung her legs to the floor and sat up on the chaise. 'But I trust you will understand if I do not join you?' She quirked mocking brows.

She knew she should pick up her gown—her beautiful gown of cream silk which had been thrown aside so uncaringly only minutes ago!—and cover her semi-nakedness, but the stubbornly proud part of her nature refused to let her do so. Minutes ago Hawk had seen her in all her naked glory, making it far too late for her to act like an innocent miss now.

Even if that was what she was.

Or had been...

Jane was sure she would never be completely innocent ever again now that Hawk had introduced her to such a world of physical intimacy and pleasure.

She forced herself to meet his imperiously haughty gaze. 'Would you please tell Arabella that I have retired to my room with a headache?' Her voice was husky, the headache she had just mentioned actually becoming a reality as Hawk's face darkened ominously at her words. 'I think it better if we do not return to the house together after such a long absence,' she added.

Hawk knew that the gossips present tonight would be sure to make much of the fact that although Jane had left the ballroom earlier in the company of the Earl of Whitney it was on the arm of the Duke of Stourbridge that she returned some time later. And he had already caused Jane enough distress for one evening without adding the ruination of her reputation in Society to his list of crimes. As it was, his return and Jane's absence were sure to be noted.

He nodded abruptly. 'I will make your excuses to Arabella. But do not remain out here alone for too long, Jane,' he continued harshly. 'I was not the only man attracted by your beauty this evening,' he added, with a disapproval he had no control over.

Her eyes widened briefly before her gaze became mocking. 'I do believe that one lover in an evening is more than enough for any woman!'

His mouth tightened at the mere thought of Jane ever sharing of her lush beauty with any man but himself. It was unacceptable. Insupportable. Unbearable.

She belonged to *him*, damn it!

His jaw clenched. 'If it really is your wish to avoid being seen again this evening, then I suggest that you go to your room by way of the back stairs.'

Like one of the servants, Jane acknowledged dully. But was that not what she was? Here on sufferance only? As a temporary companion to Lady Arabella?

And as occasional lover of the powerful Duke of Stourbridge…?

Her chin rose proudly. 'I think not, Hawk.' Her tone was coldly dismissive as she deliberately used his given name. 'I have no intention of behaving in the manner of a serving girl returning to her room after an illicit tryst with the master of the house!' she added, as he frowned darkly.

His face darkened ominously. 'I do not think of you as a servant, Jane—'

'Then do not suggest that I behave like one!'

As was usual for them, Hawk acknowledged grimly, they were arguing now they were not caught in the throes of physical desire. But for Jane to even suggest that he thought of her in the same terms as one of the maids at Mulberry Hall was utterly ridiculous. Utterly provoking!

His mouth twisted grimly. 'I believe you were the one to suggest that as your given role, Jane. Not I.'

Her eyes sparked with temper. 'You implied it, Your Grace,' she snapped.

'No, Jane, I did not,' he sighed. 'But who am I to argue with a woman when she has made her mind up to something?' he added grimly.

Her eyes glittered. 'You are the arrogant Duke of Stourbridge!'

'Undoubtedly,' he drawled, with an acknowledging inclination of his head, absolutely positive that Jane was trying to provoke an argument with him. Another argument with him... 'I believe, Jane, that we will resume this conversation when you are feeling less argumentative.'

'And I believe we will not!' Jane snapped, as she stood up to begin pulling on her gown.

Hawk's breath caught in his throat as he watched, stood transfixed at her agitated movements.

Jane could have no idea how beautiful she looked, with her red hair falling in loose curls almost to her waist, that silky chemise barely covering the fullness of her breasts and the alluring curve of her thighs before she pulled her gown over that nakedness. But Hawk was very aware of it as his body once more ached, throbbed with the return of his desire, leaving him in no doubt that he would find little rest tonight in the loneliness of his ducal bed.

It had been this way since he had first met Jane, he acknowledged ruefully. At Markham Park she had been a constant source of disruption, as he had been at first irritated by her and then amused by her. She had become more than an irritation on his journey to Mulberry Hall, and even the work that had kept him so busy about the estate the last few days had not been enough to dispel thoughts of Jane once he retired to his suite for the night. The added memory of their time together in the stables was enough to totally chase away any idea of rest.

But tonight, with the taste and feel of Jane still upon his lips and hands, he knew that he would find sleep impossible!

'As is your wish, Jane,' he bit out tersely. 'But that has been the usual way of things in our acquaintance to date, has it not?' he added hardly.

Did he really believe that? Jane wondered frowningly. Did he really believe that, given a choice, she would leave his side ever again?

She loved this man. Loved him as Hawk St Claire. Loved the Duke of Stourbridge.

And there lay the real problem.

As Hawk St Claire there might have been some hope, albeit a slim one, of him one day returning her love. But as the Duke of Stourbridge—a man destined to marry well in order to provide the ducal heir, to take as his wife a woman of a status and breeding suitable to be the mother of that heir—there was absolutely no hope of Jane, a woman who did not even know who her real father was, being able to measure up to his exacting standard.

She forced a deliberately mocking smile. 'As you say.' She gave a derisive nod. 'Please do not let me delay you a moment longer from returning to your sister's guests.'

His eyes glittered dangerously. 'You will not dismiss me in that contemptuous tone, Jane!'

Jane's soft laugh was deliberately taunting. 'I am so sorry, Your Grace.' She made him an exaggerated curtsey. 'Please forgive me, Your Grace.' She eyed him tauntingly as she straightened. 'For one very brief moment I actually believed you when you said you did not believe I was subservient to you!'

Hawk wanted to shake her. Wanted to put her over his knee and spank her.

But more than either of those things he wanted to take her in his arms once again and make love to her! Completely this time. Wanted to bury himself deep inside her silken sheath before losing himself in the inferno of her inner heat.

But as he dared not trust himself to do either of those first two things, knowing either would immediately lead to the third, he took the only other course open to him—he turned sharply on his heel and strode forcefully, determinedly, away from her and from the privacy the summerhouse offered to his real needs and desires.

Jane waited only long enough to ensure that the Duke had really gone before falling down onto the chaise in a devastation of grief-stricken tears so heated they seemed to burn as they cascaded unchecked down her cheeks, knowing she had alienated Hawk for ever with the wantonness of her behaviour.

Chapter Twelve

'Come in, Jane, and close the door behind you.'

Jane had been sitting alone in the parlour eating a late breakfast, Arabella being still upstairs in her rooms, following the dinner party the previous evening, when one of the maids had come to inform her that the Duke wished to see her at once in the library. Jane had lingered—delayed—at the breakfast table long enough to finish her cup of tea as she contemplated the reason for Hawk wanting to speak to her again so soon after they had parted so angrily the evening before.

Perhaps to tell her she would have to leave his household?

Immediately?

If so it was the same conclusion Jane herself had come to during her long hours of sleeplessness.

The tone of his voice now—undoubtedly the Duke of Stourbridge's voice, cold and imperious—was more than enough to compel her into stepping softly into the library and carefully closing the door behind her before once more turning to face him.

The tall, imposing, imperious man who stood so broodingly silhouetted in front of the window—dark clothing expertly tailored, hair brushed neatly back from that arrogant brow, hands linked behind his rigidly straight back—bore very little resemblance to the piratical lover of the previous evening, with his clothes in disarray and the darkness of his hair curling onto his broy.

As she, Jane hoped, bore no resemblance to the tumble-haired, half-naked woman he had aroused to such unimagined pleasure!

She quirked one auburn brow as those gold-coloured eyes continued to look at her so chillingly. 'I have entered, sir, and I have also closed the door behind me...'

Hawk drew in a sharp breath at her barely concealed derision. 'I warn you, Jane, do not even attempt to annoy me this morning!'

Her eyes widened with beguiling innocence. 'By doing as you bade me to do...?'

Hawk's mouth thinned at Jane's display of innocent subservience, very aware that she was the least subservient woman he knew! 'This is not a time for humour, Jane,' he assured her harshly.

'No?' Her brows rose even higher before she walked gracefully across the room to sit in one of the armchairs that flanked the empty fireplace, smoothing her gown neatly into place and folding her hands demurely on her knees before lifting her head to look at him. 'Then what *is* it a time for, Your Grace?'

Hawk's hands clenched behind his back in a supreme

effort to prevent himself from marching across the room and lifting Jane to her feet before shaking her unmercifully.

As he had known it would be, his night had been a disturbed rather than a restful one, as images of Jane, with her loosely curling red hair reaching to her slender waist, her breasts bared and pert, her thighs parted invitingly, had tortured and tormented him until morning light.

At which time he had finally given up all hope of sleeping and instead dressed before going down to the stables to saddle his stallion Gabriel and riding across the surrounding hillside for several hours. The brisk morning air had cleared his senses—if not his mind—of those tantalising memories of Jane in her half-naked abandon.

Not so now, as he looked at her sitting there so primly, her disapproving expression much like his old nanny's had been when she'd wished to rebuke him for some childish misdemeanour. On Jane a totally ineffective expression—because memories of her sensual beauty the previous evening crowded his already tormented mind.

His mouth thinned, nostrils flaring, as he refused to let those memories deter him from the reason he had summoned her here this morning. 'I have decided that it is time—past time—for us to discuss exactly why it was you decided to leave the home of your guardian so abruptly.'

Jane was so stunned by the Duke's topic of conversation that for a moment she could think of no reply. She had thought—believed—he had asked her to come here so they might talk about the events of the previous evening. Had prepared herself for that as she had lingered in the breakfast parlour drinking her cup of tea—had even thought of several replies she might make on the subject.

She could not think of a single response to the question

he had just asked her! Instead she answered with a question of her own. 'Why, Your Grace...?'

'Why.' He nodded abruptly, his golden gaze totally unreadable as he looked down the long length of his nose at her.

Jane frowned. 'But you know why, Your Grace.'

'No, Jane, I do not,' he rasped harshly. 'As I recall, your only explanation at the time was that you no longer felt you could reside under the same roof as Lady Sulby.'

And that was true, as far as it went. But there was more, so much more, to Jane's flight from Markham Park. Reasons she could not share with this stranger who looked at her so coldly. For at this moment he was every inch the haughtily superior Duke of Stourbridge.

'I stated the truth,' she confirmed tightly.

'But what caused you to feel that way, Jane?' He took two long steps so that he towered over her.

She blinked at the intensity of that golden gaze as it seemed to bore down into hers. 'My reasons are entirely personal to me—'

'Not when you now reside in my home!'

'That can easily be remedied, sir!' Jane stood up abruptly, too restless to remain seated any longer—although she had not been completely prepared for how close the Duke was now standing to her. Her arm brushed against his as she attempted to step past him, instantly sending a tingling thrill of awareness down to her fingers and up to her breasts.

The Duke reached out and curled steely fingers about one of her wrists, preventing her from moving away from him. 'We will discuss the subject of your departure from Mulberry Hall later, Jane,' he rasped coldly. 'First I would like—I demand—a full explanation as to your reasons for leaving Markham Park.'

First? Hawk intended for her to go soon, then? Might even have made arrangements for her immediate departure once she had answered his questions...?

Because of what had occurred between them the previous evening? Or because of something else...?

Jane looked up searchingly into that hard, implacable face. Hawk's gaze was coldly compelling as it met hers, his expression unreadable. 'What has occurred, sir, to suddenly bring about the need for this conversation?' she ventured cautiously.

Hawk had never for a moment during their acquaintance underestimated Jane's intelligence. He did not underestimate it now. 'This morning I received word of your guardians' reaction to your disappearance.'

'I did not disappear!' Her cheeks were flushed with indignation. 'I simply left a place where I had never been made welcome!'

'Indeed, Jane?'

'Indeed, Your Grace,' she echoed impatiently. 'I—Would you release my arm please? You are hurting me.' She frowned up at him, and his fingers tightened briefly before he gave a disgusted snort of frustration and released her.

Hawk turned away, knowing that if he did not he might do a lot more to hurt Jane than merely grasp her wrist and hold her against her will.

He was furious. Livid. Wanted to hit out and hurt someone. Anyone. Even Jane. Especially Jane—for putting him in the untenable position he now found himself in.

He kept his back firmly turned towards her as he bit out,

'No matter how unwelcoming, the Sulbys are nevertheless your guardians. Uncaring ones, perhaps—'

'Perhaps?' Jane scorned incredulously.

Hawk nodded abruptly. 'You were fed and clothed within their home, Jane. Which is more than many other penniless orphans can boast.'

'And I am to be *grateful* for that?' she challenged contemptuously. 'I am to bow and scrape and feel grateful for every morsel of food I have allowed to pass my lips these past twelve years?'

'Yes!' The Duke reached out once again to grasp her arm, his expression one of stingingly cold fury. 'Admittedly, I too have found Lady Sulby to be a contemptible woman. I have no doubt that you felt wronged by her, but that cannot be offered as an excuse for your own actions!'

Jane blinked up at him, more than a little alarmed by the fierceness of his expression. She had seen the Duke's anger before—had been the reason for that anger more times than she cared to remember!—but it had never been like this. Had never been underlined by this steely edge of absolute coldness.

'My own actions...?' she repeated slowly. 'What did I do that was so wrong?' She gave a puzzled shake of her head. 'Exactly what have you learned of my guardians' reaction to my sudden departure from their home, Your Grace? And from whom?'

His mouth tightened. 'It does not matter from whom—'

'It matters, Your Grace!' Jane cried emotionally. 'Your tone is accusing, and I believe it is unfair of you to talk to me in this way without first telling me the name of my accuser.'

He looked down at her wordlessly for several long,

searching seconds before abruptly releasing her arm to turn sharply away and stride over to stand in front of the window once again, his back to the room. And to Jane.

'When we returned here four days ago I sent word to Andrew Windham, my man of business in London, asking him to make enquiries—to ascertain, if he could, your guardians' actions following your disappearance. I felt— justifiably, I believe—that it was wrong of me to harbour you within my household without at least some effort being made on my part to discover if in fact the Sulbys were scouring the countryside looking for you.'

'I assure you they were not!' Jane scorned knowingly. 'And you had no right to make such enquiries—'

'I had every right!' the Duke grated harshly as he swung fiercely back to face her. 'Damn it, woman, the Sulbys could have been dragging neighbouring ponds and searching the woods for miles around for your dead body!'

Jane frowned at his vehemence. 'And were they?' she finally ventured, with a return of her earlier caution.

He flexed his tensed shoulder muscles. 'The report I received this morning claims that Lady Sulby has suffered a complete collapse of the nerves following your disappearance, and has had to be removed to her brother's home in Great Yarmouth in order to take advantage of the bracing air to be found there.' His tone was grim.

Jane's frown became scathing. 'Are you saying that I am the cause of Lady Sulby's supposed collapse?'

Hawk's mouth was a thin, uncompromising line. 'You doubt the information acquired by my man of business?'

'Not at all.' Jane gave a weary shake of her head, sure that anyone the Duke employed was certain to be impeccably meticulous in his duties. 'What I doubt is that Lady

Sulby would feel anything but jubilation at having finally rid herself of my unwanted presence in her household!'

The Duke did not speak for several long, tense seconds. 'Perhaps,' he finally rasped icily. 'But I am given to understand that it was not only your own departure that caused that lady's collapse, but the loss of her jewellery.'

Jane stared at him blankly. Lady Sulby's jewellery? Could Hawk possibly be referring to the only jewels that Lady Sulby possessed of any value? The Sulby diamond earrings and necklace given to her by Sir Barnaby on the event of their marriage twenty-five years ago?

But what relevance did they have to Jane?

'Several of Lady Sulby's jewels disappeared on the same day you did, Jane,' the Duke continued flatly.

Her eyes widened incredulously, her face paling. Was Hawk saying—? Could he possibly be accusing her of—?

'I know absolutely nothing of their disappearance!' Jane burst out incredulously, her expression anxious. 'Hawk, you do not seriously believe that I—'

'What I do or do not believe about this matter does not signify, Jane.' His mouth was set grimly.

Her hands clenched at her sides. 'It matters to me!'

He shook his head. 'The fact is that on the day you left the Sulby household Lady Sulby's jewels also disappeared. The matter has been reported to the appropriate authorities and an order issued for their recovery. And for your arrest. Do you understand what that means, Jane?' he prompted impatiently.

Jane understood exactly what it meant. But the fact that the authorities were actively looking for her, that they would arrest her for the theft of Lady Sulby's jewels when they found her, paled into insignificance when compared to the fact that Hawk obviously did not believe her when she told him she had no knowledge of the disappearance of Lady Sulby's jewels...

Hawk's frustrated anger with the situation increased as he looked upon Jane's bewildered countenance. If she thought for one moment that he was enjoying this conversation...

'I know how upset you were that day, Jane.' His tone gentled slightly. 'I appreciate that Lady Sulby had deeply wounded you in some way—'

'How dare you?' Jane cut in furiously, angry colour having returned to her cheeks now, and the green of her eyes glittering with that same anger. 'How dare you stand there as my accuser and my judge on the word of a woman who on the last occasion we met expressed nothing but hatred towards me?'

The last thing Hawk wanted to do was judge Jane, or condemn her. He wished only to help her. But he could not do that if Jane would not tell him why she had left the Sulbys' that day.

'It is not only Lady Sulby's word, Jane,' he told her softly.

'Who else accuses me?' she demanded angrily.

'Miss Olivia Sulby—'

He was interrupted by Jane's dismissive snort. 'She is of the same mould as her mother, and her opinion does not count.'

'In that you are wrong,' Hawk told her impatiently. 'I can assure you that Olivia Sulby's testament against you is as valid as any other. And Olivia Sulby claims that on the day prior to your sudden flight she remembers accompanying her mother to her bedchamber, and that both of them chanced upon you there, in possession of Lady Sulby's jewellery box.'

Jane thought back to that day a week ago. It was the day the guests had been arriving for Lady Sulby's house party. The day Hawk himself had arrived...

She remembered going upstairs to collect Lady Sulby's shawl and noticing the jewellery box had been left out on the dressing table before being totally distracted by the arrival of the magnificent black coach bearing the Duke of Stourbridge.

Then there had been that momentous first meeting with the Duke on the stairs, followed by Lady Sulby's scathing comment that Jane had brought her the wrong shawl and she was to return to her bedchamber at once and collect the correct one—and Jane's own embarrassment when she had returned up the stairs and realised that the Duke had stood on the gallery above as silent witness to the whole exchange.

Jane also remembered Lady Sulby's reaction when she had burst into the bedroom a short time later, Olivia behind her, and found Jane loitering in the room, the jewellery box still sitting on the dressing table.

Jane recalled how bewildered she had felt—how Olivia had looked at her with such triumphant satisfaction when the older woman had questioned Jane accusingly as to whether or not she had looked at the contents of her jewellery box.

But the following day Jane had learnt the reason for Lady Sulby's sharpness when the other woman had acknowledged that she had hidden there the letters Jane's mother had written to her married lover...

And now Hawk—the man who had made love to Jane so

intimately the evening before—chose to believe the word of the two vindictive Sulby women over her own...

'Jane, I cannot even attempt to help you if you will not be honest with me,' he reasoned frustratedly.

Jane drew herself up proudly, determined not to show how hurt she was by his lack of faith in her complete innocence in this matter. 'I do not remember asking for your help, Your Grace.'

'You prefer to be arrested and imprisoned?' Hawk could barely contain the anger he felt at her stubborn refusal to confide in him.

Her mouth twisted scathingly. 'For something I did not do?'

Hawk was a local magistrate. He knew far better than Jane how the law worked. And with two such credible witnesses against her as Lady Sulby and her daughter, coupled with her own sudden flight from Markham Park, Jane would be found guilty before the case was even presented in a court of law.

He stepped forward to grasp her shoulders impatiently and shake her into looking up at him. 'Can you not see, Jane, that it will not matter whether or not you are guilty of the crime?'

'Of course it will matter!' she assured him fiercely, the glitter in her eyes not just from anger now, but also unshed tears. 'I know nothing of the theft of Lady Sulby's jewellery. *Nothing!*' she repeated vehemently. 'I do know that Lady Sulby hates me, as she hated my mother before me—'

'Your mother, Jane?' Hawk probed softly, when she broke off abruptly. 'Did you not tell me that your mother died when you were born?'

'She did. But—' Jane broke off again as she realised she

had been about to tell more than she wanted him to know. Bad enough that he believed her to be a thief and a liar, without adding illegitimacy to that list of sins. 'Lady Sulby was acquainted with my mother.' Jane chose her words carefully. 'She told me she did not like her—that she did not approve at all when Sir Barnaby accepted guardianship of Janette's daughter.' Jane paled as a sudden thought—truth?—hit her with the force of a blow.

Her mother's letters to her lover confirmed Lady Sulby's claim that he had been a married man.

Twenty-three years ago Sir Barnaby had already been married to Lady Sulby for two years. Lady Sulby hated and despised Jane, she had told her, as she had hated and despised her mother before her.

Could it be that it was *Sir Barnaby* who had been Janette's lover twenty-three years ago? That Jane was *his* illegitimate daughter?

It would explain so many things if that were the case—most of all Jane being left to the guardianship of a man she had never even heard her adopted father mention, let alone one whom Jane had actually met before he and Lady Sulby had come to collect her from Somerset on that desolate day twelve years ago.

Could it be that Jane's mad flight to find her real father had been completely unnecessary? That she had been living under his guardianship all along...?

It was difficult to imagine the rotund Sir Barnaby as the dashingly handsome lover who had swept her mother off her feet all those years ago, whom her mother had so described in her letters when she had expressed the hope that her unborn child would resemble him. But Sir Barnaby could have—must have—looked far different twenty-three years ago...

'Jane...?'

She blinked dazedly as she focused on Hawk. On the condemning Duke of Stourbridge. 'I will leave Mulberry Hall immediately.'

'No, Jane, you will not!' Hawk cut in forcefully, having been angered seconds ago at Jane's sudden distraction of thought. What could possibly be more urgent for her to contemplate than the dire situation she found herself in?

And, no matter how Jane might choose to dismiss the whole incident, it *was* dire. An accusation of theft had been made against her, her arrest ordered, and mere claims of innocence on Jane's part would not suffice to cancel that order.

But as the powerful Duke of Stourbridge Hawk did have some influence. 'I am willing to help you, Jane—'

'As I said before, I do not remember asking for your help, Your Grace,' she cut in coldly.

Hawk looked down at her searchingly. Did Jane really not see how precarious her position was?

'Neither do I ask for it now, Your Grace,' she continued haughtily as she attempted to shake off his hold on her shoulders. 'Release me, sir,' she ordered coldly when she was unsuccessful in that attempt.

He shook his head impatiently. 'Jane, if you leave Mulberry Hall without my protection you will be exposed to immediate arrest and imprisonment.'

She gave him a pitying look. 'I am willing to take my chances.'

Even the thought of Jane exposed to the harshness of a

prison cell, to the cold and the rats and the untender mercies of the turnkey, was enough to make Hawk shudder.

She would rather suffer all that than accept his help...?

His hands dropped from her shoulders before he stepped back. 'Then you are a fool, Jane!' he assured her harshly.

Her eyes glittered challengingly. 'I would rather be thought a fool than live any longer under the protection of the Duke of Stourbridge!'

Hawk flinched as if Jane had physically struck him. Was that really how she felt? Did Jane despise him—hate him so much after what had occurred between them yesterday evening that she was willing to suffer imprisonment rather than accept his help?

The defiant expression on her face, the scorn directed towards him that she made no effort to hide, was answer enough...

He drew in a ragged breath before speaking again. 'Jane, I advise you to put aside your feelings of enmity towards me and instead concentrate on the matter at hand.' His expression was grim. 'I can intercede for you with Sir Barnaby. I have found him to be a kind and reasonable man, and I am sure—'

'No!' Jane cut forcefully across the Duke's reasoning speech. 'I will speak to Sir Barnaby myself, when I return to Markham Park.'

'You mean to go back there?' The Duke looked incredulous.

Yes, Jane intended going back to Markham Park.

She had thought to find answers to her past in Somerset, but now it seemed that Sir Barnaby might be the person who had those answers. That he might be her real father...

Whether he was or he was not, Jane knew she needed

to return to Markham Park in order to clear her name as a thief. To expose Lady Sulby for the liar that she was.

For Jane became more and more convinced by the second that Lady Sulby's jewels were not missing at all—that Lady Sulby herself had hidden the jewels away somewhere, and merely taken advantage of Jane's flight in order to blacken her name even further.

She refocused on the Duke, her lips curving into a humourless smile at the disbelief in his expression. 'Yes, of course I mean to go back there.'

'Jane, you cannot—'

'I must go,' she assured him firmly, implacably.

And, whether she planned to return to Markham Park or not, Jane knew that she could not remain under the Duke's roof for a moment longer. He could not be further from the truth when he said Jane had feelings of enmity towards him. How could she possibly have feelings of ill-will towards the man she loved with all her heart?

The man who minutes ago had broken that heart when he refused to believe in her innocence...

Hawk looked down at Jane searchingly, knowing by the stubborn expression on her face that he would not be able to change her mind either by argument or cajolery. 'If you insist on this foolhardy course of action—'

'I do!'

'Then I will come with you.'

'No, you will not!' she refused with a vehement shake of her head. 'I am grateful for the help you have given me thus far, but whatever happens next I must deal with myself. Do you not understand, Hawk, that I do not want you to come anywhere with me?' she continued impatiently, as he would have once again protested. 'As you have mentioned on more than one occasion—' a slight, self-derisive smile curved her lips now '—you were forced into the role of my protector by my own impetuous actions. It is an obligation I now release you from.'

He gave a weary shake of his head. 'Have I not just explained that it is not as simple as that, Jane?'

'I assure you, Your Grace, our conversation has made several things clear to me,' she said enigmatically.

Hawk grimaced his impatience at her stubborn refusal to listen to him. 'Perhaps you are right, Jane, and we should talk of this again later. When you have had more time to think the matter through?'

'Perhaps,' she responded unhelpfully, giving a slight inclination of her head before turning to leave.

Hawk's expression was one of brooding frustration as he watched her cross the study to the door, her movements elegantly graceful, her head angled proudly.

But how long would Jane maintain that elegance and grace, let alone her pride, if Lady Sulby had her way and Jane was imprisoned for theft…?

Chapter Thirteen

'Jane...?'

Jane did her best to ignore the curricle—and its driver—as it drew alongside her, and walked determinedly along the lane that would take her to the road to London.

'Is it you beneath that bonnet, Jane?' The query was repeated impatiently.

She turned her face to the curricle, her smile rueful as she looked into the frowningly handsome face of Justin Long, Earl of Whitney, where he sat atop his curricle in complete control of a pair of lively-looking greys. 'It is indeed I, sir,' she confirmed dryly as she continued to walk.

'What the deuce are you doing wandering around the countryside unchaperoned?' he demanded disapprovingly.

Jane raised mocking brows. 'Our conversation yesterday evening led me to believe that you are the last person to be concerned with the proprieties, sir.'

He looked irritated by the jibe. 'Some of those proprieties are unavoidable, Jane. The unsuitability of a single young lady roaming the countryside unchaperoned is one of them,' he added with a frown. 'You—Jane, will you stop marching along in that military style and tell me what the devil you think you are doing?'

'Partaking of the air?' she returned tauntingly as she continued to 'march'.

Blond brows met over censorious blue eyes. 'I do not believe my question was an invitation to facetiousness, Jane.'

No, Jane was sure that it was not. It was only that if she didn't answer him in this offhand manner she knew that she would in all probability burst into the tears that had been threatening since she had packed her small bag and departed from Mulberry Hall an hour ago.

And she didn't want to cry—was sure that once she started she would not be able to stop.

'Jane, have I not instructed you to cease this infernal marching?' the Earl reminded her sternly.

Jane came to an abrupt halt in the lane and turned to glare up at him, an angry flush to her cheeks. 'I no more take orders from you, sir, than I do the Duke of Stourbridge!'

'Ah.'

Jane bristled at his knowing expression. 'And exactly what is meant by *that*, My Lord?' she demanded resentfully.

His expression was mockingly derisive. 'Argued with the young Duke, have you?'

'And what business is it of yours if I have?' Jane eyed him challengingly.

The Earl gave a rueful smile. 'Only that I would dearly have liked to witness that unusual occurrence!'

'Because you are still annoyed at his conquest of your Countess?'

The Earl gave an appreciative shout of laughter. 'Please tell me that you and the Duke did not argue over dear Margaret?'

'We did not,' Jane snapped, deeply irritated by his amusement at their expense. 'Now, if you will excuse me, My Lord, I must be on my way—What are you doing?' She frowned as he secured his reins before leaping agilely down from the curricle to stand at her side, looking as rakishly handsome as ever, in a tailored blue jacket that matched the colour of his eyes, breeches so tight in fit it was obvious that he owed none of his physique to padding, and a pair of highly polished Hessians.

'My dear Jane,' the Earl drawled, 'you do not seriously think that even the Earl of Whitney, having been made aware of your lonely state here on a public byway, would simply continue his journey back to London as if nothing untoward had happened?'

That was exactly what Jane had been hoping. Although the Earl's mention of his destination changed her thoughts somewhat...

She forced a smile. 'If you really wish to be of help to me, sir, then you will offer me a seat in your curricle to London.'

The frown returned to his brow as he eyed her speculatively. 'And what happens then, Jane? Does your guardian challenge me to another duel? Or will you settle for those damned matriarchs of Society demanding that as I have compromised you I must now marry you?'

Jane gasped. 'I wish for neither of those things, My Lord! I care nothing for the demands of the matriarchs of Society. The Duke and I have—parted ways. It is my belief that he is no longer concerned with what becomes of me.'

No doubt Hawk, once he got over his anger at Jane for having disobeyed him once again, would actually be relieved at having her disruptive presence removed from his household. Especially as she was now accused of being a thief!

'Then, my dear Jane, it is *my* belief that you do not know the Duke of Stourbridge as well as he might wish.' The Earl eyed her pityingly. 'The man is enthralled by you, you little goose!' he added impatiently at Jane's blank expression.

She could not deny that the Duke found her physically appealing—that would be impossible after the events of yesterday evening!—but he most certainly was not 'enthralled' by her. If Hawk had felt any affection for her at all then surely he would have believed her earlier this morning, when she had assured him of her innocence concerning the disappearance of Lady Sulby's jewels?

'I assure you that you are mistaken, My Lord,' she said flatly.

He smiled. 'And I assure *you* that I am not,' he drawled, staring at her wordlessly for several long minutes before giving an impatient inclination of his head. 'Very well, Jane,' he murmured slowly. 'For you I will break the rule of a lifetime and allow a woman up into my curricle with me.'

Her face lit up with pleasure. 'Oh, thank you, My Lord! You will not regret your decision, I promise you,' she vowed, as she plucked up her skirts in order that he might help her climb into the elegance of his open carriage.

'Believe me, Jane, I already do!' the Earl muttered, his expression grim as he moved to climb in beside her and take up the reins once more.

Jane smiled happily as the greys moved forward, completely unconcerned by the Earl's sarcasm now that he had agreed to take her to London with him. Although she did seem to be making rather a habit of accepting lifts in the

carriages of unmarried gentlemen, she acknowledged ruefully. Rakishly handsome unmarried gentlemen.

'I may rethink my decision if you do not cease looking
so smugly self-satisfied, Jane!' the Earl warned her with
a scowl.

Jane at once lowered her head to look at him demurely
from beneath her bonnet.

The Earl raised scathing brows. 'If anything, that is
worse!'

She gave a relaxed laugh. 'You are very difficult to
please, My Lord.'

'Am I...?' He easily maintained control of the greys as
he continued to look at her frowningly.

'Yes...' Jane found herself disconcerted by that look.
None of the consummate flirt of the evening before was
now evident in the seriousness of the Earl's expression. Her
smile faded. 'Why do you look at me so intently, My Lord?'

He turned sharply away. 'It is of no matter, Jane.'

Jane continued to look at him for several long seconds.
'It is my belief, sir, that you are not quite as others see
you...' she finally murmured slowly.

His gaze was puzzled as he glanced at her. 'What can
you mean, Jane?'

She shook her head. 'You would have people believe
there is no more to the Earl of Whitney that the flirtatious
rogue.'

His mouth twisted. 'But Jane Smith does not believe
that to be so?'

'I know it is not so, My Lord.' She nodded. 'There is a
kindness in you—the same kindness as coming to my rescue just now—that you do not like others to see.'

His mouth twisted into a grimace. 'You are far too astute for a young lady of such tender years, Jane Smith.'

'So I have already been informed, My Lord.'

'By Stourbridge, no doubt.' He nodded knowingly. 'Poor devil.' He gave a rueful shake of his head. 'You seem to have succeeded in shaking him from his pedestal of untarnished superiority.'

She shook her head. 'Not so untarnished, My Lord, considering that the two of you appear to have recently shared a mistress!'

The Earl gave a shout of appreciative laughter. 'Far too forthright, Jane!'

She shrugged. 'I am merely stating the facts. It is you and the Duke who must take credit for the contents of that truth.'

The Earl's attention was drawn to the greys for several minutes. 'I believe, Jane,' he said grimly, once he had the lively greys under control, 'that we will save the rest of this conversation until I can give it—and you—my full attention.'

As far as Jane was concerned they could continue the rest of their journey in silence. Her only interest was in reaching London and from there continuing on to Norfolk. Talking of Hawk only caused her pain. Discussing his most recent mistress with the man who had been the Countess's previous lover only reminded Jane of her own immodest behaviour with Hawk the previous evening.

From there it was only a short distance to remembering their conversation earlier this morning.

And the disturbing conclusion she had made during that conversation.

Could it truly be that Sir Barnaby was her real father?

All the evidence—the previously unknown Sir Barnaby being appointed her guardian, Lady Sulby's hatred of her and her mother—pointed to that being the case.

In those circumstances it had perhaps been unwise of her adopted father to have made Sir Barnaby her guardian, but the fact that there had been no one else he could leave Jane's future care to had probably meant he had had no choice in the matter.

No, any mistake must lie at Sir Barnaby's door, by his even attempting to introduce his illegitimate daughter into his own household, let alone expecting her to be accepted by his wife and legitimate child...

'This is not the way to London, My Lord!' Jane realised frowningly as they passed a sign at the side of the road that indicated London was in the opposite direction from the one in which they were now travelling.

The Earl gave an abrupt inclination of his head. 'It really is most unsuitable for you, a woman alone, to go to London with me, Jane.'

She glared at him fiercely. 'It is for me to decide where I will go and who I will go with, My Lord!'

'No, Jane, it is not.' He gave a firm shake of his head.

'Where are you taking me?' Jane demanded. But she already knew the answer to that question. The countryside about the Stourbridge estate was familiar to her...

'I am sure that you believe your reasons for leaving Mulberry Hall to be valid ones—'

'They most certainly are!'

'Perhaps,' the Earl allowed grimly. 'But I somehow doubt Stourbridge would agree with you.'

'I believed you to be a man who was not frightened of the high-and-mighty Duke of Stourbridge!' Jane scorned.

'I am not, Jane,' the Earl assured her softly. 'It is you that frightens me,' he added enigmatically.

'Me?' she echoed impatiently, her desperation rising as she saw the mellow outline of Mulberry Hall in the distance.

'You.' He nodded frowningly, his mouth twisting derisively. 'Did you not fear what might happen to you once you found yourself alone and unprotected in London?'

'No, of course not.'

'That is precisely the reason you frighten me, Jane,' he said grimly. 'You are too innocent, Jane.'

'I am not such an innocent, My Lord,' she assured him dully, fully aware that yesterday evening she had all but given that innocence to Hawk St Claire, Duke of Stourbridge.

The Earl pulled his greys to a halt before turning to study Jane, and her cheeks coloured under the intensity of that experienced gaze.

'Stourbridge made love to you last night?' he finally rasped harshly.

Jane gasped. 'That is none of your concern, sir—'

'I am making it so, Jane!'

She was tired, so very tired, of the Duke of Stourbridge and now the Earl of Whitney taking such an interest in the innocence that was surely hers to give where she pleased.

'I will find some other way in which to travel to London,' she dismissed impatiently, and she turned to climb from the carriage.

The Earl moved swiftly, already on the ground at her side as she stepped down from the curricle. Steely fingers grasped her arm. 'You are not going anywhere until I have got to the bottom of this situation.'

'Can you not see that I do not require your help, My Lord?' Jane demanded impatiently, glaring up at him as he refused to release her.

His mouth twisted derisively. 'I do not believe that I asked for your permission to help you.'

Jane's brows rose disgustedly. 'Heaven preserve me from interfering, over-protective men such as you!'

He gave a humourless smile. 'And Stourbridge?'

'I neither wish to speak of nor see the Duke of Stourbridge ever again!'

The Earl shrugged. 'That is rather unfortunate.'

Jane eyed him suspiciously. 'Why?'

The Earl's gaze moved over and past her flushed face to a distance over her left shoulder. 'Because, unless I am very much mistaken, we are about to be joined by the man himself,' he drawled pointedly.

Jane turned sharply on her heel to look at a horse and rider some distance away, the colour draining from her cheeks as she recognised—as, obviously, had the Earl of Whitney!—that rider to be none other than Hawk, Duke of Stourbridge.

She found herself too surprised to move as horse and rider drew steadily nearer. In fact, as they drew near enough for her to see the grim savagery of Hawk's expression, Jane actually found herself moving a step closer to the Earl of Whitney.

'Now the fun begins,' the Earl murmured dryly, as Hawk drew the prancing black horse to a halt only feet away, before jumping lithely to the ground and striding purposefully towards them.

Fun? Jane was sure that she had never felt less like having 'fun' in her life!

* * *

Hawk had never experienced such rage. It filled him. Consumed him. Until he could see nothing but Jane, as she stood looking at him so defiantly next to the Earl of Whitney. A man Hawk was rapidly coming to view as his enemy.

When Hawk had realised Jane had once again fled—after being assured by Arabella that Jane was nowhere to be found, either in the house or about the estate, that in fact she feared Jane had left without a word to either of them—he had hurried to Jane's room to confirm her disappearance for himself.

As Arabella had claimed, the bedroom was empty except for the new cream lace gown and gloves she had worn the previous evening, which he had taken such delight in removing.

And, tauntingly, on the dressing table, lay his mother's pearl necklace and earbobs...

To then seek her, and find her in the company—pre-arranged?—of a man such as Whitney was intolerable.

'So,' he bit out between gritted teeth as he came to a halt only inches from the pair. His hands clenched at his sides as the fierceness of his gaze moved from the paleness of Jane's face to the mockingly challenging face of the Earl of Whitney.

'Indeed,' Whitney drawled derisively. 'As you can see, Stourbridge, despite protests to the contrary by the lady concerned, I have safely returned your little bird to the nest.'

A nerve pulsed in Hawk's rigidly clenched jaw. 'Before or after you have seduced her?'

'Oh, the former, of course,' the older man taunted. 'The latter, it seems, I may leave to you,' he added hardly.

Hawk's narrowed gaze met the censoriousness of that hard blue look. 'You will explain that remark!'

Whitney shrugged broad shoulders. 'Do I really need to do so?'

No, he did not. Hawk was only curious as to what could have prompted Jane to confide the events of yesterday evening to a man like Whitney.

Which in no way excused his own behaviour, Hawk acknowledged in self-disgust. He had taken advantage of a young woman he had promised to protect. A young woman who had subsequently needed to seek protection from *him*.

But could Jane not see that Whitney was the last man—the very last man—she should have run to for that protection?

'Do stop the self-flagellation, Stourbridge,' Whitney dismissed dryly. 'Just accept for once in your ordered life that you have behaved like any other man when presented with such a tasty morsel as Jane.'

Hawk's eyes glittered coldly. 'You will not talk of Jane in such a familiar manner.'

'Will I not?' the other man challenged. 'May I point out, Stourbridge, that it was Jane's intention to leave for London with me rather than remain here with you...?'

Hawk was well aware of the choice Jane had made. That she had preferred the uncertainty of Whitney's intentions towards her rather than remain at Mulberry Hall with him. That choice only made his own role in this situation more unbearable.

Jane had been momentarily stunned by Hawk's sudden appearance following so quickly her realisation that the Earl of Whitney had not been taking her to London with him at all but instead returning her to Mulberry Hall.

But, as always seemed to happen when these two men met, the conversation had taken a ludicrous turn. 'I was not leaving *with* you, My Lord, only accepting a ride in your curricle,' she reminded the Earl snappily. 'As for you, Your Grace.' She turned to glare at Hawk. 'I believe the events of this morning have nullified any promises I might previously have made concerning the need to inform you of my movements.'

'This morning as well as yesterday evening?' the Earl scowled. 'You have been busy, Stourbridge!'

'You—'

'Gentlemen, please!' Jane's voice rose sharply as she saw the conversation once again rapidly deteriorating into insults.

'Anything for you, dear Jane,' the Earl drawled.

Jane looked at him censoriously. 'You will cease this deliberate provocation, My Lord!'

'I will? Oh, very well,' he conceded dryly, as Jane continued to glare at him fiercely.

Jane turned to the Duke. 'And *you* will cease behaving as if you actually care what becomes of me,' she told him scathingly.

Behaving as if he cared? Hawk frowned darkly. Damn it, he had made love with this woman last night—of course he cared what became of her!

The fact that the two of them had argued yet again this morning, resulting in Jane fleeing Mulberry Hall as well as himself, did not—could not—alter the intimacy that existed between them.

His mouth set grimly. 'I wish you to return to Mulberry Hall, Jane, so that we might discuss this like two reasonable adults.'

'You *wish* it?' she repeated scornfully, shaking her head. 'It is my own wishes that are important to me now, Your Grace. And I do not feel any desire to return to Mulberry Hall with you—either now or at any time in the future.'

'Dear, dear, Stourbridge—can your powers of persuasion, both last night and this morning, really have been so clumsily inelegant?' the Earl of Whitney murmured scathingly. 'I would have thought you a more accomplished lover than that.'

Hawk really was going to be forced into resorting to physical violence if the conversation continued in its current vein!

His patience—what little he possessed—was being stretched to the limit, both by Jane's stubborn refusal to accompany him back to Mulberry Hall and the unwanted presence of Whitney at their exchange.

'Perhaps Jane was right to leave you, after all, in order to seek out a more…experienced protector,' Whitney continued tauntingly.

'Will you cease this nonsense, sir? You know as well as I that our paths crossed this morning only by accident!' Jane instructed impatiently.

'But I assure you, dear Jane, I consider it a most fortuitous accident…' the Earl drawled with a narrow-eyed look at the younger man. 'It is my belief that someone needs to make Stourbridge answerable for his behaviour!'

'You will explain that remark, sir!'

Jane felt her face pale and turned slowly to look up at Hawk, a shiver of apprehension slithering down the length of her spine when she saw the coldness of his expression as he looked at the other man with eyes of icy gold.

In that moment he was neither the haughty Duke of

Stourbridge nor her lover Hawk St Claire. He was instead a man who looked capable of cold-blooded murder...

The Earl of Whitney looked just as implacable. 'I am sure we are both aware of how inappropriate your behaviour has been regarding Jane—'

Jane didn't quite see what happened next. Hawk had moved so quickly, so assuredly, that before she knew it, it seemed, the Earl of Whitney lay prostrate on his back in the lane, his rapidly reddening jaw indicating exactly where Hawk had struck him.

Chapter Fourteen

'What have you done, Hawk?' Jane murmured faintly, before moving down on her knees beside the prostrate Earl. 'Are you hurt, sir?' She touched his arm. 'Can I—?'

'I have knocked him to the ground, as he deserves!' the Duke rasped, and he reached out to grasp her arm with steely fingers.

'Unhand me!' She turned to glare at him even as she tried to shake off his hold on her arm. A useless exercise, as it happened, because his fingers refused to be dislodged. 'How dare you?' Jane rose sharply to her feet. 'How dare you treat me so abominably this morning and then proceed to attack the defenceless man who has been kind enough to assist me in escaping such injustice?'

Hawk believed he had never met a less kind or defenceless man than Whitney. As he knew only too well, besides having the tongue of a viper, the man went several rounds thrice a week with 'Gentleman' John Jackson—and won as many times as he lost!

But the bright wings of angry colour in Jane's cheeks, the accusation in her gleaming green eyes, told Hawk that he had committed a tactical error in giving Whitney the beating he deserved—that by doing so he had only helped to convince Jane he was an unprincipled savage.

Whitney added to that impression as he gave a pained groan. 'I believe you may have broken my jaw, Stourbridge!'

Hawk transferred the coldness of his gaze to the other man. 'If I had broken your jaw you would not be able to talk—which would be a blessing for us all!'

'Cold, sir, when you have rendered me almost senseless.' Whitney gave another pained groan. 'Is he not cold and unfeeling, Jane?' he murmured weakly, as she moved to kneel beside him once more and carefully placed his head upon her lap.

'Very cold and unfeeling, sir,' Jane confirmed tautly, and turned to give Hawk another brief, censorious glare.

So totally missing the conspiratorial wink that Whitney gave Hawk over her left shoulder!

The man was feigning, damn it! Simply acting more hurt than he was in order to gain Jane's sympathy! And he was succeeding!

'I think perhaps you will have to remove me to Mulberry Hall and send for the doctor, Stourbridge,' the Earl murmured from his comfortable position cradled on Jane's lap, and only the glint of a mocking eye was visible as Jane ran a soothing hand across his brow.

It was a move guaranteed to once again fill Hawk with an unaccountable fury of emotions—the strongest one being a wish to knock Whitney to the ground for a second time!

'Perhaps you might help me into my curricle, Stour-bridge...?' the other man goaded.

'Yes—do help him, Hawk,' a distracted Jane encouraged worriedly. 'We must put a cold compress on that jaw as quickly as possible. Hawk?' she prompted impatiently.

Hawk conceded that there were the beginnings of redness appearing on Whitney's jaw, but he certainly did not feel it merited the other man leaning quite so heavily on his shoulder as Hawk helped him to his feet and over to his curricle.

'A bad tactical error on your part, Stourbridge,' Whitney murmured, so softly that Jane, having moved to climb into the other side of the curricle so that she might help from there, couldn't hear him. 'Did no one ever tell you that where a woman is concerned it is usually the case that to the loser go the spoils of war?'

Hawk's mouth tightened at the deliberate taunt. 'Jane is not a prize to be won!'

'Perhaps that has been your mistake...' The other man arched a derisive brow. 'You—'

'Did I not tell you Jane is a woman to be "priced above pearls"...?' the Earl reminded him softly.

Hawk had no opportunity to reply as the other man assumed a pained expression as he stepped into the curricle, and allowed himself to once again be given into Jane's solicitous care.

'You will have to secure your horse here, Hawk, and take charge of the curricle,' Jane instructed sharply, as she made the Earl's head comfortable upon her shoulder.

Returning to Mulberry Hall had not been her plan, Jane acknowledged frustratedly, but in the circumstances she really had little choice.

What had possessed Hawk to attack the Earl in that way? Admittedly the Earl had been being his usual provocative self, but that really was no excuse for Hawk to resort to using fisticuffs. The Earl would be perfectly justified, after this, in issuing Hawk with yet another challenge to a duel.

At which time Jane would probably get her previous wish that the two men might kill each other!

'What on earth—?' A stunned Arabella came to an abrupt halt halfway down the stairs as the three entered the house—the Earl of Whitney being supported by Jane on one side and the Duke on the other. 'Has the Earl met with an accident...?' Arabella's face was pale with concern as she hurried down the long staircase.

'Only your eldest brother's fist, Lady Arabella,' the Earl roused himself to reply dryly, his arm draped about Jane's shoulder as he leaned heavily against her.

Arabella looked suitably shocked by this disclosure. 'Hawk...?'

'Do not fret yourself, Lady Arabella. I can assure you that dear Jane has already more than soothed my fevered brow,' the Earl said softly. 'Although a medicinal brandy would probably help speed my recovery,' he added wryly.

'Jane...?' Arabella looked bewildered now.

'Do not concern yourself, Arabella. I am sure that the Earl's injury is not serious.'

It was a conviction Jane had become more and more convinced of during their short journey in the curricle to Mulberry Hall. The Earl's jaw seemed in no danger of swelling, and only a slight discolouration to the skin had appeared, rather than the bruising she had feared.

In fact, Jane was not completely convinced that the

whole thing had not been an exaggeration on the Earl's part in order that he might return her, without further argument on her part, to Mulberry Hall!

'Cruel, Jane,' he murmured now in dramatic rebuke. 'Too, too cruel!'

Jane gave Hawk a glance from beneath lowered lashes, knowing by the cold disgust in his expression as he stepped away from the other man that he was no more convinced by the Earl's incapacity than she now was.

She extricated herself from beneath the Earl's arm, having her suspicions confirmed when he remained perfectly steady on his feet without their support. 'I believe it is time—' past time! '—that I continued on my way,' she said.

'On your way where, Jane?' Arabella still looked totally bewildered by this sequence of events, although her eyes widened as she took in Jane's appearance in travelling cloak and bonnet. 'You really are leaving us?'

'I—'

'No, Jane is not going anywhere.' Hawk was the one to answer grimly.

Jane looked up at him, but the cold implacability of his expression told her none of his inner thoughts. 'Is it now your intention to hand me over to the appropriate authorities?'

'Authorities?' The Earl was the one to echo her sharply, making a very speedy recovery indeed as he straightened to his full height without assistance from anyone. 'What nonsense is this, Stourbridge?' He turned frowningly to the Duke.

Jane and Hawk's gazes were locked in a silent battle of wills as she answered the Earl. 'I believe it is the intention of His Grace, the Duke of Stourbridge, to have me arrested as a jewel thief. Is that not so, Your Grace?' she added challengingly.

'Arrested...? Jewel...?' Arabella repeated sharply. 'Hawk, what have you done?' She looked at her brother accusingly.

Why was it, Hawk wondered impatiently, that everyone, including Jane herself, believed he was capable of all manner of misdeeds—including cold-bloodedly giving Jane up to the caprices of English law?

'Surely you are mistaken, Jane?' Arabella frowned. 'I saw my mother's pearls and earbobs upon the dressing table in your room myself only an hour ago—'

'It is not those jewels I am accused of stealing,' Jane assured her wearily. 'But those of my guardian in Norfolk.'

'Guardian in Norfolk...?' Whitney looked stunned. 'I thought that you had claimed Jane as your own ward, Stourbridge?'

Hawk's mouth tightened. 'I have that dubious honour, yes.'

'I believe I relieved you of that temporary responsibility during the unpleasantness of our conversation earlier this morning!' Jane cut in firmly.

Hawk was breathing hard as he looked at her from between narrowed lids. 'And it is my belief that you deliberately chose to misunderstand me this morning, Jane.'

'Did I misunderstand when you accused me of stealing Lady Sulby's jewels? Did I misunderstand when you suggested I hand those jewels over to you, so that you might return them in an effort to persuade Sir Barnaby to drop the charges against me? Tell me, Your Grace, did I misunderstand any of that?' Her eyes glittered with challenge and unshed tears.

'Yes, damn it—' Hawk broke off his angry exclamation as Jenkins came into the hallway from the servants' quarters. 'I believe we should retire to the privacy of the drawing room if we are to continue with this conversation, Jane,' he bit out tautly.

'But we are not going to continue with it, Your Grace,' she assured him determinedly. 'You have insulted me enough—'

'You are recently come from Norfolk, Jane?' the Earl of Whitney cut in harshly.

Jane frowned at the interruption. 'I have, sir.'

Whitney shook his head frowningly. 'But when you spoke to my nephew at dinner yesterday evening I distinctly heard you talk of Somerset as having been your home...'

'My childhood home—yes, My Lord. But I have not lived there for some years now. Not since my father died twelve years ago and I was sent to live with—with acquaintances of my mother's.' Jane's face was extremely pale beneath the green of her bonnet.

'And would the name of these acquaintances be Sir Barnaby and Lady Gwendoline Sulby, Jane?' the Earl pressed forcefully.

Hawk gave the Earl a sharply questioning look. Did the other man know the Sulbys? From the look of almost distaste on Whitney's face as he spoke of them Hawk believed that he must.

Although he couldn't say he particularly cared for the intentness with which Whitney was now staring at Jane...

'Jenkins, bring a tray of tea things through to the drawing room, would you?' he instructed the hovering butler.

'Tea!' the Earl echoed disgustedly.

'Tea,' Hawk repeated firmly. 'For four,' he added dryly as he saw it was both the Earl's and Arabella's intent to accompany them.

Arabella moved to walk beside the obviously reluctant Jane, leaving Hawk to fall into step beside Whitney.

'What do you know of the Sulbys, Whitney?' Hawk prompted evenly.

Whitney seemed not to hear him for a moment, his gaze fixed intently on the rigid tension of Jane's back as she walked ahead of them. 'Who is she, Stourbridge?' he finally managed to grind out harshly, every last trace of the flirtatious rake gone from his face and manner.

Hawk gave a shrug of his shoulders. 'I know no more about her antecedents than you.'

Blue eyes glittered fiercely as the other man turned to look at him. 'But it's true she is the ward of Sir Barnaby Sulby?'

'She is.' Hawk gave a terse inclination of his head.

'Good God...!' Whitney groaned hollowly.

Hawk looked at the other man searchingly, wondering why this information should so disturb him. To his certain knowledge, nothing and no one had been allowed to disturb the capricious Justin Long, Earl of Whitney during the last twenty years. Hawk had sensed that even Whitney's enmity towards him over the conquest of the Countess of Morefield had been more of an affectation than any genuine feelings of ill-will.

'I take it from your response that you *do* know the Sulbys?'

'I am acquainted well enough with Lady Sulby at least to know I would not even *consider* allowing her the care of one of my hounds, let alone a young lady of Jane's tender years!' the other man confirmed harshly.

Hawk's mouth thinned as he recalled that Jane herself had once made a similar comment to him concerning her guardians.

Jane...

Hawk could still remember his feeling of impotence earlier when he had discovered Jane gone, and grudgingly acknowledged that, if not for the timely intervention of the Earl of Whitney, he might have been too late to find her, allowing her to reach London and just disappear amongst the crowd of people there.

'I offer you my thanks for—for Jane's safe return to Mulberry Hall,' he bit out hardly.

The other man eyed him derisively. 'How much did that hurt?'

Hawk's brows rose. 'No doubt much more than the blow I delivered to your jaw!'

Whitney grimaced. 'No doubt,' he acknowledged dryly.

Jane had no idea what the two men were discussing so intently as they walked behind her and Arabella down the hallway to the drawing room. Her own attention was focused on Arabella, as the other woman questioned her concerning the accusations levelled by Jane's real guardians.

'But it is surely just a coincidence, Jane?' Arabella frowned. 'I have come to know you these last few days, and I do not believe for one moment that you could have taken Lady Sulby's jewellery.'

Arabella's absolute faith in Jane's innocence only highlighted Hawk's total disbelief in that innocence!

She chose to position herself as far away from him as possible once they had entered the drawing room, standing beside the fireplace while Hawk moved to stand before a window, his face in shadow as the sun shone in at his back.

Not that Jane needed to see his expression to read his mood. The stiffness of his stance—shoulders rigidly back, spine ramrod-straight, chin angled arrogantly—was enough to inform her that this interview was going to be no more pleasant than the one that had taken place in the library earlier that morning.

No one seemed inclined to speak at all until after Jenkins had delivered the tea tray, and Jane took advantage of this lull in the conversation to remove her cloak and bonnet, and shake her curls loose after their confinement.

'What is your connection to the Sulbys, Jane?'

Her eyes widened on the Earl of Whitney as the harshness of his tone disturbed the silence. 'I believe I have already stated, sir, that they were acquaintances of my mother.'

'Your mother who died in childbirth?'

Jane gave a humourless smile. 'I had only one mother, sir.' Two fathers, she might have added, but didn't. The Duke already had a bad enough opinion of her without regaling him with the tale of her illegitimacy. She turned to him as he stood so still and silent in front of the window. 'If, as you claim, sir, it is not your immediate intention to have me arrested—'

'It is not!' the Duke rasped harshly.

Jane gave an acknowledging inclination of her head. 'Then what are your immediate plans for me, Your Grace?'

That was a very pertinent question. And one that Hawk did not have an answer to. What he wanted to do—sweep Jane up in his arms and carry her to his bedchamber, and once there make love to her until they were both weak and in need of sustenance other than each other—was obviously out of the question in the presence of Whitney and Arabella.

But that did not mean he couldn't at least try to correct Jane's impression that he intended consigning her to a prison cell at the first opportunity!

'I would like the two of us to talk, Jane,' he said stiffly.

'Talk?' She raised surprised brows. 'About what, Your Grace?'

Hawk drew in a ragged breath. 'Let us start, Jane, with the coldness with which you continue to address me!'

It was apparent from the way Jane's cheeks coloured so prettily that she was well aware of the reason he disclaimed the need for such formality between them.

She shrugged. 'I feel it is for the best, Your Grace.'

'Whose best?'

'Yours as well as my own!' Her eyes glittered warningly.

If only Whitney and Arabella were not present Hawk would have wasted no time in demonstrating just how much he disagreed with that claim. Yesterday evening he and Jane had shared a degree of intimacy usually reserved for the marriage bed, and as such her coldness towards him this morning was intolerable.

'Such formality between the two of us is unpalatable to me, Jane,' he assured her hardly.

'Then perhaps it is only I who feels that need, Your Grace!' Jane shot him another quelling glance.

'What is happening, Hawk...?' Arabella prompted uncertainly.

He held Jane's rebellious gaze for several more meaningful seconds before turning to address his sister. 'I have not had an opportunity to discuss this matter with Jane yet, Arabella, and until I do I feel it would not be…wise on my part—' his mouth twisted ruefully '—to relay our news to others.'

'What news?' Jane echoed incredulously. 'That you believe me to be a thief and a liar—?' She broke off as Hawk quickly crossed the room, his expression one of savage fury as he grasped the tops of her arms and shook her. 'Hawk…!' she gasped when she managed to regain her breath. 'Hawk, you are hurting me!'

'As you are hurting me,' he ground out between gritted teeth. 'Damn it, Jane, I do not believe you to be a thief or a liar!'

'But—'

'I did not believe it this morning and I do not believe it now!'

'But—'

'My advice is to take him at his word, Jane,' the Earl of Whitney told her laconically.

'Oh, do be quiet!'

'Stay out of this, Whitney!'

Jane's eyes widened on the fierceness of Hawk's expression as they both answered the Earl at the same time, her gaze searching now as she looked into the dangerous glitter of those predatory gold eyes. 'I do not understand…' she finally murmured, with a puzzled shake of her head.

His mouth thinned in the arrogant austerity of his face. 'Perhaps it will help your understanding if I tell you it is my wish to make you my Duchess at the earliest opportunity?'

Jane felt the colour drain from her cheeks even as she stared up at him disbelievingly.

Chapter Fifteen

Hawk, the Duke of Stourbridge, wished to marry her?

And yet everything in his manner since their shared intimacy the evening before had pointed to him wishing the opposite—that he had never so much as set eyes upon her!

If that was so then what possible reason could the arrogant Duke of Stourbridge now have for making such an announcement—

The arrogant, but so impeccably honourable Duke of Stourbridge!

Could it be that despite her orphaned state, her lack of a place in Society, Hawk felt honour-bound—compelled, following their intimacy of the evening before, to make her an offer of marriage?

Jane's hope—that brief bubble of happiness that had risen so swiftly on hearing his announcement, on so fleetingly believing that Hawk might return the love she felt for him—burst painfully within her chest.

Her mouth twisted with regret. 'I cannot believe that you truly wish to take an accused thief as your wife.'

'You are not accused by me, Jane!' His face was stony.

'No?' She viewed him sadly. 'That was not my impression earlier today.'

'You misunderstood the content of my conversation earlier, Jane, and did not give me a chance to explain.'

'I will not allow you to propose the idea of a marriage between us, Your Grace.' She firmly extricated herself from the hands that no longer gripped her arms as tightly as they had. 'I could not—would not—marry you if you were the last man upon this earth!'

'Oh, cutting, Jane,' the Earl of Whitney murmured frowningly. 'Very cutting.'

Hawk ignored the other man. 'Why not, Jane?' A nerve pulsed in the tightness of his clenched jaw.

She eyed him stonily. 'Is it not enough that I have refused to even contemplate the very idea, Your Grace?'

It had never occurred to Hawk—he had not expected, never considered—that Jane might turn down his offer of marriage!

He had waited one and thirty years to make such an offer. Had evaded the avaricious clutches of young women and their marriage-minded mothers too numerous to recall. And now, when he finally felt compelled to make an offer, Jane had refused without hesitation.

Hawk had realised when he'd found Jane had fled Mulberry Hall without so much as a word of goodbye that he must find her and bring her back. Had known without a doubt, when he had found her again, that the thought of Jane leaving his life never to be seen again was unacceptable to him.

All for nought.

Because Jane did not feel the same reluctance at being parted from him.

He stepped back. 'I apologise if I have offended you by so much as mentioning the possibility of marriage between us,' he said stiffly. 'I assure you it was not my intention to cause you distress.'

Jane held her chin regally high. 'Your apology is accepted. Now, if there is nothing else you wish to say to me, I would like to be on my way.'

'Ah, but there is something else *I* would like to say to you, Jane.' It was the Earl of Whitney who addressed her this time.

Jane turned to look at him, her gaze mocking. 'Surely you are not about to make me an offer of marriage too, My Lord?'

'Hardly!' He looked horrified at the idea. 'I would, however, like to hear more about these guardians of yours...'

Jane stiffened warily. 'Why?'

He gave a shrug. 'I believe I may once have been acquainted with Lady Sulby. If her name was previously Gwendoline Simmons, that is,' he added.

Jane's wariness increased. 'I believe that was her name prior to her marriage to Sir Barnaby, yes,' she confirmed reluctantly.

She didn't want to talk of Lady Sulby or Sir Barnaby. She badly needed to leave this place—to get as far away from Hawk as she possibly could—before she broke down in front of him and begged him to love her as she loved him!

She gave a shake of her head. 'I do not believe such a conversation would serve any purpose, My Lord.' She turned away to pick up her cloak and bonnet. 'Now, if you will excuse me—'

'Jane, I have to know if—Was your mother's name Janette?'

Jane froze. Halted in mid-flight. Barely able to breathe. Her eyes deep green pools of pain as she turned slowly, oh-so-slowly, to face the Earl of Whitney. 'How is it that you know my mother's name, sir...?'

'Dear God...' the Earl groaned weakly, his face—that rakishly handsome face, that had been breaking female hearts for over thirty years—having gone deathly pale. 'You are Janette's daughter!' He reached out a hand to tightly grasp the back of a chair, his knuckles showing white. 'I thought—I was drawn to you yesterday evening because you had the look of her. The same red hair and sparkling green eyes.' He shook his head self-derisively. 'But you see, Jane, I have looked for her face in so many others over the years,' he acknowledged heavily. 'So many women. But none of them ever Janette...'

Hawk took a protective step towards Jane as she seemed to sway slightly, her eyes limpid green pools in a face now gone white with shock.

His expression darkened warningly as he looked at the other man. 'Can you not see that you are distressing her, Whitney?' he rasped frowningly.

The Earl had eyes only for Jane. 'Am I distressing you, Jane? *Am* I?' He reached out to grasp her hands tightly within his.

Jane looked up at him searchingly. 'How—when did you know my mother?'

'When, Jane?' the Earl repeated harshly. 'Would you like

the exact date and hour of when I last set eyes upon her? Or will you settle for just the month and year...?'

Jane moistened lips gone stiff with shock. 'Please, My Lord, just tell me what you know of my mother!'

'Hawk, I really think that Jane should sit down,' Arabella cut in concernedly. 'She is ill...'

'No, I am not ill, Arabella,' Jane turned to reassure her huskily. 'I am merely—Please, My Lord.' She turned back to the Earl. 'Tell me all that you know of my mother.'

Hawk felt his heart clench in his chest at the wistfulness he detected in Jane's voice as she pleaded for knowledge—any knowledge—of the mother who had died giving birth to her.

He did not even begin to understand why the conversation had become so intense. He only knew that, like Arabella, he feared for Jane's health if this interminable situation continued. 'Pour the tea, Arabella,' he advised abruptly. 'Hot and strong for Jane, with plenty of sugar.'

Jane shook her head. 'I have refused sugar ever since my father explained the cruelty associated with its origins.'

'Today you will take sugar, Jane,' Hawk assured her firmly. 'Today you are in need of it.' He sent Whitney a censorious glance.

The Earl blinked, as if awakening from a dream. 'Yes, you must take tea, Jane,' he encouraged huskily, as he led her over to one of the armchairs and sat her down upon it. 'Perhaps I will join you,' he added gently, and he sat in the chair opposite, his gaze intent upon her face, her hands still held tightly within his own. 'You really are so very like her, you know,' he murmured softly.

Hawk continued to look at Jane concernedly as she released her hands from Whitney's in order to drink the tea

Arabella had carried over to her. Some of the colour returned to her cheeks as she sipped the hot, sugary brew. And all the time Jane's gaze remained riveted upon the Earl's face. As if she dared not let him out of her sight. As if she feared that if she did so he might simply disappear.

That hungry need in Jane's face as she looked at the other man caused Hawk's heart to clench inside his chest like a fist.

Could it be—had Jane fallen in love with the Earl of Whitney? Could that be the reason she would not even countenance the idea of a marriage proposal from Hawk?

Jane placed her empty cup carefully upon the tea tray. 'Please tell me all that you know of my mother, My Lord,' she encouraged the Earl huskily.

'Where to start?' The Earl grimaced, his own tea ignored as it sat upon the table beside him. His gaze remained on Jane in unhidden fascination. 'I cannot believe—it is incredible, after all this time, to meet Janette's daughter. I— Forgive me, Jane. I digress.' He gave a dazed shake of his head. 'Tell me what you already know of her...'

Jane gave a rueful smile. 'From my father, I know that she was good and kind and beautiful.'

'She was, Jane.' The Earl nodded. 'Oh, yes, she was all of those things!'

Jane grimaced. 'From Lady Sulby I know that my mother was none of those things. That she was wild and sinful. That her wanton behaviour brought disgrace upon her family and friends—'

'The witch!' The Earl stood up impatiently, a dark frown upon his brow. 'You did not believe her, Jane?' He scowled his impatience.

Jane shrugged. 'I tried not to, sir—'

'But you *must* not, Jane!' The Earl protested vehemently, his hands clenched into fists at his sides. 'Gwendoline Simmons—Lady Sulby—' he grimaced with distaste '—is a spiteful, vindictive woman. She was jealous of Janette's beauty always. Of the warmth that so easily drew people to her. Of the fact that from the day I met Janette I loved her more than life itself...' he added, in voice gone husky with pain.

Jane stared up at him. Justin Long, Earl of Whitney, had once been in love with Janette...?

Hawk stared at the Earl too. Whitney was twenty years older than himself—had already been established as a rake beyond compare when Hawk had entered Society fourteen years ago. The other man's behaviour had never quite gone beyond the pale, but had certainly flirted along the edges of it. His Countess was reputed to have died of a broken heart rather than of the influenza that was claimed to have taken her life and that of her young son.

If Jane's mother had died at her birth, twenty-two years ago, then surely Whitney had to have been already a married man when he claimed to have loved Janette...?

Hawk looked searchingly at Jane, wondering what she was making of the Earl's conversation. She didn't look as surprised as he might have expected. In fact she looked almost calm at Whitney's claim to having been in love with her mother...

'Perhaps, Hawk,' Arabella put in quietly, 'it might be better if you and I were to absent ourselves from what appears to be a very personal conversation?'

Hawk scowled across at his sister for her suggestion. Jane might have turned down his marriage proposal out of hand, but that did not lessen the protectiveness he felt towards her.

'There is no need for that, Arabella,' Jane assured her warmly. 'In fact, I believe it might be informative for you both if you were to remain,' she added, with a brief glance in Hawk's direction.

A glance that contained—what? Hawk could not be sure. Apprehension, certainly. But what else…?

Whitney seemed to gather his thoughts together with an effort. 'First, Jane, I have to tell you of Gwendoline Simmons—of her obsession. With me.' He grimaced as Jane looked puzzled. 'I was twenty-four when she came to London for her first Season. I was rather full of myself, I am afraid. Engaging in discreet affairs with married ladies while flirting outrageously with all the new debutantes of the Season.' He gave a disgusted shake of his head. 'I was full of conceit, Jane.'

'You were single and eligible and only twenty-four years old, My Lord,' she excused him softly.

'That is no excuse, Jane,' he assured her hardly. 'Gwendoline Simmons took my interest to heart, you see, and fancied herself in the role of my future Countess.' He sighed. 'Of course my intentions towards her were not serious. I was merely playing with her. Honing my seduction skills. But Gwendoline's pursuit of me became—intense. Whenever I turned around, it seemed she was there—at my elbow, simpering and flirting and generally making a nuisance of herself. In the end I had to be cruel to be kind.' He frowned darkly. 'She did not take my rejection well.'

'I can imagine.' With the personal knowledge Jane had of Lady Sulby's greedy and manipulative nature, she could imagine the scenario the Earl described only too well!

The Earl's mouth tightened. 'I am sure that you can, Jane.' He grimaced. 'Unfortunately my father deplored my rakish behaviour, and demanded that I find myself a wife and settle down. That I became a more worthy heir to the Earldom.'

'And did you?' Jane prompted huskily.

'I did.' He nodded. 'I cast my eye uninterestedly over the rest of the debutants that Season and chose the one I believed would cause me the least inconvenience. Not a pretty tale, is it, Jane?' he prompted self-disgustedly.

'Not one you can be proud of—no, My Lord.'

He gave a brief, humourless laugh. 'Now I know you are truly Janette's daughter! She said exactly the same thing when I told her my reasons for having taken Beatrice as my wife,' he explained, at Jane's questioning look.

Jane nodded, already able to see where this tale was leading. Except she still wasn't completely sure of the Earl's role in Janette's life. In her own life, perhaps...

The Earl sighed. 'Gwendoline returned to Norfolk, and it was almost five years later when she made her appearance back in London Society as Lady Sulby, chaperon to her young sister-in-law.' He looked grim. 'I had been married for five years by this time, and had an infant son. I am not proud of what happened next, Jane.' He shook his head. 'But I—I took one look at Janette and knew myself well and truly lost! She was everything that was beautiful, Jane. With glorious red hair and emerald-green eyes. Her vivacity, her joy in life, was contagious. I was drawn to her in a way I had never experienced before. And, miraculously, she felt the same attraction. Oh, we tried for weeks to deny how we felt about each other, to fight our attraction, but it was impossible. Every time we met the attraction, the love, became more intense. We were like two halves of a whole suddenly come together, and to deny that connection was—We could not, Jane.' He groaned. 'The two of us became lovers—'

'Stop, My Lord!' Jane instructed breathlessly when finally she found her voice. 'Are you saying—?' She swallowed hard. 'Janette was *sister* to Sir Barnaby?'

'His young half-sister from his father's second marriage.' The Earl looked surprised by the question. 'But you must know that already, Jane? Did you not say that Sir Barnaby has been your guardian in the twelve years since your father died?'

She had said that—yes. And for all of those years she had believed—had been led to believe—that she was merely a distant poor relation of the Sulbys.

Someone who had been foisted upon them and whom they had taken into their household only because there was nowhere else for her to go, no one else who wanted her...

Sir Barnaby was her *uncle*? Truly her uncle? By blood? Had been Janette's older half-brother?

'Drink, Jane.'

She looked up dazedly at the Duke as he stood in front of her, holding out a glass of what looked to be brandy, knowing by the compassion she could read in his gaze that he too realised the deception that had been practiced upon her all these years. That he pitied her for that deception.

First obligation.

And now pity.

Neither emotion was what Jane wanted from him.

And she was sure, once Hawk had heard the whole story of her claim to existence, those would probably no longer exist either!

'Thank you.' She accepted the glass and took a restorative sip of what was indeed the finest brandy, her fingers remaining curved about the cut glass as if even its delicacy might give her the strength she needed to continue this conversation. 'I did not know of the connection, My Lord,' she informed the Earl dully.

'You did not know...?' The Earl frowned darkly. 'But how can this be? How can you not have known, Jane?'

Her smile contained no humour, only sadness. 'For the simple reason that no one ever thought to inform me.'

'That makes no sense, Jane.' The Earl looked angry now.

'It does if you are acquainted with Lady Sulby.' Jane sighed heavily. She was sure—had no doubts—that it was at that lady's instigation that the deception had been made. That Sir Barnaby, a meek and mild man who wanted only a quiet, untroubled life, had simply been too weak to fight against his much stronger-willed wife.

Was there nothing that Lady Sulby was not capable of?

Remembering the deceptions of the last twelve years, the accusations Lady Sulby had levelled at Janette that last morning, and the lies the other woman had told about Jane concerning the theft of her jewellery, Jane truly did not believe there was...

'Dear God!' the Earl grated harshly, as he finally seemed to realise what had been done to Jane.

'Indeed.' Jane inclined her head in acknowledgement.

The Earl was very pale now. 'Jane, was Janette happy with her parson?'

'I believe she was—content,' Jane replied carefully. 'Sir, you said earlier that you know the exact date and time of day that you last saw my mother...?'

'I do indeed, Jane,' he confirmed grimly.

'And it was…?'

He frowned. 'Jane…'

'For God's sake answer her, Whitney!' Hawk interjected harshly, the tension of this conversation becoming altogether too much to endure.

He could not pretend to understand all that was taking place here, knew only that he could not bear Jane's pain a moment longer. Although he would dearly have liked at that moment to have Lady Gwendoline Sulby in his clutches!

'I—But—' The other man shook his head as Hawk continued to look at him compellingly. 'Janette was but nineteen years of age, and the existence of my marriage had never sat well with her. I had told her that I would leave Beatrice, that the two of us would go abroad, live together there. But Janette would not hear of it. She insisted that I must stay with my wife and young son—that she must be the one to go. I last saw Janette on the day she informed me that we would not meet again, that she was to—to marry a parson, a young man she had known from childhood, and retire from Society.'

'Whitney!' Hawk grated forcefully, as Jane seemed to pale more with every word the other man spoke.

'I last saw Janette at ten o'clock in the morning of the tenth of November, 1793.' Whitney's voice broke emotionally. 'I tried to do as Janette wished me to do. I tried to make a life with my wife and young son. But I could not do it. I could not, Jane! I loved Janette—was only half alive without her. And so, out of desperation, I went to Norfolk to ask for news of her. Sir Barnaby was away from home, but Lady Sulby was there. She took great delight in telling me that I was too late—that Janette was already dead.

She had died after giving birth to her parson's child. You, Jane.' He looked at her hungrily.

Hawk was no longer looking at Whitney, but instead watched as incredible joy lit Jane's features, to be quickly followed by sudden tears that brightened her eyes as she stared at the Earl.

'She lied, My Lord,' Jane told him breathlessly.

Whitney looked bewildered. 'Janette was not dead...?'

'Oh, yes, she was dead. But Lady Sulby lied,' Jane repeated forcefully, and she slowly stood up, appearing strangely delicate, almost fragile, rather than the strong-willed young woman Hawk was used to seeing. 'I believe I have some things in my bag that belong to you—that will explain...' She smiled shakily at Whitney.

Whitney looked startled. 'That belong to me, Jane...?'

'Oh, yes, I believe so,' she confirmed breathlessly, at the same time seeming unable to take her eyes from him.

Hawk felt that clenching in his chest once again as he saw the love shining in Jane's mesmerising green eyes. Not for him. But for another man.

'Some letters, My Lord,' Jane continued softly.

'Letters, Jane? For me? From Janette?' Whitney suddenly prompted sharply.

Jane nodded. 'You will wait here while I fetch them, My Lord?'

'I—Yes, of course.'

Whitney looked no less confused than Hawk felt himself and he watched Jane as she hurried across the room. She halted, hesitated once she reached the door, her face still lit with that inner light as she turned back to face them all.

But once again it was to Whitney that she addressed her next remark. 'Janette did not leave you because she wanted to, My Lord. It is my belief that she left because she felt she had to do so.'

'Had to...?' the Earl repeated dazedly.

'Had to, My Lord.' Jane nodded. 'Perhaps it will help you to understand—to realise... I believe the contents of Janette's letters will be less of a—a shock to you, My Lord, if I tell you that Janette was three months with child when she married Joseph Smith. That it was not his child she brought into the world before she died. You see, My Lord, I was born on the second of May in the year seventeen hundred and ninety-four.'

With a swirl of her skirts Jane quickly departed the room.

Hawk watched transfixed as the Earl of Whitney—a confirmed rake, a man who made no secret of the self-ishness of the life he had led the last twenty years—col-lapsed white-faced into a chair, a look of shock upon his still-handsome face as he stared hungrily at the spot where only seconds ago Jane had stood.

'Hawk, can it be...?' Arabella had moved silently to Hawk's side. 'Is the Earl Jane's father, Hawk?'

Exactly the conclusion Hawk had just come to himself!

Chapter Sixteen

'Are you not relieved now, Your Grace, that I did not so much as entertain the idea of a marriage between the two of us?' Jane prompted teasingly a short time later, when the two of them found themselves alone in one of smaller drawing rooms at Mulberry Hall.

It was painful for Jane to realise how vicious and cruel Lady Sulby had been—both lately and in the past. But that pain was superceded by the knowledge that her father had not rejected her, or her mother. He simply hadn't known of her existence.

She had excused both the Duke and Arabella, as well as herself, from the Earl of Whitney's—her father's—presence in the drawing room, sure that he would prefer to be alone when he read such private letters as her mother's had been to her lover.

Unfortunately for Jane, once outside the library Arabella had further excused herself, on the pretext of needing to talk to Cook concerning the luncheon arrangements. Leaving Jane alone in the small room in the icily silent company of Hawk, Duke of Stourbridge. Hence the reason for the brightness of her chatter.

'Although it is perhaps as well that you had this opportunity to—to practise, Your Grace,' she continued dryly, when he remained coldly uncommunicative. 'It really was not well done, you know,' Jane added, and he at last raised one dark, arrogant brow in the otherwise austere handsomeness of his harshly sculptured face.

The Duke—for he was every inch the loftily forceful Duke of Stourbridge at this moment!—drew in a sharp breath before answering. 'In what way was it "not well done", Jane?' he encouraged coolly.

'For future reference, Your Grace?'

He gave a haughty inclination of his head. 'For future reference, Jane.'

'Very well.' She nodded. 'Firstly, I would suggest that you do not make an offer of marriage in front of any third parties. It could not be considered in the least romantic, and is more likely to end in embarassment for everyone concerned. Secondly—' she drew in a deep breath '—I do believe, no matter what your own intentions might be, that most women, of any age or temperament, would like to feel that they are at least loved a little when proposed to.'

A nerve pulsed in his jaw. 'You believe that, do you, Jane?'

It became difficult for Jane to withstand the intensity of that piercingly golden gaze, so she busied herself with straightening the skirt of her gown instead. 'Oh, yes, I think so, Your Grace.' She nodded, red curls bobbing.

'And thirdly, Jane...?' he drawled dryly, at the same time moving from his stance in front of the empty fireplace to stand beside the chaise on which Jane sat. The muscled length of his thigh in buff-coloured breeches was visible from the corner of her eye.

She looked up. 'Thirdly...?'

She should not have looked up! Should not have acknowledged how close Hawk was now standing. Her every nerve ending, her every sense of sight, sound and smell, was now totally aware of him. Of his masculinity. His sheer physical presence.

'Oh, yes. Thirdly.' She made a concerted effort to concentrate on the matter in hand rather than allowing herself to become enthralled—overwhelmed!—by Hawk's brooding proximity. She moistened lips gone stiff and unresponsive. 'Thirdly, no woman would feel happy accepting a proposal of marriage from a man who obviously makes it out of a sense of duty, of honour, rather than love.'

'I believe we have already covered the subject of love in the second piece of advice you gave me, Jane.'

Her lids fluttered nervously at what she was sure was a deceptive mildness in his tone. 'Oh, I would not presume to offer you advice, Your Grace!'

'No?' That dark brow rose once again. 'Then perhaps it is only that you mean to help ensure that any marriage proposal I might make in future will not be met by the same rejection?'

'I did not reject you, Hawk—Your Grace.' Her hands shook slightly in her agitation, and she hurriedly laced her fingers together so that he might not see their trembling. 'You were not sincere in your suggestion of marriage to me.'

'Was I not?'

'No!' She eyed him exasperatedly. 'You merely felt bound by a sense of—of—'

'Duty and honour?' he put in helpfully.

'Yes, duty and honour.' She nodded quickly. 'Although quite how you would have explained to your family, let alone the ton, how your future bride came to be accused of theft, I cannot imagine,' she continued, with some return of her normal spirit.

His mouth thinned. 'I am sure I would have managed somehow, Jane.'

She gave an impatient toss of her head. 'In any case, it is an offer you would have had to withdraw once you were made aware of my—my illegitimate connection to the Earl of Whitney.'

Silence greeted her outburst, and Jane accepted that at last she had pierced Hawk's aloof superiority.

How could she not have done when she had just made it clear that any doubts he might have harboured in that direction were completely unfounded? That she was indeed the illegitimate daughter of Janette Sulby and the Earl of Whitney!

Her heart still ached as she recalled the way in which the Earl had taken Janette's letters from her. How he had cradled them tenderly against his chest, almost as if they were Janette herself. How the tears had begun to fall down his cheeks as soon as he had begun to read the first of those letters.

'Jane?'

She swallowed hard, almost undone by the husky intensity of Hawk's tone. She could not bear it if he was kind to her. Not now! Not when she was already so close to tears.

She loved this man with every fibre of her being. Had

briefly, oh-so-briefly, been offered the opportunity of becoming his wife.

Could he not see that simply being alone with him like this was torture for her? Was more painful than anything that had come before?

'Look at me, Jane.'

She closed her eyes briefly, her heart fluttering in her chest. She had been almost completely undone the last time she had looked at him, and was not sure she could withstand another onslaught of the longing she had to simply throw herself into his arms and beg to stay in his life in any guise he wished!

'Jane, I insist that you look at me!'

Her eyes flashed deeply emerald and she raised her head sharply, her chin high. 'You insist, sir?'

Despite the gravity of the situation, Hawk once again felt the familiar twitch of his lips as he recognised the indignant anger in Jane's face. The anger he had deliberately incited...

He gave a mocking inclination of his head. 'May I now be permitted to make several claims in my own defence, Jane?'

She blinked. 'Your defence, Your Grace?'

'Certainly, Jane.' He grimaced. 'For I have surely been as judged and found wanting, as you accused me of doing with you earlier this morning.'

'Oh, but—' She frowned, her expression one of increasing puzzlement as she gave a slow nod. 'You may proceed, Your Grace.'

'Thank you, Jane.' He moved to sit beside her on the chaise, at once able to feel the warmth of her thigh only inches from his own. 'Firstly,' he began determinedly, 'you misunderstood my intentions when we spoke earlier this morning.'

'When you accused me of being a liar and a thief?'

His mouth thinned at her too-sweet tone. 'When I offered my sympathy and understanding that you had felt compelled to strike back at Lady Sulby by removing her jewellery before you left Markham Park!'

'It is no more flattering to be accused of spite than of being a liar and a thief!'

Hawk sat forward tensely. 'Why do you continue to deliberately misunderstand me, Jane?' he demanded impatiently. 'It was because you learnt of the existence of those letters to Whit—to your father from your mother, that you felt compelled to leave Markham Park so suddenly, was it not, Jane?' he added gently, remembering how distraught she had looked that morning when she had pleaded with him to take her away with him in his carriage.

That Gwendoline Sulby was capable of such cruelty he had no doubts. That he intended dealing personally with Gwendoline Sulby at the first opportunity was also in no doubt!

'I learnt much more than that, Your Grace.' Jane's voice was flat. 'Until Lady Sulby took such pleasure in informing me otherwise, I had no idea that Joseph Smith was not my father. That I was the bastard daughter of my mother's previous lover!'

Oh, yes, Hawk intended dealing *very* personally with Gwendoline Sulby!

He drew in a ragged breath. 'This morning, Jane, after receiving news of the Sulbys' actions following your disappearance, I was furiously angry—'

'No doubt at the thought that you had almost made love to such a creature.'

'At the thought that the Sulbys, after all their previous cruelties to you—cruelties that I am only now beginning to appreciate fully—could do such a thing as demand your arrest and apprehension for a few baubles that I am sure can be of little real value anyway!' Hawk stood up in his agitation. 'Do you really have so little faith in my perception of people, Jane? In my perception of you?' he rasped harshly. 'For if you do then you were right to turn down any idea of marriage between us!'

Jane breathed shallowly as she stared up at him uncomprehendingly. Could it really be that he had *not* believed her capable of stealing Lady Sulby's jewellery? That his anger this morning had not been directed at her but at the Sulbys?

Towards her aunt and uncle…?

She still found it incredible that Sir Barnaby had been her true uncle all along. And Lady Sulby her aunt by marriage. Olivia her first cousin.

For the last twelve years Jane had longed for a family. To belong. But now that she knew exactly who that family was—her father excepted!—Jane could not help but think she had been happier in her ignorance.

And Hawk, Duke of Stourbridge, must surely now realise what a lucky escape he had made when she had refused his offer of marriage…

She shook her head wryly. 'Do you not see, Your Grace, that I refused your offer for your own sake rather than my own?'

His gaze sharpened. '*My* sake, Jane…?'

She gave a weary sigh. 'I am accused of being a thief,

and now you have learnt—must know—that I am also the
illegitimate child of Janette Sulby and the Earl of Whitney.'

'And I am the Duke of Stourbridge—and I shall marry
where I see fit!' A nerve pulsed in his tightly clenched jaw.
'I shall marry whom I please, Jane,' he continued huskily.
'I shall marry where I love!'

Jane swallowed hard. 'I—where you love, Your Grace?'

'Jane, I swear that if you do not cease—' He broke off
his angry tirade, breathing deeply as he brought his emotions back under control. 'You are the only person I know,
Jane, who can almost drive me to my knees one moment
by refusing to marry me and then totally infuriate me the
next by telling me that it is for my own good! Yes, I love
you, Jane. I have loved you, I believe, since the moment
you threw yourself into my arms upon the staircase at
Markham Park.' His face was grim.

'Oh, but—'

'I loved you when you wore that hideous yellow gown. I
loved you later that evening, when you stood amongst the
dunes with the wind rippling through your glorious hair
and the moon reflected in your eyes. I loved you when you
burst into my bedchamber the following day. I loved you
even more when you appeared at the inn that evening.' He
allowed a brief smile to curve his lips. 'I loved and adored
you when I held you in my arms and made love to you. Like
Whitney with his Janette, I have loved everything about
you in every moment of every day since the moment I first
laid eyes on you, Jane!'

This could not be happening! Hawk could not have just
told her that he loved her—not once, but several times!

She breathed raggedly. 'Hawk, I—'

'Please do not interrupt, Jane,' he instructed her curtly.

'Allow me the privilege of making a complete and utter fool of myself when I get down on my knees and beg you to reconsider your decision.' He suited his action to his words and knelt on the rug at her slippered feet, taking both her hands in his. 'Will you not marry me, Jane? Will you not forgive and forget the clumsiness of my earlier proposal? Will you not accept that I meant no insult by it? That I merely wished to secure you as my own before another minute had passed? That when I discovered you gone this morning my first and only wish was to see you returned to Mulberry Hall so that I might never let you out of my sight again? Jane, will you please agree to become my wife, my Duchess!'

Hawk loved her! He truly, truly loved her!

Nothing else mattered at that moment. Nothing!

'I love you too, Hawk!' She launched herself into his arms, knocking them both off balance so that they fell onto the rug before the fire. Jane rested lightly on his chest as she looked down at him, her face glowing. 'I have loved you since before we met on the staircase—for you see I saw you out of the window as you arrived. You quite took my breath away! And I have loved you ever since, I am sure.' She smiled down at him tremulously. 'I truly, truly love you, Hawk!'

'Oh, Jane... Jane!' he groaned achingly, and his fingers became entangled in her hair as he tilted her head down to receive his kiss.

It was a kiss completely different from any other they had shared, as Hawk sipped and tasted, claimed and then conquered.

'Am I a wanton to want you in this shameless way?' she

murmured some time later, with Hawk's arms like protective steel bands about her waist.

Hawk's chest moved convulsively beneath her cheek as he chuckled. 'It is not wanton to want, to desire, to love in the way that we love each other. Darling Jane, you are warm and loving—and if that means you are a wanton then I thank God for it!'

She was Hawk's wanton. Wanted no other man but him. Never had and knew she never would.

'I am glad of it,' she murmured happily. 'You know, I am not sure it is completely proper for the Duke of Stourbridge to be romping on the rug with his sister's companion!'

This time Hawk's chest reverberated with his chuckle. 'As it is something that I intend to happen frequently once we are married, it would perhaps be as well for me to issue a new instruction to the household—that no one is to enter a room in which the two of us are alone without first knocking and being bade to enter!'

He claimed her lips once again, and Jane was rendered breathless when the kiss finally ended. 'I am sure it is all well and good that we love each other—'

'Well and good?' Hawk repeated teasingly as he rolled over so that she lay beneath him on the rug. 'It is wonderful, Jane! It is miraculous to feel so much love and know that you are loved in return!'

'Well. Yes. But—'

'Why do I have the feeling I am not going to like what you are about to say...?' His face was serious above hers, his gaze searching. 'Jane, whatever obstacle you see in our path, preventing us from being together, I advise you to put it firmly from your mind. Now that I know you love me too I will not allow anyone or anything to keep us from marrying each other.'

'But I am still accused of theft by Lady Sulby—'

'You may safely leave Lady Sulby to me,' he assured her grimly. 'And I am sure that your father, the Earl of Whitney, will also have some things he wishes to discuss with that lady!'

'But that is my next point, Hawk.' Jane looked up at him concernedly. 'How can you—how can the Duke of Stourbridge—possibly marry the illegitimate daughter of the Earl of Whitney? Perhaps it would be better if we were to just—?'

'Do not even suggest it, Jane!' he interrupted harshly, his arms tightening about her. 'You will not besmirch or belittle the love we feel for each other by suggesting that there can be anything less than marriage between us! Not even for my own sake will you suggest such a thing, Jane,' he added warningly. 'I am the Duke of Stourbridge, and your father is the Earl of Whitney. Between the two of us we will manage something that is acceptable.'

Jane believed him. Utterly. Completely. For he was the omnipotent Duke of Stourbridge. And he loved her.

Hawk, the Duke of Stourbridge, and the adopted daughter of the Earl of Whitney, Janette Justine Long—for the had learned from the church register in Somerset that Jane's full name was indeed Janette, for her mother, Justine, for her father—were married one month later in St George's church in Hanover Square. All of the St Claire and Whitney families were in attendance, as well as the ton, as they all wised the Duke and his new Duchess well.

'Do you still believe that "love has nothing to do with

marriage"?' Jane teased her husband, even as she snuggled into his arms as the carriage drove the two of them away for their wedding trip.

'Minx!' Hawk chuckled softly. 'I was arrogant, ridiculous, in that assertion.'

'You were,' Jane concurred, even as she sat up to kiss along the arrogant line of his jaw. 'Oh, Hawk, I wish that everyone could be as happy as we are!'

'I too, my love,' Hawk assured her gruffly, knowing that he held all his future happiness in his arms.

'My father's family have been wonderful.'Jane glowed up at him. 'And Arabella is already like a sister to me—'

'And Sebastian and Lucian like brothers, I hope?' he growled possessively.

Jane laughed softly. 'Sebastian is the dearest—and did you find occassion to ask Lucian how he came by his bruised knuckles?' she prompted frowningly, as she remembered Arabella's distress earlier when she'd seen the bruises upon her brother's hand.

Tall, dark-haired and wickedly handsome, Lord Lucian St Claire had stood as witness for his older brother.

'He claims to have scraped it upon a wall.' Hawk's frown echoed Jane's.

Jane's eyes widened. 'And you believe him?'

'No, of course I do not.' He grimaced.

There had been no chance this last month to see or talk to his brother, following Arabella's concern.

There had been the wedding to organise—once he had Whitney's permission Hawk had allowed nothing to delay those arrangements. There had also been Lady Gwendoline and Sir Barnaby for them to visit in Norfolk—a most unpleasant interview, to say the least.

Most of all, there had been Jane!

At Whitney's behest Hawk had accepted that it was better if the Earl and Jane were to stay with her aunt, Lady Pamela Croft, on the estate that adjoined his until after the wedding. The arrangement had allowed Jane to become better acquainted with her father and his family, but had also allowed Hawk to see Jane every day. To talk with. To walk with. To make love with!

Hawk had not believed it possible to love Jane any more than he already did, but that had not proved to be the case. Jane was now everything and all things to him.

But the arrival of Lucian at their weddng today, sporting bruised knuckles and an expression that dared any to question the reason for it, was definitely a cause for concern.

A concern that would now have to wait until after Hawk and Jane had returned from their honeymoon trip to Europe.

'I will deal with Lucian when we return in six weeks.' His arms tightened about her. 'Not, Jane, I forbid you to think or talk of any other man but me—at least for the duration of our honeymoon!'

'You "forbid" me, Your Grace…?' she echoed softly.

Hawk kissed her long and deeply. 'I forbid you, Jane,' he repeated challengingly. The lure of the seat opposite was proving too much of a temptation. There was something about Jane and the privacy of an enclosed carriage…!

The mischievous glow deepened in those wonderful green eyes as Jane easily read his intent. 'I bow to your superior authority, Your Grace,' she murmured throatily as she gave him a deceptively demure look from beneath lowered lashes.

Hawk chuckled softly as he lifted her in his arms an

moved with her to the seat opposite. 'I have no doubt you are going to lead me a merry dance, Jane!'

Jane looked up into the face of the man she loved aboce and beyond all things. 'You are dissatisfied with your wide already, Your Grace?' Once again she deliberately used the title she knew infuriated him. Usually into making love to her!

'Never, Jane!' Hawk assured her fiercely, even as his arms tightened about her and his mouth claimed hers.

His Duchess.

Janette St Claire.

But most of all and always, his beloved Jane.

* * * * *

THE LADY GAMBLES

Author Note

Welcome to the first in the trilogy featuring the Copeland sisters! Caroline, Diana and Elizabeth Copeland, eager to escape their new guardian's unacceptable marriage plans, decide to leave the comfort and safety of their home in Hampshire for the first time and embark on exciting, and separate, adventures in London.

They certainly find adventure—and danger—and most importantly of all, the men destined for each of them, and by doing so begin the biggest adventure of their lives: love.

The sisters are totally different in temperament, of course, but all are feisty and brave. And I do believe I fell in love with each and every one of the heroes during the writing of this trilogy. I hope you do, too.

Enjoy!

Prologue

April 1817—Palazzo Brizzi, Venice, Italy

'Have I mentioned to either of you gentlemen that I had thought of offering for one of Westbourne's daughters?'

Lord Dominic Vaughn, Earl of Blackstone, and one of the two gentlemen referred to by their host, Lord Gabriel Faulkner, found himself gaping inelegantly across the breakfast table at the other man in stunned disbelief. A glance at their friend Nathaniel Thorne, Earl of Osbourne, showed him to be no less surprised at the announcement as he sat with his tea cup arrested halfway between saucer and mouth.

Indeed, it was one of those momentous occasions when it seemed that time itself should cease. All movement. All sound. Indeed, when the very world itself should simply have stopped turning.

It had not, of course; the gondoliers could still be heard singing upon their crafts in the busy Grand Canal, the ped-

lars continued to call out as they moved along the canal
selling their wares, and the birds still sang a merry tune.
That frozen stillness, that ceasing of time, existed only between the three men seated upon the balcony of the Palazzo Brizzi, where they had been enjoying a late breakfast
together prior to Blackstone and Osbourne's departure for
England later today.

'Gentlemen?' their host prompted in that dry and amused
drawl that was so typical of him, one dark brow raised
mockingly over eyes of midnight blue as he placed the letter he had been reading down upon the table top.

Dominic Vaughn was the first to recover his senses.
'Surely you are not serious, Gabe?'

That mocking dark brow was joined by its twin. 'Am
I not?'

'Well, of course not.' Osbourne finally rallied to the occasion. '*You* are Westbourne!'

'For the past six months, yes.' The new Earl of Westbourne acknowledged drily. 'It is one of the *previous* Earl's
daughters for whom I have offered.'

'Copeland?'

Westbourne gave a haughty inclination of his dark head.
'Just so.'

'I—but why would you do such a thing?' Dominic made
no effort to hide his disgust at the idea of one of their number willingly sacrificing himself to the parson's mousetrap.

The three men were all aged eight and twenty, and had
been to school together before serving in Wellington's army
for five years. They had fought together, drunk together,
eaten together, wenched together, shared the same accommodations on many occasions—and one thing they had all
agreed on long ago was the lack of a need to settle on one

piece of succulent fruit when the whole of the basket was available for the tasting. Gabriel's announcement smacked of a betrayal of that tacit pact.

Westbourne shrugged his wide shoulders beneath the elegance of his dark-blue superfine. 'It seemed like the correct thing to do.'

The correct thing to do! When had Gabriel ever bothered himself with acting correctly? Banished to the Continent in disgrace by his own family and society eight years ago, Lord Gabriel Faulkner had lived his life since that time by his own rules, and to hell with what was correct!

Having inherited the extremely respected title of the Earl of Westbourne put a slightly different slant on things, of course, and meant that London society—the marriage-minded mamas especially—would no doubt welcome the scandalous Gabriel back into the *ton* with open arms. But even so...

'You *are* jesting, of course, Gabriel.' Osbourne felt no hesitation in voicing his own scepticism concerning their friend's announcement.

'I am afraid I am not,' Westbourne stated firmly. 'My unexpected inheritance of the title and estates has left the future of Copeland's three daughters to my own tender mercies.' His top lip curled back in self-derision. 'No doubt Copeland expected to see his three daughters safely married off before he met his Maker. Unfortunately, this was not the case, and as such, the three young women have become my wards.'

'Are you saying that you have been guardian to the three Copeland chits for the past six months and not said a word?' Osborne sounded as if he could barely believe it.

Westbourne gave a cool inclination of his arrogant head.

'A little like leaving the door open for the fox to enter the henhouse, is it not?'

It was indeed, Dominic mused wryly; Gabriel's reputation with the ladies was legendary. As was his ruthlessness when it came to bringing an end to those relationships when they became in the least irksome to him. 'Why have you never mentioned this before, Gabriel?'

The other man shrugged. 'I am mentioning it now.'

'Incredible!' Osborne was still at a loss for words.

Gabriel gave a hard, humourless grin. 'Almost as incredible as my having inherited the title at all, really.'

It was certainly the case that it would not have occurred if the years of battle against Napoleon's armies had not killed off Copeland's two nephews, the only other possible inheritors of the title. As it was, because Copeland only had daughters and no sons, the disgraced Lord Gabriel Faulkner had inherited the title of Earl of Westbourne from a man who was merely a second cousin or some such flimsy connection.

'Obviously, the fact that I am now the young ladies' guardian rendered the situation slightly unusual, and so I had my lawyer put forward an offer of marriage on my behalf,' Westbourne explained.

'To which daughter?' Dominic tried to recall whether or not he had ever seen or met any of the Copeland sisters during his occasional forays into society this past two Seasons, but drew a complete blank. He did not consider it a good omen that none of the young women appeared to be attractive enough to spark even a flicker of memory.

Westbourne's sculptured mouth twisted wryly. 'Never having met any of the young ladies, I did not feel it necessary to state a preference.'

'You did not!' Dominic stared at the other man in horror. 'Gabriel, you cannot mean to say that you have offered marriage to *any* one of the Copeland chits?'

Westbourne gave a cool smile. 'That is exactly what I have done.'

'I say, Gabe!' Osbourne looked as horrified as Dominic felt. 'Taking a bit of a risk, don't you think? What if they decide to give you the fat and ugly one? The one that no other man would want?'

'I do not see that as being a problem when Harriet Copeland was their mother.' Westbourne waved that objection aside.

All three men had been but nineteen when Lady Harriet Copeland, the Countess of Westbourne, having left her husband and daughters, had tragically met her death at the hands of her jealous lover only months later. The woman's beauty was legendary.

Dominic grimaced. 'They may decide to give you the one that takes after her father.' Copeland had been a short and rotund man in his sixties when he died, and with little charm to recommend him, either—was it any wonder that a woman as beautiful as Harriet Copeland had left him for a younger man?

'What if they do?' Westbourne relaxed back in his chair, his dark hair curling fashionably upon his nape and brow. 'In order to provide the necessary heir, the Earl of Westbourne must needs take a wife. Any wife. Any one of the Copeland sisters is capable of providing that heir regardless of her appearance, surely?' He shrugged those elegantly wide shoulders.

'But what about—I mean, if she is fat and ugly, surely you will never be able to rise to the occasion in order to provide this necessary heir?' Osbourne visibly winced at the unpleasantness of the image he had just portrayed.

'What do you say to that, Gabe?' Dominic chuckled.

'I say that it no longer matters whether or not I would be able to perform in my marriage bed.' Westbourne picked up the letter he had set aside earlier to peruse its contents once again with an apparent air of calm. 'It would appear that my reputation has preceded me, gentlemen.' His voice had become steely.

Dominic frowned. 'Explain, Gabriel.'

That sculptured mouth tightened. 'The letter I received from my lawyer this morning states that all three of the Copeland sisters—yes, even the fat and ugly one, Nate...' he gave a mocking little bow in Osbourne's direction '... have rejected any idea of marriage to the disreputable Lord Gabriel Faulkner.'

Dominic had known Gabriel long enough to realise that his calm attitude was a sham, and that the cold glitter in those midnight-blue eyes and the harsh set of his jaw were a clearer indication of his friend's current mood. Beneath that veneer of casual uninterest he was coldly, dangerously angry.

A fact born out by his next statement. 'In the circumstances, gentlemen, I have decided that I will shortly be following the two of you to England.'

'The ladies of Venice will all fall into a decline at your going,' Osbourne predicted drily.

'Perhaps,' Gabriel allowed dispassionately, 'but I have decided that it is time the new Earl of Westbourne took his place in London society.'

'Capital!' Osbourne felt no hesitation in voicing his approval of the plan.

Dominic was equally enthusiastic at the thought of having Gabriel back in London with them. 'Westbourne House in London has not been lived in for years, and must resemble a mausoleum, so perhaps you would care to stay with me at Blackstone House when you return, Gabriel? I would welcome your opinion, too, on the changes I instructed be made at Nick's during my absence.' He referred to the gambling club he had won a month ago in a game of cards with the previous owner, Nicholas Brown.

'I should have a care in any further dealings you might have with Brown, Dom.' Gabriel frowned.

An unnecessary warning as it happened; Dominic was well aware that Nicholas Brown, far from being a gentleman, was the bastard son of a peer and a prostitute, and that his connections in the seedy underworld of England's capital were numerous. 'Duly noted, Gabe.'

The other man nodded. 'In that case, I thank you for your invitation to stay at Blackstone House, but it is not my intention to remain in town. Instead, I will make my way immediately to Shoreley Park.'

An occurrence, Dominic felt sure, that did not bode well for the three Copeland sisters...

Chapter One

*Three days later—Nick's gambling club,
London, England*

Caro moved lightly across the stage on slippered feet before arranging herself carefully upon the red-velvet chaise, checking that the gold-and-jewelled mask covering her face from brow to lips was securely in place, and arranging the long ebony curls of the theatrical wig so that they cascaded over the fullness of her breasts and down the length of her spine, before attending to the draping of her gold-coloured gown so that she was completely covered from her throat to her toes.

She could hear the buzz of excitement behind the drawn curtains at the front of the small raised stage, and knew that the male patrons of the gambling club were anticipating the moment when those curtains would be pulled back and her performance began.

Caro's heart began to pound, the blood thrumming hotly

in her veins as the introductory music began to play, and the room behind the drawn curtains fell into an expectant silence.

Dominic hesitated at the entrance of Nick's, one of London's most fashionable gambling clubs, and one of his favourite haunts even before he had taken possession of it a month ago.

Newly arrived back from Venice that afternoon, he had decided to visit the club at the earliest opportunity, and as he handed his hat and cloak over to the waiting attendant, he could not help but notice that the burly young man who usually guarded the doorway against undesirables was not in his usual place. He also realised that the gambling rooms beyond the red-velvet curtains were unnaturally silent.

What on earth was going on?

Suddenly that silence was bewitchingly broken by the sultry, sensual sound of a woman singing. Except that Dominic had given strict instructions before his departure for Venice that in future there were to be no women working—in *any* capacity—in the club he now owned.

He was frowning heavily as he strolled into the main salon, seeing at once the reason for the doorman's desertion when he spotted Ben Jackson standing transfixed just inside a room crowded with equally mesmerised patrons, all of them apparently hearing only one thing. Seeing only one thing.

A woman, the obvious source of that sensually seductive voice, lay upon a red-velvet *chaise* on the stage, a tiny little thing with an abundance of ebony hair that cascaded in loose curls over her shoulders and down the length of her slender back. Most of her face was covered by a jewelled mask much like the ones worn in Venice during carnival, but her bared lips were full and sensuous, her throat a pearly white. She wore a gown of shimmering gold, the voluptuousness of her curves hinted at rather than blatantly displayed, and the more seductive because of it.

Even masked, she was without a doubt the most sensually seductive creature Dominic had ever beheld!

The fact that every other man in the room thought the same thing was evident from the avarice in their gazes and the flush to their cheeks, several visibly licking their lips as they stared at her. A fact that caused Dominic's scowl to deepen as his own gaze returned to that vision of seduction upon the stage.

Caro tried not to reveal her irritation with the man who stood at the back of the salon glowering at her, either by her expression or in her voice, as she brought her first performance of the evening to an end by slowly standing up to move gracefully to the edge of the stage as she sang the last huskily appealing notes.

It did not prevent her from being completely aware of that pale and disapproving gaze or of the man that gaze belonged to.

He was so extremely tall that even standing at the back of the salon he towered several inches over the other men in the room, his black superfine tailored to widely muscled shoulders, his white linen impeccable and edged with Brussels lace at his throat and wrist. His fashionably styled hair was the colour of a raven's wing, so black it almost seemed to have a blue sheen. His eyes, those piercingly critical eyes, were the pale colour of a grey silky mist, and appeared almost silver in their intensity. He had a strong, aristocratic face: high cheekbones, a straight slash of a nose, firm sculptured lips, and a square and arrogantly determined jaw. It was a hard and uncompromising face, made more so by the scar that ran down its left side, from just beneath his eye to that stubbornly set jaw.

His pale grey eyes were currently staring at Caro with an intensity of dislike that she had never encountered before in all of her twenty years. So unnerved was she by his obvious disdain that she barely managed to maintain her smile as she took her bows to the thunderous round of applause. Applause she knew from experience would last for several minutes after she had returned to her dressing-room at the back of the club.

It was impossible not to take one last glance in the scowling man's direction before she disappeared from the stage, slightly alarmed as she saw that he was now in earnest conversation with the manager of the club, Drew Butler.

'What is the meaning of this, Drew?' Dominic asked icily under cover of the applause for the beauty still taking her bows upon the stage.

The grey-haired man looked unperturbed; as the manager of Nick's for the past twenty years, the cynicism in his tired blue eyes stated that he had already seen and done most things in his fifty years, and was no longer disturbed by any of them, least of all by the disapproving tone of the man who had become his employer only a month ago. 'The patrons love her.'

'The patrons have neither drunk nor gambled since that woman began to sing some quarter of an hour ago,' Dominic pointed out.

'Watch them now,' Drew said softly.

Dominic did watch, his brows rising as the champagne began to flow copiously and the patrons placed ridiculously high bets at the tables, the level of conversation rising exponentially as the attributes of the young woman were loudly discussed, along with more bets being placed as to the chances of any of them being privileged enough to see behind the jewelled mask.

'You see.' Drew gave an unconcerned shrug as he turned back to Dominic. 'She's really good for business.'

Dominic shook his head impatiently. 'Did I not make it clear when I was here last month that this is to be a gambling club only in future, and not a damned brothel?'

'You did.' Again Drew remained completely unruffled. 'And as per your instructions the bedchambers upstairs have remained locked and unavailable to all.'

A gentleman, an earl no less, owning a London gambling club of Nick's reputation was hardly acceptable to society. But it had been a matter of honour to Dominic, when Nicholas Brown had challenged him to a game of cards the previous month for ownership of Midnight Moon, the prize stallion kept at Dominic's stud at his estate in Kent. In return, Dominic had demanded that Nicholas put up Nick's as his own side of the wager and obviously Dominic had won.

Owning a gambling club was one thing, but the half-a-dozen bedchambers on the first floor, until recently available to any man who had wished for some privacy with… whomever, were totally unacceptable; Dominic drew the line at being considered a pimp! As such, he had ordered a ban on women—all women—inside the club, and the bedrooms upstairs to be immediately closed off. With the exception of the mysterious young woman, who had so recently held the club's patrons enthralled—and not just with her singing!—those instructions appeared to have been carried out.

Dominic's mouth compressed. 'I believe my instructions were to dispense with the services of all the...ladies working here?'

'Caro ain't—is not, a whore.' Drew visibly bristled, his shoulders stiffening defensively.

Dominic frowned darkly. 'Then what, pray, is she?'

'Exactly as you saw,' Drew said. 'Twice a night she simply lays on the *chaise* and sings. And the punters drink and gamble more than ever once she leaves the stage.'

'Does she bring a maid or companion with her?'

The older man looked amused. 'What do you think?'

'What do *I* think?' Dominic's eyes had narrowed to icy slits. 'I think she is a disaster in the making.' He scowled. 'Which gentleman has the privilege of escorting her home at the end of the evening?'

'I does.' The doorman, Ben Jackson, announced proudly as he passed them on his way back to his vigil at the entrance to the club, his round face looking no less cherubic for all that his nose had obviously been broken more than once. His ham-sized fists did not come amiss in a brawl, either.

Dominic raised sceptical brows. '*You* do?'

Ben beamed contentedly, showing several broken teeth for his trouble. 'Miss Caro insists on it.'

Oh, she did, did she?

Ben Jackson could make grown men quake in their boots just by looking at them, and Drew Butler was a cynic through and through, and yet *Miss Caro* appeared to have them both eating out of her delicate little hand!

'Perhaps we should continue this discussion in your office, Drew?' Dominic turned away, expecting rather than waiting to see if the older man followed him, his impatience barely held in check. Nevertheless, he still managed to greet and smile at several acquaintances as he moved purposefully towards the back of the smoke-filled club to where Drew's office was situated.

He barely noticed the opulence of that office as Drew followed him into the room before closing the door behind him and effectively shutting out the noise from the gaming rooms. Although Dominic did spot a decanter of what he knew to be a first-class brandy, and he swiftly poured himself a glass and took an appreciative sip before offering to pour one for the manager, too.

The older man shook his head. 'I never drink during working hours.'

Dominic made himself comfortable as he leant back against the front of the huge mahogany desk. 'Well, who is she, Drew? And where is she from?'

The manager shrugged. 'Do you want my take on her or what she told me when she came to the back door asking for work?'

Dominic's gaze narrowed. 'Both.' He took another sip of his brandy, giving every appearance of studying the toe of one highly polished boot as the other man began to relate the young woman's tale of woe.

Caro Morton claimed to be an orphan who had lived with a maiden aunt in the country until three weeks ago, the death of the elderly lady leaving her homeless. Consequently she had arrived in London two weeks earlier with very little money and no maid or companion, but with a determination to make her own way in the world. Her intention, apparently, had been to offer herself as companion or governess in a respectable household, but her lack of references had made that impossible, and so she had instead been driven to begin knocking on the back door of the theatres and clubs.

Dominic looked up sharply at this part of the story. 'How many had she visited before arriving here?'

'Half a dozen or so.' Drew grimaced. 'I understand she did receive several offers of…alternative employment along the way.'

Dominic gave a humourless smile as he easily guessed the nature of those offers. 'You did not feel tempted to do the same when she came knocking on the door here?' He had no doubt that Miss Caro Morton was a young woman most men, no matter what their age, would like to bed.

The older man shot him a frowning glance as he moved to sit behind the desk. 'My lord, I happen to have been happily married for the past twenty years, with a daughter not much younger than she is.'

'My apologies.' Dominic gave a slight bow. 'Very well.' His gaze sharpened. 'That would appear to be Miss Morton's version of her arrival in London; now tell me who or what *you* think she is.'

Drew looked thoughtful. 'There may have been a maiden aunt, but somehow I doubt it. My guess is she's in London because she's running away from something or someone. A brutish father, maybe. Or perhaps even a cruel husband. Either way she's far too refined to be your usual actress or whore.'

Dominic eyed him speculatively. 'Define refined?'

'Ladylike,' the older man supplied tersely.

Dominic looked intrigued; a woman of quality attempt-

ing to conceal her identity would certainly explain the
wearing of that jewelled mask. 'And you do not think that
actresses and whores are capable of giving the impression
of being ladylike?'

'I know they are,' Drew answered. 'I just don't happen
to think Caro Morton is one of them.' His expression became closed. 'Perhaps it would be best if you were to talk
to her and decide for yourself?'

That the manager felt a fatherly protectiveness towards
the 'refined' Miss Caro Morton was obvious. That the doorman, Ben Jackson, felt that same protectiveness was also
apparent. If she really were a runaway wife or daughter,
then Dominic felt no such softness of emotions. 'I fully
intend doing so,' he assured the other man drily as he
straightened. 'I merely wished to hear your views first.'

Drew looked concerned. 'Are you intending to dismiss her?'

Dominic gave the thought some consideration before answering. There was no doubting Drew Butler's claim that
Caro Morton's nightly performances were a draw to the
club, but even so she might just be more trouble than she
was worth if she really were a runaway wife or daughter.
'That will depend upon Miss Morton.'

'In what way?'

He raised arrogant brows. 'I accept that you have been
the manager of Nick's for several years, Drew. That you
are, without a doubt, the best man for the job.' He smiled
briefly to soften what he was about to say next. 'However,
that ability does not give you the right to question any of
my own actions or decisions.'

'No, my lord.'

'Where is Caro Morton now?'

'I usually ensure that she has a bite to eat in her dressing-room between performances.' Drew's expression challenged Dominic to question that decision of *his*.

Remembering the girl's slenderness, and the pallor of her translucent skin, Dominic felt no inclination to do so; from the look of her, that 'bite to eat' might be the only food Caro Morton had in a single day.

'I'd like to be informed if you decide to let her to go. She has wages owing to her,' Drew defended as Dominic looked surprised.

She also, Dominic decided ruefully as he agreed to the request before leaving the office, had the cynical club manager wrapped tightly about her tiny little finger, and no doubt the older man would offer her his assistance in finding other employment should Dominic decide to let her go.

Deciding for himself who or what Miss Caro Morton was promised to be an interesting experience. It was a surprising realisation for a man whose years in the army, and the two years since returning to England spent evading the clutches of every marriage-minded mama of the *ton*, had made him as cynical, if not more so, as the much older Drew Butler.

Caro gave a surprised start as a brief knock sounded on her dressing-room door. Well, not a dressing-room as such, she allowed ruefully, more a private room at the back of the gambling club that Mr Butler had put aside for her use in between her performances.

A room that he had assured her was completely off-limits to any and all of the men who frequented Nick's...

She stood up slowly, nervously making sure that her robe was securely tied about her waist before crossing the tiny room to stand beside the locked door. 'Who is it?' she asked warily.

'My name is Dominic Vaughn,' came the haughty reply.

Just like that, Caro *knew* that the man standing on the other side of the locked door was the same man who had looked at her earlier with those disdainful silver-coloured eyes. She was not sure why or how she knew that, she just did. There was an arrogance in the deep baritone voice, a confidence that spoke of years of issuing orders and having them instantly obeyed. And he was obviously now expecting her to obey him by unlocking the door and allowing him inside...

Her hands clenched in the pockets of her robe, the nails digging painfully into the palms. 'Gentlemen are not allowed to visit me in my dressing-room.'

A brief silence followed her statement, before the man replied with hard impatience, 'I assure you that my being here has Drew Butler's full approval.'

The manager of Nick's had been very kind to Caro this past week, and, what's more, she knew that she could trust him implicitly. But having a man approach her dressing-room in this unexpected way and simply stating that Mr Butler approved of his being here and expecting her to believe his claim was not good enough. 'I am sorry, but the answer is still no.'

'I assure you, my business with you will only take a few moments of your time,' came the irritated response.

'I am in need of rest before my next performance,' Caro insisted.

Dominic's mouth firmed in frustration at this woman's stubborn refusal to so much as open the door. 'Miss Morton—'

'That is my final word on the subject,' she informed him haughtily.

Drew had claimed that Caro Morton was 'ladylike', Dominic recalled with a narrowing of his eyes. He could hear that quality himself now in the precise diction of her voice. A subtle, and yet unmistakable authority in her tone that spoke of education and refinement. 'You will either speak to me now, Miss Morton, or I assure you there will be no "next performance" for you at Nick's.' Dominic stood with his shoulder leaning against the wall in the darkened hallway, arms folded across the broad width of this chest.

There was a tiny gasp inside the room. 'Are you threatening me, Mr Vaughn?' There was a slight edge of uncertainty to her voice now.

'I feel no need to threaten, Miss Morton, when the truth will serve just as well.'

Caro was in something of a quandary. Having fled her home two weeks earlier, sure that she would find employment in the obscurity of London as a lady's companion or governess, instead she had found herself being turned away from those respectable households, time and time again, simply because she did not have the appropriate references.

Everything in London had been so much more expensive than Caro had imagined it would be, too. The small amount of money she had brought with her, saved over the months from her allowance, had diminished much more rapidly than she had imagined it would, leaving her with no choice, if she were not to return to an intolerable situation, but to try her luck at the back door of the theatres. She had always received compliments upon her singing when she'd entertained after dinner on the rare occasions her father had invited friends and neighbours to dine. Those visits to the theatres *had* resulted in her receiving several offers of employment—but all of them were shocking to a young woman brought up in protected seclusion in rural Hampshire!

She owed her present employment—and the money with which to pay for her modest lodgings—completely to Drew Butler's kindness. As such, she was not sure that she could turn Dominic Vaughn away from her dressing-room if for some reason the older man really had approved the visit.

Her fingers shook slightly as she took her hands from the pockets of her robe to slowly turn the key in the lock, only to step back quickly as the door was immediately thrust open impatiently.

It *was* the silver-eyed devil from earlier! He looked even more devilish now as the subdued candlelight illuminating the hallway threw that scar upon his cheek into sharp relief and his black jacket and white linen only added to the rawness of the power that seemed to emanate from him.

Caro took another step backwards. 'What is it you wished to speak to me about?'

Dominic deliberately schooled his expression to reveal none of the shock he had felt as he looked at Caro Morton for the first time without the benefit of that concealing jewelled mask. Or the ebony-coloured wig, which had apparently concealed her own long and gloriously golden curls. Those curls now framed sea-green, almond-shaped eyes, set in a delicate, heart-shaped face of such beauty it took his breath away.

An occurrence, if she were indeed a disobedient daughter or—worse—a runaway wife, that did not please him in the slightest. 'Invite me inside, Miss Morton,' he demanded dictatorially.

Long-lashed lids blinked nervously before she arrested the

movement and her pointed chin rose proudly. 'As I have already explained, sir, I am resting until my next performance.'

Dominic's mouth hardened. 'Which I understand from Drew does not take place for another hour.'

The slenderness of her throat moved convulsively, drawing his attention to the bare expanse of creamy-white skin revealed by the plunging neckline of her robe. His hooded gaze moved lower still, to where the silky material draped down over small, pointed breasts. Her waist was so slender that he was sure his hands could easily span its circumference. He also privately acknowledged, with an unlooked for stirring of his arousal, that his hands could easily cup her tiny breasts before lowering to the smooth roundness of her bottom and lifting her against him for her to wrap those long, slender legs about his waist...

Caro found she did not much care for the way Dominic Vaughn was looking at her. Almost as if he could see beneath her robe to the naked flesh beneath. Her cheeks became flushed as she straightened her shoulders determinedly. 'I would prefer that you remain exactly where you are, sir.'

That silver gaze returned to her face. 'My lord.'

She blinked. 'I beg your pardon?'

He introduced himself. 'I am Lord Dominic Vaughn, Earl of Blackstone.'

Caro felt a tightness in her chest as she realised this man was a member of the *ton*, a man no doubt as arrogant as her recently acquired guardian. 'If that is meant to impress me—*my lord*—then I am afraid it has failed utterly.'

He raised dark brows as he ignored the sarcasm in her tone. 'I believe it is the usual custom at this point for the introduction to be reciprocated?'

Her cheeks burned at the intended rebuke. 'If, as you claim, you have spoken to Mr Butler, then you must already know that my name is Caro Morton.'

He looked at her shrewdly. 'Is it?'

Her gaze sharpened. 'I have just said as much, my lord.'

'Ah, if only the saying of something made it true,' he jeered.

That tightness in Caro's chest increased. 'Do you doubt my word, sir?'

'I am afraid I am of an age and experience, my dear Caro, when I doubt everything I am told until proven otherwise.'

There was no doubting that the cynicism and mockery of this man's expression gave him a world-weary appearance, and that scar upon his left cheek an air of danger, but even so she would not have placed him at more than eight or nine and twenty. Not so much older than her own twenty years.

Nor was she his 'dear' anything! 'How very sad for you.'

Not the response Dominic had expected. Or one he wanted, either; the wealthy and eligible Earl of Blackstone did not desire or need anyone's pity. Least of all that of a woman who hid her real appearance behind a jewelled mask and ebony wig.

Could Butler's assessment of her be the correct one? Had this young woman run away to London to hide from possibly an overbearing father, or a brutish and bullying husband? She was of such a tiny and delicate appearance that Dominic found the latter possibility too distasteful to contemplate.

Whatever the mystery surrounding this woman, he was of the opinion that neither he, nor his gambling club, was in need of the trouble she might bring banging upon the door. 'Are you even of an age to be in a gambling club, Caro?'

She looked startled. 'My lord?'

'I simply wondered as to your age.'

'A gentleman should never ask a lady her age,' she retorted primly.

Dominic slowly allowed his gaze to move from the top of that golden head, over the slenderness of her body, the delicacy of her tiny wrists and slender hands, to the bareness of her feet, before just as slowly returning to her now flushed and slightly resentful face. 'As far as I am aware, *ladies* are always accompanied by a maid or companion; nor do they cavort upon the stage of a gentlemen's gaming club.'

Her little pointed chin rose once more. 'I do not cavort, my lord, but simply lie upon a *chaise*,' she bit out tartly. 'I also fail to see what business it is of yours whether or not I have a maid or companion.'

Dominic glanced into the room behind her, noting the tray on the dressing table, with its bowl of some rich and still-steaming stew and a platter of bread beside it, a plump and tempting orange upon another plate, obviously intended as her dessert. No doubt that 'bite to eat' Butler had mentioned providing for her.

'I appear to have interrupted your supper,' he acknowledged smoothly. 'I suggest that we finish this conversation later tonight when I, and not Ben, act as your escort home.'

Her eyes widened in alarm before she gave a firm shake of her head. 'That will not be possible, I am afraid.'

'Oh?'

This was not a man used to receiving no for an answer, Caro realised ruefully as she took in the glittering arro-

gance in those silver eyes beneath one autocratically raised
brow. And her lack of maid or companion was easily explained—if she had felt inclined to offer this man any explanation, which she did not! To have brought either maid
or companion with her when she fled Hampshire two weeks
ago would have placed them in the position of having abet-
ted her in that flight, and she was in enough trouble already,
without involving anyone else in her plight.

'No,' she reaffirmed evenly now. 'It would hurt Ben's
feelings terribly if he were not allowed to walk me home.
Besides,' she added as his lordship would have dismissed
that excuse for exactly what it was, 'I do not allow gentlemen I do not know to escort me to my home.' A man she
had no wish to know, either, Caro could have added.

Mocking humour glittered briefly in those pale grey
eyes. 'Even if Drew Butler were to vouch for this gentleman?'

'I have yet to hear him do so. Now, if you will excuse
me? I wish to eat my supper before it becomes too cool.'
Caro's attempt to close the door in Dominic Vaughn's face
was thwarted by the tactical placing of one of his booted
feet against the door jam. Her eyes flashed a warning as she
slowly reopened the door. 'Please do not force me to call
upon Ben's help in having you removed from the premises.'

A threat that did not seem to bother the arrogant Dominic Vaughn in the slightest as he continued to smile down
at her confidently. 'That would be an…interesting experience.'

Caro eyed him uncertainly. Ben was as tall as the earl,
and obviously more heavily built, but there was an underlying air of danger lurking beneath this man's outward
show of fashionable elegance. An aura of power that im-

plied he could best any man against whom he chose to pit the strength of those wide shoulders and tall, lithely muscled body. Besides which, Caro very much doubted that the Earl of Blackstone had received that scar upon his face by sitting comfortably at home by his fireside!

She forced the tension from her shoulders as she smiled up at him. 'Perhaps we might defer discussing your offer to escort me home until after I have spoken to Mr Butler?'

And perhaps, Dominic guessed, this young lady would choose to absent herself without so much as bothering to talk to Drew Butler. 'I will be waiting outside for you when you have finished your next performance.'

The irritated darkening of those beautiful sea-green eyes told him that he had guessed correctly. 'You are very persistent, sir!'

'Just anxious to acquaint myself with one of my own employees.'

She gasped, those sea-green eyes wide with alarm. 'Your...? Did you say *your* employee?'

Dominic gave an affirmative nod, and took great pleasure in noting the way the colour drained from the delicacy of her cheeks, as she obviously realised he did indeed have the power to ensure she never performed at Nick's again. 'Until later then, Miss Morton.' He bowed elegantly before returning to the gaming rooms, a smile of satisfaction curving his lips.

Chapter Two

'I would prefer to walk, thank you.' It was a little over two hours later when Caro firmly dismissed even the idea of getting inside Dominic Vaughn's fashionable carriage as it stood waiting outside Nick's—a man Drew Butler had confirmed to Caro was not only the Earl of Blackstone, but also the man who had recently taken ownership of the gambling club at which they were both employed. That aside, she had no intention of placing herself in the vulnerable position of travelling alone in his carriage with him!

'As you wish.' He indicated for the driver of the carriage to follow them, his raven-black hair now covered by a fashionably tall hat, and a black silk cloak thrown about those widely muscled shoulders.

Caro shot him a sideways glance from beneath her unadorned brown bonnet, only a few of her golden curls now showing at her temples and nape. The brown gown she wore beneath her own serviceable black cloak was equally as modest in appearance, with its high neckline and long sleeves.

She had bought three such gowns when she'd arrived in London two weeks ago, this brown one, another in a dull green, and the third of dark cream, having very quickly realised that the few silk gowns she had brought to town with her stood out noticeably in the genteelly rundown area of London where she had managed to find clean and inexpensive lodgings. And being noticed—as herself, rather than as the masked lady singing at Nick's—was something she dearly wished to avoid.

To say that Dominic had been surprised—yet again!—by Caro Morton's appearance on joining him a few minutes ago would be an understatement. In fact, it had taken him several seconds to recognise her beneath that unbecoming brown bonnet that hid most of those glorious golden curls, and the equally unfashionable cloak that covered her from neck to ankle, so giving her every appearance of being a modest and unassuming young lady of meagre means.

That dark modesty of her clothing opened up a third possibility as to why Caro Morton was living alone in London and so obviously in need of work in order to support herself. Her slender hands were completely bare of rings, but that did not mean she was not one of those starry-eyed young ladies who, during the years of war against Napoleon, had abandoned all propriety by eloping with their unsuitable soldier beau before he marched off to battle, only to find themselves widowed within weeks, sometimes days, of that scandalous marriage having taken place.

No matter what the explanation, there was certainly very little danger of any of the patrons of Nick's recognising this drably dressed young woman as the ebony-haired siren whose seductive performance had so easily bewitched and beguiled them all so completely twice this evening.

Himself included, he readily admitted.

'Perhaps you would care to enlighten me as to why an unprotected young woman should choose to work in one of London's fashionable gambling clubs?'

It was a question she seemed to have been expecting as her expression remained cool. 'For the money, perhaps?'

Dominic scowled. 'If you must work, then why did you not find more respectable employment? You have the refinement to be a lady's maid, or, failing that, to serve in a shop.'

'How kind of you to say so,' she returned over-sweetly. 'But one needs references from previous employers to become either of those things. References I do not have,' she added pointedly.

'Perhaps because you have never worked as a lady's maid or served in a shop?' he pressed.

'Or perhaps I was just so inadequate at both those occupations that I was refused references?' she suggested tartly.

Dominic gave an appreciative smile at her spirited answer. 'So instead you have chosen to put yourself in a position where you are ogled by dozens of licentious men every night?'

Caro came to an abrupt halt, her own humour fading at the deliberate insult, both in his tone and expression, as he paused beside her in the flickering lamplight and allowed that silver gaze to rake over her critically from her head to her toes. 'It appears that I needed no references for that,' she informed him with chilling hauteur.

Dominic knew that it really was none of his concern if she chose to expose herself to the sort of ribald comments he had been forced to listen to following her second performance this evening, when the bets as to who would even-tually become her lover and protector had increased to a level he had found most unpleasant. And yet... 'Do you have so little regard for your reputation?'

Her cheeks became flushed. 'The jewelled mask I wear ensures my reputation remains perfectly intact, thank you!'

'Perhaps.' Dominic's jaw tightened. 'I am surprised you did not consider a less...taxing means of employment.'

She looked puzzled. 'Less taxing?'

He shrugged. 'You are young. The comments of your numerous admirers this evening are testament to your desirability. Did you not consider acquiring a single male protector, rather than exposing yourself in this way to the attentions of dozens?'

Caro felt the flush that warmed her cheeks. 'A protector, my lord?'

'A man who would see you housed and suitably clothed in exchange for the pleasure of your...company,' he elaborated.

Caro's breath caught in her throat, that flush covering the whole of her body now as she realised that the earl was suggesting she should have taken a lover when she arrived in London rather than 'singing for her supper' at Nick's.

A lover!

When Caro's father had been so averse to any of his three daughters appearing in London society that he had not even allowed any of them to have so much as a Season, but instead had kept them all secluded at his estate in Hampshire. Had ensured his daughters were so overprotected that Caro had never even been alone with a young gentleman until now.

Although that description was hardly appropriate in regard to the arrogant Dominic Vaughn; that scar upon his otherwise handsome face, and the mockery that glittered now in those narrowed silver-coloured eyes, proclaimed him to be a gentleman in possession of a cynicism and experience that far exceeded his calendar years...

'I believe it would not be merely my *company* that would be of interest in such an arrangement, my lord.' She arched pert blonde brows.

Dominic was beginning to wish that he had never broached this particular subject. Indeed, he had no idea why he was taking such an interest in the fate of this particular young woman. Perhaps his sense of chivalry was not as dead as he had believed it to be? 'Surely the attentions of one man would be preferable to being undressed, mentally at least, by dozens of men, night after night?' he bit out harshly.

Her gasp was audible. 'You are attempting to shock me, sir!'

Yes, he was. Deliberately. 'I am attempting to stress, madam, how foolishly you are behaving by repeatedly placing yourself in such a vulnerable position.'

Her eyes widened indignantly. 'I assure you, sir, I am perfectly capable of taking care of myself. I am in absolutely no danger—' Dominic put an end to this ridiculous claim by the simple act of pulling her effortlessly into his arms and taking masterful possession of the surprised parting of her lips.

He did it as a way of demonstrating the vulnerability of which he spoke. As a way of showing Caro how easily a man—any man—could take advantage of her delicacy. How the slenderness of her tiny body was no match for a man bent on stealing a kiss. Or worse!

He curved that willowy body against his much harder

one as he took possession of the softness of those parted lips. With deliberate sensuality, his tongue swept moistly across her bottom lip before exploring farther, his hands moving in a light caress down the slenderness of her back before cupping her bottom and pulling her even more firmly against him as that marauding tongue took possession of the hot cavern of her mouth. Thrusting. Jousting. Demanding her response.

Nothing in Caro's previous life, not the twenty years spent in seclusion in Hampshire, or these past two weeks in London, had prepared her for the rush of sensations that now assaulted her and caused her to cling to Dominic Vaughn's wide and powerful shoulders rather than faint at his feet.

She was suffused with a heart-pounding heat, accompanied by a wild, tingling that began in her breasts, causing them to swell beneath her gown and the tips to harden so that they felt uncomfortable and sensitised as they chafed against her shift, that heat centring, pooling between her thighs, in a way she had never imagined before let alone experienced. She—

'What ho, lads!'

'Don't keep her all to yourself, old chap!'

'Give us all a go!'

Caro found those hard lips removed from her own with a suddenness that made her gasp, the earl's hands hard about her waist as those silver-coloured eyes glittered down at her briefly before he put her firmly away from him. He turned and bent the fierceness of that gaze upon the three young gentlemen walking slightly unsteadily towards them.

Caro staggered slightly once released, knowing herself badly shaken by the searing intensity of Dominic Vaughn's kiss—a punishing, demanding assault upon her lips and senses that in no way resembled any of her previous youthful imaginings of what a kiss should be. There had been none of the gentleness she had expected. None of the shy thrill of emotions. Only that heart-pounding heat and the wild tingling in her breasts and thighs.

Emotions not reflected in the hard intensity of his lordship's expression as he signalled to his coachman and groom that he was as in control of this present situation as he had obviously been whilst kissing her!

The young gentlemen had come to an abrupt and wary halt as they suddenly found themselves the focus of Dominic's glittering silver gaze, the three of them backing up slightly at the chilling anger they obviously recognised in his expression, that savage slash of scar running the length of his left cheek adding to the impression of impending danger.

'We meant no offence, old chap,' the obvious ringleader of the trio offered in mumbled apology.

'A little too much to drink, I expect,' the second one excused nervously.

'We'll just be on our way.' The third member of the group grabbed a friend by each arm before turning and staggering back in the direction they had just come.

Leaving a still-trembling Caro to the far from tender mercies of Dominic Vaughn!

That trembling increased as he turned the focus of his glowering attention back on to her. 'I believe you were assuring me that you are perfectly capable of taking care of yourself and that you believe yourself to be in absolutely no danger from any man's unwanted attentions?'

Caro felt a shiver run the length of her spine as she

looked up into that harshly forbidding face; no wonder those three young gentlemen had decided that retreat was the best and safest course of action. She felt like retreating herself as she recalled how demanding and yet arousing that firmly sculptured mouth had felt against her own...

Her shoulders straightened determinedly. 'You kissed me deliberately, my lord, purely in an effort to demonstrate your superior strength over me.'

His nostrils flared as that silver gaze raked over her. 'In an effort to demonstrate how *any* man's strength would be superior to your own—even those three drunken young pups who just ran away with their tails between their legs.'

Caro raised a haughty brow. 'You exaggerate, sir—'

'On the contrary, Miss Morton,' he snapped coldly, 'I believe myself to be better acquainted than you with the lusts of my own sex.' His mouth twisted in distaste. 'And if I had not been here to protect you just now then I guarantee you would now find yourself in an alley somewhere with your skirts up about your waist whilst one of those young bucks rutted between your thighs and the other two awaited their turn!'

Caro felt herself pale and the nausea churn in her stomach at the vividness of the picture he painted. A vividness surely designed to shock and frighten her—and succeeding? Those three young gentlemen had obviously over-imbibed this evening, and were feeling more than a little playful, but surely they would not have behaved as shockingly as the earl suggested?

She looked at him in challenge. 'Then it is a pity that there was no one here to protect me from your own unwanted attentions, was it not?'

Dominic drew in a swift breath at the accusation. In

the circumstances, it was a perfectly justified accusation, he allowed fairly. He had meant only to teach a lesson, to demonstrate her vulnerability by taking advantage of her himself. Instead he had found he enjoyed the honeyed taste of her as he explored the heat of her mouth, as well as the feel of her slender curves pressed against his much harder ones. To the extent that he had taken the kiss far beyond what he had originally intended.

He straightened, the expression in his eyes now hidden behind hooded lids. 'I meant only to demonstrate how exposing yourself on a stage night after night has left you open to physical as well as verbal abuse.'

'You are being ridiculous,' she dismissed briskly. 'Neither am I a complete ninny. It was for the very reason of protecting my reputation that I donned the mask and wig at Nick's. Indeed, I doubt that anyone would ever recognise the woman I am now as the masked and ebony-haired woman who sings in a gambling club each evening.'

There was some truth in that; Dominic had barely recognised Caro himself when she had joined him earlier. Even so... 'The fact that you are masked, and your own blonde curls hidden beneath those false ebony tresses, would, I am afraid, only protect your identity as far as the bedroom.'

Her throat moved convulsively as she continued to look up at him proudly. 'My...identity?'

Dominic gave an exasperated sigh. 'Your voice and manner proclaim you as being a lady—'

'Or a disgraced lady's maid,' she put in quickly.

'Perhaps,' Dominic allowed tersely. 'I have no idea what your reasons are for taking the action you have—and I doubt you are about to enlighten me, are you?'

Her mouth firmed. 'No.'

'As I thought.' He gave an abrupt nod. 'Of course, the simplest answer to this predicament would be for me to simply terminate your employment. At least then I would not feel honour bound to take responsibility for your welfare.'

She gave an inelegant snort. 'That would only solve the problem for *you*, my lord; *I* would still need to find the means with which to earn my own living.'

She was right, Dominic allowed sourly. But there was another alternative... He could offer to become her protector himself—his enjoyment of their kiss earlier proved that his senses, at least, were not averse to the idea. And no doubt, with a little coaching as to his physical preferences, Caro would be more than capable of satisfying his needs.

But in the ten years since Dominic had first appeared in town he had never once taken a permanent mistress, as many of his male acquaintances chose to do, preferring instead to take his pleasures whenever and with what women he pleased. He had no wish to change that arrangement by making the spirited and outspoken Caro Morton his mistress.

'Of course, if you were to decide to terminate my employment then you would leave me with no choice but to seek the same position elsewhere.' She shrugged those slender shoulders. 'Something that should not prove too difficult now that the masked lady has, as you say, gained something of a...male following,' she added.

It was a solution, of course. Except at Nick's, whether the chit was aware of it or not, Caro at least had the protection of the attentive Drew and Ben. And, apparently, now Dominic himself. 'If it is only question of money—'

'And if it were?' Caro had immediately bristled haughtily.

His mouth thinned. 'In those circumstances I might perhaps see my way clear to advancing you sufficient funds to take you back to wherever it is you originate from.'

'No!' Those sea-green eyes sparkled up at him rebelliously. 'I have no intention of leaving London yet.'

Dominic was unsure as to whether Caro's vehemence was due to his offer to advance her money, or his suggestion that she use that money to take herself home, so he decided to probe further. 'Is the situation at home so intolerable, then?'

She attempted to repress a shudder and failed. 'At present, yes.'

Dominic studied her through narrowed lids, noting the shadows that had appeared in those sea-green eyes, and the pallor of her cheeks. 'That remark would seem to imply that the situation may change some time in the future?'

'It is to be hoped so, yes,' she confirmed with feeling.

'But until it does, it is your intention to remain in London, whether or not I continue to employ you at Nick's?'

Her mouth set firmly. 'It is.'

'You are very stubborn, madam.'

'I am decisive, sir, which is completely different.'

Dominic sighed heavily, not wishing to send Caro back to a situation she obviously found so unpleasant, but also well able to imagine the scrapes this reckless young woman would get herself into, if she were once again let loose to roam the streets of London seeking employment. 'Then I believe, for the moment, we must leave things as they are.' He looked away. 'Shall we continue to walk to your lodgings?'

Caro shot him a triumphant glance. 'We have been standing outside them for some minutes, my lord!'

Dominic gave her an irritated scowl before glancing at the house behind them. It was a three-storied building so typical of an area that had once been fashionable, but which was no longer so, and as such had fallen into genteel decay. Although the owner of this particular lodging had at least attempted to keep up a veneer of respectability, the outside being neat and cared for, and the curtains at the windows also appearing clean.

He turned back to Caro. 'In that case it remains only for me to bid you goodnight.'

She gave an abrupt curtsy. 'My lord.'

'Miss Morton.' He nodded curtly.

Caro gazed up at Dominic quizzically as he made no move to depart for his waiting carriage. 'There is no need for you to wait to leave until you are assured I have entered the house, my lord.'

He raised an eyebrow. 'In the same way you were in "absolutely no danger" earlier on?'

Her cheeks coloured prettily. 'I find your manner extremely vexing, my lord!'

'No more so than I do your own, I assure you, Miss Morton.'

Caro had never before met anyone remotely like Dominic Vaughn. Had never dreamed that men like him existed, so tall and fashionably handsome, so aristocratic. So arrogantly sure of themselves!

Admittedly her contact with male acquaintances had been severely limited before she came to London, usually only consisting of the few sons of the local gentry, and occasionally her father's lawyer when he came from London to discuss business matters.

Even so, Caro knew from Drew Butler's respectful attitude towards the earl earlier this evening, and the hasty departure of those three young gentlemen just minutes ago, that Dominic Vaughn was a man whose very presence demanded respect and obedience.

Except, after years of having no choice but to do as she was told, Caro no longer wished to obey any man. Not least of all the guardian she had so recently acquired…

She flashed the earl a bright meaningless smile before turning to walk to the front door of her lodgings, not even glancing back to see if he still watched as she quietly let herself inside with the key the landlady had provided for Caro's personal use when she had taken the rooms two weeks ago.

She waited several heartbeats before daring to look out through the lace-covered window beside the front door. Just in time to see the earl climbing inside his carriage before the groom closed the door behind him and hopped neatly on to the back of the vehicle as it was driven away.

But before it did so Caro saw the pale oval of Dominic Vaughn's grimly set face at the carriage window as he glanced towards where she stood hidden. She moved away quickly to lean back against the wall, her hands clutched against her rapidly beating heart.

No, being kissed by the Earl of Blackstone had been nothing at all as she imagined a kiss would be.

It had been far, far more exciting…

'So, where did you get to last night, Dom?' Nathaniel Thorne, Earl of Osbourne, prompted lazily the following evening, the two men lounging in opposite wingchairs beside the fireplace in one of the larger rooms at White's.

'I was…unavoidably detained.' Dominic evaded answering his friend's query directly. The two men had arranged to meet late the previous evening, an appointment Dominic obviously had not kept as he had instead been occupied with seeing Caro Morton safely delivered back to her lodgings. For all the thanks he had received for his trouble!

Nathaniel raised a blond brow. 'I trust she was as insatiable as she was beautiful?'

'Beautiful—yes. Insatiable? I have no idea.' In truth, hours later, Dominic still had no idea what to make of Caro Morton, of who and what she was. He had taken the trouble, however, to send word to Drew Butler to continue feeding her, as well as arranging for Ben Jackson to escort her home at the end of each night's work; Caro might have no care for her own welfare, but whilst she continued working for Dominic, he had every intention of ensuring that no harm befell her.

'Yet,' Nathaniel drawled knowingly.

Both of Dominic's parents had died years ago, and he had no siblings, either, making Nathaniel Thorne and Gabriel Faulkner the closest thing he had to a family; the years they had all spent at school together, and then in the army, never knowing whether they would survive the next battle, had made them as close as brothers. Even so, Dominic could have wished at that moment that Nathaniel did not know him quite as well as he did.

Thankfully he had the perfect diversion from his lack of appearance the night before. 'I received a note from Gabriel today. He expects to arrive in England by the end of the week.' He lifted his glass of brandy and took an appreciative sip.

'I received one, too,' Nathaniel revealed. 'Can you imagine the looks on the faces of the *ton* when Gabe makes his entrance back into society?'

'He reaffirmed it was his intention to first go to Shoreley Park and confront the Copeland sisters,' Dominic reminded him.

Osbourne snorted. 'We both know that will only take two minutes of his time. By the time Gabriel returns to town, past scandal or not, I have no doubt that all three of the silly chits will be clamouring to marry him!' Nathaniel made a silent toast of appreciation to their absent friend.

It was a fact that Gabriel's years of banishment to the Continent and the army had in no way affected his conquests in the bedchamber; one look at that raven-black hair, those dark indigo eyes and his firmly muscled physique, and women of all ages simply dropped at Gabriel's feet. Or, more accurately, into his bed! No doubt the Copeland sisters would find themselves equally as smitten.

'What shall we do with the rest of the night?' After the dissatisfaction he had felt at the end of the previous evening, Dominic knew himself to be in the mood to drink too much before falling into bed with a woman who was as inventive as she was willing.

Nathaniel eyed him speculatively. 'I have heard that there is a mysterious beauty currently performing at Nick's...'

As close as the three men were, Dominic knew that some things were best kept to oneself—and his meeting with Caro Morton the previous night, his uncharacteristic, unfathomable sense of protectiveness where she was concerned, was certainly one of them! Although Dominic could not say that he was at all pleased that she was already so great a source of gossip at the gentlemen's clubs after only a week of appearing at his.

He grimaced. 'I believe the only reason she is considered such a mystery is because she wears a jewelled mask whilst performing.'

'Oh.' The other man's mouth turned down. 'No doubt to hide the fact that she's scarred from the pox.'

'Possibly,' Dominic dismissed in a bored voice, having no intention of saying anything that would increase his friend's curiosity where Caro was concerned.

Nate sighed. 'In which case, I believe I will leave the choice of tonight's entertainment to you.'

That choice involved visiting several gambling clubs before ending the evening at the brightly lit but nevertheless discreet house where several beautiful and accomplished ladies of the *demi-monde* made it only too obvious they would be pleased to offer amusement and companionship to two such handsome young gentlemen.

So it was all the more surprising when those same two gentlemen took their leave only an hour or so later, neither having taken advantage of that willingness. 'Perhaps we should have gone to view the mysterious beauty at Nick's, after all.' Osbourne repressed a bored yawn. 'Scarred from the pox or not, I doubt I could find her any less appealing than the ladies we have just wasted our time with!'

Dominic frowned, knowing that to demur a second time would definitely incur Nate's curiosity. 'Perhaps we are becoming too jaded in our tastes, Nate?' he murmured drily as he tapped on the roof of the carriage and gave his driver fresh instructions.

The other man raised a questioning brow. 'Do you ever miss the excitement of our five years in the army?'

Did Dominic miss the horror and the bloodshed of war? The never knowing whether he would survive the next battle or if it was his turn to meet death at the end of a French sword? The comradeship with his fellow officers that arose from experiencing that very danger? He missed it like the very devil!

'Not to the point of wanting to renew my commission, no. You?'

Osbourne shrugged. 'It is a fact that civilian life can be tedious as well as damned repetitious.'

Dominic felt relieved to know that he was not the only one to miss those years of feeling as if one walked constantly on the knife edge of danger. 'I am told that participating in a London Season often resembles a battlefield,' he mused.

'Do not even mention the Season to me,' the other man groaned. 'My Aunt Gertrude has taken it into her head that it is high time I took myself a wife,' he explained at Dominic's questioning look. 'As such she is insisting that I escort her to several balls and soirées during the next few weeks. No doubt with the expectation of finding a young woman she believes will make me a suitable Countess.'

'Ah.' Dominic began to understand his friend's restlessness this evening; Mrs Gertrude Wilson was Osbourne's closest relative, and one, moreover, of whom he was extremely fond. She reciprocated by taking a great interest in her nephew's life. To the point, it seemed, that she was now attempting to find him a wife. Reason enough for Dominic to be grateful for his own lack of female relations! 'I take it that you are not in agreement with her wishes?'

'In agreement with the idea of shackling myself for life to some mealy-mouthed chit who has no doubt been taught to lie back and think of king and country when we are in bed together? Certainly not!' Osbourne barely suppressed his shiver of revulsion. 'I cannot think what Gabriel is about even contemplating such a fate.'

It was a fact that all three gentlemen would one day have to take a wife and produce the necessary heir to their respective earldoms. Fortunately, it seemed that Osbourne, at least, was as averse to accepting that fate as Dominic was. Although there was no doubting that Mrs Gertrude Wilson was a force to be reckoned with!

Dominic's humour at his friend's situation faded, his mouth tightening in disapproval, as the two gentlemen stepped down from his carriage minutes later and he saw that Ben Jackson was once again absent from his position at the entrance to Nick's; obviously they had arrived in time for Nathaniel to witness Caro Morton's second performance of the evening.

However, the sound of shouting, breaking glass and the crashing of furniture coming from the direction of the main gaming room as they stepped into the spacious hallway of the club in no way resembled the awed silence Dominic had experienced on his arrival the previous evening.

Especially when it was accompanied by the sound of a woman's screams!

Chapter Three

Caro had never been as frightened in her life as she was at that moment. Even with Ben and two other men standing protectively in front of her, and keeping the worst of the fighting at bay, it was still possible for her to see men's fists flying, the blood freely flowing from noses and cut faces as chairs, tables and bottles were also brought into play.

In truth, she had no idea how the fighting had even begun. One moment she had been singing as usual, and the next a gentleman had tried to step on to the stage and grab hold of her. At first Caro had believed the second gentleman to step forwards was attempting to come to her aid, until he pushed the first man aside and also lunged towards where she had half-risen from the *chaise* in alarm.

After that all bedlam had broken loose, it seemed, with a dozen or more men fighting off the first two with fists and any item of furniture that came readily to hand.

And through it all, every terrifying moment of it, Caro

had been humiliatingly aware of Lord Dominic Vaughn's dire warnings of the night before...

'Care to join in?' Osbourne invited with glee as the two men stood in the doorway of the gaming room still hatted and cloaked.

Dominic's narrowed gaze had taken stock of the situation at a glance. Thirty or so gentlemen fighting in earnest. Several of the brocade-covered chairs broken. Tables overturned, and shattered glasses and bottles crunching underfoot. Drew Butler was caught in the middle of it all as he tried to call a halt to the fighting. And on the raised stage, Ben Jackson stood immovable in front of where a head of ebony curls was just visible above and behind the *chaise*.

'Head towards the stage,' Dominic directed Osbourne grimly as he threw his hat aside. 'If we can get the girl out of here, I believe the fighting will come to an end.'

'I sincerely hope it does not!' Nathaniel grinned roguishly as he stepped purposefully into the mêlée.

Most of the gentlemen fighting seemed to be enjoying themselves as much as Osbourne, despite having bloody noses, the occasional lost tooth and several eyes that would no doubt be black come morning. It was the three or four gentlemen closest to Ben Jackson, and their dogged determination to lay hands on Caro as she crouched down behind the *chaise*, that concerned Dominic the most. Although to give Ben his due, he had so far managed to keep them all at arm's length, and even managed to shoot Dominic and Osbourne an appreciative grin as they stepped up beside him.

At which point Caro Morton emerged from behind the

chaise and launched herself into his arms. 'Thank goodness you are come, Dominic!'

Osborne grinned knowingly at the spectacle. 'You take the girl, Dom; this is the most fun I've had in years!' He swung a fist and knocked one of the men from the stage with a telling crunch of flesh against teeth.

At that moment Dominic was so angry that he wanted nothing more than to break a few bones for himself. A satisfaction he knew he would have to forgo as Caro's arms tightened about his neck, a pair of widely terrified sea-green eyes visible through the slits in the jewelled mask as she looked up at him.

Dominic's gaze darkened as he saw that her gold gown was ripped in several places. 'Did I not warn you?' Dominic's voice was chilling as he pulled her arms from about his neck and swung off his cloak to cover her in it before bending down to place his arm at the back of her knees and toss her up on to his shoulder as he straightened.

'I— What— Put me down this instant!' Tiny fists pummelled against his back.

'I believe now would be as good a time as any for you to learn when it is wiser to remain silent,' Dominic rasped grimly as several male heads turned his way to watch jealously as he carried her from the stage and out to the private area at the back of the club.

The last thing that Caro had needed in the midst of that nightmare was for Lord Dominic Vaughn to tell her 'I told you so'. She had already been terrified enough for one evening without the added humiliation of being thrown over this man's shoulder as if she were no more than a sack of potatoes or a bail of straw on her father's estate!

Caro struggled to be released as soon as they reached the relative safety of the deserted hallway. 'You will put me down this instant!' she instructed furiously as her struggles resulted only in her becoming even more hot and bad-tempered.

'Gladly.' Dominic slid her unceremoniously down the hard length of his body before lowering her bare feet on to the cold stone floor.

'I do not believe I have ever met a man more ill mannered than you!' Caro looked up at him accusingly even as her flustered fingers tried to secure the engulfing cloak about her shoulders and hold the soft silk folds about her trembling body.

'After I have tried to save you from harm?' His voice was silky soft as those silver eyes glittered down at her in warning.

'After you have manhandled me, sir!' Caro was unrepentant as she tried to bring some semblance of order to the tangled ebony curls, all the time marvelling at how the jewelled mask and ebony wig had managed to stay in place at all. 'Your own anger a few minutes ago seemed to imply that you believe *I* am to blame for what just took place—'

'You *are* to blame.'

'Do not be ridiculous!' Caro gave him a scornful glance. 'Every woman knows that men—even so-called gentlemen—will find any excuse to fight.'

She might very well be in the right of it there, Dominic acknowledged as he remembered Osbourne's glee before he launched himself into the midst of the fighting. But that did not change the fact that this particular fight had broken out because Caro had refused to see the danger of flaunting herself night after night before a roomful of intoxicated men.

As it was, Dominic had no idea whether to beat her or kiss her senseless for her naïvety. 'I have a good mind to take out the cost of this evening's damages on your backside!' he grated instead.

Her eyes widened and her cheeks flushed a fiery red even as her chin rose in challenge. 'You would not dare!'

Dominic gave a disgusted snort. 'Do not tempt me, Caro.'

Caro gave up all attempt to bring order to those loosely flowing locks and instead removed the jewelled mask in order to glare at him. 'I believe you are just looking for an excuse to beat me.'

Dominic stilled, his gaze narrowing searchingly on her angrily defiant face. Just the thought of some nameless, faceless man ever laying hands on this delicately lovely woman in anger was enough to rouse Dominic's own fury. Yet at this particular moment in time, he totally understood the impulse; he badly wanted to tan Caro's backside so hard that she would not be able to sit down for a week! 'I assure you, where you are concerned, no excuse is necessary,' he growled.

'Oh!' she gasped her indignation. 'You, sir, are the most overbearing, arrogant, insulting man it has ever been my misfortune to meet!'

'And you, madam, are the most stubborn, wilfully stupid—'

'*Stupid?*' she echoed furiously.

'*Wilfully* stupid,' Dominic repeated unrepentantly as he glared back at her.

Caro had never been so incensed. Never felt so much like punching a man on his arrogant, aristocratic nose!

As if aware of the violence of her thoughts those sculptured lips turned up into a mocking smile. 'It would be most unwise, Caro.' His warning was silkily soft and all the more dangerous because of it.

Sea-green eyes clashed with silver for long, challenging moments. A challenge she was almost—almost!—feeling brave enough to accept when an amused voice broke into the tension. 'I came to tell you that Butler and his heavies have thrown out the last of the patrons and are now attempting to clean up the mess, but I can come back later if now is not a convenient time...?'

Dominic was standing directly in Caro's line of vision and she had to lean to one side to see around him to where a tall, elegantly dressed man leant casually against the wall of the hallway. His arms were folded across the width of his chest as he watched them with interest, only the ruffled disarray of his blond and fashionably long hair about the handsomeness of his face to show that he had only moments ago been caught up in the thick of the fighting.

'I believe our earlier assessment of the...situation to have been at fault, Blackstone.' The other man gave Dominic an appreciative smile before turning his dark gaze back to pointedly roam over the unblemished, obviously pox-free skin of Caro's beautiful face.

It was a remark she did not even begin to understand, let alone why he was looking at her so intently! 'To answer your earlier question, sir—I believe Lord Vaughn and I have finished our conversation.'

'Not by a long way.' One of Dominic's hands reached out, the fingers curling about Caro's wrist like a band of steel, as she would have brushed past him. 'I trust not too many heads were broken, Osbourne?'

The blond-haired man shrugged. 'None that did not deserve it.' He straightened away from the wall. 'Care to introduce me, Blackstone?' A merry brown gaze briefly met his friend's before he looked at Caro with open admiration.

'Caro Morton, Lord Nathaniel Thorne, Earl of Osbourne,' Dominic said coldly.

'Your servant, ma'am.' Lord Thorne gave an elegant bow.

'My lord.' Really, did every man she met in London have to be a lord and an earl? she wondered crossly as she pondered the ridiculousness of formally curtsying to a gentleman under such circumstances.

'If you were thinking of leaving too now all the excitement is over, Osbourne, then by all means do so,' Dominic said. 'I fear I will not be free to leave for some time yet.'

His gaze hardened as he glanced down pointedly at Caro Morton, his mouth thinning as those sea-green eyes once more stared back at him in silent rebellion.

She broke that gaze to turn and smile graciously at the other man. 'Perhaps, if you are leaving, I might prevail on you to take me with you, Lord Thorne?'

To all intents and purposes, Dominic recognised impatiently, as if she were a lady making conversation in her drawing room! As if a fight had not just broken out over who was to share her bed tonight. As if Dominic's own property had not been destroyed in that mêlée.

As if she were not standing before two elegant gentlemen of the *ton* dressed only in a ripped gown, and with her ebony wig slightly askew!

Dominic gave a frustrated sigh. 'I think not.'

Those sea-green eyes flashed up at him with annoyance

before Caro ignored him to turn once again to Nathaniel. 'I would very much appreciate it if you would agree to escort me home, Lord Thorne.' A siren could not have sounded or looked any more sweetly persuasive!

Dominic easily read the uncertainty in his friend's expression; a gentleman through and through, Osbourne never had been able to resist the appeal of a seeming damsel in distress. Seeming, in Dominic's estimation, being a correct assessment in regard to Caro Morton. The woman was an absolute menace and had become a veritable thorn in Dominic's side since the moment he'd set eyes upon her.

'I am afraid that is not possible,' Dominic answered smoothly on the other man's behalf.

Those delicate cheeks flushed red. 'I believe my request was made to Lord Thorne and not to *you*!'

Dominic allowed some of the tension to ease from his shoulders, aware that he had been in one state of tension or another since first meeting her. 'Lord Thorne is gentleman enough, however, to accept a prior claim, are you not, Osbourne?'

Osbourne's eyes widened. As well they might, damn it; Dominic had as good as denied all knowledge of this woman earlier tonight, a denial that had been made a complete nonsense of the moment Caro had launched herself into his arms and, in her agitation, called him by his given name.

Hell and damnation!

'I believe you were quite correct in your assertion earlier, Blackstone,' Osbourne's drawled comment interrupted Dominic's displeasing thoughts. 'Personally I would say exquisite rather than beautiful!'

Dominic nodded irritably. 'Just so.'

'That being the case, Blackstone, I believe I will join Butler and Ben and enjoy a reviving brandy before I leave. My respects, Miss Morton.' Osbourne gave a lazy inclination of his head before leaving the two of them alone.

Caro blinked at the suddenness of Lord Thorne's departure. 'I do not understand.' Neither did she have any idea what tacit agreement had passed between the two men in the last few moments. But something most certainly had for the gentlemanly Lord Thorne to have just abandoned her like that.

Dominic released her wrist before stepping away from her. 'You should go to your room now and change. I will be waiting in Drew Butler's office when you are ready to leave.'

Caro frowned. 'But—'

'Could you, for once, just do as I ask without argument, Caro?' The scar on Dominic's cheek showed in stark relief against his clenched jaw.

She looked up into that ruthlessly hard face, repressing a shiver of apprehension as she saw the dangerous glitter in those pale silver eyes. Of course—this man had already told her that he held her responsible for the occurrence of the fight and the damages to his property, and he had also threatened to take out the cost of those damages on her backside!

Never, in all of her twenty years, had Caro been spoken to in the way the arrogant Dominic Vaughn spoke to her. So familiarly. So—so…intimately. A gentleman should not even refer to a lady's bottom, let alone threaten to inflict harm upon it!

Her chin rose haughtily. 'I am very tired, my lord, and would prefer to go straight home once I am dressed.'

'And I would prefer that you join me in Butler's office first so that we might continue our conversation.'

'I had thought it finished.'

'Caro, I have already been involved in a brawl not of my making, and my property has been extensively damaged. As such, I am really in no mood to tolerate any more of your stubbornness this evening.' His hands had clenched at his sides in an effort to control his exasperation.

'Really?' She arched innocent brows. 'My own patience with your impossible arrogance ended some minutes ago.'

Yes, Dominic acknowledged ruefully, this young woman was undoubtedly as feisty as she was beautiful. To his own annoyance, he had also spent far too much time today allowing his thoughts to dwell on how delicious Caro's mouth had tasted beneath his the night before.

'Would you be any more amenable to the suggestion if I were to say please?'

She eyed him warily, distrustfully. 'It would be a start, certainly.'

He regarded her for several seconds before nodding. 'Very well. I insist that you join me in Butler's office shortly so that we might continue this conversation. Please.'

A second request that was intended to be no more gracious than the first! 'Then I agree to join you in Mr Butler's office shortly, my lord. But only for a few minutes,' Caro added firmly as she saw the glitter of triumph that lit those pale silver eyes. 'It is late and I really am very tired.'

'Understandably.' He gave a mocking bow. 'I will only require a few more minutes of your time this evening.'

That last remark almost had the tone of a threat, Caro

realised worriedly as she made her way slowly to her dressing-room to change. And for all that she had so defiantly
told Dominic Vaughn the previous evening that she would
simply seek employment elsewhere if he chose to dismiss
her, after this evening's disaster she could not even bear
the thought of remaining in London without the protection
of Drew and Ben.

She had been completely truthful the evening before
when she'd assured Dominic that she had every intention
of returning home as soon as she felt it was safe for her to
do so. Unfortunately, Caro did not believe that time had
come quite yet…

Dominic made no attempt to hide his pained wince as
he looked at the dull green gown Caro was wearing when
she joined him in Drew's office some minutes later; it was
neither that intriguing sea-green of her eyes, or of a style
in the least complimentary to her graceful slenderness.
Rather, that unbecoming colour dulled the brightness of
her eyes to the same unattractive green, and gave the pale
translucence of her skin an almost sallow look. The fact
that the gown was also buttoned up to her throat, and her
blonde curls pulled tightly back into a bun at her nape as
she stood before the desk with her hands demurely folded
together, gave her the all appearance and appeal of a nun.

Dominic stood up and stepped lithely around the desk
before leaning back against it as he continued to regard
her critically. 'You appear none the worse for your ordeal.'

Then her appearance was deceptive, Caro acknowledged
with an inner tremor. Reaction to the horrors of this evening's fighting had begun in earnest once she had reached
the safety and peace of her dressing-room, to the extent

that she had not been able to stop herself trembling for some time. It had all happened so suddenly, so violently, and the earl's rescue effected so efficiently—if high-handedly—that at the time, Caro had not had opportunity to think beyond that.

She was still shaking slightly now, and it was the reason her hands were clasped so tightly together in front of her; she would not, for any reason, show the arrogant Dominic Vaughn any sign of weakness. 'I did not have opportunity to thank you earlier, my lord, for your timely intervention. I do so now.' She gave a stiff inclination of her head.

Dominic barely repressed his smile at this show of grudging gratitude. 'You are welcome, I am sure,' he replied. 'Obviously it is going to take several days, possibly a week, to effect the repairs to the main salon—'

'I have no money to spare to pay for those repairs, if that is to be your next suggestion,' she instantly protested.

Dominic looked at her from underneath lowered lids, seeing beyond that defiant and nunlike appearance to the young woman beneath. Those sea-green eyes were still slightly shadowed, her cheeks pale, her hands slightly trembling, all of those things evidence that Caro had been more disturbed by the violence she had witnessed earlier than she wished anyone—very likely most especially him—to be aware of.

He found that he admired that quality in her. Just as he admired her pride and the dignity she'd shown when faced with a situation so obviously beyond her previous experience.

Did that inexperience extend to the bedchamber? he could not help but wonder. After her initial surprise the previous evening, she had most definitely returned the passion of his kiss. But then afterwards she had appeared completely unaware of the danger those three young bucks had represented to her welfare.

Just as she had seemed innocent of the rising lusts of the men who returned night after night to watch her performance at Nick's. Perhaps an indication that she was inexperienced to the vagaries of men, at least?

Caro Morton was fast becoming a puzzle that Dominic found himself wishing to unravel. Almost as much, he realised with an inward wince, as he wished to peel her out of that unbecoming green gown before exploring every inch of her delectably naked body...

'It was not,' he answered. 'I was merely pointing out that Nick's will probably have to be closed for several days whilst repairs and other refurbishments are carried out. A closure that will obviously result in your being unable to perform here for the same amount of time.'

She looked at him blankly for several moments, and then her eyes widened as the full import of what he was saying became clear to her. She licked suddenly dry lips. 'But you believe it will only be for a few days?'

Dominic studied her closely. 'Possibly a week.'

'A week?' Her echo was distraught.

Alerting him to the fact that she was in all probability completely financially reliant upon the money she earned each night at the gambling club—her clothes certainly indicated as much! It also proved, along with her determination to remain in London 'for the present', that her situation at home must be dire indeed... 'There is no reason for you to look so concerned, Caro,' he assured her. 'Whether you wish it or not, for the moment, it would appear you are now under my protection.'

Her eyes went wide with indignation. 'I have absolutely *no* intention of becoming your mistress!'

Any more than it was Dominic's wish to take her—or any other woman—as his mistress...

His parents had both died when he was but twelve years old. Neither had there been any kindly aunt to take an interest in him as there had with Nathaniel. Instead Dominic's guardianship had been placed in the hands of his father's firm of lawyers until he came of age at twenty-one. During those intervening years, when he was not away at school, Dominic had lived alone at Blackstone Park in Berkshire, cared for only by the impersonal kindness of servants.

It would have been all too easy once he reached his majority, and was at last allowed to manage his own affairs, to have been drawn into the false warmth of affection given by a paid mistress. Instead, he had been content with the friendship he'd received from and felt for both Gabriel and Nathaniel. He knew their affection for him, at least, to be without ulterior motive. The same could not be said of a mistress.

'I said protector, Caro, not lover. Although I am sure that most of the gentlemen here tonight now believe me to already have that dubious honour,' he pointed out.

She stiffened at the insult in his tone. 'How so?'

'Several of them witnessed you throwing yourself into my arms earlier—'

'I was in fear of my life!' Two indignant spots of colour had appeared in the pallor of her cheeks.

Dominic waved a dismissive hand. 'The why of it is not important. The facts are that a masked lady is employed at my gambling club, and tonight that lady threw herself into my arms with a familiarity that was only confirmed when she called out my name for all to hear.' He shrugged. 'Those things are enough for most men to have come to the conclusion that the lady has decided on her protector. That she is now, in all probability, the exclusive property of the Earl of Blackstone.'

If it were possible, Caro's cheeks became even paler!

Chapter Four

For possibly the first time in her life, Caro was rendered bereft of speech. Not only was it perfectly shocking that many of the male members of society believed her to be the exclusive property of Lord Dominic Vaughn, but her older sister, Diana, would be incensed if such a falsehood were ever related to her in connection with her runaway sister, Caroline!

Caro had left a note on her bed telling her sisters not to worry about her, of course, but other than that she had not confided her plan of going to London to either Diana or her younger sister, Elizabeth, before fleeing the family home in Hampshire two weeks ago, before their guardian could arrive to take control of all their lives. A man none of the Copeland sisters had met before, but who had nevertheless chosen to inform them, through his lawyer, that he believed himself to be in a position to insist that one of them become his wife!

What sort of man did that? Caro had questioned in

outraged disbelief. How monstrous could Lord Gabriel Faulkner, the new Earl of Westbourne, be that he sent his lawyer in his stead to offer marriage to whichever of the previous earl's daughters was willing to accept him? And if none chose willingly, to *insist* upon it!

Never having been allowed to mix with London society, none of the Copeland sisters had any previous knowledge of their father's heir and second cousin, Lord Gabriel Faulkner. But several of their close neighbours had, and they were only too happy to regale the sisters with the knowledge—if not the details—of his lordship's banishment to the Continent eight years previously following a tremendous scandal, with talk of his having settled in Venice some years later. Other than that, none of the sisters had ever heard or seen anything of the man before being informed that not only was he their father's heir, but also their guardian.

They had all known and accepted that a daughter could not inherit the title, of course, but it was only when their father's will was read out after his funeral that the three sisters learnt they were also completely without finances of their own, and as such their futures were completely dependent upon the whim and mercy of the new Earl of Westbourne.

But as the weeks, and then months, passed, with no sign of the new earl arriving to take possession of either the Shoreley Hall estate, or to establish any guardianship over the three sisters other than the allowance sent to them by the man's lawyer each month, they had begun to relax, to believe that their lives could continue without interference from their new guardian.

Until, that is, the earl's lawyer had arrived at Shoreley

Hall three weeks ago to inform them that the new Earl of Westbourne was very generously prepared to offer marriage to one of the penniless sisters. An offer, the lawyer had informed them sternly, that as their guardian, the earl could insist—and indeed, would insist—that one of them accept.

Diana, the eldest at one and twenty, was half-promised to the son of the local squire and so was safest from the earl's attentions. Elizabeth, only nineteen and the youngest of the three, had nevertheless declared she would throw herself on the mercy of a convent before she would marry a man she did not love and who did not love her. Caro's plan to avoid marrying the earl had been even more daring.

Desperate to bring some adventure into her so far humdrum existence, Caro had decided she would go to London for a month, perhaps two, and seek obscurity as a lady's companion or governess. And when Lord Gabriel Faulkner arrived in England—as his lawyer had assured them he undoubtedly would once informed of their refusal of his offer—then Diana, incensed by the disappearance of one of her sisters, would reduce the man to a quivering pulp with the cutting edge of her legendary acerbic tongue, before sending him away with his cowed tail tucked between his legs.

A month spent in London, possibly two, should do it, Caro had decided as she excitedly packed her bag before creeping stealthily from the house to walk the half a mile or so to the crossroads where she could catch the evening coach to London.

None of Caro's plans had worked out at she had expected, of course. No respectable household would employ a young woman without references, nor the dress shops, either, and the small amount of money Caro had brought with her had been seriously depleted, as instead of being taken into the warmth and security of the respectable household of her imaginings, she was forced to pay a month in advance for her modest lodgings.

In fact, until Drew Butler had taken pity on her, allowing her to sing at Nick's, Caro had feared she would have to return home with her own tail between her legs, before the earl had even arrived in England, let alone been sent on his way by the indomitable Diana!

Dominic had been watching Caro's expressive face with interest as he wondered what her thoughts had been for the past few minutes. 'You know, you could simply put an end to all this nonsense by returning from whence you came,' he said persuasively.

A shutter came down over that previously candid sea-green gaze, once again alerting Dominic to Caro's definite aversion—maybe even fear?—of returning to her previous life. Once again he wondered what, or who, this beautiful young woman was running away from.

And what possible business was it of his? Dominic instantly rebuked himself. None whatsoever. And yet he could not quite bring himself to insist that Caro must go home and face whatever punishment she had coming to her for having run away in the first place.

What if it were that bullying father she was running away from? Or the brutish husband? Either of whom would completely crush the spirit in Caro that Dominic found so intriguing...

She shook her head. 'I am afraid that returning to my home is not an option at this point in time, my lord.'

He raised dark brows. 'So you have already informed me. And between times, is it your intention to continue turning my hair prematurely grey as I worry in what scrape you will next embroil yourself?'

'I do not see a single grey hair amongst the black as yet, my lord.' Amusement glittered in those sea-green eyes as she glanced at those dark locks.

'I fear it is only a matter of time.' Dominic pulled a rueful face, only to then find himself totally enchanted as she laughed huskily at this nonsense. He realised, somewhat to his dismay, that he was as seriously in danger of falling under this woman's spell as Butler and Ben—and possibly Osborne—so obviously were.

It was a spell Dominic had no intention of succumbing to. Bedding a woman was one thing; allowing his emotions to become engaged by one was something else entirely. It was about time he changed his tactics; if he couldn't persuade Caro to leave London by simply asking her, he would have to try a more direct approach...

Caro took an involuntary step back, her eyes widening warily, as Dominic rose slowly to his feet, his movements almost predatory as he moved around the desk to cross over to the door and slowly turn the key in the lock.

'So that we are not disturbed,' he murmured as he moved so that he now stood only inches away from her.

She moistened suddenly dry lips as she tilted her head back so that she might look up, fearlessly, she hoped, into that arrogantly handsome face. 'It is time I was leaving—'

'Not quite yet, Caro,' the earl murmured huskily as one of his hands moved up to cup the side of her face and the soft pad of his thumb moved across the pouting swell of her bottom lip.

'I— What are you doing, my lord?'

'You called me Dominic earlier,' he reminded her huskily.

Caro's throat moved convulsively as she swallowed. 'What are you doing, Dominic?' she repeated breathlessly.

He shrugged those broad shoulders. 'Endeavouring, I hope, to show you there could be certain…benefits to becoming my mistress.'

Caro's knees felt weak just at the thought of what method this man intended using to demonstrate those 'benefits'. She so easily recalled the feel of that hard and uncompromising mouth against her own the night before, the feel of his hands as they ran the length of her spine to cup her bottom and press the hardness of his body intimately into hers. 'This is most unwise, my lord.'

He made no answer as he moved to rest back against the edge of the desk, taking her with him, those strange, silver-coloured eyes fixed caressingly upon Caro's slightly parted lips, the warmth of his breath stirring the tendrils of hair at her temples.

Dominic was standing much too close to her. So close that she could feel the heat of his body. So close that she was aware of the way that he smelt; the delicate spice of his cologne, and a purely male smell, one that appeared to be a combination of a clean male body and musky heat, uniquely his own.

Caro made every effort to gather her scattered senses. 'Dominic, I have no intention of allowing you to—oh!' she gasped as he encircled her waist and pulled her in between his parted legs, her thighs now pressed against him, as her breasts were crushed against the firm muscles of his chest.

She placed her hands upon his shoulders with the intention of pushing him away.

'I think not,' Dominic murmured as he realised her intention, his arms moving about her waist to hold her more tightly against him, quelling her struggles as he looked to where her hair was secured in that unbecoming nunlike bun. 'Remove the pins from your hair for me, Caro.'

She stilled abruptly. 'No!'

'Would you rather that I did it?' He quirked dark brows.

'I would rather my hair remain exactly—oh!' She gave another of those breathless gasps as Dominic reached up and removed the pins himself. It was a breathless gasp that he found he was becoming extremely fond of hearing.

'Better.' He nodded his approval as he reached up to uncoil her hair and allow it to cascade in a wealth of golden curls over her shoulders and down the length of her spine. 'Now for the buttons on this awful gown—'

'I cannot possibly allow you to unbutton the front of my gown!' Caro's fingers clamped down over his, even as she glared up at him.

Dominic found himself smiling in the face of this display of female outrage. 'It has all the allure of a nun's habit,' he said drily.

'That is exactly what it is supposed to—' Caro broke off the protest as she saw the way those silver eyes had narrowed to shrewdness.

'Do…?' Dominic finished softly for her. 'As no doubt the wearing of that unbecoming bonnet was designed to hide every delicious golden curl upon your head?'

'Yes,' she admitted.

He shook his head as he resumed unfastening the buttons on the front of her gown. 'It is a sacrilege, Caro, and one I am not inclined to indulge.' He folded back the two sides of her gown to reveal the thrust of her breasts covered only by the thinness of her shift above her corset.

Caro had no more will to protest as she saw the way those silver eyes glittered with admiration as Dominic gazed his fill of her. Indeed, she found she could barely breathe as she watched him slowly raise one of his hands to pull aside that gauzy piece of material and bare her breast completely. Her cheeks suffused with colour as, even as she watched, the tiny rose-coloured nub on the crest of her breast began to rise and stiffen.

'You are so very beautiful here,' he said huskily, the warmth of his breath now a tortuous caress against that burgeoning flesh. He looked up at her enquiringly. 'I wish to taste you, Caro.'

She found herself mesmerised by the slow flick of Dominic's tongue across his lips. Mesmerised and aching, the tip of her breast deepened in colour as it became firmer still. In anticipation. In longing, she knew, to feel that hot tongue curling moistly over it.

Where had these thoughts come from? Caro wondered wildly. How was it that she even knew the touch of Dominic's lips and mouth against her breast would give her more pleasure than she had ever dreamt possible? Woman's intuition? A legacy of Eve? However Caro knew these things, she surely could not allow Dominic to—

All thought ceased, any hope of protest dying along with it, as he gave up waiting for her answer and instead lowered his head to gently draw the now pulsing tip of Caro's breast into the heat of his mouth. His hand curved beneath it at the same time as he laved that aching bud with the moist heat of his tongue, and sending rivulets of pleasure into her other breast and down the soft curve of her abdomen to pool between her thighs.

Caro was filled with the strangest sensations, her breasts feeling full and heavy under the intimacy of Dominic's ministrations, the muscles in her abdomen clenching, that heat between her thighs making her swell and moisten there. She discovered she wanted to both squeeze her thighs together and part them at the same time. To have Dominic touch her there and ease that ache, too.

Her back arched instinctively as his hand moved to capture her other breast, the soft pad of his thumb now flicking against that hardened tip in the same rhythm with which he drew on its twin.

Dominic's lovemaking had been intended as a way of showing Caro that she did not belong here in London, that she was no match for him or other experienced men of the *ton*. Instead he was the one forced to recognise that he had never tasted anything quite so delicious as her breast, the nipple as sweet as honey as he kissed her there greedily, the hardness of his erection pulsing in his pantaloons testifying to the strength of his own arousal.

He drew back slightly to look at that pouting, full nipple, stroking his tongue across it before moving slightly to capture its twin, drawing on it hungrily before looking up at her flushed face and feverishly bright eyes. 'Tell me how you wish me to touch you, Caro,' he murmured against her swollen flesh.

Her fingers dug into his shoulders. 'Dominic!' she groaned a throaty protest.

He took pity on her shyness. 'Do you like this?' He swept his thumb lightly over that pouting nipple.

'Yes!' she gasped, shuddering with pleasure.

'This?' He brought his mouth down to her breast once more, even as he allowed his hand to fall to her ankle and push her gown aside and began a slow caress to her knee.

'Oh, yes!'

'And this?' Dominic ran his tongue repeatedly over that swollen nipple even as his hand caressed higher still to weave a pattern of seduction along her inner thigh, the heat of her through her drawers, her dampness, telling him of her arousal.

Nothing in Caro's life had prepared her to be touched with such intimacy. How could it, when she had never realised that such intimacies existed? Such achingly pleasurable intimacies that she wished would never end.

'I would like you to touch me in the same way, Caro,' Dominic encouraged gruffly.

She swallowed hard. 'I—' She broke off her instinctive protest as someone rattled the door handle in an effort to open the locked door.

'My lord?' Drew Butler sounded both disapproving and concerned at this inability to enter his own office.

Dominic turned his head sharply towards the door. 'What is it?'

'I need to speak with you immediately, my lord.' The other man sounded just as irritated as Dominic.

He scowled his displeasure as Caro took advantage of his distraction to extricate herself from his arms before turning away to begin fastening the buttons of her gown with fingers that were shaking so badly it took her twice as long as it should have done. What had she been thinking? Worse, how much further would she have allowed these intimacies to go if not for Drew's timely intervention?

'Caro—'

'Mr Butler requires your attention, my lord, not I!' Caro protested, her cheeks aflame.

Dominic's gaze narrowed in concern on her flushed and disconcerted face, knowing, and regretting, being the obvious cause of her discomfort. He had not meant things to go so far as they had. As for demonstrating to Caro how ill equipped she was to withstand the advances of the gentlemen of the *ton*, Dominic knew full well that *he* had been the one seriously in danger of overstepping that line! 'Caro—'

'Mr Butler requires you, my lord,' she reminded him.

Dominic stood up impatiently to stride over to the door and unlock it, his expression darkening as the other man's gaze instantly slid past him to where Caro stood with her back towards the door. Dominic deliberately stepped into the other man's line of vision. 'Yes?'

Speculative blue eyes gazed back at him. 'There is… something in the main salon I believe you should see.'

Dominic frowned. 'Can it not wait?'

'No, my lord, it cannot,' Drew stated flatly.

'Very well.' He nodded before turning to speak to Caro. 'It appears that I have to leave you for a few minutes. If you will be so kind as to wait here for me—'

'No.'

Dominic's eyes widened. 'No?'

'No.' Caro rallied, still embarrassed by the intimacies she had allowed this man, but determined not to allow that embarrassment to render her helpless. She carefully lifted her cloak and bonnet from the chair she had placed them on earlier. 'Mr Butler, is Ben available to escort me home now?'

'Yes, he is.'

'I would prefer that you wait for me here, Caro,' Dominic insisted firmly.

She met his gaze unflinchingly. 'And I would prefer that Ben be the one to accompany me to my lodgings.'

A nerve pulsed beside that savage slash of a scar on Dominic's left cheek. 'Why?'

Caro looked away as she found she could not withstand the probing of that narrowed silver gaze. 'I would simply prefer his company at this time, my lord.'

'Drew, could you wait outside for a moment, please?' Dominic did not even wait for the man's compliance before stepping back into the room and firmly closing the door behind him.

'I have nothing more to say to you, my lord—'

'Dominic.'

Caro gasped. 'I beg your pardon?'

The earl gave a graceful shrug. 'You did not seem to have any difficulty calling me Dominic a few minutes ago,' he reminded her wickedly.

Caro's cheeks burned with mortification as she recalled the most recent circumstances under which she had called this man by his first name. 'I do not even wish to think about just now—'

'Do not be so melodramatic,' Dominic interjected. 'Or perhaps, on consideration, it is the hideousness of my scars you would rather not dwell upon?' His voice hardened even as he raised a hand to his scarred cheek.

'I trust I am not so lily-livered, my lord,' Caro protested indignantly. 'No doubt you obtained that scar during the wars against Napoleon?'

'Yes.'

She nodded. 'Then it would be most ungrateful of me—

of any woman—to see your scar as anything less than the result of the act of bravery it undoubtedly was.'

Dominic was well aware that some women found the scar on his face unsightly, even frightening. He should have known that the feisty Caro was made of sterner stuff. 'I will endeavour to conclude my business with Butler as quickly as is possible, after which I will be free to escort you home. No, please do not argue with me any further tonight,' he advised wearily as he saw that familiar light of rebellion enter those sea-green eyes.

'You are altogether too fond of having your own way, sir.' She frowned her disapproval at him.

And his efforts to frighten this young woman into leaving London had only succeeded in alarming himself, Dominic recognised frustratedly. 'And if I once again add the word please?'

'Well?' she prompted tartly as he added nothing further.

Dominic found himself openly smiling at her waspishness. '*Please*, Caro, will you wait here for me?' he said drily.

Her chin remained proudly high. 'I will consider the idea whilst you are talking to Mr Butler.'

Dominic shot her one last exasperated glance before striding purposefully from the room. He forgot everything else, however—kissing and touching Caro, her response to those kisses and caresses, his own lack of control over that situation—the moment he entered the main salon of the club and saw a bloodstained and obviously badly beaten Nathaniel Thorne lying recumbent upon one of the couches there...

Chapter Five

'Dominic, why—?'

'Not now, please, Caro,' he cut in as he sat broodingly across from her inside the lamp-lit coach.

Not that the lamp was really necessary, dawn having long broken, and the sun starting to appear above the roof-tops and chimneys of London, by the time they had delivered Nathaniel safely to his home. The two of them had remained long enough to see him settled in his bedchamber and attended by several of his servants before taking their leave.

Caro had given a horrified gasp earlier when she'd ventured from Drew's office and entered the main salon of the club to see a group of men standing around Lord Thorne as he lay stretched out upon one of the couches, with blood covering much of his face and hands and dripping unchecked on to his elegant clothing.

Not that Dominic had spared any time on the pallor of her cheeks or her stricken expression as he'd turned and seen her standing there. 'Someone take her away from here!' he had ordered as Caro stood there, simply too shocked to move.

'Dom—'

'Stay calm, Nate.' His voice softened as he spoke soothingly to the injured man, some of that softness remaining in his face as he turned back to Caro. 'It really would be better for all concerned if you left, Caro.'

'I'll take her back to my office,' Drew offered before striding across the room to take a firm hold of her arm and practically drag her from the room.

She barely heard the older man's comforting words as he escorted her to his office before instructing Ben to remain on guard outside the door. Caro had paced the office for well over an hour whilst the two men obviously dealt with the bloody—and Caro sincerely hoped not too seriously injured—Nathaniel Thorne.

Dominic had grimly avoided answering any of her questions when he'd finally arrived to escort her home. Caro had gasped in surprise as he had thrown his cloak over her head just as she was about to step outside. 'What are you doing?'

He had easily arrested her struggles to free herself. 'Continue walking to the coach,' he had instructed.

Caro had thrown that cloak back impatiently as soon as she'd entered the carriage, any thought of further protest at Dominic's rough handling of her dying in her throat as she saw Lord Thorne reclining upon the bench seat opposite, the dressings wrapped about both his hands seeming to indicate that he had received the attentions of a doctor since she had seen him last. His face had been cleansed of the blood, revealing his many cuts and bruises, injuries that could surely only have been inflicted by fists and knives.

Caro felt herself quiver now as she remembered the full extent of those numerous gashes and bruises, and the imagined violence behind them. 'How——?'

'I am in no mood to discuss this further tonight,' Dominic rasped, the attack on Nathaniel having been a brutal awakening, a timely reminder that there was no place for a vulnerable woman like Caro in his world.

Sea-green eyes gazed back at him reproachfully. 'But why would someone do such a thing to Lord Thorne?'

'I should have realised that asking you for silence, even for a few minutes, was an impossibility.' Dominic sighed heavily. 'The simple answer to your question is that I do not know. Yet,' he added grimly. But he had every intention of discovering who was responsible for the attack on Nathaniel and why.

Caro flinched. 'He appeared to be badly injured...'

Dominic nodded curtly. 'He was beaten. Severely. Repeatedly. By four thugs wielding knives as well as their fists.' He knew more than most how strong a fighter Nathaniel was, but the odds of four against one, especially as they had possessed weapons, had not been in his friend's favour.

She gasped as her suspicions were confirmed, one of her hands rising to the slenderness of her throat . 'But *why*?' She appeared totally bewildered.

Nathaniel had remained conscious long enough to explain that he had been set upon the moment he'd stepped outside the club earlier, the wounds on his hands caused both from the blows he had managed to land upon his attackers, and defensively as he'd held those hands up in front of him to stop the worst of the knife cuts upon his face. Once he'd fallen to the ground, he had not stood a chance against the odds, as he was kicked repeatedly until one of those blows had caught him on the side of the head. After which he knew no more until he awoke to stagger back inside the club and ask for help.

Considering those odds of four against one, Dominic was sure that if murder had been the intention, then Nathaniel would now be dead. Also, his purse had still been in his pocket when he'd regained consciousness, the diamond pin also in place at his throat, so robbery was not the motive, either. From that Dominic could only surmise that the thugs had achieved what they had set out to do, and that the attack had been a warning of some kind.

But a warning to whom exactly...?

The words of caution Gabriel had given Dominic before he'd left Venice, in regard to Nicholas Brown, the previous owner of Nick's, had immediately come to mind. Dominic was well aware of the other man's violent reputation; while publicly Brown behaved the gentleman, privately he was known to be vicious and vindictive, his associates mostly of the shady underworld of London's slums. Also, the other man had been most seriously displeased to lose Nick's in that wager to Dominic.

No, the more thought he gave to the situation—when Caro allowed him the time to think about it, that was— the more convinced he became that Nicholas Brown was somehow involved. That tonight's attack might not been meant for Nathaniel at all...

Dominic had left for Venice only days after winning the wager that had cost Brown his gambling club, only returning back to London two days ago, a fact that would no doubt have reached the other man's ears as early as yesterday. As such, it would have been all too easy for the four thugs lying in wait outside the club to have assumed that the gentleman leaving alone, long after the last patron had left, with his face hidden by both the darkness and the hat upon his head, was Dominic himself.

He had discussed the possibilities briefly with Drew, the older man having agreed that his previous employer was more than capable of sending some of his paid thugs to attack Dominic. Except those thugs had not dealt the lethal blow to the man they had attacked. Drew had offered the possibility that it might not have been a case of mistaken identity at all; that Brown could well be deliberately hurting people known to be associated with Dominic, as both a threat and a warning, before later extracting his revenge from Dominic himself.

Dominic gave a grimace as he anticipated Caro's reaction to what was to be the subject of their next conversation. 'I have no idea as yet. But in view of the fact that the attack occurred outside Nick's, it has been decided that, for the next few days at least, all of us associated with the club should take the necessary precautions.'

Caro stared across at him blankly. 'But surely *I* am in no danger? No one except you, Lord Thorne, Drew Butler, and Ben Jackson has even seen the face of the masked lady singing at Nick's. That is the reason you threw your cloak over me when we were leaving the club earlier!' she realised suddenly, looking shocked.

He nodded grimly. 'It is not my intention to frighten you, Caro.' He frowned darkly as she obviously became so. 'But, until we know more, Drew and I are agreed that the masked lady must disappear completely, whilst at the same time every precaution taken to ensure the safety of Caro Morton.'

'Perhaps I might go to stay with Mr Butler and his family?'

'Drew and I dismissed that possibility,' Dominic explained. 'Unfortunately, Drew and his family share their modest home with both his wife's parents and his own so there is simply no room.'

'Oh.' Caro frowned. 'Then perhaps I might move to the obscurity of an inexpensive hotel—'

The earl gave a firm shake of his head. 'A hotel is too public.'

She sighed her frustration with this situation. 'Is there any real danger to me, or is this just another way for you to ensure that it is impossible for me to do anything other than return from "whence I came"?'

Dominic looked at her thoughtfully. 'Would you even consider it if I were to suggest it?'

'No, I would not,' she stated firmly.

'No,' Dominic conceded flatly. In truth, it was no longer an option; if Brown really were responsible for tonight's attack, there was also every possibility he was already aware of Caro's identity as the masked lady. He undoubtedly had informers and spies everywhere. As such, Caro returning to her home unprotected could put her in more danger than if she were to remain in London. 'Drew and I have come up with another solution.'

Caro eyed him warily. 'Which is...?'

'That I now escort you to your lodgings, where you will pack up your belongings and return to Blackstone House with me.' Not an ideal solution, he allowed honestly, but one that more easily enabled him to ensure her safety. The fact that she would at the same time be all too available to the desire he was finding it more and more difficult to resist was something he had tried—and failed—not to think about.

No wonder Caro stared at him so incredulously!

He raised an eyebrow. 'If you choose to accompany me to Blackstone House, then I will do all in my power to ensure your stay there is a temporary one. If it appears that it is to be longer than two, or possibly three days, then I will endeavour to find alternative accommodations for you. In any event, my offer of protection is one of expediency only. A desire, if you will, not to find one, or more, of my employees dead in a doorway during the next few days.'

Caro felt her face grow pale. 'You truly do believe those thugs will attack again?' She was totally confused as to what she should do. She had managed her escape from Hampshire easily enough, but she knew her older sister well enough to realise that Diana would not allow that situation to continue for long. That, despite Caro's letter of reassurance, once Diana had ascertained she was nowhere to be found in Hampshire, then her sister would widen her search, in all probability as far as London.

Diana's wrath, if she should then discover Caro living in the household of a single gentleman of the *ton* would, she had no doubt, be more than a match for this arrogant man!

She shook her head. 'Surely Mr Butler did not agree with this plan?'

'On reflection Drew agreed with me that at the moment your safety is of more importance than your…reputation.' Dominic's mouth twisted derisively.

She shook her head. 'I simply cannot—'

'Caro, I am grown weary of hearing what you can or

cannot do.' He sat forwards on the seat so that their two faces were now only inches apart, his eyes a pale and glittering silver in the weak, early morning sunlight. 'I have told you of the choices available to you—'

'Neither of which is acceptable to me!'

He gave her a hard smile. 'Then it seems you must choose whichever you consider to be the lesser of those two evils.'

Caro understood that Dominic was overset concerning the injuries inflicted upon his friend this evening, and the damage also caused to his gambling club before the attack, that he was genuinely concerned there might be another attack on those working or associated with the gambling club. But having already suffered twenty years of having her movements curtailed out of love and respect for her father, she had no intention of being told what she could or could not do, either by her guardian, or a man she had only met for the first time yesterday. 'And if I should refuse to do either of those things—go home or accompany you?'

Dominic had admired this young woman's courage from the start. Appreciated that feistiness in her, her lack of awe, of either him or his title, as well as her willingness to disagree with him if she so chose. But at this moment he could only wish she was of an obedient and compliant nature! 'It is late, Caro—or early, depending upon one's perspective.' He sighed wearily. 'In any event, it has been a very long night, and as a consequence perhaps it would be best if we waited until later today to make any firm decision one way or the other?'

She nodded. 'Then we are in agreement that once you have returned me to my lodgings I will remain there until we are able to talk again?'

Caro had all the allure of a prim old maid in that unbecoming brown bonnet that once again hid most of her hair, Dominic decided dispassionately. In fact, she looked nothing at all like the delicious, half-naked woman he had made love to earlier. Which was perhaps as well, given the circumstances! Dominic had thought to teach her a lesson earlier, and instead he had been taught one—that at the very least, Caro Morton was a serious danger to his self-control.

'We are not agreed at all,' Dominic contradicted, making no effort to continue arguing with her, but instead tapping on the roof of the carriage and issuing instructions to his groom to drive directly to Blackstone House. 'I will send to your lodgings for your things later today,' he informed her.

'You—'

'Caro, I have already assured you that should my enquiries take longer than those two or three days, then I will make other arrangements for you; let that be an end to the matter,' he said as he relaxed back in his seat, one dark brow raised in challenge.

A challenge she returned. 'It is seriously your intention to introduce me—even temporarily—into your household?'

'Seriously,' Dominic said.

She gave a disgusted snort. 'As what, may I ask?'

'Should any ask for an explanation—' his tone clearly implied that there were few who would dare ask the Earl of Blackstone for an explanation concerning any of his actions! 'then I will suggest that you are my widowed and impoverished cousin—so many young women were left widowed after Waterloo. That you are newly arrived from the country on the morning coach, with the intention of staying with me at Blackstone House whilst I arrange a modest household for you in London.'

'Without clothes or a maid?' Caro scorned.

Dominic shrugged unconcernedly. 'An impoverished widow cannot afford to employ a maid until I arrange for one, and your trunk will be delivered later today.'

She eyed him impatiently. 'Does the Earl of Blackstone even have a widowed and impoverished cousin?'

'No.'

'Do you have *any* cousins?'

'No.'

She eyed him quizzically. 'Any family at *all*?'

'Not a single one.'

Caro could not even imagine a life without her two sisters in it. Admittedly she had put a distance between them now, but it had been done in the knowledge that she could return to them as soon as Gabriel Faulkner had been convinced by Diana that none of the Copeland sisters had any intention of ever marrying him.

'Do not waste any of your pity on me.' Dominic's tone was laden with warning as he obviously saw that emotion in her expression. 'Having witnessed the complications that so often attend having close family members, I have come to regard my own lack of them as being more of a blessing rather than a deprivation.'

Could that really be true? Caro wondered with a frown. Could Dominic really prefer a life derelict of all family ties? A solitary life that allowed for only a few close friends, such as Lord Thorne?

She was given no more time to dwell on that subject or any other as the coach came to a halt, a glance outside revealing a large town house in an obviously fashionable dis-

trict of London. Mayfair, perhaps. Or St James's? Whatever
its location, Blackstone House was a much grander house
than any she had ever seen before.

Shoreley Hall was a rambling red-bricked house that
had been erected for the first Earl of Westbourne in the
sixteenth century. It had been built upon haphazardly by
succeeding earls until it now resembled nothing more than
a rambling monstrosity surrounded by several thousand
acres of rich farmland.

In contrast, Dominic Vaughn's home was of a mellow
cream colour, four storeys high, with gardens all around
covered in an abundance of brightly coloured spring flowers, the whole surrounded by a high black wrought-iron
fence.

'Caro?'

She had been so intent on the beauty of Blackstone
House, so in awe of its grandeur, that she had not noticed
that one of the grooms had opened the door and folded
down the steps, and was now waiting for her to alight.
'Thank you.' She accepted the aid of the young man's hand
as she stepped down on to the pavement, Dominic's obvious wealth making her more than ever aware of her own
drab and unfashionable appearance.

Vanity, her sister Diana would have called it. And she
would have been right. But that did not make Caro feel it
any less!

Again, she was allowed no more time for protest as Dominic took a firm hold of her arm to pull her along beside
him as he ascended the steps up to the front of the house.
The door opened before they reached the top step—despite
it being barely past dawn—by a footman in full livery. If
he was in the least surprised to see his employer accom-

panied by a drably clothed young woman he introduced as his cousin, Mrs Morton, then the man did not show it.

The inside of Blackstone House was even grander than the outside, if that were possible—the floor of the entrance hall a beautiful mottled green-and-cream marble, with four alabaster pillars either side leading to the wide staircase and up to a gallery that surrounded the whole of the first floor. High above them, suspended from a domed and windowed ceiling, a beautiful crystal chandelier glittered and shone in the sunlight. Caro had every expectation that the rest of Dominic's home would be just as beautiful.

'Would you take Mrs Morton up to the Green Suite, Simpson?' Dominic ignored Caro's awestruck expression as he turned to address the butler who had now appeared in the entrance hall. 'And provide her with whatever refreshment she requires.' He turned away with the obvious intention of passing her into the care of the servants.

'My lord!'

He was frowning slightly as he turned. 'What is it now?'

She nervously ran the tip of her tongue across her lips before answering him. 'I—you recall my trunk will not be arriving until later today...'

Dominic's frown deepened at this further delay. 'I am sure that Simpson will be only too happy to provide you with anything that you require.' He nodded abruptly to the attending butler before turning on his heel and striding down the hallway to where his study was situated at the back of the house.

Dominic needed time in which to think. Time, now that both he and Caro were safely ensconced in Blackstone House, in which to try to make some sense of everything that had occurred during these past few hours.

And unfortunately, he recognised darkly, he was unable to think in the least bit clearly whilst in Caro Morton's company…

It was Caro's indignation at the abruptness of Dominic's departure that helped her through the next few minutes, as she was shown up to a suite of rooms on the first floor, that indignation not in the least mollified by the delightful private sitting room that adjoined the spacious bedchamber. Both rooms were decorated in a warm green and cream— the reason it was named the Green Suite, no doubt!—with cream furniture in the sitting room and a matching four-poster in the bedchamber, the latter surrounded by the same beautiful cream-brocade curtains that hung at the huge windows overlooking the front of the house and the square beyond.

Yes, it was all incredibly beautiful, she acknowledged once she had been left alone with warm water in which to wash, and a maid had delivered a pot of fresh tea to revive her flagging spirits. But the beauty of her surroundings did not change the fact that she should not be here.

Running away to London and posing as Caro Morton in order to avoid her guardian's marriage proposal was one thing, but chancing the possibility of ever being found out as Lady Caroline Copeland was something else entirely, and had certainly never entered into any of her hastily made plans.

It was not a part of her plans now, either. Just because Dominic had chosen to bring her here, supposedly for her own protection, did not mean that she had to remain. As such, she would escape at the first opportunity—

'I would seriously advise against it…'

Caro was so surprised to hear the softness of Dominic's voice behind her that she almost dropped the cup she had been nursing in her hands. As it was, some of the hot tea tipped and spilled over her fingers as she turned to find him lounging in the open doorway of the sitting room. 'Advise against what, may I ask?' she demanded crossly even as she placed the cup back in its saucer before inspecting her scalded fingers.

'What have you done now?' The concern could be heard in the deep timbre of Dominic Vaughn's voice as he threw something down on a chair before striding across the bedchamber towards her.

She turned to glare at him at the same time as she clasped her hands tightly together behind her back. 'What have *I* done? *You* were the one who startled me into spilling my tea!'

'Let me see your hands.' Those silver eyes glowered down at her even as he reached behind her to easily pull her hands apart before bringing them both forward for his minute inspection.

Caro's protest died in her throat as she saw how pale and tiny her hands looked as he cradled them gently in his much larger ones. He was also standing far too close to her, she realised a little breathlessly, the light from the candelabra giving his hair that blue-black sheen as he bent over her so attentively, his strong and handsome face appearing all savagely etched hollows and sharp angles in the candlelight.

'Why are you here, Dominic?'

'Why?' He could no longer remember the reason why as he felt his response to the way she spoke his name so huskily; his chest felt suddenly tight, his arousal stirring, rising, inside his pantaloons. 'It was certainly not with the intention of hurting you,' he murmured ruefully as he lifted her hand to sweep the moistness of his tongue soothingly over that slightly reddened skin, even as he looked up and held her gaze captive.

'I—it was an accident.' Her lips were slightly parted as she breathed shallowly.

'One that would not have happened if I had not startled you,' he apologised ruefully as he continued to stroke his tongue against her silky soft skin.

The slenderness of her throat moved convulsively. 'I—I believe my hand is feeling better now, my lord.' But she made no effort to release her fingers from either Dominic's hand or the attentions of his lips and tongue.

She tasted...delicious, he recognised achingly as he placed delicate kisses between each individual finger, a combination of lightly scented soap and the natural saltiness of her skin, the trembling of her hand as he held it gently in the palm of his an indication of the pleasure she felt from his caressing attentions.

Dominic's thighs ached now, throbbed, his arousal more engorged and swollen just from the eroticism of kissing Caro's fingers than he had ever known it to be under the ministrations of the most accomplished of courtesans.

She had removed her bonnet and cloak since he'd last seen her, several golden curls having escaped the confinement of the pins designed to keep them in place, those curls shining like the clearest gold in the mellow candlelight. Her eyes had grown dark and misty, her cheeks slightly flushed, the full swell of her lips slightly parted as if waiting to be kissed.

She snatched her hands from his now before stepping back, her eyes wide with alarm. 'I believe we are already agreed that I have no intention of ever becoming your mistress, my lord.'

Dominic drew in several deep and controlling breaths as he acknowledged he had once again fallen under the sensuous spell of this woman. A woman who refused to tell him anything about herself other than her name—and he suspected even that was a fabrication!

He gave a slight shake of his head as he straightened. 'It would appear, Caro, because Butler and Jackson make no effort to hide their admiration of you, that you are under the misapprehension that every man you meet must necessarily be as smitten as they are,' he drawled mockingly.

Caro's cheeks flushed a fiery red at the accusation. 'Of course I am not—'

'Perhaps that is as well.' He looked down the length of his arrogant nose at her with those pale and glittering eyes. 'I assure you, my own jaded tastes require a little more stimulation than the touch of a woman's fingers—moreover, a woman with an eye for fashion that would surely make even a nun weep!' That silver gaze raked over her critically.

Caro had no idea why, but she felt that he was being deliberately harsh with her. Not that this green gown was not as unbecoming as the brown one she had worn the night before, because she knew that it was. But that had been the purpose in buying them, had it not? Besides, Dominic had not seemed to find her gown so awful when he'd made love to her earlier! 'I chose my gowns to suit myself, my lord, and not you,' she said calmly.

'Your choices are deplorable.' His top lip curled. 'I will arrange for a dressmaker to visit you later today. Hopefully she will have some suitable day dresses already made that can easily be altered to fit you, but you will also need to choose some materials for an evening gown or two.' He scowled. 'If I must have you as a guest in my home for the next few days, then I can at least ensure you are a decorative one.'

'I am your unwilling guest, remember?'

Dominic shrugged. 'Your reasons for being here are not important—what is far more pressing is not having the delicacy of my senses constantly offended by your drab appearance, even for the short time you will reside here!' He was being deliberately cruel, he knew. Because he had not cared earlier, or even a few minutes ago, how unbecoming Caro's gown was, or even who she might be; he had only been interested in the alluring curves of the silken body he knew lay beneath that gown.

Those sea-green eyes sparkled up at him angrily now. 'You are offensive, sir!'

He looked completely unaffected by her annoyance. 'If you choose to find the truth offensive, then who am I to argue?' He turned to walk over to the door, coming to a halt halfway across the room as the garment he had thrown on the chair earlier drew his attention. 'In view of your earlier reticence, it occurred to me that you might feel uncomfortable asking Simpson to find you something suitable in which to sleep, and so I brought you this.' He indicated the white robe draped across the chair.

The thought was a kind one, Caro acknowledged—the offhand method of bestowing that kindness was not! Any more than she appreciated having Dominic Vaughn arrange for a dressmaker to call on her here later today. 'I cannot possibly—' She broke off abruptly as she recalled this man's scathing comment earlier when she'd stated what she could and could not allow. 'I am afraid, where my gowns are concerned, that your "delicate senses" will just have to continue to be offended, my lord!'

He eyed her incredulously. 'You are saying you do not care for pretty gowns?'

Of course she liked pretty gowns—did she not secretly long for all the beautiful gowns she had left behind at Shoreley Hall? If only so that she could wear one of them to show Dominic Vaughn how fashionable she really was!

But she did not long for those pretty confections of silk and lace enough to agree to have a dressmaker attend her here—almost as if she really were about to become Dominic's mistress! 'Not at the moment, no,' she said mendaciously, only realising the error of answering so unguardedly as she saw the earl's eyes narrow shrewdly.

'And why is that, Caro?' he prompted slowly. 'Could it be because you believe yourself to be less conspicuous in those shabby gowns?'

She instantly bridled at the description. 'I will have you know that these gowns cost me several crowns.'

'Then it was money obviously wasted,' he drawled, before adding softly, 'I should warn you, Caro, that every attempt you make to hide your true identity from me only makes me more curious to learn exactly what or who it is you are hiding from...'

A shiver of apprehension quivered down her spine. 'You are imagining things, sir!' Her scorn sounded flat—and patently untrue—even to her own ears.

'We shall see,' Dominic said as he continued his stroll to the doorway before looking back at her briefly. 'I trust you will bear in mind what I said to you earlier?'

She gave a weary sigh, as tired now as he had claimed to

be earlier. 'You have said so many things to me tonight—
to which nugget of wisdom do you refer?'

'I also seem to recall we have said a great many things to
each other—and most of them impolite.' The earl's mouth
twitched ruefully. 'But the advice I am referring to now is
not to attempt to leave here without my knowledge. As I
have said, it is not my wish to alarm you,' he added more
gently as she visibly tensed. 'But, until I know more about
the events of this evening, I cannot stress strongly enough
your need for caution.'

Her throat moved convulsively as she swallowed.
'Truly?'

'Truly,' he echoed grimly.

Caro could only stand numbed and silent as Dominic
closed the door softly behind him as he left, the walls of
the bedchamber instantly seeming to bear down on her,
making her their captive.

No—making her Lord Dominic Vaughn's unwilling
captive…

Chapter Six

Caro awoke refreshed, a smile curving her lips as she felt the sun shining upon her face while she lay snuggled beneath the warmth of the bedclothes. That smile swiftly faded as she remembered exactly where she was. Or, more exactly, who owned the bed she had been asleep in. That arrogant, silver-eyed devil Lord Dominic Vaughn, Earl of Blackstone!

Her eyes opened wide and she looked about her in alarm as she tried to gauge what time of day it was. The sun had not been shining in the bedchamber when she'd finally drifted off to sleep earlier, and now it completely lit up and warmed the room, meaning that she must have slept for several hours, at least.

Sleeping during the day had seemed decadent to her a week ago, but she had quickly learned that it was impossible for her to do anything else when the gambling club did not open until—

No, Nick's would now not be opening at all for several

days, according to Dominic, which meant she could not work there in the evenings, either. She had enough money for the moment, courtesy of Drew Butler having paid her when she'd arrived for work the previous evening. But how was she supposed to fill her time now, incarcerated at Blackstone House for several days at least?

Caro had always disliked the usual pursuits expected of women of her class; her embroidery work was nondescript, and she had no talent for drawing or painting. She rode well, but doubted she would enjoy the sedateness of riding in the London parks. Perhaps Dominic had a decent library she might explore? She had always liked to read—

What was she doing? she wondered with disgust; as she had realised earlier this morning, she was not to be a guest here, but held virtually as a prisoner, albeit in a gilded cage, until Dominic Vaughn deemed it was safe for her to leave.

She threw the bedclothes back restlessly and swung her legs to the floor before standing up, only to become instantly aware of the garment the earl had provided for her to sleep in. White in colour, and reaching almost down to her knees, with buttons from the middle of her chest to throat and at the cuffs of the long sleeves, the garment could only be one of Dominic's own silk evening shirts.

A sensuously soft and totally decadent gentleman's white silk evening shirt. A garment that, once it had slid softly over Caro's nakedness, had evoked just as sensuous and decadent thoughts of the gentleman it belonged to…

Caro dropped down upon the side of the bed as she recalled the wickedness of her thoughts before she had drifted off to sleep. Of how those memories, of Dominic's lips and tongue upon her bared breasts earlier, had once again made her breasts swell and the strawberry tips to become hard and engorged, evoking a warm rush of moisture between her thighs that had sent delightful rivulets of pleasure coursing through her when she'd clenched them tightly together. She—

'You're awake at last, madam.' A young maid had tilted her head around the slightly opened door, but she pushed that door completely open now before disappearing back into the hallway for several seconds.

Long enough, thankfully, for Caro to climb quickly back beneath the bedclothes and pull them up to her chin before the maid reappeared carrying a silver tray she dearly hoped had some tea and toast upon it; she had not eaten for some time and just the thought of food caused her stomach to give an unladylike growl. She grimaced self-consciously as the smiling maid bustled about opening up the small legs beneath the tray before placing the whole across Caro's thighs above the bedclothes.

Not only was there tea and toast, Caro realised greedily, but two perfectly poached eggs and several slices of sweet-smelling ham. 'This looks delicious.'

'I'm sure it will be, madam.' The young girl bobbed a curtsy. 'His lordship surely has the best cook in London.'

Unfortunately Caro's appetite had suddenly deserted her. The maid's continual use of the title 'madam' was a timely reminder that she was supposed to be Dominic Vaughn's poor and widowed cousin, a deception that did not please her at all. She didn't want to be connected to Dominic in any way, even in a falsehood!

'Eat up, madam,' the maid encouraged brightly as she hovered beside the bed. 'The dressmaker has been waiting downstairs for quite some time already.'

The dressmaker Caro had told the earl she did not require. She should have known that the arrogant man would completely disregard her instruction. Just as she fully intended to disregard his!

She smiled up at the maid. 'What is your name, dear?'

'Mabel, ma'am.'

Caro nodded. 'Then, Mabel, could you please go downstairs and inform the dressmaker that there has been a mistake—'

'No mistake has been made, Caro,' Dominic drawled as he strolled uninvited into the bedchamber, crossing the room on booted feet until he stood beside the bed looking down mockingly at a red-faced Caro. That silver gaze raked over her mercilessly before he turned to the blushing young maid. 'That will be all, thank you.'

'My lord. Madam.' The young girl bobbed a curtsy to them both before hurrying from the room.

Caro wished that she might escape with her, but instead she once again found herself the focus of those chilling silver eyes as the earl stood tall and dominating beside the bed. And looking far too handsome, she thought resentfully, in buff-coloured pantaloons above black Hessians, a severe black superfine stretching the width of those wide shoulders, with a grey waistcoat and snowy white shirt beneath.

No doubt a white silk shirt similar to the one that she now wore as a nightgown!

'Impoverished widowed cousin or not, I do not believe that entitles you to enter my bedchamber uninvited, my lord,' Caro hissed when she at last managed to regain her breath.

Dominic could not help but admire how beautiful Caro looked with her golden curls loose upon the pillows and the pertness of her breasts covered only by the white silk of one of his own dress shirts, the nipples standing firm and rosy beneath the sheer material.

His jaw clenched now as he once again resisted the urge to push that material aside and feast himself on those firm and tempting buds. 'Eat up, Caro; the dressmaker does not have all day to waste while you laze about in your bed.'

Her cheeks coloured with temper. 'I distinctly remember telling you that I did not require the services of a dressmaker.'

'And I distinctly recall telling you that I refuse to see you dressed in one of those drab gowns a moment longer.' Dominic bent calmly to pluck a slice of ham from the plate upon the laden tray after making this announcement.

Caro found her gaze suddenly riveted upon his finely sculptured lips and the white evenness of his teeth, as he took a bite of the delicious-smelling ham, unsure if the moisture that suddenly flooded her mouth was caused by that mouthwatering ham or the unexpected sensuality of watching Dominic eat...

Those lips and teeth had been upon her breasts only hours ago, the tongue he now used to lick his lips having swirled a delicious pattern of pleasure on her flesh.

She wrenched her gaze away from the earl's dangerously handsome face as the contents of the tray placed across her thighs rattled in rhythm with her trembling awareness. 'I fear I am no longer hungry.' Her fingers curled about the handles of the tray as she attempted to remove it.

'Careful!' Dominic Vaughn took the tray from her shaking fingers to lift it and place it on the dressing-table before turning back to face her, the sunlight shining in through the window once again giving his hair the blue-black appearance of a raven's wing as that silver gaze narrowed on her critically. 'Speaking as a man who prefers a little more meat on the bones of the women he beds, I do believe you need to eat more,' he finally drawled.

Her chin rose challengingly. 'Speaking as a woman who has no interest in your preferences regarding "the women you bed", I prefer to remain exactly as I am, thank you very much!'

Dominic gave an appreciative grin; Caro had obviously lost none of her feistiness in the hours since he last saw her.

They had been busy hours for him, as he first set some of his associates from the army ranks, now civilians, the task of investigating Nicholas Brown's dealings over the past few days, before dispensing with his own household and estate business, and then returning to Nathaniel's home to see how his friend fared. Dominic's mouth tightened grimly as he thought of the other man's discomfort and obvious pain.

'Before you dismiss the dressmaker so arbitrarily, I believe you should be made aware that when your things were brought from your lodgings earlier, I instantly instructed one of the maids to consign all of the gowns inside into the incinerator,' he announced with satisfaction.

Caro gasped. '*All* of them?'

'All.'

Her startled gaze moved to the chair where she had placed her green gown earlier, only to find that chair now empty apart from her underclothes. And if the earl had indeed sent all her other gowns to be burned, then he must have included the three fashionable gowns Caro had brought to London with her two weeks ago. She turned back to him accusingly. 'You had no right to touch my things!'

'You were refusing to replace them.' Dominic gave an unapologetic shrug. 'It seemed easier to leave you with no choice in the matter rather than continue to argue the point.'

Her eyes sparkled indignantly. 'And I suppose I am now expected to go down to the seamstress dressed only in my shift?'

It was a pleasant thought, if an impractical one, Dominic accepted. 'She will come up here to you, of course. With, I might add, two gowns at least that you should be able to wear immediately.' He had personally instructed the dressmaker to bring a gown of sea-green and another of deep rose, the one reminding him of Caro's eyes, the other the tips of her breasts when they were aroused.

'Have you received word on how Lord Thorne fares?'

Dominic's thoughts of the anticipated changes to Caro's appearance completely dissipated at this reminder of the attack on one of his two closest friends. Not that he would ever forget that first moment of seeing Osbourne covered in blood in the early hours of this morning.

How could he, when it was such a stark reminder of the last memories Dominic had of his mother sixteen years ago?

He moved away from the bed to stand in front of one of the picture windows, his back to the room, his hands clasped tightly together behind his back as he fought back those memories. Memories that had returned all too vividly after Caro had questioned him concerning his family...

He breathed in deeply before answering. 'I have done better than that; I have been to see him.' He went on to explain that Nathaniel's aunt, Mrs Gertrude Wilson, having learnt that her nephew had suffered injuries and was confined to his bed, had wasted no time in having her own physician visit him, and fully intended removing Osbourne to her own home in St James's Square later this afternoon. An occurrence that aided Dominic's determination to ensure the future protection of his friend.

Dominic hoped to have some news later today concerning the enquiries into last night's attack, but if those enquiries should prove unhelpful, then he had plans of his own for later this evening that may give him some of the answers, if not all of them.

'And?' Caro prompted with concern as Dominic fell broodingly silent.

'And the physician has discovered he has two cracked ribs to go with his many cuts and bruises.'

Caro knew by the harshness of the Dominic's tone that he was far from happy at this news of his friend's condition. 'I am sure that he will recover fully, my lord.'

He did not look in the least comforted by her reassurances. 'Are you?'

'He is otherwise young and healthy,' Caro nodded. 'Now if—if you would not mind, I should like to get out of bed now.' She had not had time to deal with her morning ablutions before her bedchamber was invaded, first by the maid, and then Dominic Vaughn, and that need was becoming more pressing by the moment.

He raised dark brows. 'I was not aware I was preventing you from doing so?'

'You know very well that your very presence here is preventing me from getting out of bed.'

He gave a disbelieving laugh. 'You have flaunted yourself in a gambling club for this past week, in front of dozens of men, but now take exception to my seeing you clothed in one of my own shirts?'

Caro gave a pained frown. 'The gown I wore at those performances covered me from neck to toe.'

'And titillated and aroused the interest of your audience all the more because of it!'

Had it titillated and aroused this man's interest? she wondered breathlessly. Obviously something had, if his passion earlier this morning was any indication. A passion she had responded to in a way that still made her blush. 'Then it would seem the sooner I am clothed in one of my new gowns, the better it will be for everyone.'

His gorgeous mouth curved into a pleased smile. 'You are sufficiently recovered from your previous outrage to now accept the new gowns?'

Caro bristled. 'I believe it is more a case of having little choice in the matter when you have had all of my own gowns burned. I should become a prisoner of this bedchamber rather than just the house if I did not accept the new gowns, would I not?'

He winced. 'You are not to be a prisoner here, Caro, only to take the precaution of being accompanied if you should decide to go about.'

'I do not even know where "here" is!' she snapped caustically.

'Blackstone House is in Mayfair,' he elaborated. 'And as soon as you are dressed, and the seamstress has gone about her business, I will be only too happy to take you out for a drive in my carriage.'

'Accompanied by the maid I do not have?' she came back derisively.

'We are believed to be cousins, Caro,' he reminded her drily. 'Making such a fuss about the proprieties would be a nonsense.'

'In that case, if you would send the dressmaker up to me now I should very much like to go out for a drive.'

Her tone, Dominic noted ruefully, was almost as imperious as Osbourne's Aunt Gertrude's. Further evidence, if he should need it, that Caro Morton was a woman used to instructing her own servants and having those instructions obeyed. Because she was, in fact, a lady of quality?

He crossed the room to once again stand beside the bed. 'Have you considered the possibility, Caro, that I might be more…amenable, if you did not constantly challenge me?'

'I have considered it, my lord—and as quickly dismissed it.' Her expression was defiant as she glanced up at him. 'It goes completely against my nature, you see.'

Dominic could not prevent his throaty chuckle as he looked down at her admiringly. No, he never found himself bored in Caro's company, even when he was not making love to her! 'I will arrange for the carriage to be brought round in an hour's time.' He gave her a brief bow before taking his leave.

Caro did not move for several minutes after he had left the bedchamber, still slightly breathless from the transformation that had overcome his austere features when he laughed. Those silver eyes had glowed warmly, with laughter lines fanning out at their sides, the curve of those sculptured lips revealing the white evenness of his teeth. Even that savage scar upon his cheek had softened. The whole rendered him so devastatingly handsome that just looking at him had stolen her breath away…

'Relax, Caro,' Dominic drawled softly as she sat tensely beside him as he controlled the reins of his curricle, his two favourite greys stepping out lively in the sun-dap-

pled park. 'By this time tomorrow, all of society will be
agog to know who was the beautiful young lady riding in
the park with Blackstone in his curricle.' And she looked
every inch a lady of quality in her rose-coloured gown
and matching bonnet, with several golden curls framing
the delicate beauty of her face, and her hands covered in
pale cream gloves.

'How disappointed they will be when they learn it is
only your impoverished and widowed cousin up from the
country,' she came back tartly. 'And the last thing I desire
is to become the talk of London society,' she added with
a delicate shudder.

It was rather late for that, when to Dominic's certain
knowledge the male members of the *ton*, at least, had been
avidly discussing the masked woman who had sung at
Nick's for the past week! Not that any of those men would
recognise the blonde woman sitting so demurely beside
him in his curricle as the same masked and ebony-haired
siren who had entertained them so prettily at Nick's; several of those gentlemen had already greeted Dominic as
they passed in their own carriages, with no hint of recognition in their gazes as they'd glanced admiringly at the
golden-haired beauty at his side.

'A beautiful woman, impoverished or otherwise, is always a source of gossip amongst the members of the *ton*,'
he said.

Caro glanced at him beneath long golden lashes, noting how easily he kept the two feisty greys to a demure
trot as he drove his elegant curricle through the park. She
had also noted the admiring glances sent his way by all
of the ladies in the passing carriages, before those covet-
ous glances had shifted coldly on to Caro, no doubt due to

the fact she was the one sitting beside the eligible Earl of Blackstone in his carriage.

Wearing a beautiful gown, and being driven through a London park in a fashionable carriage, with a wickedly handsome man at her side, had long been one of Caro's dreams. But in those girlish dreams the man had been totally besotted with her, something she knew Dominic would never be with regard to her.

Admittedly, the circumstances under which they had first met had been less than ideal, but if Lady Caroline Copeland and Lord Dominic Vaughn, Earl of Blackstone, had met in a fashionable London drawing room, he would certainly have behaved more circumspectly towards her.

Except she was not, at this moment, Lady Caroline Copeland, and the earl's casualness of manner towards her was reflective of that fact. 'I believe I would like to return to Blackstone House now, if you please,' she said stiffly.

Dominic glanced down at Caro, frowning slightly as he saw the way her lashes were uncharacteristically cast down. 'There is a blanket beside you if you are becoming chilled?'

'I am not in the least chilled; I would just prefer to leave now.' Her voice was huskily soft, but determined.

Dominic transferred both reins to his right hand before reaching down with his left to lift Caro's chin so that he might look into her face. Far from invigorating her, she seemed to have grown paler during the drive, and, unless he was mistaken, the glitter in her eyes was not due to her usual rebellion. 'Are you about to cry?' His voice sounded as incredulous as he felt.

'Certainly not!' She wrenched her chin out of his grasp and turned away. 'I merely wish to return home, that is all. To Blackstone House, I meant, of course,' she added awkwardly.

Dominic had known exactly what Caro meant. Strange, in all the years he had been the Earl of Blackstone, he had never particularly regarded any of his houses or estates as being his home—how could he, when all of them were a reminder of the parents who had both died when he was but twelve years old?

Or how, along with those memories, came the nightmare reminder of the part he had played in their deaths! Memories that were usually kept firmly at bay, but had haunted him this past few hours...

'Of course.' Dominic gave a curt nod before turning the greys in front of the curricle back towards Blackstone House. 'Perhaps you should go to your bedchamber and rest before dinner?'

'I am simply grown bored of driving in the park, Dominic; I am not decrepit!'

He gave an appreciative smile as Caro answered with some of her usual spirit, all trace of what he had thought were tears having disappeared as she glared up at him. 'I assure you, Caro, I would not have brought you out driving with me at all if I thought you decrepit.'

'Is that because only women you consider beautiful are allowed in your curricle?' she asked, regarding him with a scornful purse to her mouth.

Dominic dearly wished to kiss that expression from her lips. Damn it, he had wanted nothing more than to kiss her again since she had appeared downstairs earlier looking breathtakingly beautiful in the rose-coloured gown and bonnet!

'No woman, beautiful or otherwise, has ever been invited to accompany me to the park in my curricle before today,' he admitted after a moment of silence.

She eyed him curiously. 'Should I feel flattered?'

'Do you?' Dominic asked.

'Not in the least,' she said with a return of her usual waspishness. 'No doubt, as far as the gentlemen of the *ton* are concerned at least, it will only add to your considerable reputation if you are believed to have the ebony-haired masked lady from Nick's in your bed at night, and a golden-haired lady in your curricle by day.'

Dominic gave her a mocking glance. 'No doubt,' he agreed.

Caro's eyes flashed deeply green. 'You—Dominic, there is a dog about to run in front of the carriage!' She reached out to grasp his forearm, half-rising in her seat as the fluffy white creature ran directly in front of the hooves of the now-prancing greys, quickly followed by a young girl in a straw bonnet who seemed to have the same disregard for her own welfare as the dog as she narrowly avoided being trampled under the hoofs of the rearing horses before following the animal across the pathway, and on to the grass, and then running into the woodland in hot pursuit without so much as a glance at the occupants of the carriage.

It took Dominic several minutes to bring the startled greys back under his control, by which time the dog and the girl had both completely disappeared, leaving Caro with the startled impression that the young girl in the straw bonnet had looked remarkably like her younger sister, Elizabeth!

Chapter Seven

'Bring brandy into the library, would you, Simpson?' Dominic instructed the butler as he kept a firm hold of Caro's arm, unsure as to whether or not she might faint away at his feet if he did not.

Admittedly, the near-miss in the park had been of concern for several seconds, but even so he had been surprised to see Caro so white and shaking after the event. Damn it, she was *still* white and shaking!

His hand tightened on her arm. 'At once, if you please,' he said to the butler briskly before taking Caro into the library and closing the door against curious eyes. He led her gently across the room and saw her seated in the chair beside the fireplace.

Ordinarily, he would have been impatient with a woman's display of nerves. But having already witnessed Caro's fortitude several times—when faced with the ribaldry of three young bucks, in the midst of a brawl, and then again when Osbourne had received a beating by those four thugs—Dominic could only feel concern that a minor incident, such as the one that had happened in the park just now, should have reduced her to this trembling state.

He moved down on to his haunches beside the chair in which she now sat, before placing one of his hands on top of her clasped and trembling ones. 'No harm was done, Caro. In fact,' he continued drily, 'I believe that young girl to be completely unaware of the near-accident that she caused.'

The young girl who had reminded Caro so much of her younger sister, Elizabeth...

For it could not really have been Elizabeth, could it? No, the young and ebony-haired girl in the blue gown and spring bonnet could not possibly have been Elizabeth, only someone who looked a little like her—because Elizabeth was safely ensconced at Shoreley Hall with their sister, Diana.

Caro had been reminding herself of that fact for the ten minutes or so that it had taken Dominic to drive the curricle back to Blackstone House—all the while shooting her frowning glances from those silver-coloured eyes, at what he obviously viewed to be her overreaction to the near-accident.

An assumption she dared not refute, for fear he would then demand an explanation as to what had really upset her.

She pulled both her hands from beneath his much larger, enveloping one. 'Do not fuss, Dominic. I assure you I am now perfectly recovered!'

Dominic straightened to step away and lean his arm casually upon the top of the mantel as he looked down at her; this caustic Caro was much more like the one he had come to know these past two days. 'I am glad to hear it.' He gave a mocking inclination of his head, giving away none, he hoped, of his own disturbed emotions with regard to the near-accident.

It was difficult, nearly impossible after all that had already happened this past twelve hours, for the incident not to have once again reminded Dominic of the carriage accident that had killed his mother sixteen years ago, and resulted in the death of his father, too, only days later. Especially when Caro had obviously been rendered so upset by it all.

'Ah, thank you, Simpson.' He turned to the butler as he entered to place the tray containing the brandy decanter and glasses down upon the table in the centre of the room.

'I trust Mrs Morton is feeling better, my lord?' The remark was addressed to Dominic, but the elderly man's gaze lingered in concern on Caro as she sat so white and still beside the fire.

She turned now to bestow a gracious smile upon the older man. 'I am quite well now, thank you, Simpson.' She continued to smile warmly as she removed her bonnet.

Dominic listened incredulously to the exchange—when, by all that was holy, had Caro managed to beguile his butler? An elderly man who was usually so stiffly correct he was in danger of cutting himself from the starch in his collar. 'That will be all, Simpson,' he dismissed the servant curtly.

Caro waited until the two of them were alone before speaking. 'I believe, Dominic, that you might find your servants were happier in their work if you were to treat them with a little more politeness.'

Brought to task by this little baggage, by damn! 'And what, pray, would *you* know about servants' happiness in their work?' Dominic decided to attack rather than defend, and was instantly rewarded with the flush that coloured her cheeks. 'Unless, of course, you were once a servant yourself?'

Her chin rose. 'And if I were?'

Then Dominic would be surprised. *Very* surprised! 'I will know the story of your past one day, Caro,' he warned softly as he moved to pour brandy into two glasses.

She eyed him coolly. 'I doubt you would find it at all interesting, my lord.'

He moved to hand her one of the bulbous glasses. 'Oh, I believe that I might…'

Rather than answer him, Caro took a sip of her brandy, her eyes widening as the fiery alcohol hit the back of her throat and completely took her breath away. 'My goodness…!' she gasped, her eyes watering as the liquid continued to burn a path down to her stomach.

Dominic eyed her with amusement. 'I take it that you have never drunk brandy before?'

She placed the glass carefully down upon the table beside her. 'It is dreadful stuff. Disgusting!'

'I believe it may be something of an acquired taste.' He took another appreciative sip.

Caro gave a delicate shudder, her stomach still feeling as if there were a fire lit inside it. 'It is not one I ever intend to acquire, I assure you.'

'I am glad to hear it,' he smiled. 'There is nothing so unattractive to a man as an inebriated woman.'

Caro wrinkled her nose delicately. 'Really? In what way?'

'Never mind. Would you care for some tea, instead?'

'That will not be necessary—oh. Do you play?' Caro had taken the time to glance about the comfortable library as the two of them talked, spotting the chess pieces set up on the table beside the window.

Dominic followed her line of vision. 'Do you?'

'A little,' she answered noncommittally.

His brows rose. 'Really?'

'You do not sound as if you believe me?' Her eyes sparkled with challenge.

He shrugged. 'In my experience, women do not usually play chess.'

'Then I must be an unusual woman, because I believe I play rather well.'

Dominic didn't doubt she was an unusual woman; she had been the source of one surprise after another since he had first met her.

'Would you care for a game before dinner?' she challenged lightly.

He grimaced. 'I think not. I was taught by a grand master,' he explained as Caro looked up at him enquiringly.

As the undisputed chess champion in her family and that included her father, she felt no hesitation in pitting her own considerable ability against Dominic Vaughn's or anyone else's. She was certainly a good enough player that she would not embarrass herself.

She stood up to cross over to the chess-table. The pieces appeared to have been smoothly carved out of black-and-white marble, the table inlaid with a board of that same beautiful marble. She glanced back to where Dominic still stood beside the fireplace. 'Surely you cannot be refusing to play against me simply because I am a woman?'

'Not at all,' Dominic drawled. 'I simply prefer to play against an opponent I consider to be my equal in the game.'

Her eyes widened. 'How do you know I am not until we have played together?'

He quirked a brow. 'A game in the nursery with your nanny does not equip you to play a champion.'

Caro bristled. 'You are being presumptuous, sir!'

'Concerning your game or the nanny?'

'Both!' Caro was all too well aware how determined Dominic was to learn more of her past. 'But being a gentleman of the *ton*, perhaps you would find it more of a challenge if I were to propose a wager?'

He eyed her guardedly. 'What sort of wager?'

'Are you any further forwards in your enquiries concerning the attack upon Lord Thorne?'

Dominic's expression became even more cautious. 'I am hoping to receive news on the subject later today.'

'But you are not sure?' she pressed.

Dominic's mouth tightened. 'At this precise moment, no.'

Caro nodded briskly. 'In that case, if I win, I would like for you to find me other accommodation sooner rather than later.'

Those silver eyes narrowed. 'Why?'

'I do not have to state a reason, my lord, merely name a forfeit,' she pointed out primly. 'And if you win—'

'Should I not be allowed to choose your own forfeit for myself?' Dominic interjected softly, those silver eyes glittering in challenge.

She drew in a deep breath, not at all sure she had not ventured beyond her depth, after all; Dominic seemed utterly convinced that he would win any game of chess between them. But she could not back down now; she owed it to other females who played chess to defend their reputation against such obvious male bigotry! Besides which, she dearly wished to escape Blackstone House. And the disturbing Lord Dominic Vaughn... 'Name your forfeit, my lord.'

'Dominic.'

Her eyes widened. 'That is your forfeit?'

'That is only an aside request, Caro, and not the actual forfeit,' he said. 'I am sure you will not find it too difficult to do; you seem to have no trouble at all in calling me Dominic before launching yourself into my arms!' Those silver-coloured eyes openly laughed at her now beneath long dark lashes.

Caro's cheeks burned, not at all sure which occasion he was referring to—there had been so many, it seemed! 'Very well, name my forfeit... Dominic.'

He seemed to give the matter some thought. 'You will reveal something of your true self to me, perhaps?'

Caro looked at him warily. She knew of her own ability in playing the game of chess, but Dominic's self-confidence could not be overlooked, either; he was so obviously sure of his ability that he had not even attempted to dispute the forfeit she would demand of him if she were the victor. To agree to tell him something of her true self was not something she had ever intended doing, either now or in the future. But then, neither did she intend allowing him to win this game of chess... 'Very well, I agree.' She gave a haughty inclination of her head.

Dominic lounged back in his chair, his expression one of boredom as the game began, sure that he was wasting both his own time and hers by playing at all.

After only a few more moves in the game he knew that victory was not going to be so easily won. Caro's opening gambit had been an unusual one, and one Dominic had put down to her lack of experience in the game, but as he now studied the pieces on the board he saw that if the game continued on its current path, then she would have him in check for the first time in only three more moves.

'Very good,' he murmured appreciatively as he moved his king out of danger.

Caro could see that, instead of continuing to lounge back uninterestedly, she now had all of Dominic's attention. 'Perhaps we might play in earnest now?' Her heart did a strange leap as he looked up to smile across the table at her. A warm and genuine smile that owed nothing to his usual expression of mockery or disdain, and instead leant a boyish charm to the usual severe austerity of his face.

'I am looking forward to it, Caro,' he replied, his attention now fully on the chessboard.

The maid, Mabel, had come in and attended to the fire, and Simpson had arrived to light several candles whilst the game continued, but neither opponent had even been aware of their presence as they concentrated completely on the chessboard between them.

It had become more than a game of chess to Caro; it had come to represent the inequality of the relationship that currently existed between the two of them. An equality that would not have existed between Lord Dominic Vaughn and Lady Caroline Copeland, but which most definitely existed between Lord Dominic Vaughn and Caro Morton. As such, it had become more than a battle of wills to Caro, and she played like a fiend in her determination not to be beaten.

Something that Dominic was well aware of as he studied her flushed and determined face between narrowed lids. Her eyes were more green than blue in their intensity, and the flush added colour to her otherwise porcelain white cheeks and down across the full swell of her breasts. Those rosy tips were no doubt deeper in colour, too, and were perhaps swollen and begging for the feel of his—

'Check!' Caro announced with barely concealed excitement.

Dominic's attention was reluctant to return to the board rather than considering the taste of Caro's breasts. He moved his own piece out of danger.

Irritation creased Caro's brow before clearing again as she made another move. 'Check.'

Dominic studied the board intently for several seconds. 'I believe that we will only continue in this vein *ad nauseam*, and that this game, therefore, must be declared a draw.'

She eyed him mockingly. 'Unless you were to concede?'

'Or you were?'

She sat back in her chair. 'I think not.'

'Then we will call it a draw.' Dominic said. 'And hope that one of us will be the victor on the morrow.'

'We could play again now—'

'It is time for dinner, Caro,' he murmured after a glance at the clock on the mantel, surprised to learn that a full two hours had passed since they had began to play. Surprised, also, at how much he had enjoyed those two hours.

Caro did not talk as she played, but neither was the silence awkward or uncomfortable. More, despite the fact they were in opposition to one another, it had been a companionable and enjoyable silence. And he, Dominic, decided as the realisation caused him to rise abruptly to his feet, was not a man to be domesticated to his fireside by any woman. Least of all a woman who steadfastly refused to reveal anything of her true self to him!

'Does this mean that we both concede our forfeit or that neither of us does?' she asked.

Dominic's eyes narrowed as he glanced back to where Caro had now risen gracefully from the table. 'Stalemate would seem to imply that neither of us do,' he replied. 'As we are so late I suggest that neither of us bothers to change before dinner.'

'Oh, good.' She gracefully crossed the room on slippered feet as she confided, 'I am so ravenously hungry.'

Dominic found himself laughing despite his earlier uncomfortable thoughts concerning domesticity. 'Has no one ever told you that ladies are supposed to have the appetite and delicacy of a sparrow?' he drawled.

'If they did, then I have forgotten,' Caro retorted as they strolled through the hallway and into the small candlelit dining room together, another fire alight in the hearth there to warm the room.

'I take it you are now, out of pure contrariness, about to show that you have the appetite and delicacy of an eagle.' Dominic pulled her chair back, lingering behind her a few seconds longer than was strictly necessary as he enjoyed the floral perfume of her hair.

Caro, in the act of draping her napkin across her knee, paused to give the matter some thought before answering. As far as she was aware, she had eaten nothing so far today. 'Perhaps a raven.' Not a good comparison, she realised with an inner wince, when the colour of Dominic's hair reminded her of a raven's wing...

Dominic was chuckling softly as he took his seat opposite hers at the small round table. Not so intimate that their knees actually touched beneath it, but certainly enough to create an atmosphere Caro could have wished did not exist.

She ignored Dominic to smile at Simpson as he entered the room with a soup tureen and began to serve their first course. It was a delicious watercress soup that Caro enjoyed so much that the butler served her a second helping.

'As I said, an eagle…' Dominic muttered so that only she could hear, wincing slightly, but not uttering a sound, as she kicked him on the shin beneath the table with one slipper-covered foot; no doubt it had hurt her more than it had hurt him!

He inwardly approved of the fact that she made no effort to hide her appetite; he had spent far too many evenings with women who picked at their food, and in doing so totally ruined his own appetite. In contrast to those other women, Caro ate just as heartily of the fish course, and her roast beef and vegetables, all followed by some chocolate confection that she ate with even more relish than the previous courses.

So much so that Dominic found himself watching her rather than attempting to eat his own dessert. 'Perhaps you would care to eat mine, too?' He pushed the untouched glass bowl towards her.

Her eyes lit up, before she gave a reluctant shake of her head. 'I really should not…'

'I believe it is a little late for a show of maidenly delicacy,' Dominic teased as he placed the bowl in front of her before standing up to pour himself a glass of the brandy Caro had so obviously disliked earlier. He sat down again to study her as he swirled the brandy round in the glass, easily noting the colour in her cheeks. 'I was commenting on the subject of food, of course…'

That colour deepened. 'If you are going to start being ungentlemanly again—'

'I was not aware that in your eyes I had ever stopped?' Dominic said, raising dark, mocking brows.

Perhaps not, Caro conceded, but there had been something of a ceasefire during and since their game of chess. In fact, she had believed she had even seen a grudging respect in those silver-coloured eyes when the game had ended in a draw. 'What shall we do with the rest of the evening?' She opted for a safer subject.

'I, my dear Caro, am going out—'

'Out?' She frowned after a glance at the gold clock on the mantel. 'But it is almost eleven o'clock.'

He gave an inclination of his head. 'And if Nick's were open, you would still have a second performance of the evening to get through.'

True. But having spent most of the day sleeping, Caro was not ready to retire to her bedchamber just yet. 'Are you going to see Lord Thorne? If so, perhaps I might come with you?'

'No, on both counts, Caro,' Dominic said; engrossed as he had been in their game of chess, and much as he had enjoyed his dinner, he had nevertheless been continually aware of the fact that the news he had been waiting for concerning Nicholas Brown had not been delivered, leaving him no choice but to now instigate his own plans for the evening. 'I have already visited Osbourne once today, and doubt that a second visit this late in the day would be welcome.' Mrs Gertrude Wilson would most definitely frown upon it! 'And where I am going tonight you definitely cannot follow.'

'Oh.'

Dominic quirked one eyebrow as he saw how flushed Caro's cheeks had become. 'Oh?'

Caro frowned her irritation, with her own naïvety as much as with Dominic Vaughn. Just because he kissed her whenever the mood took him did not mean that he did not have a woman he occasionally spent the night with. That he was not going out in a few minutes to spend the rest of the night in bed with such a woman!

Strange how much even the idea of that should seem so distasteful to her...

She had, Caro realised in dismay, enjoyed Dominic's company this evening. The verbal exchanges. The challenge of trying to best him at chess. Even the teasing in regard to her appetite. She now found it more than unpleasant to be made aware of the possibility he might be spending the rest of the night in bed with some faceless woman.

Which was utterly ridiculous!

She stood up abruptly. 'In that case, with your permission, I believe I will go back into the library and choose a book to read.'

It wasn't too difficult for Dominic to guess what Caro's thoughts had been during these last few minutes of silence: that she imagined it was his intention to spend the night in some willing woman's bed. Much as the idea appealed—it had been some time since Dominic had bedded a woman; those few unsatisfactory forays with Caro did not count when they had left him feeling more physically frustrated than ever—it did not actually enter into his plans for the rest of the night.

No, Dominic's immediate destination had absolutely nothing to do with bedding a woman and more to do with personally paying a visit to Nicholas Brown... 'Do not bother to wait up for me, Caro. I expect to be very late,' he said after he emptied the last of the brandy before placing the glass down upon the table.

Her cheeks were flushed with temper. 'As if I have any interest in what time it will be when—or even if—you should return!'

Dominic chuckled softly as he strolled over to the door. 'Sweet dreams, Caro.'

'As long as they are not of you then I am sure they will be!' she snapped.

He paused in the doorway to glance back at her. 'I very much doubt that I shall ever have the dubious pleasure of featuring in any young girl's dreams,' he said drily before closing the door softly behind him.

Dominic could not be sure, but he thought he might have heard the tinkling sound of glass shattering on the other side of that closed door...

Chapter Eight

It was some hours later when Dominic finally returned to Blackstone House, and he could not help smiling slightly as the attentive Simpson opened the door for him as if it were three o'clock in the afternoon rather than the morning.

'Mrs Morton is in the library, my lord,' the butler advised softly.

Dominic came to an abrupt halt halfway across the marble entrance hall and turned back sharply. 'What the devil is she still doing in there?'

The butler turned from locking and bolting the front door. 'I believe she fell asleep whilst reading, my lord. She looked so peaceful, I did not like to wake her.'

Dominic felt no such qualms as he glanced in the direction of the library, his expression grim. 'Get yourself to bed, man. I will deal with Mrs Morton.'

'Very good, my lord.' The elderly man gave a stiff bow. 'I—I believe that Mrs Morton may have been upset earlier, my lord.' he added as Dominic walked in the direction of the library.

Dominic was slower to turn this time. 'Upset?'

'I believe she was crying, my lord.' Simpson looked pained.

What the hell! The last thing he felt like dealing with tonight was a woman's tears. Or, as was usually the case, having to guess the reason for those tears. Whatever could have happened to reduce the indomitable Caro to tears? Perhaps the danger he had warned her of had become all too real to her once she was left alone for the evening?

Whatever the reason it gave him a distinctly unpleasant sensation in the pit of his stomach to think of Caro alone and upset...

He could see the evidence of her tears on the pallor of her cheeks once he had entered the library and stood looking down at her as she lay curled up asleep in the wing-backed armchair beside the fire, the book she had been reading still lying open upon her knees.

He was also struck by how incredibly young and vulnerable she looked without the light of battle in her eyes and the flush of temper upon her cheeks. So young and vulnerable, in fact, that Dominic questioned how she could ever have survived her first week in London without falling victim to some disaster.

Not that he imagined for one moment that Caro would have succumbed quietly—she did not seem to do anything quietly!—but she wasn't physically strong enough to fight off a male predator, and her youth and lack of a protector would have made her easy prey for the seedy underworld of a city such as this one. As it was, he had no doubt that

Caro had Drew Butler's visible protection to thank for her physical well being this past week, at least.

If Dominic had needed any reassurance that he had done the right thing in now placing Caro in his protection, then he had received it this evening when he'd visited Nicholas Brown at his home in Cheapside.

The bastard son of a titled gentleman and some long-forgotten prostitute, Brown, whilst now giving the appearance of wealth, had in fact grown up on the streets of London, and was as hardened and tough as any of the cut-throats that walked those darkened streets. A toughness he had taken advantage of by building himself a lucrative business empire that often catered to the less acceptable excesses of the *ton*; Nick's had been the more respectable of the three gambling clubs the man owned.

Within minutes of Dominic being admitted to Brown's house earlier, the other man had had the unmitigated gall to offer to allow the masked lady to sing at one of his other clubs, until such time as Nick's reopened. An offer Dominic had felt no hesitation in refusing on Caro's behalf!

Looking down at her now as she slept the sleep of the innocent, he could only shudder at the thought of her ever being exposed to the vicious and seedy underbelly of Nicholas Brown's world. At the same time Dominic feared that Brown, with his many spies in the London underworld, might already know that the young woman now staying with him and masquerading as his widowed cousin was that same masked lady...

Brown had not by word or deed revealed whether or not this was the case, but the fact that the other man had denied hearing any gossip or rumours concerning the perpetrators of yesterday's attack on Nathaniel Thorne, when directly asked by Dominic, was suspicious in itself; Brown was a man privy to all the secrets of the London underworld.

Like the officer and soldier he had once been, Dominic had now only retreated in order to decide how best to deal with the villain.

But first he must see Caro safely delivered to her bed...

Dominic's expression softened as he picked the book up from her knee and placed it on the side table before bending down to scoop her up into his arms. She stirred only slightly before placing her arms about his neck and sighing contentedly as she lay her head down against his shoulder.

For all that she'd had such a hearty appetite earlier, she weighed almost nothing at all, and it was no effort for Dominic to carry her up the wide staircase to her bedchamber, to where the fire was alight, and candles were burning on the dressing table to light the room in readiness for when Caro retired for the night.

Dominic crossed the room to lay her down upon the bedcovers, having every intention of straightening and leaving her there, only to discover that he could not as her arms were still clasped tight about his neck. 'Release me, Caro,' he instructed softly. Her only answer was to tighten that stranglehold to the point that Dominic had to sit down on the side of the bed or risk causing her discomfort.

As he had absolutely no intention of having to remain in this uncomfortable position for what was left of the night, he had no choice but to wake her. The Lord knew she was going to be indignant enough when she awoke and found he had carried her up to bed, without exacerbating the situation by giving into the temptation Dominic now felt to take off his boots, lie down beside her and then fall asleep with his head resting upon her breasts! 'Wake up, Caro,' he encouraged gruffly.

An irritated frown creased her brow and she wrinkled her nose endearingly before her lids were slowly raised and she looked up at him with sleepy sea-green eyes. 'Dominic?'

He raised mocking brows. 'Were you expecting someone else?'

Caro stilled, knowing by the candle lighting the room and the silence of the house that it must be very late. Which posed the question—what was Dominic doing in her bedchamber? More to the point, how did she come to be in her bedchamber? The last thing she remembered was sitting beside the fire in the library reading a book—

'You fell asleep and I carried you up the stairs to bed,' Dominic answered the puzzle for her.

Even if it did not provide the answer as to what he was still doing here! Or why her fingers were linked at his nape, and in doing so bringing his face down much too close to Caro's own?

She slowly unlinked those fingers, although her arms stayed about his shoulders. 'That was—very kind of you.'

He gave a hard smile. 'I am sure we are both aware that kindness is not a part of my nature.'

Caro could not agree. How could she, when he had saved her time and time again, from dangers she had not even been aware existed when she had left Hampshire to embark on what she had thought would be a wonderful adventure?

And in doing so, had left her two sisters, and everything in life that was familiar to her...

It was a fact that had been brought sharply home to Caro earlier today, when she had seen that young girl in the park who reminded her so much of Elizabeth. It did not matter that it had not actually been her sister; the familiarity, along with the game of chess she and Dominic had played earlier and which had so reminded her of the times she had played the board game with her father, had been enough to incite an aching homesickness once Caro was left alone, for both her home and family.

Dominic frowned as he saw the emotions flickering across her expressive face. 'Simpson seems to believe you have been…upset, whilst I was out this evening?'

That open expression immediately became a frown as she finally drew her arms from about his neck to push the curling tendrils of her hair back from her face. 'If I was, then I assure you, it had absolutely nothing to do with your own absence.'

This was more like the Caro he was used to dealing with! 'With what, then?'

She looked more cross than upset now. 'Does there have to be a reason?'

Where this particular woman was concerned? Yes. Most definitely. Dominic did not believe her to be the type of woman to give in to tears without good reason. Just as her pride would not allow her to now reveal to him the reason for those tears. 'Perhaps you have found the events of the past few days more disturbing than you had first thought?'

'I believe they would have reduced any woman of sensitivity to tears,' she came back tartly.

And far too quickly for Dominic to be convinced that the excuse he had so conveniently given her was the true reason for Caro's upset. But he could see, by the stubbornness of her expression, that this was the only explanation she was about to give. 'I should leave you now and allow you to prepare for bed,' he rasped.

'You should.' Caro nodded agreement.

Still neither of them moved, Caro lying back against the pillows, Dominic sitting beside her on the bed looking so dark and handsome in the candlelight, the hard and handsome savagery of his face made to appear even more so with that jagged scar upon his cheek.

It was a ragged and uneven scar, as if the skin had been ripped apart. 'How did it happen?' Caro finally gave in to the longing she had felt to lightly touch that scar with her fingertips.

Dominic flinched but did not move away. 'Caro—'

'Tell me, please,' she encouraged huskily.

His mouth tightened. 'It was a French sabre.'

Caro's eyes widened before her gaze returned to the scar. 'It does not have the look of the clean stroke of a sword…'

Dominic gave a dismissive shrug, more than a little unnerved at the gentle touch of her fingertips against his ragged flesh. 'That is because I did not make a good job of it when I sewed the two sides together!'

Her eyes widened. 'You sewed the wound yourself?'

'It was a fierce battle, with many injured, and the physicians were too busy with my seriously wounded and dying men for me to trouble them over a little cut upon my face.'

'But—'

'Caro, it is late— What the—?' Dominic broke off, shocked to his very core, when she sat up to place her lips against the scar on his cheek. 'What on earth do you think you are doing?' He grasped hold of her arms to hold her firmly away from him as he glared down at her.

Caro ignored Dominic's anger and the firm grasp of

his fingers upon her arms, too concerned—disturbed—by thoughts of the terrible wound he had suffered and then stitched himself. No doubt completely without the aid of the alcohol that would have numbed the pain but at the same time impaired his judgement. Just the thought of it was enough to make her shudder. 'War is barbaric!'

Dominic gave a ruefully bitter smile. 'So is tyranny.'

Reminding Caro that, although this man now gave every appearance of being a fashionable and dissolute man about town, he had admitted to being a soldier, an officer in charge of men, all of them fighting to keep England safe from the greedy hands of Napoleon.

Her gaze was once again drawn back to the scar upon his cheek. A daily reminder to him, no doubt, of the suffering and hardships of that long and bloody war. 'You were a hero.'

'Do not attempt to romanticise me, Caro!' Dominic stood up abruptly, a nerve pulsing in his tightly clenched jaw as he scowled down at her.

In doing so, he could not help but notice the way her breasts swelled over the top of her gown as she rested back on her elbows. Or how several enticing curls had come loose from their pins and now lay against the bareness of her shoulders. He acknowledged that at this moment his arousal was hard and throbbing, and that he wanted nothing more than to push her back against the pillows before ripping the clothes from her body and taking her with a fierceness that caused his engorged erection to ache and throb anew!

'I am not, nor will I ever be, any woman's hero,' he dismissed harshly.

Caro swallowed hard as she saw the fierce desire in

those glittering silver eyes. She knew instinctively that Dominic was poised on the very edge of control; that one wrong word from her and he would in all probability lose it completely.

Caro, her emotions already so raw—from her fear during the brawl that had broken out at Nick's the previous night, the brutality of the attack against Lord Thorne that had followed, being whisked away by Dominic to the indulgent splendour of Blackstone House, and then that sighting earlier today of the young girl that had so reminded her of her younger sister—could not help but relish the very idea of Dominic losing the firm grip he was attempting to maintain upon his control.

She moistened her lips with the tip of her tongue. 'That scar upon your face says otherwise, Dominic.'

Dominic knew that women were more often than not repulsed by the ugly scar that ran the length of his face from eye to jaw; Caro had already assured him she felt no such repulsion. But then, Dominic already knew that she was unlike any other woman he had ever met...

He should leave. He needed to put distance between himself and Caro. Now!

And yet something in her expression held him back. The soft sea-green of her eyes, perhaps. The flush upon her cheeks. The pouting softness of her parted lips...

'You should tell me to go, Caro!' Even as he said the words Dominic was striding back to the bedside and pulling her roughly up on to her knees. He looked down at her fiercely. 'If it should transpire that you are a married woman—'

She gasped. 'I am not—'

It was all the encouragement Dominic needed as his

mouth came down crushingly against hers and cut off further speech.

Caro felt on fire as his lips against hers gave no quarter, no gentleness, his arms like steel bands about her waist as he curved her body up into the uncompromising hardness of his, allowing her no time or chance for further thoughts as her fingers clung to the wide width of his shoulders.

Nothing else existed at that moment but Dominic. His lips hungry, his body hard and unyielding. His hands warm and restless as they caressed down the length of her spine before cupping her bottom and lifting her into him, a low growl sounding in his throat as he ground his thighs against her.

Caro seemed to melt from the inside out, as she felt the evidence of his desire pressing against her, so hard, so hot and pulsing, and inducing a reciprocal and aching heat inside her as her breasts swelled and between her thighs moistened. That heat increased, intensified as one of Dominic's hands cupped the full swell of one of her aching breasts before he pulled the material down and bared the fullness of that breast to his caress, capturing the hardened tip to roll it between fingers and thumb.

Caro groaned low in her throat as those caresses bordered on the very knife-edge between pleasure and pain, and rendering them all the more arousing because of it as she arched her breast into that caress even as Dominic's mouth continued to hungrily devour hers.

Her lips parted, invited, as Dominic ran his tongue moistly between them, gently at first, and then more forcefully as he thrust into the heat of her mouth in the same rhythm as he caressed the hard tip of her breast—

'No!' Dominic suddenly wrenched his mouth from hers,

eyes glittering furiously as he straightened her gown before he put her away from him.

Caro felt dazed, disorientated, hurt by the suddenness of his rejection. 'Dominic—'

'I may be accused of many things, Caro,' he bit out harshly, hands clenched behind his back as though to resist more temptation. 'And I have no doubt that I am guilty of most of them.' His mouth twisted self-derisively. 'But, married or not, I do not intend to add seducing an unprotected female guest in my own home to that list, even when I am invited to do so!'

Could it be called seduction when Caro had been such a willing participant? When she still longed, ached, for the touch of Dominic's hands and mouth upon her? When just thinking of those things made her tremble in anticipation?

When his last comment showed that he was aware of all those things...

One glance at the savage fury on Dominic's hard and uncompromising face was enough to tell Caro that the moment of madness had passed. For him, at least... All that remained was for her to try to salvage at least some of her own pride. 'I did not invite you to seduce me, Dominic!'

His mouth thinned. 'You invite seduction with every glance and every word you speak.'

'That is unfair!' Caro gasped at the accusation. Yes, her body still ached with longing, but she had only to look at Dominic to see the evidence of his own hard arousal beneath his pantaloons.

'Is it?' Dominic's nostrils flared as his gaze raked over her mercilessly. This woman tempted him, seduced him, with just her presence. So much so that he did not believe he could be under the same roof with her for even one more night and retain his honour. 'Go to bed, Caro,' he instructed harshly. 'We will talk of this again in the morning.'

'I—what is there to talk about?' She looked confused.

Dominic's lids narrowed until his eyes were only visible as silver slithers. 'As I said, the morning will be soon enough—'

'I would rather we talked *now*!' Her eyes flashed in warning.

A warning that Dominic had no intention of heeding. Damn it, he had been a commissioned officer in the army for five years, had been responsible for the lives and discipline of the dozens of men under his command; the temper of one tiny woman did not concern or impress him. 'I have said the morning will be soon enough, Caro,' he repeated firmly.

Caro's cheeks flushed hotly. 'I am beginning to find your arrogance a little tiresome, Dominic.'

He gave a humourless smile. 'Then let us both hope that you do not have to suffer it for much longer.'

Caro sincerely hoped that meant his arrangements for her removal from Blackstone House were progressing as quickly as he had hoped they might; she really did not think she could bear to stay here with him for too much longer.

She sank back on the bed once Dominic had left her bedchamber and closed the door softly behind him; the tears that fell down her cheeks now were for a completely different reason than those she had shed earlier tonight.

What was it about Dominic Vaughn that made her behave so shamelessly? To the point that just now Caro had been practically begging for the return of his kisses, for his hands upon her breasts? Whatever the reason, she knew she was seriously in danger of succumbing to the temptation of those kisses and caresses if she remained at Blackstone house with him for much longer…

'Will Lord Vaughn be down soon, do you think, Simpson?' Caro enquired lightly of the butler at nine o'clock the next morning as she sat alone at the breakfast table, drinking tea and eating a slice of buttered toast.

What had remained of the night, once Dominic had left her bedchamber, had been long and restless for Caro, as she'd tried to fall asleep but was unable to do so, her thoughts too disturbed after yet another incident of finding herself in the earl's seductive arms. All of those disturbing thoughts had come down to the simple fact that it was becoming nearly impossible for Caro to remain at Blackstone House, under Dominic Vaughn's protection.

'His lordship breakfasted and left the house some time ago, Mrs Morton,' the butler answered her question.

Caro's eyes widened. 'He did?'

'Yes, madam.'

Caro's heart sank. Much as she appreciated the grandeur of Blackstone House, and the attentiveness of the servants, the mere thought of having to idle away the morning here alone was unthinkable, reminding her as it did of the tediousness of the life she had been forced to lead at Shoreley Hall for the first twenty years of her life.

Strange, it had only been two weeks since she had come to London, and yet during that time—and despite some of the more *risqué* aspects of her behaviour!—Caro had come to enjoy having control over her own actions. So much so that she could no longer bear the thought of having her movements restricted in this way, least of all by a man whose emotions she could not even begin to understand…

She looked up to smile at the attentive Simpson as he stood ready to provide her with more tea or toast. 'Does his lordship have another carriage that I might use?' Caro held her breath as she waited to see if Dominic had acted with his usual efficiency and left instructions with the servants to restrict her comings and goings from Blackstone House.

The elderly man nodded. 'His lordship keeps four carriages for his use when in London, Mrs Morton.'

Caro's heart began to pound loudly in her chest. 'And do you suppose I might use one of these other carriages?'

The butler gave a courtly bow. 'If you wish, I am sure one can be readied for your use as soon as you have finished breakfast.'

Caro released her breath slowly, her features carefully schooled so as not to give away her inner feelings of elation; Dominic had not had the time—or, as was more likely, in his arrogance, he had decided he did not need to bother—to issue the instruction that Caro was never to leave Blackstone House unaccompanied.

Not that it was her intention to leave for good. She was not so foolish, and knew enough to believe Dominic when he'd warned of the danger that might be lurking outside these four walls—indeed, the attack on Lord Thorne was proof enough! But a drive in one of Dominic's own carriages, driven by his own servants, was surely safe enough?

'I do wish, Simpson,' she told the butler brightly. She stood up. 'In fact, I will go back upstairs this minute and collect my bonnet and gloves.' Caro hurried from the room to run lightly up the stairs, anxious to absent herself from Blackstone House before Dominic had the chance to return and prevent her from going.

Chapter Nine

Had Dominic ever been this angry in his life before?

He thought not; after all, until three days ago he had been in blissful ignorance of Caro Morton's very existence! Now, after years spent totally in control of his emotions, Dominic found himself the opposite; one minute aroused by her, the next enchanted, but more often than not, furiously angry. At this moment he was most definitely the latter as he had returned to Blackstone House at a little after ten o'clock, only to learn from Simpson that Caro had taken advantage of Dominic's absence and fled to heaven knew where. More insultingly, that she had made that escape in one of his own carriages!

Dominic paced the hallway as he waited for the return of that carriage so that he might learn where, exactly, the driver had taken her. And while he paced he listed all the ways in which he was going to punish Caro for her reck-lessness when he finally caught up with her. As he most assuredly would. He wanted an explanation as to exactly what she had thought she was doing by placing herself in danger in this way—

'I believe Mrs Morton has every intention of returning, my lord.' Simpson spoke diffidently, tentatively, behind him, having been made aware several minutes ago as to his employer's displeasure at finding Caro gone.

Dominic turned sharply, gaze narrowed. 'And what gives you that impression, Simpson?'

The other man gave a slight flinch at he obviously heard his employer's continued displeasure. 'I took the liberty, after our earlier conversation, of having one of the maids to go upstairs and check Mrs Morton's bedchamber.'

'And?' Dominic frowned darkly.

'All of Mrs Morton's things are just as she left them, my lord.' The man looked relieved at being able to make this pronouncement.

As far as Dominic was aware, all of her things now consisted of only the few belongings left to her after her other gowns had been consigned to the incinerator and he did not believe Caro felt strongly enough about any of them to return for them.

Just as Caro had felt no hesitation in leaving Blackstone House the moment Dominic's back was turned, despite his warnings. That, perhaps more than anything else, was what rankled, when Dominic's whole existence seemed to have been invaded by her in the three days since they had met. Not a pleasant realisation for a man who had long ago decided he would never allow any woman, even the wife needed to provide his heir, to dictate how he should live his life, let alone take charge of it in the way protecting Caro seemed to have done.

Nevertheless, the circumstances of the Nicholas Brown situation were such that Dominic could not—as he told himself he dearly wished to do—rid himself of that particular imposition just yet. The fact that Caro had not only attempted to leave Blackstone House unaccompanied this morning, but had succeeded, showed that one of them, at least, needed to have a care for her welfare.

Damn it.

Dominic gave a weary sigh as he answered his butler, 'I greatly admire your optimism, Simpson, but I am afraid in this instance I feel it is sadly misplaced. It would seem that Mrs Morton is dissatisfied with London society and has decided to return to her previous life.' He spoke with care, mindful of the fact that no matter what the household servants might think or say of this situation in private, publicly, at least, Dominic must continue to claim Caro as his widowed cousin.

The more Dominic considered her disappearance this morning, the less inclined he was to believe that she would have left without first saying her goodbyes to Drew Butler and Ben Jackson...and Dominic knew both those men were at Nick's this morning, overseeing the repairs.

'I believe I will go out again, Simpson.' Dominic collected up his hat and cane. 'If Mrs Morton should return in my absence...'

'I will advise her of your concern, my lord,' the older man assured as he held the door open attentively.

His concern? Dominic's feelings, as he climbed back into his curricle, were inclined more towards wringing her pretty neck than showing her concern. A pleasure he continued to relish for the whole of the time it took to manoeuvre the greys through the busy London streets to Nick's.

* * *

He had been too hasty earlier, Dominic acknowledged as he entered the gambling club some half an hour later—now was the time he felt more angry than he ever had in his life before!

And, once again, Caro was the reason for that emotion.

As was usual at this time of day, the gambling club appeared closed and deserted from the outside, but almost as soon as Dominic had entered the premises by the back door he had been aware of the murmur of voices coming from the main salon. The deep rumble of Drew Butler and Ben Jackson's voices were easily recognisable, as was the lightness of Caro's laughter, but there was also a third male voice that Dominic found shockingly familiar.

The reason for that became obvious as Dominic stood in the doorway of the salon looking through narrowed lids at the four people seated around one of the tables: Drew Butler, Ben Jackson, Caro—and, of all people, the previous owner of the club, Nicholas Brown!

Admittedly, Drew and Ben were seated protectively on either side of Caro, with Brown sitting opposite. But that protection was completely nullified by the admiration gleaming in Brown's calculating brown gaze as he looked across the table at Caro beneath hooded lids.

The fact that the four of them appeared to be enjoying a bottle of best brandy, at only eleven o'clock in the morning, only increased his displeasure. 'I take it from your lack of activity, Drew, that all of the repairs have been completed?'

Caro gave a guilty start at the silky and yet nevertheless unmistakable sarcasm in Dominic's tone, and instantly saw that guilt reflected in the faces of at least two of the three men seated at the table with her. Drew Butler and Ben Jackson instantly rose to their feet and excused themselves before returning to the aforementioned repairs.

Only the relaxed and charming Nicholas Brown appeared unperturbed at the unexpected interruption as he turned to smile unconcernedly at the younger man. 'I am to blame for the distraction, I am afraid, Blackstone. After our conversation last night I felt I ought to come and see things here for myself. Finding the beautiful Mrs Morton here, too, has been an unexpected pleasure.' He turned to bestow a warm smile on her.

Caro blushed prettily at the compliment, although that colour faded just as quickly, and a shiver of apprehension ran the length of her spine, as she saw the dark scowl on Dominic's face as he looked across at her; his eyes were that steely grey that betokened banked fury, his cheekbones hard beneath the tautness of his skin, his mouth a thin and uncompromising line, and his jaw set challengingly. Although whether that displeasure was because of Nicholas Brown's admiration for her, or because Caro had so blatantly disobeyed his instruction earlier concerning leaving Blackstone House unaccompanied, she was as yet unsure.

Caro was inclined to think it might be the latter; after the way in which he had left her bedchamber so abruptly during the night after rejecting her, she could not think of any reason why he should be in the least upset by Nicholas Brown's attentions towards her. Although that man's comment, concerning the two men having spoken together last night, seemed to indicate that Dominic had been telling the truth when he'd claimed he was not going out with the intention of visiting a mistress.

* * *

'You must excuse my cousin, Brown. I am afraid she is fresh from the country, and unfamiliar with the dictates of London society that prevent her from venturing out without her maid,' Dominic bit out coldly as he strode across the room to stand beside the table where Caro and Brown now sat facing each other. Although a brief glance at the tabletop at least revealed that she had a half-drunk cup of tea in front of her rather than having joined the men in a glass of brandy. Dominic wondered with abstract amusement where in the gambling club Butler had managed to obtain the china cup, let alone the tea to put in it!

'I assure you, no apology is necessary, Blackstone,' Brown came back smoothly. 'Indeed, I find such independence of nature in a beautiful woman refreshing.'

Caro's cheeks had coloured at the rebuke in Dominic's tone. 'I had thought to offer my assistance to Mr Butler after you informed me of the damage that had occurred here.'

Dominic raised dark brows. 'And I had similarly expected you at Blackstone House when I returned.'

Caro raised her brows. 'You had already left the house when I came down for breakfast, and I did not relish the idea of spending the rest of the morning alone.'

'Perhaps I should withdraw and allow the two of you to continue this conversation in private?' Brown offered lightly.

Dominic's narrowed his gaze on the older man, not convinced for a moment by the innocence of the other man's expression. With his dark and fashionable clothes and politeness of manner, he gave every outward appearance of being the gentleman and yet he most certainly was not; it was well known that he would sell his mother to the highest bidder if it was found to be in his own best interests.

Nor was Dominic unaware of the significance of the older man's visit here so soon after their conversation about the attack on Nathaniel the evening before. It was only whether or not Brown knew of Caro's identity as the masked lady appearing at Nick's that was still in question...

Although Dominic could not attach blame to any young woman—including Caro—for being flattered by the older man's marked attention; at forty-two, with dark and fashionable styled hair, and a roguishly handsome face, no doubt the rakish Nicholas Brown was enough to set the heart of any young woman aflutter.

'Not at all, Brown,' Dominic dismissed with a casual tone he was far from feeling as he took the seat that Drew Butler had recently vacated. 'My rebuke was only made to indicate my disappointment at not finding my cousin at home when I returned earlier.'

Caro glared at him beneath lowered lashes, knowing very well that his emotion had not been 'disappointment' at not finding her exactly where he had left her—he had been, and obviously still was, furious. 'I am to come and go as I please, I hope, my lord,' she said airily, choosing to ignore the retribution promised in Dominic's pale silver eyes for this open challenge to his previous instructions concerning her movements to and from Blackstone House.

'Not without your maid—'

'Perhaps we should, after all, discuss this later?' Caro interrupted what she was sure was going to be yet another verbal reprimand concerning the inadvisability of her having ventured out alone on to the London streets. 'I am sure that neither of us wishes to bore Mr Brown any further with the triviality of what is merely a family disagreement.'

'On the contrary, Mrs Morton, I find I am highly diverted by it.' The older man eyed them both speculatively.

It was a speculation that Caro did not in the least care for. 'You must forgive poor Dominic, Mr Brown.' She reached out to lightly rest her gloved hand on the back of Dominic's as it lay on the tabletop. 'I am afraid my widowed state has made him feel he has been placed in a position where he has to act the role of my protector. Much like an older brother, or perhaps even a father.'

Dominic was not fooled for a moment by the coy flutterings of silky lashes over those blue-green eyes, knowing from experience that she did not have a coy bone in her gracefully beautiful body. Nicholas Brown was just as aware of her insincerity, if the appreciative humour sparkling in the darkness of his eyes as he looked at her was any indication…

Dominic turned his hand over and captured Caro's gloved fingers tightly within his grasp. 'I assure you, my dear cousin, my feelings towards you have never been in the least fraternal *or* paternal.' He lifted her hand, his gaze easily holding her widened one captive as he slowly, and very deliberately, placed a kiss within her gloved palm. He then had the satisfaction of watching as the indignant colour warmed her cheeks.

'I see the way of things now…' Nicholas Brown gave an appreciative laugh as he rose elegantly to his feet. 'I hope I did not cause offence by any of my earlier comments, Blackstone?' His movements were languid as he straightened his cuffs beneath his expertly tailored black superfine.

Dominic's fingers tightened even more firmly about Caro's, preventing her from snatching her hand away, as he looked up at the older man challengingly. 'Not in the least, Brown. I can see that in future I shall have to make sure I remain constantly at Caro's side in order to provide her with suitable amusement.' His voice had hardened in warning over that last statement, a warning he knew the other man was fully aware of as that calculating brown gaze met his in shrewd assessment.

Caro was very aware that Dominic had been manipulating the conversation these past few minutes. And in a way that she did not in the least care for; after the things he had both said and implied, she believed that the handsome and charming Mr Nicholas Brown could come to only one possible conclusion concerning the Earl of Blackstone's relationship with his 'cousin'!

'Perhaps, if you have time, Mr Brown, you would care to come for a turn about the park with me before taking your leave?'

Dominic had the grim satisfaction in seeing Caro's triumphant expression turn to a wince as his fingers tightened about hers. 'I do not think that advisable, Caro,' he grated harshly. 'For one thing, it has turned a little chill.' His tone implied that it was going to get a lot chillier! 'I am afraid Caro and I must also go to another appointment, Brown,' he informed the other man distantly.

Nicholas Brown turned to give Caro a courtly bow before handing her his card. 'You have only to contact me if you should ever again feel a need for company during another of your jaunts about London, Mrs Morton.'

Nicholas Brown would only ever be allowed to accompany Caro anywhere over Dominic's dead body! Which,

he allowed grimly, was a distinct possibility if she continued to behave so recklessly...

'You little fool!' Dominic's teeth were tightly clenched
together as he returned from dismissing the carriage Caro
had arrived in earlier, a nerve now pulsing in the hard set
of his jaw, the scar upon his cheek once again a livid slash
as he lifted her up into his curricle as if she weighed no
more than a feather.

She bristled indignantly. 'I do not think there is any
need—'

'Believe me, Caro, you do not want to hear what my
particular needs are at this moment in time.' He gave her
a silencing glare.

'You—' Caro's second protest was arrested in her throat
as Dominic urged his highly strung greys on to what she
considered to be a highly dangerous speed. Not that she
did not have every confidence that he was in complete
command of the sleek and powerful horses, but she did
fear for the safety of the occupants of the other carriages
who were driving at a more sedate pace along the busy
cobbled streets.

Streets that did not look in the least familiar... 'This does
not look like the way back to Blackstone House?'

If anything Dominic's jaw clenched even tighter. 'Possibly because it is not.'

'But—'

Dominic had turned and speared her with eyes that glittered a pale and dangerous silver. 'Unless you wish for me
to stop the curricle this instant, and warm your bottom to
the degree that you will not be able to sit down again for a

week, then I urgently advise that you not say another word
for the duration of our journey!'

Caution was not normally a part of Caro's nature, but
she decided that in this instance it was perhaps the wisest
course; Dominic was angry enough at this moment to actually carry out that scandalous threat!

That Dominic had been angry at finding her gone from
Blackstone House in his absence was in no doubt. That
he had been put to the trouble of seeking her out had obviously not improved his temper. That he had found her
in the company of the charming Mr Nicholas Brown only
seemed to have added to that displeasure.

Why any of those things should necessitate Dominic
now behaving with the savagery of a barbarian, Caro had
no idea. Neither did she think it sensible at this moment—
indeed, it might be highly detrimental to her health—to
question him further.

She looked about her curiously as Dominic turned the
curricle on to one of the city's quieter residential streets,
the wide arc of cream-fronted town houses along this tree-
lined avenue nowhere near as magnificent as Blackstone
House, but of a style that was nevertheless elegant as well
as quietly genteel. She turned to Dominic with a guarded
frown. 'Are we to go visiting?'

His mouth twisted scathingly. 'Hardly.'

'Then why are we here?'

They were here because Dominic had realised, after almost making love to her last night, that for Caro's sake, as
well as his own, he could not allow her to remain within
his own household for a single night longer. That having
her so freely available to him at Blackstone House was a
temptation he was finding it increasingly hard to resist.

The only solution to that dilemma, he'd felt, was to move Caro to other premises as quickly as was possible. With the added security of being able to staff that establishment with men and women Dominic could trust to ensure that she did not repeat this morning's recklessness.

In fact, the sooner she was made aware that the oh-so-charming Mr Nicholas Brown was, in fact, the danger Dominic was attempting to protect her from, the better for them all!

Dominic brought the curricle to a halt in front of the three-storeyed terraced house he'd had prepared for Caro's arrival only that morning, allowing an immediately attentive groom to take hold of the horses before he jumped lightly down to the pavement. He moved around to the other side of the carriage to raise his hand with a politeness he was far from feeling. 'Caro?' he prompted tersely as she remained seated.

Caro's earlier puzzlement had obviously turned to wariness as she stubbornly refused to take his hand and step down from the curricle. 'What are we doing here, Dominic?'

Dominic was not a man best known for his patience, and what little he possessed had already been pushed to its limit this morning by this infuriating young woman. Neither did he care to explain himself in the middle of the street. 'Will you step down voluntarily, or must I employ other, perhaps less dignified, measures?'

Her eyes flashed the same sea-green as her gown. 'You did not seem to have the slightest thought for my dignity earlier when you made a show of me in front of Mr Brown!'

'It is my dignity I referred to now, and not your own.' Dominic eyed her quellingly.

'Then let me assure you that I have absolutely no intention of going anywhere with you until you have explained— Dominic…!' The last came out as a surprised squeak as he wasted no further time on argument but took Caro by the hand to pull her forwards on the seat before throwing her over one of his shoulders. 'How dare you? Put me down this instant!'

No, Dominic acknowledged grimly as he began to walk down the path towards the house, dignity certainly had no part in these proceedings!

Chapter Ten

It was a little difficult for Caro to take in the unfamiliarity of her surroundings when she was hanging upside-down over one of Dominic Vaughn's broad shoulders. Even so, she did manage to take note of the quiet elegance of the hallway once they were inside the house, and several doors leading off it to what were probably salons and a dining room.

Several servants stood just inside the hallway as the Earl of Blackstone calmly handed one of them his hat before he began to ascend the staircase with Caro still thrown over his shoulder.

'Not a word!' he warned softly as he obviously guessed she was about to voice another protest.

Caro clamped her lips together, her cheeks red with mortification as the servants below continued to watch the two of them until Dominic had rounded a corner to enter a long hallway. 'You will be made to regret this indignity if it is the last thing I ever do!' she hissed furiously.

He gave a scathing snort. 'If I could be sure that was the outcome, I might allow you that privilege!'

'You are despicable! An overbearing, arrogant bully—' Her flow of insults came to an abrupt halt as Dominic entered one of the bedchambers and tilted her forwards over his shoulder before throwing her unceremoniously down on to a bed. Caro barely had time to glare her annoyance up at him before she suffered the further indignity of having her bonnet tilt forwards over her eyes as she bounced inelegantly upon the mattress.

Her eyes glittered up at him furiously as she pushed the bonnet back into place. 'How dare you treat me in this high-handed manner?'

'How dare you completely disobey my instructions this morning and leave Blackstone House unaccompanied?' Dominic thundered, appearing completely unaffected by her indignation as he glowered down at her.

Her eyes narrowed in warning. 'I do not consider myself in need of your permission concerning anything I may, or may not, choose to do!' She drew in an angry breath. 'Neither does anything I have done this morning compare to your outrageous behaviour of just now.'

'I beg to differ.' He eyed her coldly, dark hair rakishly ruffled, although the rest of his appearance was as elegantly fashionable as always: perfectly tied neckcloth against snowy white linen, a deep grey superfine over a paler grey waistcoat and black pantaloons above brown-and-black Hessians.

His sartorial elegance made Caro even more aware of her own dishevelled appearance. Her sea-green gown was in disarray, rumpled from where she had been thrown down on to the bed, her hair even more so as she sat up to untie and remove the matching bonnet completely.

She gave an unladylike snort as she threw the bonnet aside. 'I do not believe you have ever begged for anything in your life.'

'No,' he acknowledged unrepentantly. 'Nor am I about to start now.'

'What are we doing here, Dominic?' Caro still felt agitated by the fact that he appeared to have carried her into the home of someone she did not even know; there was no way she could know the owner of this house when she was unacquainted with anyone in London except Dominic himself. And Drew Butler and Ben Jackson, of course. And now Nicholas Brown.

Dominic watched coldly as Caro tried unsuccessfully to tidy the waywardness of her curls. 'I am more concerned at this moment with the fact that your recklessness in going to Nick's this morning may result in much more serious repercussions than what you view as the indignity of being carried against your will into this house.'

Caro ceased fussing with her hair to look up at him scornfully. 'You are being ridiculous. There was no danger involved in my choosing to visit Mr Butler and Ben—'

'And Nicholas Brown?' Dominic's nostrils flared angrily. 'Do you believe yourself to have been in absolutely no danger from him, too?'

Her chin rose. 'Mr Brown was charming, and behaved the perfect gentleman in my company.'

Dominic gave a fierce scowl. 'Ben Jackson is more of a gentleman than Nicholas Brown.'

She eyed him haughtily. 'After your most recent behaviour, I am inclined to believe Ben to be more of a gentleman than you, too!'

Dominic's eyes narrowed to icy cold slits, his jaw clenching as he once again fought the battle to retain his usual control over his emotions, rather than letting them control him. It was a battle he had been destined to lose from the moment he'd walked into Nick's earlier and saw Caro calmly sitting down and drinking tea with the man he believed responsible for the attack on Nathaniel Thorne. As for being a gentleman, Brown was a man whose rakish handsomeness often occasioned him being invited into the bedchambers of married ladies of the *ton*, but who would nevertheless never be invited into the drawing room of one.

Dominic's teeth clenched so tightly together he heard his jaw crack. 'You have absolutely no idea what you have done, do you?'

She looked unconcerned. 'I merely exerted my free will—'

'To sit down and drink tea with the previous owner of Nick's.'

'Oh.' Caro looked momentarily nonplussed by this information, before rallying once again. 'I am sure I do not understand why, when you now own the club, that you should choose to hold that against him.'

'It is an ownership Brown relinquished to me with great reluctance,' Dominic grated pointedly.

'No doubt. Even so—'

'Caro, I know you to be an intelligent woman.' Dominic spoke with controlled impatience. 'I wish that you would now stop arguing with me long enough to use that intelligence.'

She eyed him warily. 'With regard to...?'

'With regard to the fact that only minutes ago you sat down and drank tea with the man I have every reason to believe is the very same man I have these past two days been attempting to protect you from.' Dominic's hands were now clenched at his sides.

Caro looked startled. 'You are referring to Mr Brown?'

'I am indeed referring to the man *you* think is a perfect gentleman.' Dominic's tone implied he knew the man to be the exact opposite of her earlier description of him. 'I believe him to be behind the attack on Nathaniel.'

Caro swallowed. 'Are you sure?'

Dominic's expression was grim. 'After this morning, yes!'

Caro began to tremble slightly, as the full import of what she had done began to sweep over her. She had found Nicholas Brown affable and charming, had flirted with him lightly, as he had flirted with her. She had even invited him to go walking with her! Admittedly that had been in response to what she had considered to be Dominic Vaughn's overbearing attitude, but that did not change the fact that she had made the invitation. And all the time, the man was a complete villain!

'If you truly know this for certain, then I do not understand why you did not instantly challenge him with the despicable deed?' Caro, uncomfortably aware of the severity of her error, decided to attack rather than defend, only realising her mistake as she noted the anger smouldering in the depths of Dominic Vaughn's ice-grey eyes once more flare into a blaze.

'I was an officer in the King's army, Caro, and a soldier does not confront the enemy before he has his own troops firmly in place and, more importantly than that, the civilians removed from harm's way.'

She gave a dismissive snort. 'Apart from myself, there were but the two of you present this morning.'

'And Brown's cut-throats were no doubt waiting outside in the shadows, eager to assist him if the need should arise.' Dominic looked down at her coldly. 'One of my dearest friends has already suffered a beating on my behalf, I was not about to see the same happen to you this morning, or indeed Butler and Jackson.'

Her eyes widened. 'You believe the attack on Lord Thorne to have been meant for *you*?'

'Only indirectly. It would appear that, for the moment at least, Brown is enjoying playing a cat-and-mouse game of inflicting harm on my friends rather than a direct attack upon me.'

'Then that is even more reason, surely, for you to have confronted him this morning?'

'Caro, it sounds distinctly as if you are accusing me of lacking the personal courage to confront him.' Dominic's tone was now every bit as glacial as his eyes.

It would be very foolish indeed of her to accuse him of such cowardice, when three nights ago she had personally witnessed him challenging those three young bucks well into their cups. When he had not hesitated to come to her rescue in the middle of a brawl. When she knew him to have been a gallant officer as the mark of that gallantry was slashed for ever upon his face.

But foolish was exactly how Caro felt at learning how mistaken she had been concerning Nicholas Brown's nature. Foolish, and embarrassed, to have been flattered by the attentions of the man she now knew him to be.

Her chin rose proudly. 'I would have thought you might, at the very least, have allowed him to see that you are aware of his guilt.'

Dominic gave a hard smile. 'Oh I am sure he is well aware of that fact.'

'How could he be, when apart from making such a show of implying our relationship is that of more than cousins, you were politeness itself?' Caro asked.

'The fact that I implied our relationship to be that of more than cousins, as you so delicately put it, was done with the intention of warning Brown, should he even consider the idea, of the inadvisability of harming one golden hair upon your head.' A nerve pulsed in Dominic's tightly clenched jaw. 'Which is not to say that I now feel that same reluctance myself.' The very softness of his tone was indicative of the depth of his anger.

Caro's trembling deepened as she realised too late her mistake in questioning Dominic when he was already so displeased with her; the grey of his eyes had become so pale and glittery that they glowed a shimmering silver, the scar standing out harshly in the tautness of his cheek, and his mouth had thinned to a dangerous line.

If those things were not enough to tell Caro of her mistake, then the purposeful look in his eyes as he moved to kneel on the bed beside her before pulling her roughly up against him and lowering his mouth to capture hers certainly did!

There was no gentleness in him as he ground his lips against hers before his tongue became as lethal as an arrow as it speared between her lips to thrust deeply into the heat of her mouth, and one of his hands moved to cup and then squeeze the fullness of her breast in that same remorseless rhythm.

Caro knew she should have been at the least frightened, if not repulsed, by the force of Dominic's passion, but instead she found herself filled with an aching excitement; her cheeks felt hot, her breasts full and aroused, and between her thighs became damp and swollen.

Dominic roughly pulled the bodice of her gown and chemise down to her waist and pushed the two garments down about her knees, before his mouth once again captured hers. His hand cupped firmly about one of Caro's exposed breasts and his fingers began to tweak and tug on the hardened nipple.

She forgot everything else but Dominic. Her neck arched invitingly as he finally wrenched his mouth from hers to lay a trail of fire down the column of her throat, her arms moving up over his shoulders and her fingers becoming entangled in the dark thickness of hair at his nape, as his head moved lower still and he drew one of those hardened nipples deep into the heat of his mouth.

Caro gave a choked gasp as there seemed to be a direct line of pleasure from Dominic's rhythmic tugging at her breast to the dampness between the bareness of her thighs, her movements becoming restless as she pressed into his hardness in search of some sort of relief for that throbbing and hungry heat.

Dominic had meant only to punish Caro for her disobedience, for her questioning his courage, but as he kissed and caressed her he instead found himself more aroused than he had ever been in his life before. So much so that he had not hesitated to pull down her gown and chemise and expose the silky paleness of her naked body to his heated gaze. Her breasts were high and firm, her waist narrow and flat, with a tiny thatch of enticing golden curls in the vee of her thighs.

He continued to lay siege to both her breasts with his lips, tongue and teeth as one of his hands gently parted those thighs before cupping her silky mound with his palm and allowing his fingers to explore the heat beneath. Caro was so hot and wet as he parted those sensitive folds to caress a finger along the heat of her opening, slowly, gently, circling but not yet touching the swollen nub nestled amongst those curls, in no rush to hurry her release, but instead savouring every low aching groan she gave as he caressed ever closer to that sensitive spot.

He touched her there once, lightly, feeling the response of that hard and roused little nubbin as it pulsed against his finger, hearing but ignoring Caro's low moan as he resumed caressing the swollen opening below, fingers testing, dipping slightly inside, and feeling the way her muscles contracted greedily about his finger even as she pushed her hips forward in an effort to take him deeper still. An invitation Dominic resisted as he continued to tease and torment her.

'Dominic, please!'

He raised his head slightly in order to look into Caro's flushed and reproachful face. 'Please what?'

Her eyes flashed deeply green and her fingers clenched on his shoulders. 'Do not tease me, Dominic.'

'Tell me precisely what you want from me, Caro,' he encouraged gruffly. 'You have only to issue an instruction and I will obey.'

Could she do that? Caro wondered wildly. Could she really tell Dominic plainly, graphically, what it was she re-

quired from him in order to give her relief from the heat
threatening to consume her?

'Do you want some part of me inside the sweetness of
you, Caro?' Dominic prompted softly as he seemed to take
some little pity on her desperate silence.

'Yes!' she groaned achingly.

'Which part, Caro?' he pressed. 'My fingers? My tongue?
My shaft?'

Oh, help! Those satisfying fingers? The hot and probing moistness of his tongue? His swollen arousal that she
could clearly see hard and throbbing beneath his pantaloons? From not knowing what she needed, Caro now knew
she wanted to experience having all three of those things
inside her.

'Perhaps we should experiment? See which it is you like
the best?' Dominic looked down at her nakedness with
eyes that had become both dark and hungry as he once
again swirled his fingers into the silky curls between her
thighs to unerringly find and gently stroke against that secret part of her.

Caro felt the instant return of that earlier pleasure, stronger now, more demanding, as she instinctively began to
move into those caresses, knowing she was poised on the
brink of—Caro had no idea what she was poised on the
brink of, she only knew that she wanted, needed it, with a
desperation she had never known before.

She moaned again in her throat as one long finger probed
her before slipping inside her heat. Deeper. Then deeper
still. At last giving her some relief for that aching need as
she moved her hips in rhythm with that finger as it thrust
slowly in and out of her.

'Lie back upon the bed, Caro,' Dominic instructed

throatily even as he eased her back against the pillows, continuing that slow and penetrating thrust inside her as he discarded her gown and chemise completely before moving to kneel between her legs to lower his head between her parted thighs.

Caro's hips jerked up from the bed at the first hot sweep of his tongue against her sensitised flesh, her fingers contracting, clutching at the bedclothes beside her, at the second sweep. She cried out, her neck arching her head back into the pillows, as unimagined pleasure ripped through her, Dominic thrusting a second finger deep inside her at the same time as he administered a third sweep of his tongue against that pulsing nubbin.

Caro became pure liquid heat. She felt as if she were on fire as wave after wave of pleasure radiated from deep between her thighs, only to surge through the whole of her body, each caress of his tongue and fingers creating yet another, deeper, swell of that mind-shattering pleasure.

Dominic watched Caro's face even as he continued to lave her with his tongue and slowly thrust with his fingers, knowing the exact moment she became lost in the throes of her climax; her eyes were a wide and stormy blue-green, her cheeks flushed, lips slightly parted, her breasts thrusting, the nipples hard as pebbles, her thighs a parted invitation as the nubbin pulsed beneath his tongue and she convulsed greedily about his thrusting fingers.

As he looked at her Dominic knew he had never experienced anything more beautiful, more physically satisfying, than watching Caro lost in the pleasure she felt from the touch of his mouth and hands. He found it more satisfying even than attaining that climax for himself.

He had been so angry with her earlier, so absolutely furious, not least because by behaving in that reckless way she had exposed her whereabouts to Nicholas Brown. But he did not want to dwell on that here and now, when Caro still quivered and trembled from the ministration of his lips and hands. Not with her all but naked beneath him, her only clothing now a pair of white silk stockings.

Besides, he had no answer as yet to his earlier question: fingers, tongue, or shaft?

Caro lay back weak and satiated against the pillows as she watched Dominic quickly strip off his boots, jacket, waistcoat, neckcloth and shirt, to reveal a hard and muscled chest covered in a light dusting of dark hair that disappeared beneath the top of his pantaloons. Pantaloons he now unfastened and pushed down and off equally hard and muscled legs to reveal the surging power of his engorged arousal.

Caro had never seen a naked man in her life before, but even so she was sure that Dominic was a physically well-endowed man. Her gaze rose to look at his face, and she swallowed convulsively as she saw the flush to his cheeks and the slightly fevered glow in those silver eyes as he wrapped a hand around that impressive length before moving forwards to rub it slowly against the opening between her thighs.

Caro felt herself quiver with each stroke of that hardness against her sensitivity, breathing heavily as she felt the return of that heat between her thighs. Surely she could not feel that pleasure again so quickly?

She could, Caro discovered only seconds later as Dominic continued to stroke that silky hardness against her own reawakened nubbin, her breasts becoming firm, nipples thrusting achingly even as she felt herself moisten in anticipation.

'Fingers? Tongue? Or shaft?' Dominic prompted gruffly even as he moved his hips forwards into her opening, one inch, two, before pulling back and starting again. One inch. Two. Three this time, before he pulled out and started again.

Caro had never experienced pleasure like this in her life before. Never imagined anything so exquisite as looking down at Dominic as he knelt between her parted thighs and slowly breached her, inch by glorious inch.

Each time Dominic thrust inside Caro she felt full and satisfied. Each time he pulled out again she felt bereft and empty. And each time he thrust inside her a little deeper she was sure she had reached her limit, that she had inwardly stretched and accommodated him as far as she was able. Until Dominic pulled out before thrusting even deeper inside her the next time.

Caro had been convinced when she first saw the size of Dominic's arousal that she would never be able to accommodate anything so large—

'Oh, my God!' Caro tensed suddenly, eyes wide with shock as she felt herself start to rip apart inside the moment Dominic took his weight on his arms to thrust forwards urgently with his hips so that he surged into her completely. It felt as if she were being torn in two as she finally took his whole length inside her.

'What the—!' Dominic froze above her, his face suddenly pale, his eyes glittering like opaque silver as he stared down at her incredulously.

'It is all right, Dominic,' Caro assured breathlessly. And, incredibly, it was, that first searing pain having now faded, and so allowing her to once again become aware of the pleasure of having his fullness completely inside her.

His face was grim. 'It most certainly is *not* all right!'

'I assure you that it is,' she encouraged softly. Dominic's arousal had looked hard and fierce earlier, but now that he was completely inside her Caro realised that fierce hardness was encased in skin of seductive and silky velvet. She moved her hips up, and then down again, the better to feel that sleek and velvety smoothness as it moved against her sensitive flesh.

'Do not move like that again, Caro, or I cannot be responsible for the consequences.' Dominic's jaw was clenched, his expression pained, a fine sheen of moisture upon his brow.

But of course Caro must move! How could she not move, when every part of her, every sensitised inch of her, cried out for the relief of having that pleasure-giving hardness stroking inside her?

Dominic had been stunned into immobility the moment he discovered Caro's innocence. 'Why did you not tell me?' His gaze was fierce as he looked down at the flushed beauty of her face, angry with himself at the moment rather than Caro, knowing he should have put a stop to this long before it had come to the point of his breaching her virginity.

And he had every intention of putting a stop to it now!

Dominic moved up and carefully away from her as he slowly disengaged himself, frowning as he saw Caro's wince of discomfort as he slipped from her obviously sore entrance. That frown turned to a dark scowl as he looked down and saw the blood smeared between her thighs as well as on him.

'Do not move,' he instructed harshly as he stood up to cross the room to the jug and bowl on the washstand, pouring some of the water from the jug into the bowl before moistening a cloth and cleaning Caro's blood from his own body before returning it to the bowl to rinse it in preparation for her. The water was cold, of course, but would hopefully be all the more soothing because of it.

Caro had watched Dominic beneath her lashes as he stood up to cross the bedchamber, completely unconcerned by his own nakedness, his movements gracefully predatory, like the sleek movements of a large jungle cat. He stood with his back towards her now, his shoulders wide, his back long and muscled, his buttocks a smooth curve above heavily muscled thighs and legs. If a man could be described as beautiful, then Caro knew that he could be called such.

The colour warmed her cheeks, however, when he returned to sit on the side of the bed and began to bathe between her thighs with a cool and soothing washcloth, his face a study of unreadable hauteur. Caro attempted to push those attentive hands away. 'There really is no need—'

'There is every need.' Dominic barely glanced up at her before continuing that studied bathing between her sensitive thighs.

Caro felt embarrassed, both by the intimacy of his ministrations, and the fact that their lovemaking had come to so abrupt an end once he'd been made aware of her innocence.

Surely there should have been more to it than that? A completion? A reciprocal pleasure? Dominic had certainly not shown signs of experiencing anything like the pleasure that Caro had.

All whilst in the bedchamber of house she had never visited before!

Caro moistened her lips, instantly aware of how swollen and sensitive they still were from the force of his kisses.

'Exactly where are we, Dominic?'

He looked at her briefly before turning away to place the cloth back in the bowl. 'I hope you are a little more comfortable now.' He stood up abruptly, his arousal already noticeably depleted. 'Perhaps I should send for a physician and he might give you some sort of soothing balm to apply—'

'I have no intention of being attended by a physician!' Caro's cheeks were hot with embarrassment as she imagined having to explain this situation to a third party. 'Dominic, is it possible I might become with child from—from what just occurred between us?'

Dominic closed his eyes even as he gave a groan of self-disgust. An innocent. Damn it, he had just deflowered a complete innocent!

Chapter Eleven

'It is very doubtful,' Dominic answered stiffly.

'But possible?'

'Perhaps,' he allowed abruptly.

Caro turned away. 'Whose house is this?'

Dominic looked down at her between narrowed lids, her cheeks flushed, her mouth slightly trembling as she pulled the sheet over her nakedness. It was a little late in the day for maidenly modesty, of course, but now was possibly not the right time for Dominic to allude to that fact.

'I do not believe that to be important at this moment—'

'I do.' There was a stillness about Caro now. A wariness that bordered on anger, perhaps?

He gave a humourless smile. 'You had made it obvious from the first that you did not wish to remain at Blackstone House, and last night it became just as obvious to me that the two of us could not continue to reside under the same roof any longer—'

'At which point in last night's proceedings did this

become so obvious to you, Dominic?' Caro interrupted sharply. 'Perhaps at the point where you announced the inappropriateness of seducing a female guest in your own home?' Angry colour now heightened the delicacy of her cheeks.

Looking down at her, the warmth of their lovemaking still visible upon her body, Dominic knew that she had never looked lovelier: her eyes sparkled, her cheeks were flushed, her lips slightly swollen from the passion of their kisses, and the skin across her shoulders and the exposed tops of her creamy breasts was slightly pink from the abrasion of the light stubble upon Dominic's jaw.

That jaw hardened at the accusation he heard in her tone. 'If you are somehow meaning to imply that I brought you to this house in order to seduce you—'

'Did you not?' She stood up, her movements agitated as she held the sheet tightly to her breasts to pace the bedchamber.

'Do not be ridiculous, Caro.' Dominic's quickly rising anger was more than equal to her own. Damn it, he was the one who had been in complete ignorance of her innocence until a few minutes ago!

The signs had been there if he had cared to see them, Dominic instantly rebuked himself. Caro's naïvety concerning the interest of the men who had come to Nick's night after night just to see her. The frequent indications of her being a young lady of refinement. The often imperious manner that hinted at her being used to issuing orders rather than receiving them.

That Dominic was now assured he had not been guilty these past three days of attempting to make love to a married woman or a member of the servant class was poor consolation when he had instead robbed a young woman of the innocence she should one day have presented to her husband.

'Ridiculous?' Caro now repeated softly, eyes gleaming as dark as emeralds. 'You strode into this house earlier as if you owned it—and perhaps that is because you do?' She didn't wait for Dominic to answer before striding across the bedchamber to throw open the wardrobe doors, her expression darkening as she saw the three pretty silk gowns hanging there. She turned to shoot Dominic a scathing glance. 'The previous occupant of this house appears to have been so hastily removed that she has left several of her gowns behind!'

'There was no previous occupant of this house—'

'All evidence to the contrary, my dear Dominic!' Caro was breathing hard in her agitation—she could only hope this anger served to hide the deep hurt she really felt.

It was humiliating enough that he had not even desired her enough to complete their lovemaking once he'd become aware of her innocence, but for him to have chosen to bring her to the house he had already owned, and where another woman had obviously been hastily removed, was a much more painful insult.

Dominic was well aware that at the moment Caro did not consider him her 'dear' anything; in fact, she looked more than capable of plunging a knife between his shoulder blades if one had been readily available. Which, thank God, it was not... 'Look at the gowns more closely, if you please, Caro,' he ordered.

Her nose wrinkled delicately at the suggestion. 'I have no wish to—'

'Look at them, damn you!' Dominic demanded impatiently. 'Look at the gowns, Caro,' he repeated more evenly as he realised that it was himself he was angry with and not her. 'Once you have done so, you will see that they are the ones ordered for you yesterday.'

Caro eyed him uncertainly for several seconds before turning her attention back to the gowns hanging in the wardrobe, frowning as she realised they were indeed the ones ordered from the seamstress yesterday. Two days dresses, one of pale peach, the other of deep yellow. The third an evening gown of pure white silk and lace.

A purity Caro was all too aware she could no longer lay claim to...

'If you care to look in the drawers in the dressing table you will find your own undergarments and new nightgowns, too.'

Caro firmly closed the wardrobe door on the mockery of that white gown. 'All that proves is that you were sensible enough, after all, to remove the belongings of your mistress and replace them with my own.'

Dominic drew in a sharp breath, knowing that engaging in their usual verbal battle of wills was not going to help this already disastrous situation. And no matter what she might choose to think to the contrary, he had not brought her here with any intention of seducing her. The opposite, in fact. He had thought—hoped—that by removing her from Blackstone House, he would be removing her from his temptation. Instead of which he had merely exacerbated the situation by bringing Caro here and making love to her before he had even had chance to explain.

'Caro, I acquired ownership of this house only this morning.'

'Now who is being ridiculous?'

Dominic knew, for all that Caro was putting such a brave face on things, that she had to be keenly feeling the loss of her innocence. 'I can take you to the office of my lawyer, if you wish,' he spoke gently. 'I am sure he would be only too happy to show you today's date upon the transfer of the deeds, if that will help to convince you I am telling you the truth?'

Her chin rose. 'You not only bought this house this morning but somehow managed to engage all those servants downstairs, too?' A flush entered her cheeks as she obviously recalled the curious gazes of those servants earlier as he'd carried her through the entrance hall and up the stairs.

An impulse he now deeply regretted when it had resulted in him taking Caro's innocence... 'They are, one and all, men and women already known to me. Men who served under me in the army, and their wives, whom I knew could be trusted to protect you,' he admitted ruefully.

Her eyes glittered, whether with anger or tears, Dominic was unsure. 'Obviously they did not feel that protection was necessary when it applied to *yourself*!'

'Caro—'

'Do not touch me, Dominic!' Her warning was accompanied by a step away from him, the knuckles on her fingers showing white as she tightly gripped the bedcover about her nakedness. 'I believe, if this truly is to be my home for the immediate future, that I should like you to leave now.'

No more so than Dominic wished to remove himself, he felt sure. At this moment, all he wanted to do was walk away from Brockle House and forget he had ever met Caro Morton. Forget especially that he had taken her innocence.

'Perhaps on your way out you might ask for a bath and

hot water to be brought up to me?' Caro requested stiltedly as Dominic pulled on his pantaloons and shirt before sitting on the side of the bed to pull on his boots.

Dominic inwardly winced at the thought of the soreness she must now be experiencing following their lovemaking. 'Please believe me when I tell you I did not plan for what happened here this morning—'

'Planned or otherwise, it is done now.'

There was so much sadness in her tone, that if that knife had been available, then Dominic believed himself to be capable of plunging it into his own heart at that moment. 'I cannot express how much I…regret what has happened.'

Caro looked up at him searchingly, not sure whether she felt reassured by Dominic's claim, or insulted by it. Their lovemaking had been a mistake, of course, a shocking error on both their parts. But even so… 'I had not believed you could possibly insult to me more than you already have; I was obviously wrong.' She turned her back on him to stare sightlessly out of the window into the square below. 'I require the bath and hot water to be brought up to me now, if you please, Dominic.'

Dominic stared at the proud set of Caro's bare shoulders for several long seconds before bending to pick up the rest of his clothes from the floor. 'I will call on you later this afternoon.'

She turned sharply. 'For what purpose?'

Dominic's heart sank at the suspicion he so easily read in her expression. 'For the purpose of checking that you have not suffered any feelings of ill health from this morning's…activity.'

Caro gave a humourless snort. 'As far as I am aware,

we did not indulge in anything of an unnatural nature this morning.'

A flush warmed the hardness of Dominic's cheeks. 'No, of course we did not.'

'Then I fail to see why you might think I will suffer any ill health because of it?'

'Damn it, Caro—'

'I suppose if you think it more fitting, then I could perhaps swoon or have a fit of the vapours?' she continued scathingly. 'But only if you believe it absolutely necessary.' Her nose wrinkled. 'Personally, I have always believed that women who behave in that way, seemingly at the slightest provocation, to be complete ninnies.'

Even in the midst of what Dominic considered, at best, to be an exceedingly awkward situation, he could not help but admire her courageous spirit. She truly was a woman like no other he had ever met. What had just happened between the two of them could certainly not be termed a mere 'slight provocation'. In fact, Dominic felt sure that most women in her position would be either screaming obscenities at him or alternately demanding jewels and gowns, the latter as compensation for the loss of her innocence; Caro asked only for a bath and hot water in which she might bathe the soreness from her body.

Dominic gave a rueful smile. 'I, too, would prefer that you do not swoon or have a fit of the vapours.' That smile faded as he looked at her searchingly. 'You truly are unharmed from our encounter?'

He knew himself to have been severely provoked when he'd returned to Blackstone House earlier and found Caro gone. Even more so when he'd arrived at Nick's and found her happily engaged in conversation with Nicholas

Brown—even now Dominic dreaded to think what might have befallen Caro if he had not been present when she had been foolish enough to suggest walking with him in the park! For her to then taunt him as she'd done regarding his own behaviour towards Brown had been more than Dominic's already frayed nerves had been able tolerate.

An intolerance that Caro had paid for with her innocence...

'I am as comfortable as might be expected in the circumstances.' Caro kept her chin proudly high even as she saw the way Dominic winced at her lack of assurances. In truth, it was her pride that now hurt more than her body.

Caro eyed him uncertainly now from beneath her lashes, still so very aware of how handsome he looked with the darkness of his hair rakishly tousled, and his shirt hanging loosely over his pantaloons, the buttons still undone halfway down his chest and revealing the hard and muscled flesh beneath. Hard and muscled flesh that Caro now knew more intimately than she did her own...

She gave a decisive shake of her head. 'We were both in error earlier. Let that be an end to it.'

Dominic continued to look at her searchingly for several long seconds. A scrutiny that Caro was determined to withstand without alerting him to how distressed she felt inside. And not by their lovemaking, as Dominic presumed, but because of the emotions which Caro feared had instigated her own part in that wild and wonderful lovemaking.

He frowned. 'I have your promise that you will stay well away from Nicholas Brown?'

'Such a promise is completely unnecessary, I assure you.' Caro's brow creased with irritation that Dominic, after revealing to her that Brown was the person behind the attack on Lord Thorne and consequently was the excuse for her own incarceration in this house, could for one moment think she had any interest in ever meeting the villain again!

Dominic wanted nothing more than to take Caro in his arms and smooth the frown from her brow and the shadows from her eyes. Even knowing of the physical discomfort she must now be suffering following their lovemaking, Dominic was not enough in control of his own emotions at that moment to be sure that he would be able to stop himself from making love to her fully if he were to touch her again.

He was a man who had enjoyed his first physical encounter at the age of sixteen. And there had been many women since that first time with whom he had enjoyed the same physical release. It was disturbing to realise that almost making love with Caro had been completely unlike any of those previous encounters. More sensuous. More out of control. With the promise of being more wildly satisfying…

'Caro—'

'Dominic!' Her eyes flashed in warning as she turned to face him, the control she had been exerting over her own emotions obviously at an end. 'In the past two days I have been caught up in the midst of a brawl, seen an innocent man beaten within an inch of his life, been deposited in your own household against my wishes, drunk tea with the man you assure me is responsible for that innocent man being beaten, been literally carried away and deposited in this house like a piece of unwanted baggage, before then being made love to. I should warn you, I am seriously in danger of resorting to behaving like that complete ninny I mentioned earlier, if you do not soon take your leave!' Her voice quivered with emotion, an emotion she masked by crossing the room to ring for the maid.

Still he hesitated. 'I should also like your promise that you will not attempt to go out alone again, now that you are aware of the danger.'

Could Caro make Dominic such a promise? What choice did she have? The only place she wished to go was back to Shoreley Hall in Hampshire, where she might be with her sisters and lick her wounds in private. Something she most certainly could not do, now that she and Nicholas Brown had met, when it might also result in her taking the danger that man represented back home with her...

In truth, what Caro most wanted at that moment was the privacy to sit down and cry. To scream and shout, if necessary. And after doing those things she needed the peace and quiet in which to come to terms with the loss of her innocence and the wantonness of her own behaviour this morning in Dominic's arms.

She gave a cool inclination of her head. 'You have my promise. Now, do you not think your own time would not be better spent in dealing with Nicholas Brown, rather than in lingering here to extract superfluous promises from me?'

Dominic's eyes narrowed. 'Superfluous?'

She gave a tight smile. 'Of course it is superfluous, when I so obviously have nowhere else of safety to go.'

'Caro—' Dominic broke off what he was going to say as, after a brief knock, a maid appeared in the doorway in answer to Caro's ring. 'Your mistress requires a bath and hot water,' he instructed tightly. 'Immediately,' he added firmly as the maid seemed inclined to linger in order to satisfy her curiosity rather than be about her business. He waited until the woman had gone before turning back to Caro. 'My advice is that once you have bathed you then rest quietly—'

'Why is it, I wonder, Dominic, that when you offer advice it always has the sound and appearance of an order?' Caro eyed him with exasperation.

Dominic gave a weary sigh as he ran impatient fingers through his already tousled hair. 'Caro, this situation is already difficult enough—could we not at least try to behave in a civilised manner towards each other?'

Could they? Somehow Caro doubted that they could ever be completely civilised with each other; it seemed that whenever the two of them were together their emotions ran to extremes. Arrogance. Anger. Desire.

She sighed heavily. 'Perhaps when you return this afternoon our emotions will be less…fraught than they are now,' she allowed distantly.

Dominic certainly hoped that would be the case.

But somehow he doubted it.

Chapter Twelve

'I am afraid I cannot accurately describe any of the four men who attacked me.' Nathaniel Thorne lay propped up against the pillows in one of the bedchambers at his widowed Aunt Gertrude's house, his expression regretful as he gazed across to where Dominic stood in front of one of the long picture windows.

Dominic had been shocked by the worsening of his friend's appearance when he arrived at Mrs Wilson's home a few short minutes ago, and the elderly lady's young companion showed him into Nathaniel's bedchamber. His friend's face was extremely pale except for the myriad of brightly coloured bruises and cuts that, although they were starting to heal, still looked vicious and painful. The bandage about Nathaniel's broken ribs was visible at the unbuttoned collar of his loose white nightshirt.

Nathaniel shook his head. 'As I told you at the time, I had no sooner walked outside than I was set upon by those four men wielding knives, and fists that had the force of hammers. I was immediately too busy defending myself to take note of what any of them looked like.' He grimaced at his oversight.

In truth, Dominic had not held out much hope of Nathaniel being able to add any more light on this particular subject. Regrettably, his reasons for coming here were, in fact, as much self-interest as they were concern for Nathaniel. Much as he wished to assure himself of Osbourne's well being, Dominic had been even more in need of a diversion from his own company!

Having returned to Blackstone House earlier to bathe and change his clothes, Dominic had then found himself pacing his study, too restless, his thoughts too disturbed, for him to be able to even glance at the papers concerning estate business sitting on his desktop awaiting his attention.

How could it be any other when all he could think about was Caro's stolen innocence?

'What is it, Dom?' Nathaniel's softly probing concern was the first indication he had that he might have actually groaned his self-disgust out loud.

Dominic had believed, hoped, that he could talk to Nathaniel about his present dilemma with regard to Caro. Instead he had realised since coming here that, as close as the two men were, there was no way that he could confide his despicable deed to the other man. More importantly, that he could not speak about Caro in such a way with a third party. Even one of his closest friends.

Gabriel, Nathaniel, and Dominic had always been as close as brothers, but even so, Dominic knew that he could not reveal to one of those friends what had taken place at Brockle House that morning. Osbourne, quite rightly, could not help but consider the taking of Caro's innocence as being beneath contempt. The same contempt, in fact, that Dominic now felt towards himself...

The truth of it was that he had been suffused with feelings of helplessness when he'd discovered Caro had gone from Blackstone House this morning, but instead of feeling relieved when he found her at Nick's, he had instead been filled with anger to see her calmly sitting drinking tea with Nicholas Brown. So much so that Dominic had completely lost control of the situation once they'd reached Brockle House.

How Caro must now hate and despise him—

'Dom?'

He closed his eyes briefly before focusing on Osbourne. 'I believe it is time I left; I have no doubt tired you enough for one day,' he dismissed briskly as he stepped forwards into the bedchamber, ready to take his leave. 'Is there anything I might bring to make you more comfortable?'

Nathaniel winced. 'No, as usual my Aunt Gertrude appears to have everything well in hand.'

Dominic smiled slightly at his friend's affectionate irony. 'I did not see her when I arrived earlier.'

'She has been persuaded to go out visiting this morning.' The relief could be heard in Osbourne's tone. 'Between her over-attentiveness, and her companion's sharp tongue, I am not sure I will last out the week!'

Dominic would not have thought the quiet and gracious young lady who had shown him up to Osbourne's bedchamber capable of being sharp-tongued. 'I am sure you will manage, Nate.'

'I wish I had the same confidence.' His friend gave a shake of his head. 'Of all things, my aunt is talking of removing me to the country to convalesce once I am well enough to travel.'

The idea had merit, Dominic decided after only the briefest of considerations. Nathaniel would be removed from danger, at least, if he were safely guarded by the formidable Mrs Wilson at her country home. 'It sounds a reasonable plan to me.'

'It is not at all reasonable!' Nathaniel glared. 'The Season has barely begun and Aunt Gertrude is intending to subject me to the boredom of the country when I am in no condition to protest.'

'No hardship, surely, when she is also removing you from the avaricious sphere of all those marriage-minded mamas?' Dominic reasoned drily.

'As I have reached the age of eight and twenty without as yet falling foul of those marriage-minded mamas, I am reasonably optimistic that I will have no trouble continuing to resist the allure of their beautiful daughters.' Osbourne eyed Dominic curiously. 'Speaking of which… Was I hallucinating, due to the beating I had just taken, or did your angel accompany us home in your carriage two evenings ago?'

Dominic stiffened. 'My angel?'

He knew to whom Nathaniel referred, of course; although the last time he had seen Caro, she had, quite rightly, presented him with all the warmth of a porcelain statue…

'You know exactly to whom I am referring, Dom,' Nathaniel prodded ruthlessly.

Exactly, yes. 'Do I?'

'Do you have any idea how boring it is just lying here with nothing to do but think?' Nathaniel's scowl was disgruntled to say the least.

'If you must think, then perhaps you should give consideration to Gabriel's future rather than my own?' Dominic attempted to change the subject.

Osbourne brightened slightly. 'He should be arriving in England very shortly.'

Dominic shrugged. 'But with the intention of travelling immediately to Shoreley Hall, remember.' Fortunately. If informed, Gabriel would definitely have had something to say about the situation Dominic found himself in. 'I—'

'I am sure we are very grateful for the frequency of your visits, Blackstone, but the physician has assured me that my nephew is in need of rest rather than excessive conversation.' An officious Mrs Wilson bustled forcefully into the bedchamber to begin enthusiastically plumping up the pillows beneath Osbourne's head, obviously now returned from her visiting, and not at all pleased that Dominic was once again disturbing her nephew in his sickbed.

Dominic gave her a polite bow. 'I assure you I am just as concerned for Osbourne's welfare as you obviously are, ma'am. In fact, I was about to take my leave when you came in.'

'Oh, I say, Aunt—'

'We must all take note of Mrs Wilson, Nate, if you are to make a full and speedy recovery,' Dominic drawled mockingly over his friend's protest.

The other man shot him a narrow-eyed glare that contained the promise of retribution for Dominic's defection at some later date. A glare that he chose to ignore as he smilingly took his leave. A smile that faded as soon as Dominic stepped from Mrs Wilson's home, as he acknowledged that he could no longer put off his return to Brockle House.

And Caro…

* * *

'Lord Vaughn is here to see you, Mrs Morton.'

Caro heard the butler's words, but did not immediately respond to them.

The first thing Caro had done, once Dominic finally left earlier that morning, was to strip the soiled sheets from the bed and attempt to remove the worst of the bloodstains with some of the cold water left in the jug; bad enough that she was aware of this tangible evidence of her lost innocence, without the whole household being made aware of it, too.

Although she doubted there could be much doubt in the minds of any of the servants Dominic had engaged at Brockle House, concerning the events of this morning!

To their credit, Caro could not claim there had been any evidence of that in the demeanour of any of the servants who'd brought in the bath and hot water some half an hour after Dominic's departure, their manner both polite and attentive as the fire was lit in the hearth before the footmen placed the bath in front of it and the water was poured in.

Caro had refused the offer of help from one of the maids, however, needing to be alone as she soaked in the bath and contemplated the events of the morning just past.

Not one of those thoughts had offered any comfort to the situation in which she now found herself. Caro knew, at the very least, that she should feel angry with Dominic for having taken her innocence and yet somehow she could not bring herself to do so. Perhaps because she knew herself to be just as responsible as he—if not more so—for what had happened?

She had wanted Dominic to make love to her this morning. Had desired him as much as he had desired her, to the extent that her chief emotion had been disappointment when he had brought an abrupt halt to their lovemaking. It was a shameless admission from a young woman who had been brought up to believe that women who behaved in such a way were wantons, no better than the prostitutes who roamed the streets of any large town or city.

As to how Caro now felt towards Dominic himself...

That was a question she had considered and then shied away from answering. Whatever her feelings towards him, it would be madness indeed for Caro to care anything for the Earl of Blackstone—a man who so obviously shunned all the softer emotions in life.

That Dominic had now returned, as he had said he would, made Caro all the more determined that he not become aware of her own inner confusion of emotions. 'Show him in, please,' she instructed the butler coolly as she stood up to receive him with the same formality to be found in the sunlit drawing room in which she sat.

One glance at Caro's coolness of expression and the dignified elegance of her body was enough to tell Dominic that, even if she had not recovered from this morning, she did not intend to reveal as much by her demeanour. Aware of the presence of the butler, Dominic greeted her formally. 'Mrs Morton.'

She gave a brief curtsy in response to his abrupt bow. 'How kind of you to call again so soon, Lord Vaughn.'

Dominic wasn't fooled for a moment by the politeness of Caro's greeting, aware as he was of the utter disdain in her expression. As aware, in fact, as he was of how lovely she looked in a gown of deep lemon, with the sun shining through the window behind her and giving her delicate curls the appearance of spun gold, her light and floral perfume tantalising his senses.

He waited until the butler had left the room and closed the door behind him before answering drily. 'A visit you obviously wish I had not made.'

Caro raised her light-coloured brows. 'On the contrary, I am merely curious as to why you bothered to have yourself announced when you are the owner of this house?'

Dominic frowned his irritation. 'I may own the house, Caro, but you are the one living here—'

'Temporarily.'

'As such,' Dominic continued firmly, 'it would have been impolite of me to simply walk in unannounced.'

Her smile was more bitter than amused. 'And politeness is to be between us from now on, is it?'

Dominic's mouth compressed as he walked farther into the room. 'It is to be attempted, yes.'

'How nice.' Caro resumed her seat upon the sofa, her hands folded neatly together to rest upon her thighs as she looked across at him serenely. 'In that case, would you care to take tea with me, Lord Vaughn?'

What Dominic would rather have was a return of the old Caro. The Caro who no more cared for polite inanities than he did and who opposed him at every turn. The same Caro who had defiantly assured him on numerous occasions that she would do exactly as she pleased, when she pleased. A Caro who, as far as Dominic could tell, was nowhere to be seen in this coolly self-possessed young lady who gazed back at him so aloofly.

'Or perhaps you would care for something stronger than tea?' she prompted distantly when Dominic made no answer, not betraying by word or expression how deeply his presence here disturbed her.

She had no idea how a woman was supposed to behave towards a man who only that morning had taken her innocence, but had afterwards made it patently clear how much he considered that action to have been a mistake. She was sure, given the circumstances, that she should not be quite so aware of how magnificently handsome he appeared in a superfine of deep blue, a paler waistcoat beneath, his linen snowy-white, with buff-coloured pantaloons above brown Hessians.

Although the expression in those silver-coloured eyes, and the hard tension in his jaw, showed he was far from as confidently relaxed as he wished to appear.

The coldness that now existed between the two of them was intolerable, Caro decided heavily. Not that it was her wish for either of them to allude to the events of earlier this morning—it was, in truth, the very last thing she wished to talk, or even think, about—but she found the polite strangers they were pretending to be just as unacceptable. So much so that her emotions were once again verging on the tearful.

She stood up abruptly to tug on the bell-pull. 'You would prefer brandy? Or perhaps whisky?'

A glass of either of those held appeal, Dominic acknowledged wryly. Except he doubted that even imbibing a full decanter of alcohol would numb the feelings of guilt that had beset him as he observed the changes in Caro. 'By all means order tea for us both.' He moved restlessly to stand over by the window as she spoke softly to the butler when he arrived to take her order.

He could have been the male guest in the drawing room

of any female member of the *ton*, Dominic recognised with a frown. There was the same politeness, the same formality and stiffness of manner he could have expected to receive there. The sort of polite formality that had never existed between himself and Caro!

He drew himself up determinedly once the two of them were once more alone. 'Caro, it must be as obvious to you as it is to me that we need to talk.'

'What would you care to talk about, Lord Vaughn?' she prompted brightly as she resumed her seat on the sofa to look across at him with unreadable sea-green eyes. 'The weather, perhaps? Or the beauty of the gardens at this time of year? I am afraid, never having attended one, that I cannot talk knowledgably of the balls and parties given in the homes of the *ton*—'

'You will cease this nonsense immediately.' Dominic could no longer contain his impatience with the distance yawning between them. 'I have no more wish to discuss the weather, the garden, or the doings of the *ton*, than I believe you do.'

She raised haughty brows. 'I thought I had just assured you that I would be only too happy to converse on either of the first two subjects—'

'If you do not stop this nonsensical prattling, Caro, then I will have no other recourse but to come over there and shake you until your teeth rattle!' Dominic's hands were clenched at his sides as he resisted that impulse, a nerve pulsing in his tightly set jaw as he glared across the room at her.

She visibly bristled. 'If you even attempt to do so, then I assure you *I* will have no other recourse but to take the letter opener from the table over there and stab you with it!'

Dominic gave an appreciative grin as his tension eased slightly. Better. Much better. Almost the Caro he was used to, in fact.

He waited until the tray of tea things had been placed on the low table in front of her, and the butler once again departed about his business, before speaking again. 'I had thought you might be interested in hearing how Lord Thorne fares this afternoon?' He strolled across to make himself comfortable in the armchair facing Caro as she sat forwards on the sofa to pour the two cups of tea.

She paused to look across at him. 'He is well, I hope?'

'Slightly better, yes. But, if I read the situation correctly, he is also being thoroughly suffocated by the kindness of his doting aunt, as well as browbeaten by the sharp tongue of her young companion.'

Caro smiled slightly at the image this conjured up of the rakishly handsome Lord Thorne being fussed over by one lady and rebuked by another. 'No doubt something he considers more tiresome than his injuries.' She handed Dominic his tea before picking up her own cup and saucer and settling back against the sofa.

There was a slight pause before Dominic spoke again. 'Caro, we should have had this conversation this morning, but…' He gave a shake of his head. 'Emotions were such that I did not feel the time was right—'

'I sincerely hope you do not intend plaguing me by enquiring again after my own health, Lord Vaughn!' Her eyes flashed deeply green as she looked across at him. 'I have already assured you that I am perfectly well and do not wish to discuss this subject further.' To her dismay her hand shook slightly as she concentrated on raising her cup to her lips and took a sip of the milky unsweetened tea in order to avoid meeting the probing of that silver gaze.

It was uncomfortable to sit here drinking tea together as if they were only casual acquaintances, but Caro knew she preferred even that to the humiliation of discussing the events of this morning. Just being in the same room as Dominic was enough to make her aware of the slight aches and soreness of the different parts of her body—all of them a physical reminder of their lovemaking earlier today.

As she had hoped, the bath she had taken had eased some of her discomfort. But it seemed there had been no soothing the slight redness to her breasts from the chafing of stubble upon Dominic's jaw as it rubbed against her tender flesh, or the slight soreness between her thighs every time she moved—a constant reminder of what had happened between them.

None of them were things Caro cared to discuss with Dominic!

Or things she should think of and dwell on, when he had already made it so clear that he considered their lovemaking to have been a mistake.

If only Caro were not still so aware of him. Of the way his silky dark hair had fallen rakishly over his brow. Of how the hand he now raised to push back those dark locks had this morning been entangled in the golden curls between her thighs—

'Would that we could dismiss it so easily.' Dominic's mouth had thinned with displeasure.

She frowned as she forced her thoughts back from those memories of carnal delight. 'I do not see why we cannot.'

Could Caro really be this innocent? Dominic wondered. If so, then it was even more important that they have this discussion. 'You were the one to mention earlier that there may be consequences from our actions this morning.'

She stilled. 'Consequences I recall you saying would be extremely unlikely.'

Dominic gave up all pretence of appearing in the least relaxed as he stood up to pace restlessly on the rug in front of the fireplace. Earlier, he had been too shocked by that proof of Caro's innocence, so befuddled by the intensity of his arousal, to be in any condition to think clearly, let alone have a rational discussion on the subject.

Even now, Dominic found himself in danger of wanting to make love to her again rather than talk, as they surely must. To kiss the vulnerability of her exposed nape, to touch and caress the firm swell of her breasts, to part the soft curls between her thighs as he stroked the sensitive nubbin there before throwing up her skirts and once again thrusting his arousal into the exquisite pleasure of her!

His hands clenched at his sides. 'Consequences I said *may* be a possibility,' he corrected stiltedly.

'I do not understand?'

'Much as it pains me, Caro, there is the possibility—remote, I do acknowledge—that merely by having penetrated you, you could become with child,' Dominic explained as she looked up at him blankly.

Caro's eyes widened and all the colour drained from her cheeks as the cup and saucer she was holding slipped from her fingers and tumbled to the floor.

Chapter Thirteen

Caro could only stare down numbly at the broken cup and saucer as it was quickly surrounded by a rapidly spreading pool of milky tea that threatened to wet her satin slippers as well as the rug in front of the fire.

'Caro—'

'Ring for Denby, would you, Dominic?' Caro grabbed a napkin from the tea-tray and fell down on to her knees to wipe up the worst of the tea before starting to gather up the shattered pieces of porcelain, grateful to have this diversion as a means of avoiding answering Dominic's previous statement.

Caro was not ignorant about how babies were made; even if Diana, as the eldest, had not felt it her duty to discuss such matters with her two younger sisters once she considered them both old enough, it would have been impossible to avoid knowing about such things, when their father had often discussed the selective breeding for the deer and other livestock at Shoreley Hall with his estate manager in the presence of his three daughters.

She had simply chosen to believe—to the point of denial—that such a thing could not possibly come about from Dominic's brief penetration.

'Leave it, Caro.' He stepped forwards to take a grip of her arm and pull her effortlessly to her feet, maintaining that hold as he turned to speak to the butler who had entered the room. 'Denby, could you see that this is cleaned up whilst I take Mrs Morton outside for a refreshing walk in the garden?' Dominic's expression was grim as Caro appeared too dazed to respond with her usual aversion to being told what to do, but instead allowed him to guide her outside into the sunlit garden. In truth, he was unsure as to whether she might have collapsed completely if he had not maintained that steadying grip upon her arm. 'Caro, I realise the delicacy of this situation, but surely—'

'Not now, Dominic,' she managed to breathe. 'I—allow me a few minutes in which to think, if you please.' She stepped away from him, releasing his hold upon her arm before turning her back on him and walking over to gaze down into the murky depths of the fishpond.

She looked so delicate, Dominic realised with a frown, so very young and vulnerable, as she stood there so still and silent. Unseeing, too, he did not doubt, knowing from the stunned expression and the pallor of her face that her thoughts were troubled ones.

As troubled as Dominic's own. 'I have come here this afternoon to assure you, that if by some mischance you do find yourself with child, I will of course feel honour-bound to offer you my hand in marriage.'

'Marriage!' Caro appeared horrified by the mere suggestion of it as she turned to stare at him.

Dominic had always been aware that he would have to marry one day. As a means of providing an heir, if for no other reason. But, if he had given the matter any thought at all, then the future bride he had imagined for himself would be selected from one of the families of the *ton*, a young lady of gentleness and obedience. She would certainly not be a stubborn and forthright young woman who refused to so much as listen—worse, who wilfully went her own way no matter what advice was offered to her.

He took a deep breath. 'It is obvious to me, despite the circumstances under which we first met, that you were obviously brought up to be a lady.'

'Indeed?' Caro's tone was icy.

'And that for reasons of your own,' Dominic continued determinedly, 'you have chosen to temporarily separate yourself from your family. Luckily, no one but Butler and Jackson...' and possibly Nicholas Brown, he mentally acknowledged '...is aware that Caro Morton and the masked lady are one and the same person. It is regrettable that you ever associated yourself with a gambling den, of course, but it cannot be changed now—'

'I assure you, if I have any desire to change *anything* about my visit to London, then it is that I ever had the misfortune to meet *you*!' Caro informed him frostily.

Dominic's mouth tightened at the deliberate insult. 'Even so, if you should indeed find yourself with child, then I am prepared, in view of the fact that I know of your previous innocence, to accept my responsibility—'

'I would advise that you not say another insulting word.' Her eyes flashed in warning. 'With child or otherwise, I would never consider even the possibility of ever marrying you,' she continued scornfully. 'Not even if you were to go down upon your knees and beg me to do so!'

Dominic could never envisage any situation in which he would ever go down upon his knees and beg any woman to marry him, although the vehemence with which Caro dismissed the very notion of a marriage between the two of them was insulting rather than reassuring.

She gave a delicate shudder now. 'I knew you to be an arrogant man, *my lord*, but I had not realised you to be one so full of self-conceit, too!'

Dominic felt the angry tide of colour in his cheeks at this further added insult. 'These character faults of mine did not seem a hindrance to the desire you felt for me earlier today!'

Caro's own cheeks became flushed at this reminder of her response to his lovemaking. But having come to London in the first place in order to escape the possibility of her guardian—another Earl, no less—being able to somehow coerce her into marrying him, Caro could not help but feel slighted by Dominic's obvious aversion to the unwelcome possibility that he might have to take her as his own Countess.

'I believe we have both of us made our feelings in this matter clear, Lord Vaughn,' she dismissed. 'And this conversation is therefore at an end. It would be better if you did not lay hands upon me again!' Her eyes narrowed as she found Dominic was now standing far too close to her for comfort and about to take a grip upon her arm.

His eyes glittered down at her just as fiercely as his fingers closed around her arm. 'And if I should choose not to heed that advice?'

Caro's chin rose challengingly. 'Then you will leave me no choice but to punch you upon your arrogant chin!'

He gave a start of surprise, then the angry glitter began to fade from his eyes to be replaced by reluctant admiration as he gave a brief laugh. 'You are without doubt the most unusual woman I have ever encountered.'

Unfortunately for him, Caro's own anger remained just as intense as it had ever been. 'Because I choose to threaten you with something you would understand rather than womanly hysteria?'

'Exactly so.' His fingers relaxed slightly upon her arm, but he did not release her. 'Caro, I meant you no insult just now when I said that I am prepared to offer you marriage should there be a child—'

'Did you not?' She tossed her head. 'Am I to understand that you expect me to feel grateful, then, by your *honourbound* offer? Flattered when you express how *regrettable* you consider this situation to be? Suggesting that, as you are completely assured of my innocence before today, I should be happy that you are prepared to *accept your responsibility* as the father of any baby I might produce in the next nine months?'

'You are twisting my words—'

'Indeed I am not,' Caro denied hotly, her anger deepening the more she thought about Dominic's so-called proposal of marriage. At the moment, she really did feel capable of punching him upon his arrogant chin! 'Please accept my assurances, Lord Vaughn, that if I did happen to find myself unfortunate enough to be carrying your child, you would be the very last man I would ever think of going to for assistance.'

Dominic looked down at her sharply. 'Who else should you go to but me?'

Caro might have behaved recklessly in coming to London in the first place, most especially by remaining to become a singer in a gentleman's gambling club, even more so by allowing the lovemaking with Dominic this morning to go as far as it had, but none of those things changed the fact that she was in reality Lady Caroline Copeland, and the daughter of an Earl. A woman, moreover, who was Dominic Vaughn's social equal. That he had no idea of her true identity was irrelevant—the man was arrogance personified!

'I am not without friends, sir.' Caro looked down the length of her nose at him—not an easy feat when she was so much shorter than he. 'Good and faithful friends, who would be true to me no matter what I have done.' Caro considered her two sisters to be her best friends as well as her family. As such, she had no doubt that both Diana and Elizabeth would stand beside her, no matter what the circumstances.

His top lip curled. 'And where have these friends been these past two weeks?'

Her chin rose. 'Exactly where they have always been.' There had been comfort for Caro in knowing that her two sisters would be waiting for her at Shoreley Hall whenever she should choose to return to them. No doubt with a severe reprimand from Diana for having run away at all, and a whispered urging from Elizabeth to relate her adventures once they were alone together, but nevertheless, Caro had no doubt that her sisters would stand beside her come what may.

Dominic scowled darkly as his hand once again took a firm grip upon her arm. 'Damn it, Caro—'

'No doubt, by tomorrow, I will be in possession of as many black-and-blue bruises as Lord Thorne!' Caro protested, knowing full well he wasn't hurting her, but the implication that he was would make him release her immediately.

'I apologise.' As she had predicted, Dominic did indeed let her arm go abruptly. 'Caro, put your stubborn pride aside for one moment, and just consider—'

'The honour of becoming your Countess?' she flung back at him derisively. 'I have considered it, my lord—and as just quickly dismissed it!' She eyed him with the disdain of a queen.

Dominic was fast losing patience with this conversation. In attempting to be honest with her and proposing marriage if she should find herself with child, it appeared he had only succeeded in insulting her. And nothing he had said since appeared to have in any way rectified that situation. It appeared, in fact, that he could not regain favour in her eyes no matter what he did or said.

Yet did he wish to regain favour in her eyes? Surely it would be better for both of them if he left things exactly as they were? It was unpleasant to feel the lash of her tongue and coldness of manner towards him, but the alternative would no doubt only result in another of those passionate encounters. Dominic still burned with desire for her, despite knowing how ill advised a repeat of this morning's activities would be.

Just to look at Caro was to remember the silky smoothness of her skin beneath his fingers. To remember the hard pebbles of her nipples being drawn into his mouth. The burning heat of her slick and yet tight thighs as she took him deep inside her… No, perhaps it would be much safer to foster this lack of accord between them!

'As you wish, Caro,' he said haughtily as he turned away to studiously straighten the shirt cuffs beneath his jacket.

Caro was absolutely incensed as he turned his back on her. 'I cannot imagine what I could have been thinking of this morning, allowing you to make love to me, when you are so obviously everything that I most despise in a man!'

He turned back sharply, nostrils flared. 'Just as your own rebellious and outspoken nature is everything that I most dislike in a woman!'

Caro eyed him coldly. 'Then we are agreed we do not care for each other?'

His jaw tightened. 'Indeed we are!'

She gave a cool nod. 'Then I will wish you good day, Lord Vaughn.'

Dominic eyed her with frustration. He had never met a woman who could bring him so quickly to anger. To impatience. To fury. But most especially to desire…

Logical thought told Dominic that if he wished to retain his sanity, then any future protection he provided for Caro's safety must necessarily be given from a distance. Just to be with her was playing the very devil with his self-control—

'Am I to remain a prisoner here, as I was at Blackstone House, until this danger from Nicholas Brown is over?' Caro interrupted Dominic's disturbing train of thought. 'Or am I to be allowed out for a carriage ride, at least?'

He refocused on her, his instincts telling him, for the sake of her own safety, to deny her even that small pleasure. However, that same instinct was quickly overridden by the memory of how flagrantly Caro had chosen to defy those same instructions only this morning and what the result of that defiance had been!

His mouth twisted. If he denied her, she'd likely find a way to disobey him, and then all hell would be let loose. Far better that he knew what she was doing at all times. 'I believe a carriage ride is permissible.'

'How kind!' Her sarcasm was unmistakable. 'And am I to take a maid with me on this carriage ride?'

'I do not believe that to be necessary unless you especially wish to do so. The grooms and coachmen here are also old comrades of mine,' he added before she had the opportunity to make another scathing comment. 'I trust in their ability to ensure that no harm befalls you.'

'*Further* harm, I think you mean?'

Dominic flinched as that verbal arrow of hers hit its mark. How he longed to take this rebellious woman into his arms. To kiss her into submission, if he could achieve her obedience in no other way. Yet at the same time he knew he should not, could not do either of those things. 'I will call on you again tomorrow—'

'I am sure there is no need to trouble yourself on my account,' she cut in.

Once again Dominic bit back his frustration, knowing how badly he had already handled this situation. 'I will take my leave, then.'

She nodded coolly. 'Lord Vaughn.'

There was nothing more for Dominic to do or say. Nothing he could do or say, it seemed, that would make things as they had once been between them.

Even if he did not know, could not completely comprehend, exactly what that had been...

* * *

Caro was filled with a raw restlessness once she was sure that the Earl had gone from the house, aware as she was of the rest of the afternoon and the long evening alone that now stretched before her. Tomorrow, too, in all probability, now that she had told Dominic it was unnecessary for him to call on her.

He should not have made her so angry! Should not have said those insulting things to her. Insults, Caro acknowledged ruefully, that she had more than returned.

How different things could have been, if instead of offering her marriage in that insulting manner, Dominic had first made a declaration of having fallen in love with her.

And if he had? Caro asked herself. What would her answer have been then to his marriage proposal? Would she have returned that declaration of love before accepting his marriage proposal?

The thought that she might have done both of those things was so disturbing to Caro that she found herself hurrying from the drawing room, pausing only long enough in the entrance hall to instruct Denby to have the coach brought round, before hurrying up to her bedchamber to collect her bonnet and pelisse. The afternoon seemed to have grown chilly since Dominic's abrupt departure...

Quite where she intended going on her carriage ride Caro had no idea, aware only that she had to escape the confines—the memories!—of Brockle House, if only for a short time.

She instructed the coachman to drive through the same park as yesterday—perhaps with the hope that she might once again catch a glimpse of the young girl with the dog that had so achingly reminded her of Elizabeth. But if that was her wish then she was disappointed, and after only a short time she was also a little tired of the curious glances being directed towards where she travelled in the black carriage so obviously bearing the crest of the Earl of Blackstone.

Feeling in need of sympathetic company, Caro knocked upon the roof of the carriage and instructed the coachman to take her to Nick's; Drew Butler and Ben had been delighted when she had called to see them this morning, so surely a second visit would not be too unwelcome?

But they had not gone far in that direction before Caro looked up and noticed a huge black cloud billowing up into the sky, her attention fixed on that black haze as she once again tapped on the roof of the coach. 'What is that about, Daley?'

'I believe it might be smoke, Mrs Morton,' he answered respectfully.

Smoke? If there was smoke then there must be a fire. And fire was a dangerous thing in a city the size of London. 'Perhaps we should go and see if we can be of any assistance, Daley?'

The middle-aged man looked uncertain. 'I doubt his lordship would approve, madam.'

Dominic.

Smoke?

Fire!

Quite why Caro was so convinced those three things were connected she had no idea—she only knew that she became more convinced of it by the second!

Chapter Fourteen

'You have to stop now, Drew; there is nothing more we can do,' Dominic instructed the man wearily.

The two men were blackened from head to toe from having several times entered the burning building before them, thick black smoke now billowing out of every doorway and window of the building even as the flames and sparks shot up through a hole in the burning roof.

Butler's eyes glittered wildly in his own soot-covered face. 'Ben is still in there!'

'There is nothing more we can do,' Dominic repeated dully, his own expression grim beneath the soot and grime as he stared up at the inferno that had once been Nick's.

'But—'

'He's gone, Drew.'

The older man's arms fell helplessly to his sides, his weathered face echoing the defeat both men felt as they could only stand now and watch the fire blaze out of control despite their own efforts and that of the men who had arrived a few minutes ago to help put it out.

The fire had been well under way when Dominic himself had arrived some half an hour or so ago. Nowhere near as fierce as it was now, of course, but even so he had quickly drawn a halt to Drew and Ben Jackson's efforts as they rushed in and out of the building salvaging what they could.

Unfortunately Ben had decided to return one more time to collect some personal belongings and the account books from the desk in Drew Butler's office.

He had not come out again...

Drew's hands clenched into fists at his sides. 'I'm going to kill the bastard!'

Dominic's jaw tightened. 'Brown?'

The older man's eyes blazed with fury as he turned. 'Who else?'

It was a conclusion that Dominic had come to himself the moment he saw the fire blazing and so easily recalled Brown's air of quiet satisfaction when he had left the gambling club earlier today.

Dominic had gone into the lion's den the evening before, with the intention of ascertaining whether Brown truly was the one responsible for the attack on Osborne. The slickness with which the other man had denied all knowledge of that attack—when he was a man known to boast that he was aware of everything that happened in what he regarded as being 'his city'—had seemed to indicate those suspicions were correct.

That Brown had himself arrived at the gambling club earlier today, supposedly to pay a visit on his old friends, Butler and Jackson, as well as the guarded conversation that had transpired between Brown and Dominic in Caro's presence, was simply a measure, Dominic was certain, of the other man's audacity.

A fire in that building, only hours after Brown's visit, was to Dominic's mind tantamount to a direct challenge...

He frowned darkly. 'The law will need evidence before they will agree to act.'

The older man gave a scathing snort. 'I don't need any evidence to recognise Brown had a hand in this.'

Neither did Dominic. 'Be assured, I feel exactly the way you do about this, Drew, but nevertheless I must seriously advise against taking matters into your own hands—'

'So I'm to sit back and let him get away with murder, am I?'

Dominic had already experienced one slight on his honour in the past two days; he was not about to suffer another one. He put his hand on the older man's arm. 'I am hoping you will trust me to ensure that will not happen.'

Drew barely seemed to hear him. 'I worked for the man for almost twenty years. Had my suspicions before this of what a low-down cur he could be, but—' He gave a disgusted shake of his head. 'Brown did this as surely as my name is Andrew Butler.'

Dominic drew his breath in sharply. 'And I have assured you that I will ensure he will be made to pay for his crimes—'

'Dominic! Drew! Oh, thank goodness you are both safe!'

Dominic turned just in time to catch Caro as she launched herself into his arms.

Caro had barely been able to comprehend the sight that had met her eyes as the carriage turned into the avenue and she saw the blazing remains of the club where she had worked until two evenings ago. The whole building was ablaze, with that heavy black smoke billowing everywhere, and dozens of men hurrying back and forth as they threw water upon the blaze to prevent it passing to the vulnerable neighbouring buildings.

Her relief when she spotted Dominic, standing to one side in conversation with Drew, had been immense. So much so that she had briefly forgotten her earlier disagreement with Dominic, and simply thrown herself into his arms out of the sheer relief of seeing him safe.

Her cheeks now felt hot—and not from the effects of the fire!—as she gathered herself together and extracted herself from Dominic's embrace before turning to face the older man. 'How good it is to see that you are unharmed, Drew—'

'Never mind that now, Caro,' Dominic was the one to answer her as he pulled her firmly back from the danger of the hot timbers now starting to fall from the top of the blazing building. 'Explain what you are doing here, if you please!'

She frowned up into his dark and disapproving face. 'I had gone out for a drive, as I told you I intended, when I saw the smoke...'

'And decided to investigate,' Dominic recognised with barely restrained violence. 'Did you not realise that by doing so you might have become caught up in the blaze yourself and possibly been injured?'

She waved an airy hand. 'I hope I have more sense than to have gone close enough so that—'

'And yet here you are!' Dominic glared down at her, very aware that she was as yet unaware of Ben Jackson's absence. That when she did realise he would have another crisis on his hands; Caro's affection for the gentle giant had been obvious from the first, and once she discovered that Ben had disappeared into the blazing building some minutes ago, and not returned, she was sure to react. In truth, Dominic had no idea which direction those emotions would take, tears and cries of anguish, or anger that her friend might have perished in the fire...

She gave a pained frown. 'I was concerned—'

'And now that concern has been satisfied I want you to get back into your carriage immediately and return to Brockle House,' Dominic instructed firmly.

'But—'

'Caro, do not argue with me over this, as you seem to feel you must argue every other point in our conversations.' Dominic's jaw was as tightly clenched as Drew's fists had been minutes ago. 'You can be of no possible help here,' he added.

'Might I suggest that you leave me to continue dealing with the situation here whilst you escort Caro home?' Drew quietly drew Dominic's attention, his pointed look in the direction of some activity at the side of the building enough to tell Dominic that Ben had been found; neither man believed he could have lived through the minutes he had spent trapped in that raging inferno...

'That is unnecessary—'

'It is very necessary.' Dominic easily cut across Caro's protest even as he gave a brief nod to the older man in recognition of their silent exchange.

'To you, perhaps—'

'To me, too, Caro.' Drew gently added his own weight behind the argument as he moved forwards so that he now stood beside Dominic. 'Do as his lordship advises and return to your carriage—'

'Why are you suddenly both in such a hurry for me to leave?' Caro eyed both men suspiciously as she realised they seemed to be crowding around her. Herding her, actually. Much like her father's estate workers when they were gathering the livestock together to house them in the huge barns over the winter. 'I—where is Ben?' Her gaze moved sharply to the left and then to the right, but with Drew and Dominic standing like two sentinels directly in front of her, she found that vision limited.

Deliberately?

'Caro—'

'Where is Ben, Dominic?' Caro lifted her hands and placed one against the chest of both men with the intention of pushing them aside, nimbly stepping around them when neither man was made to move. Just in time to see that several of the men who had been fighting the fire were now carrying something from the side of the building. Something heavy. A dead weight, in fact... 'Ben?' she gasped weakly.

'No, Caro!' Dominic reached out and grasped her by the shoulders as she would have run across to where the men were now placing that cumbersome burden down upon the ground.

Her gaze was frantic as she lifted her hands to fight against Dominic's hold upon her. 'Can you not see that it is Ben?'

'We know who it is, Caro.' Once again it was Drew who spoke gently. 'If there's anything that can be done for Ben, then you can be assured that it will be,' he added grimly.

'The best thing you can do for him now is to return home without any more fuss.'

Caro became very still in Dominic's grasp as she looked first at Drew and then back to Dominic, the latter giving a slight shake of his head as he turned back from looking at the frantic activity around that scorched bundled of rags that had obviously been Ben Jackson.

Because even from this distance Caro could see that his spirit was no longer there…

An anguished cry escaped her lips even as she felt her legs buckle beneath her and began to fall slowly to the ground.

'You are perfectly safe, Caro.' Dominic's voice sounded harsher than he had intended, in the otherwise silence of the moving carriage, as he tried to still her struggles to free herself from where he held her tightly against his chest. 'Please be still, Caro,' he urged more gently.

For once in their acquaintance she heeded him, unmoving in his arms as she looked up at him with huge sea-green eyes that were rapidly filling with tears. 'Is Ben really gone, Dominic?'

He drew in a ragged breath. 'If it is any consolation then I believe he would have died from breathing in the smoke long before the fire ever came anywhere near him.' He sincerely hoped that was the case, at least.

Although the method of Ben's death did not change the fact he was indeed dead. And as a result of a fire both Drew and Dominic believed to have been deliberately set by Nicholas Brown.

'Truly, Dominic?'

He forced the rigidity from his expression at those grim

thoughts of Brown's cowardly act before looking down at Caro, knowing that she needed to believe that Ben's death had been as painless as was possible given the circumstances. 'Truly.' Dominic nodded.

He had paused only long enough, after seeing the unconscious Caro into the safety of the carriage, to converse briefly with the men who had brought out Ben's body. It seemed they had found him collapsed in the hallway leading to Drew's office situated at the back of the club, where the fire itself was the least fierce.

'He was such a kind young man.' Caro's voice caught emotionally.

Dominic had seen Ben off and on for years on his visits to the gambling club; it had been impossible not to feel an affection for the younger man's almost childlike acceptance of his lot in life.

As such, Dominic knew that it was going to be hard for all of them to accept the death of such an affable and likeable young man. 'He was,' he acknowledged flatly.

Caro pulled out of his arms to slowly sit up. 'How could it have happened, Dominic?' She gave a slightly dazed shake of her head. 'I can hardly believe I was sitting drinking tea with him only hours ago...' The tears began to fall unchecked down her cheeks.

'Yes.' Dominic's mouth tightened as he easily recalled that Brown had been seated at that table, too. 'We may perhaps have more insight into how the fire began once the flames have died down and we are able to get back inside the building.' Although in his own mind—and undoubtedly that of Drew Butler—Brown, or one of his henchmen acting on instructions, was clearly to blame.

'Do you believe Nicholas Brown to be responsible?'

Dominic was not in the least surprised at the speed of Caro's astuteness. 'Undoubtedly,' he confirmed grimly.

'As just another deliberate act to cause you as much inconvenience as possible, or do you think he really meant either Ben or Drew—or possibly both—to die?' Her face had taken on a slightly green cast as she voiced that last possibility.

As far as Dominic was aware, he had never lied to Caro; in fact, his actions, especially this morning, had possibly been too honest where she was concerned. Possibly? The whole of his behaviour today, from making love to her to the crassness of his marriage proposal, had been honest to the point of self-destruction!

That she had allowed him to hold her just now, even briefly, Dominic knew was due only to her distress over Ben's death. Once she had recovered her senses they would no doubt be back to a state of daggers' drawn.

He drew in a deep breath as he chose his words carefully. 'I believe it was the former. At the same time, I also believe Brown did not care who, or if, anyone should be hurt in the fire,' he acknowledged heavily before taking the kerchief from his pocket and wiping the worst of the soot and grime from his face and hands.

Caro breathed shakily. 'Ben would not have hurt even a fly.'

Remembering those ham-sized fists, and the several occasions upon which he had witnessed the younger man wielding them, Dominic was not quite sure of the truth of that statement! Nevertheless, he took Caro's point; there had never been any malice in Ben's actions in doing his job defending the club.

'I am sure it was pure misfortunate that Ben perished in

the fire.' Dominic was not as certain of that as he sounded, aware as he was that this morning Nicholas Brown had witnessed both Ben and Drew busily at work in the gambling club so that it might re-open as soon as was possible.

Caro looked up at him closely. 'Do you honestly believe that?'

'I…believe it is a reasonable assumption, yes,' he said carefully.

'I am neither a child nor an imbecile, Dominic, and after all that has happened, I do not expect you to treat me as such!' Caro's expression had become fierce as she obviously picked up on his evasion.

He had no doubts as to her maturity or intelligence; it was simply not in his nature to confide his thoughts and feelings to another person. 'I assure you it is not my intention to do either of those things, Caro. I simply feel it is better not to voice my concerns until I can be completely sure of my facts.'

He also had no intention of allowing her to become in the least involved in the reckoning that Dominic had every intention would shortly descend upon Nicholas Brown; Caro was impetuous enough, reckless enough, to place herself in danger if she believed it was necessary to avenge Ben.

No, Dominic had every intention of dealing personally with Mr Nicholas Brown…

Caro still looked slightly ill. 'I cannot conceive of anyone doing something so…so heinous, as to have deliberately started a fire.'

Dominic was only too aware that Brown was reputed to have done much worse things than that in the past. Just as Dominic was now aware—too late to save Ben, unfortunately—that after the attack on Osbourne two nights ago, and despite Drew's assurances that he was quite capable of taking care of himself and his own family, including Ben, Dominic should have insisted on more safeguards being put in place. The reason he had not was because he had been so distracted by the need to protect Caro that he had given little thought to anything else...

A danger that now seemed more immediate than ever; Dominic had thought to make Caro safe by offering her his protection, by moving her as quickly as he could to the obscurity of Brockle House. But Brown's visit to the gambling club this morning had exposed Caro, if not as the masked singer, then certainly as a closer acquaintance to Dominic than the cousins they claimed to be. Now he feared the man might even know that Caro resided at Brockle House as from this morning...

Dominic shared Drew's eagerness to confront Nicholas Brown, to ensure that he paid for his crimes—in fact, at that moment, he knew he would enjoy nothing more than personally strangling the man with his own bare hands— but his explanation to Caro, when she had previously dared to question his honour, was also true. A soldier, an officer, did not confront his enemy until he had all of his troops in place.

And Nicholas Brown was now most certainly Dominic's enemy!

'Caro, I believe it would be best if I were to stay at Brockle House tonight.' He looked at her from underneath lowered lids.

Her own eyes widened. 'I believed we had both made our feelings on that subject perfectly clear—'

'I did not say it was with any intention of sharing your

bed,' Dominic cut in impatiently. 'Only that it might be… safer, perhaps, if I were to stay at Brockle House tonight.'

Caro's cheeks warmed as she realised her mistake. Of course Dominic did not intend sharing her bed again tonight; he did not intend sharing her bed ever again! Something she should feel grateful for. And yet somehow did not… 'Is it your belief that we are both now in mortal danger from Nicholas Brown?'

Dominic shrugged. 'Perhaps.'

Caro was consumed with annoyance at Dominic's reticence, his refusal to share his thoughts and feelings with her. He had to be the most self-contained man she had ever met—and that was including her father, who had become so shut inside himself after their mother had left them all to go and live in London ten years ago, that he had never mentally been completely with his three daughters again. As far as she could tell, Dominic shared none of his thoughts and ideas with anyone.

Least of all a woman to whom he had only offered marriage if *by some mischance*, as he'd put it, she should find herself carrying his child!

'If you feel it is necessary, Dominic, then of course you have every right to spend the night in what is, after all, your own property.' She gave a cool inclination of her head.

Dominic breathed heavily through his nose. 'In that case, until this situation has been resolved to my complete satisfaction, I feel it best if I spend all of my nights at Brockle House.'

Caro's eyes widened. 'Are you not going to find that a little…restricting?'

He scowled darkly. 'In what way?'

She shrugged. 'Would such an arrangement not...limit your own freedom to come and go as you wished?'

Dominic drew in an angry breath. 'Caro, if you are once again suggesting that I might have a mistress set up in another house in London somewhere, and with whom I might wish to spend my nights, then let me state, once and for all, that I do not now, nor have I ever, had a mistress in the accepted sense of the word!' He eyed her coldly.

'No?' Her brows rose. 'I would be interested to know why not.'

'Then it is an interest I am afraid you will just have to continue to endure,' Dominic growled. 'After only a few days of having you as a permanent fixture in my life, of feeling responsible for you twenty-four hours a day, I am more convinced than ever that my decision never to be tied down by such an arrangement was the correct one.' He meant to be insulting, and he knew he had succeeded when he saw the sparkle of anger in the deep blue-green of Caro's eyes.

A spark of anger that Dominic had deliberately incited...

'That situation can be rectified any time you choose to let me leave both your home and your company,' she came back challengingly.

'Unfortunately, it cannot.' Dominic sighed. 'Not until Brown has been brought to justice. Never fear, Caro,' he added mockingly. 'I am sure that Brockle House is large enough for us to successfully avoid spending time in each other's company, if that is what you wish?'

'I wish it more than anything!' There was an angry flush to Caro's cheeks as she turned away from him to present him with her profile as she stared out of the carriage window.

Dominic accepted that it had been cruel of him to bedevil her in this way when their lovemaking had ended so disastrously earlier today. When she had been present as they pulled Ben's body from the burning building. His only excuse was that his baiting of her had briefly cast aside her bewilderment and pain over Ben's death, to be replaced by a little of the usual fiery spirit he so admired and which was such a large part of her nature.

A spirit Dominic dearly hoped would help see her through, what he was sure, were going to be several difficult days...

Chapter Fifteen

'Caro, when I said earlier that you might avoid my company as much as is possible for the duration of my stay here, it was not with any intention that you would eat your dinner in your bedchamber whilst I am left to dine downstairs alone.'

She was completely unmoved by the impatience in Dominic's tone as she turned to look at where he stood in the open doorway of her bedchamber.

It had been almost two hours since they had arrived back at Brockle House. Dominic appeared to have bathed and changed out of the soiled clothing of earlier into a black evening jacket and snowy white linen with a meticulously tied neckcloth. Evidence, perhaps, that in the interim he had sent to Blackstone House for both his valet and his clothes.

Caro had spent those same two hours trying to come to terms with the fact that Ben Jackson was dead. To accept that her friend had perished in a fire Dominic believed had been started deliberately by Nicholas Brown or one of his close associates.

For years she had chafed and fought against the sheltered life she had been forced to lead in Hampshire, with the result that she had not hesitated to put her plan into action once she had decided to run away to London as a means of avoiding the arrival of her guardian and his unwanted offer of marriage. She had believed herself to be thoroughly capable of taking care of herself, and that spending several weeks in London would be an exciting adventure she would remember for the rest of her life.

Nothing about her previous life could possibly have prepared her for such stark reality as she had witnessed today.

She gave a slight shake of her head. 'I have not eaten my dinner in my bedchamber.'

Dominic scowled darkly as he strode forcefully into the room. 'In that case, why haven't you?'

She gave a listless shrug. 'I am not hungry.'

'Caro—'

'Dominic, please!' She stood up restlessly, also having bathed and changed into the deep rose-coloured gown. 'How can I possibly eat when every time I so much as think of poor Ben's fate I feel utterly nauseous?'

Dominic's expression softened as he realised that, while he'd had some little relief from her tempting charms in the past couple of hours, suggesting they avoid each other's company had not been particularly beneficial to her; he could see the evidence of the tears she had obviously shed once she was alone in the slight redness about pain-darkened eyes and the pallor of her cheeks. 'It will not help anyone if you make yourself ill—'

'You cannot expect me to eat when Ben is lying dead in

the morgue!' Caro's voice broke emotionally over the last, and she buried her face in her hands, her shoulders shaking, as she once again began to sob piteously.

Dominic felt a tightening in his chest as he witnessed her distress, taking the two steps that enabled him to reach out and take her into his arms, her head resting against his chest as she wept. He had never been at ease with a woman's tears, and, after the intimacies they had shared, he found Caro's especially difficult to bear. Her close proximity was even more difficult as he felt her arms move about his waist and the warm spread of her fingers across his back...

Dear Lord! Desire, arousal were the last things he should be feeling when she was obviously so distraught. And yet, try as he might, he could exert no control over the stirring, the hardening of his thighs, as Caro nestled the softness of her body against his. She rested so trustingly against him—for Dominic was sure that she shared none of those same thoughts of desire as she continued to sob quietly. His own physical response to that trust was as inappropriate as it would no doubt be unwelcome should she become aware of it, and he grimaced with annoyance at his own body's betrayal.

As Caro's tears slowly began to abate she sensed a change in the mood between herself and Dominic. A tension, an intimacy, that invaded her senses with a subtlety that was as insidious as it was undeniable. The very air around them seemed to thicken, to deepen, and she was suddenly completely aware of the tense heat of his body and the ragged unevenness of his breathing, as his chest rose and fell beneath the increasing warmth of her cheek.

She was also aware of the thick length of his arousal as it continued to grow and press against the softness of her own thighs.

Her breath caught in her throat as she slowly raised her head to look up at him, knowing by the glittering intensity of the silver gaze that looked down and met hers that she was not mistaken concerning his present state of arousal.

She moistened dry lips before speaking. 'Dominic, how can it be that we feel this…this desire after all that has happened today?' She was utterly bewildered—almost ashamed—by the feelings now coursing hotly through her own body.

Dominic shook his head. 'I have seen it dozens of times in soldiers following a battle,' he recalled huskily. 'I believe it is a need, a desire, to reaffirm one's own place in the mortal world following confrontation with death.'

Caro breathed shallowly. 'Is it not shocking for me to feel this way now?'

His expression softened. 'Does it feel shocking to you?'

'No.' The pink tip of her tongue swept across her lips a second time. 'I— It feels as if, as you say, I have a need to know that we both still live.'

Dominic looked down at her searchingly, a gaze that she met unflinchingly. 'Will you allow me to make love to you, Caro?' he asked gently.

Her eyes widened. 'But I thought you had made it quite clear that we could not, must not, repeat the events of this morning?'

'Neither will we.'

Her frown was perplexed. 'I do not understand…'

Dominic gave a rueful smile. 'There are many ways in which to make love, my dear. Many of them do not involve the penetration that could so easily result in you becoming with child.'

Caro's cheeks felt hot. 'I see. And will you...will you show me these other ways?' Her cheeks were flushed, her eyes fever bright.

But not with awkwardness or discomfort, Dominic noted with admiration, but instead with a curiosity and underlying excitement. He knew he should not allow this to happen, that he should refuse to acknowledge the invitation in her eyes. But as he looked down at her, he clearly saw the same desire in her that now throbbed through his own body, and he knew he would not, could not, walk away from her as he surely should.

He, too, had had time to think since they had parted after arriving at Brockle House earlier. To realise that she could just as easily have gone to visit Drew and Ben at Nick's this afternoon rather than this morning. To acknowledge that she might have been inside the club with the other two men when the fire began, and easily envisage the nightmare of what might have been—Caro lying in the morgue rather than Ben Jackson...

Which perhaps explained why he had felt it so keenly when Denby had told him a short time ago that Caro had asked him to inform Dominic she would not be joining him downstairs for dinner. Whatever the reason, no matter how much more it might complicate matters if he were to make love with her again, he knew that it was something he urgently needed to do.

Caro pulled out of his arms to turn her back on him before looking at him over her shoulder. 'I believe we should start by removing my gown?'

He drew his breath in sharply as he looked at the calm

determination in Caro's expression for several long seconds before raising his hands to begin releasing the buttons down the back of her gown. Only to falter slightly once he had unfastened a half-dozen of those tiny buttons. 'Are you *sure* you want to do this?'

'I am very sure, Dominic,' she murmured even as she tilted her head forwards to reveal the fragile vulnerability of her nape.

It was more than any man could bear—more, certainly, than he could at this moment—to resist Caro's absolute conviction in what they were about to do. And once he had unfastened the rose-coloured gown, allowing it to pool on the carpet at her feet, before she stepped free of its confinement and turned to face him wearing only a shift that nevertheless revealed the firm thrust of her breasts tipped by those darker nipples, and the silky thatch of golden curls between her thighs, Dominic had no room for thoughts of resistance. His desire blazed completely out of his control as she reached up to slip the thin straps of her last garment down over the slenderness of her arms, before allowing that, too, to fall at her feet and she stood before him completely naked.

Dominic meant to be gentle with her, out of consideration for the discomfort she must still feel following their lovemaking this morning. But it was a gentleness Caro firmly rejected as she stepped boldly into his arms before raising her head so that her lips might capture his. That kiss became wild, fiercely heated, as she dispensed with his jacket and waistcoat before unfastening his shirt and pushing her hands inside the silky material to caress his bared chest.

Dominic returned the heat of that kiss even as he reached

up to rend the material of his shirt in two to allow her better access to his flesh. Caro's nails scraped over the hard nubbins nestled amongst the silky dark hair that covered his chest, the hard tips of her own breasts pressed against the muscled hardness of his abdomen. He gasped into her mouth as those caressing, confident hands moved slowly downwards to stroke the length of his erection as it jutted proudly against the confinement of his pantaloons.

It did not remain confined for long as Caro easily dispensed with the six buttons at the sides of his pantaloons before peeling that flap of material aside, the fingers of one hand curling about his engorged arousal even as she cupped him beneath with the other.

Dominic broke the kiss, his groan one of aching longing as he felt her dextrous fingers sweep across the sensitive tip before moving down along the length of him. 'Yes, Caro! Oh, God, yes!'

'Tell me how to give you pleasure, Dominic,' she encouraged softly.

His breath caught in his throat. 'Kiss me there, take me into the sweetness of your mouth!' His moan was heartfelt as Caro dropped softly to her knees in front of him, that sea-green gaze looking up to steadily meet his as she slowly and deliberately opened those kiss-swollen lips and took him into the fiery heat of her mouth.

Dominic's knees almost buckled completely as he looked down at her pleasuring him, his hands moving to become entangled in her golden curls as she continued her delicious ministrations until he knew he was going to lose control. He needed to taste her before that happened, wanted to pleasure her in the same way.

Dominic ignored her slightly reproachful look as he gently disengaged himself and pulled her back up on to her feet. He swung her up into his arms and carried her over to lie her down upon the bed, gently propping her head upon the pillows. She watched him as he first drew off his boots and then threw off the rest off his clothes before moving to kneel between her legs. The darkness of his gaze briefly held hers captive before he lowered his head between her parted thighs to run his own tongue along the length of her opening before rasping moistly over and around her sensitive bud, feeling it pulse with each rhythmic stroke. 'Watch me, Caro!' he urged.

She obeyed as he gently parted her golden curls and cried out as he lowered his head once again to stroke that pulsing bud with the hard tip of his tongue, and she felt the pleasure begin to build, to grow, deep inside her. Suffusing her with heat. Turning her limbs to water. Her head fell back against the pillows even as her thighs began to undulate against that marauding mouth and tongue.

That pleasure surged out of control as his hands moved up to cup and capture both her breasts before he rolled the nipples between finger and thumb, Caro's release hitting with the force of a tidal wave as he squeezed those roused tips at the same time as his tongue thrust into her time and time again until she lay limply back against the pillows.

Dominic moved up on to his knees to look down at Caro as she lay there, replete and naked against the pillows. 'My turn now, love,' he said throatily.

Caro was completely focused on that jutting arousal as she came up on to her knees to move down the bed and kiss him slowly from base to tip, before then taking him fully into the heat of her mouth.

It was too much, Dominic already far too aroused from

both the taste of her in his mouth and her earlier attentions, and his hands tightly gripped Caro's shoulders as he climaxed fiercely, hotly, triumphantly…

Caro's hand moved in a gentle caress against the unruly darkness of the hair at Dominic's nape, his head resting lightly against her breast as they lay naked together in the aftermath of their wild and satisfying lovemaking.

She felt no awkwardness, no shame; she knew that they had both needed what had just happened between them, that he had been correct in that they had both needed to reaffirm their precarious grip on mortality, and the silence between them now was companionable rather than uncomfortable.

Dominic raised his head slightly to look at her, that silver gaze guarded. 'I was not too rough with you?'

'Not at all,' she assured without hesitation. 'Was I too rough with you?' she added, aware that she had been somewhat less than gentle herself!

He smiled slightly before lowering his head back down on to her breast. 'Not in any way I would not like you to repeat if, or indeed whenever, the mood should take you.'

Caro's cheeks felt warm as she recalled the way in which she had caressed and kissed Dominic so intimately. She had no knowledge of lovemaking between a man and a woman other than the things he had shown her these past few days, and yet she had gloried in touching and kissing the beauty of his hard arousal.

'I no longer feel quite so…empty.' Her voice was husky with emotion.

'Nor I,' Dominic acknowledged softly.

She frowned as a thought occurred to her. 'Do you know whether or not Ben had any family?'

Dominic's shoulders tensed beneath the caress of Caro's fingers. 'He has a sister, I believe. A Mrs Grey.'

'She will be deeply saddened by his death.'

'As we all are,' Dominic said heavily. 'Drew was to go and see her as soon as he was able to get away. I have asked him to convey my regrets, and also to tell her that I will call on her tomorrow to discuss the funeral arrangements if that is what she wishes.'

'I would like to attend the funeral.'

The tension in Dominic's shoulders increased. 'I am not sure that is a good idea—'

'It was not a request, Dominic,' Caro insisted. 'Have you—have you seen much of death?' she asked before he could voice any more objections.

'More than I care to remember,' he admitted harshly.

Caro breathed a sigh. 'My own mother died when I was but ten years old, and she was not at home with us when it happened.' She gave a pained frown as she remembered the circumstances under which her mother had died. 'My father died only a few months ago, but he had been ill for some time, and in truth, it was more of a happy release for him than a shock to…to his family.'

Dominic was aware that the pieces that made up Caro's life were given rarely and sparingly, but she had said enough just now for him to know it was no more a father that she hid from than a husband.

He could not resist looking up at her and teasing her a little. 'I believe you told Drew that it was a maiden aunt who had died a few months ago, and in doing so left you homeless as well as penniless.'

Two bright wings of colour now brightened Caro's cheeks. 'I did say that, yes.'

'And...?'

She gave an irritated little snort. 'What difference does it make whether it was a father or a maiden aunt?'

'None at all—except maybe to that father or aunt.' Dominic placed a slow and lingering kiss upon the side of her breast in apology for his teasing of what they both knew to be a complete fabrication of her previous life. But he felt too relaxed, too satiated, to seriously question it at this moment. That relaxed contentment rendered him ill prepared for Caro's next question...

'Obviously you are the Earl, so your own father is no longer with us, but what of the rest of your family? Your mother, for instance?'

All relaxation fled, all contentment, as Dominic sat up sharply. 'Also dead. They both died when I was but twelve years old.'

Caro gasped. 'Both your parents?'

'Yes.'

'Together?'

'No. Caro—'

'Please do not go, Dominic!' She reached out to grasp his arm as he would have stood up, her gaze pleading as he paused to look down at her. 'If you do not wish to talk of your parents, then we will not do so,' she promised huskily.

Dominic concentrated on how her loosened curls looked, all spread out on the pillow behind her. Her eyes were a beautiful, luminous sea-green, her lips slightly swollen from the kisses they had shared. Her cheeks were flushed, as was the delicate skin of her breasts, the tips all pouting and rosy from his attentions. His expression softened as he slowly exhaled his tension away before once again lowering his head to rest against one of those kiss-reddened breasts, his hand moving to lightly cup its twin. 'There is nothing more to say about my parents other than that they are both dead.'

'But your mother, at least, must have been quite young when she died?'

Dominic sighed. 'She was but two and thirty at the time of the accident. My father was eight and thirty when he chose to follow her only days later.'

Caro stilled, her heart pounding loudly beneath Dominic's head. 'He *chose* to follow her?'

Dominic had learnt early on in their acquaintance not to underestimate Caro's intelligence, and with this question she once again proved he had been wise not to do so. 'Yes.'

Caro's throat moved convulsively as she swallowed before speaking. 'Can you possibly mean that he took his own life?'

Dominic made no attempt to halt his movements a second time, instead sitting up and moving away from her. Caro was sensible enough—or too stunned still—not to try to stop him, either by word or deed. He shrugged. 'He loved my mother very much and obviously saw no reason to continue living without her.'

'But he had a young son to care for!'

'Obviously he did not feel I was reason enough to continue living.' Dominic stood up and began pulling on the pantaloons he had discarded so eagerly only minutes ago.

Caro reached down and pulled the bedsheet up to her chin as she watched him with huge, disbelieving eyes. 'My own father loved my mother very much, too, and was devastated when she died. But even so, I do not think he ever contemplated the idea of taking his own life; he accepted that he had other responsibilities—'

Dominic's scathing snort cut off her halting words. 'Obviously your father was made of sterner stuff than my own.'

'I do not believe it was a question of that—'

'And I believe we have talked of this quite long enough for one evening!' His eyes glittered a pale and dangerous silver.

Caro lowered her gaze. 'It is just that I do not understand how any man, no matter how devastated he is by loss, could deliberately take his own life at the cost of leaving his twelve-year-old son alone in the world.'

'I have *told* you why!' Dominic paused to glare across at her once he had pulled on the tattered remnants of his shirt. 'He loved my mother so much he had no desire to live without her.'

The compassion in her eyes as she looked up at him was almost his undoing. As it was, the painful memories this conversation evoked felt like a heavy weight bearing down upon him. 'I am sure my father felt justified in his actions, Caro,' he said.

Caro looked stubborn. 'I do not believe there can be any justification for leaving a twelve-year-old boy alone and without either of his parents.'

Dominic's dark brows lifted, his expression hard and uncompromising; eyes a steely grey, cheekbones as sharp as blades beneath the tautness of his skin, that vicious scar livid from eyes to jaw, and his mouth a thin line. 'Not even if you hold that twelve-year-old boy—your own son—responsible for the death of the woman you loved?'

Caro gave a shocked gasp, all the colour draining from her cheeks as she stared up at Dominic with those huge sea-green eyes.

Chapter Sixteen

Dominic knew that the look of horrified disbelief on Caro's face was perfectly justified; no doubt that was exactly the emotion she was feeling, at even the suggestion that a twelve-year-old boy could be responsible for killing his own mother. Let alone that it might actually be the truth…

Not that Dominic had caused his mother's coach to leave the road and plunge into the river. Nor had he wedged the door of that carriage shut so that it was impossible for her to escape when the carriage began to sink and the water to flood inside it. And neither had he physically held his mother's head beneath the water until she'd drowned.

No, he had not personally done any of those things. Nevertheless, he knew he was as much to blame for his mother's death as if he had done every one of them.

Caro shook her head. 'It is utterly ridiculous to even suggest you might have done such a thing.'

'Is it?'

'Utterly,' she spoke with conviction.

'You do not believe me capable of killing someone?' He eyed her tauntingly.

'Of course you have killed in the heat of battle,' she said. 'It is the way of things. But I do not believe you capable of harming any woman, let alone killing your own mother.'

'Come now, Caro, I am sure you must know me well enough by now to realise that I am capable of all manner of things. Seducing, not once, but twice, the young woman I have taken into my care is only one of them.' He looked disgusted with himself.

'I was as instrumental as you in both those seductions.' Caro's cheeks warmed with guilty colour as she quickly stood and collected her wrap, securing the belt of that robe around her waist. 'I also believe you are only saying these things about your mother in order to shock me.'

His mouth twisted. 'Am I succeeding?'

'I am more disappointed that you feel you have to say things that cannot possibly be true—'

'Oh, but they are true,' he cut in, his voice silkily soft, eyes narrowed to challenging slits as she looked across at him. 'I, and I alone, am responsible for the death of my mother.'

Once again Caro could see the ruthlessness in Dominic's expression; yes, she had no doubt that if he deemed it necessary for someone to die, then he would be cold and decisive, even savage, in the execution of that death. But the underlying edge of gentleness, of love, she had heard in his voice as he spoke of his mother told her that he could not have had a hand in her death. Besides which, what would a twelve-year-old boy know of killing anyone?

'Tell me how she died, Dominic,' she urged.

'What difference does the manner of her death make?'

'It makes all the difference in the world,' Caro said crossly. 'Why did you tell me these things if you did not wish me to question you?' Although she might take a guess on it having something to do with him thinking that he deserved to have people—women, most especially—feeling no affection for him.

But also an indication, perhaps, that he might also fear that she was falling in love with him? Caro winced inside. That he was determined to foil any such softness of emotion, if it existed, was humiliating. Worse than humiliating, if he'd guessed her feelings correctly.

In contrast, Dominic was a difficult man to read. That was deliberate, she felt sure. On the surface he was an arrogant, hard and uncompromising man, who outwardly scorned all the softer emotions. Yet, at the same time, he'd shown a deep concern over the attack on his friend, Lord Thorne. And instead of being furious earlier at the loss of his gambling club, as many gentlemen might have been, Dominic had instead only revealed a deep sorrow and anger at the death of poor Ben.

And Dominic's concern for Caro's own safety and welfare was just as undeniable, even though he took great pains to claim he had been forced into saving her from her own reckless behaviour!

He might give himself all sorts of reasons for his behaviour, but Caro had seen the man beneath and would have no part of it. 'I will know the truth, Dominic, if you please!'

He arched mocking brows. 'And will you then reveal to me the truth about yourself?'

Caro was in a quandary. No doubt he considered such an exchange of information fair. And it probably was. Except she could not confide her own situation to him, especially now when, having thought long and hard earlier this evening, Caro had decided that, guardian or not, she must return to Shoreley Hall as soon after Ben's funeral as possible.

Once back at Shoreley Hall she would assume the mantle of Lady Caroline Copeland. That being so, there was absolutely no reason for him to know anything further concerning Caro Morton, a woman who did not exist out of the small circle of acquaintances she had made in London.

She drew in a deep breath. 'I must refuse.'

Dominic's lip curled. 'Then it would seem we are at an impasse.'

'The two situations are completely different,' Caro snapped her impatience with his stubbornness. 'I have not just laid claim to killing someone!'

'How do I know that you did not see off this "maiden aunt" or your father before making your escape to London?' Dominic eyed her mockingly.

Because there was no maiden aunt, and of course Caro had not been involved in her father's death! But the second part of his statement, concerning her having made her escape to London, was too close to the truth for comfort...

'I believe you are merely trying to fudge the issue by making ridiculous accusations,' she said.

'You may think what you please,' Dominic retorted. 'As far as the subject of my mother, and the manner of her death, is concerned, I have no wish to discuss the matter further. With you or anyone else.' The finality in his tone did not allow for further argument. 'I believe I will wish you goodnight now, Caro.' He gave her a brief bow before striding across the room, pausing briefly when he reached the door. 'If you wish it, I will have some supper brought up to you.'

'That will not be necessary, thank you.' Caro felt even less like eating now than she had earlier. Ben was still dead, and contemplating food after the intimacies she and Dominic had just shared was impossible. Also, his refusal to further discuss his mother's death had left Caro with more questions than answers, especially as she now feared she might indeed have fallen in love with him!

Dominic's face darkened in fury when he returned to Brockle House late the following morning, accompanied by Drew, and was informed by a concerned Denby that Mrs Morton and Mr Brown were taking tea together in the Gold Salon.

The fact that Nicholas Brown had come here at all was disquieting. That Caro had chosen to receive him, knowing all that she did about the other man, was more disturbing still in view of what Dominic knew to be her often reckless and impulsive nature!

'Damn it, Denby.' He glared at the man who had once been his batman in the army but was now, for the sake of expediency, posing as his butler. 'What is the good of my installing you here to protect Caro when you then let the biggest threat to her calmly walk through the front door?'

The other man gave a pained frown. 'Mrs Morton had been for a walk in the park across the way—she was accompanied by my wife,' he added quickly as Dominic looked set for another explosion. 'It was apparently as she was returning to the house that she saw Mr Brown stepping down from his coach and stopped to engage him in conversation.'

Which sounded exactly the sort of thing Caro would

do, Dominic realised frustratedly. He also realised that
Brown must have had the two of them followed yesterday
to know to find Caro at Brockle House at all. 'That still
does not explain why you allowed the man to accompany
her into the house?'

'I tried to prevent it from happening—'

'Obviously you did not try hard enough!'

'My wife is in the Gold Salon with them, my lord.'

'I am relieved to see that you have not completely lost
your senses!' Dominic barked.

'We are wasting time here, my lord.' Drew put a steadying hand upon Dominic's arm. 'Brown can be a wily cur at
the best of times, and I really don't think we should leave
Caro to deal with him alone any longer. She is also likely
to say more than she ought to him.'

'Caro has no more sense than a—'

'She is merely idealistically young,' the older man interrupted diplomatically.

'Nothing a sound beating would not cure!' Dominic assured the other man grimly as he strode across the entrance
hall to thrust open the door to the Gold Salon, taking in at a
glance the determined expression on Caro's face as she sat
on the sofa looking up at a relaxed and nonchalant Nicholas Brown as he stood beside the unlit fireplace.

'I apologise for you having to receive our guest alone,
Caro.'

She gave a self-conscious start at the icy coldness of
Dominic's tone, one glance at the fury so clearly evident
upon his face enough to show her how displeased he was
at having returned to Brockle House to find that, despite
all his warnings, she had chosen to invite Nicholas Brown

inside when he'd had the audacity to arrive outside in his carriage some minutes earlier.

Dominic was no doubt perfectly aware that her sole purpose for inviting the other man to join her for tea, knowing him to be responsible for both Ben's death and the attack upon Lord Thorne, was to confront him with his perfidy! Something she had been just about to do when Dominic had arrived accompanied by Drew Butler.

In truth, Caro knew a certain relief in the timely arrival of the two men. Every attempt on her part to challenge the villain with his terrible deeds had been smoothly and charmingly foiled by him as he had kept up a stream of polite gossip and inanities from the moment they had entered the Gold Salon. Caro had even begun to doubt both her own and Dominic's conviction that Brown was responsible for anything more than having the misfortune to have gained a bad reputation!

'To what do we owe the pleasure of your visit, Brown?' Dominic obviously felt no such doubts as he kept the icy coldness of his gaze firmly fixed upon the older man.

Brown raised dark and mocking brows. 'I merely called to pay my respects to Mrs Morton.'

'Indeed?' Dominic's teeth showed in a predatory smile.

'I understand she was present when the fire occurred yesterday afternoon?' Brown said smoothly.

Dominic's jaw clenched. 'What of it?'

'I, of course, wished to assure myself of her good health.' Brown's smile was lazily confident. 'Women are such fragile creatures, are they not?'

It was impossible for Dominic to miss the underlying threat in that single remark. For him not to feel an icy chill in his veins at the thought of this man harming one golden hair upon Caro's head. His mouth thinned. 'Which is why men were, presumably, put on the earth to protect them.' Two could engage in this particular game of veiled threats. And when that game now so obviously involved Caro it was one that Dominic had every intention of winning.

As was to be expected, Caro was unable to stop herself from commenting on Dominic's remark. 'I am sure I am perfectly capable of protecting myself, Dominic.'

'All evidence to the contrary, my dear,' he said grimly.

Her cheeks flushed prettily. 'You—'

'I, too, am pleased to see that you are quite recovered from yesterday's ordeal, Mrs Morton,' Drew cut in tactfully.

Caro gave him a grateful smile. 'And I you.'

'Oh, I believe you will find that it's going to take more than a fire to be rid of me,' he said, at the same time shooting a telling glance in Brown's direction.

'My compliments on your lucky escape, Drew,' the other man taunted.

'Would that Ben had been so lucky,' Drew said pointedly.

Hard brown eyes glittered with satisfaction. 'Such a waste of a young life…'

'A needless waste,' Drew agreed harshly.

'It would appear that you have had a busy morning, Brown?' Dominic felt it was time to intercede, before Drew's anger became such that he spoke or acted incautiously and this situation deteriorated whilst Caro was still present. Dominic and Drew had talked of this earlier and had agreed it must not be allowed to happen; if she were not present now, the conversation would no doubt have ceased being polite long ago!

Even the thought of Caro being anywhere near when

that veneer of politeness was stripped from this situation, to reveal the ugly truth they all knew lurked beneath, was enough to send a cold rivulet of fear down Dominic's spine; he had no doubt, for all Brown looked so elegant in his perfectly tailored clothes, that the other man had a knife, or possibly even a small pistol, concealed somewhere about his person. Just as Dominic also believed that Caro would be Brown's target if this situation were to explode into violence now...

'Indeed?' Brown drawled.

Dominic nodded. 'I am informed by Ben's sister, Mrs Grey, that you have assisted her by financing tomorrow's funeral arrangements.'

He gave a dismissive shrug. 'It seemed the least I could do in the circumstances.'

'And what *circumstances* might they be?' Dominic asked.

Nicholas Brown met his gaze unblinkingly. 'Ben was my employee, and as such was loyal to me, for far longer than he was to you.'

It was tantamount to a declaration that it had been this change of loyalty on Ben's part—and no doubt on Drew's, too—which had ultimately brought about the young man's demise. That Brown would have been more than happy if both Drew and Ben had perished in yesterday's fire, as retribution for the fact that they had chosen to continue being employed by the new owner of Nick's rather than leave.

Just as Brown's visit to Caro was yet another veiled threat? That the villain had so clearly shown that he was fully aware of exactly where Caro resided now was, to Dominic's way of thinking, tangible evidence of that threat...

'I believe it is time you took your leave, Brown.' Dominic had had quite enough of even attempting to be polite to this man. 'Caro is looking a little pale. No doubt she is in need of rest following the events of yesterday and all this talk of death and funerals today.' He rang the bell for Denby.

Caro knew she might look less than perfect, but she had not, as yet, had the opportunity to say all that she wished to say to Mr Nicholas Brown! Added to which, she had been rendered almost speechless by the politeness—at least on the surface—of the conversation between the three men. Why did Dominic or Drew not just confront the man? Tell him of their suspicions and demand an explanation? It was what she had intended doing until she had found herself rendered tongue-tied by the man's smooth charm!

'Having now assured myself as to your welfare, Caro, I believe I will also take my leave,' Drew said smoothly.

But not smoothly enough that Caro was not aware of the hard edge beneath the blandness of his tone. 'No doubt I will see you again at Ben's funeral tomorrow.'

Brown raised surprised brows. '*You* will be attending?'

Caro looked at him coldly. 'But of course I shall—'

'It has yet to be decided.' Dominic was the one to cut in as he stepped forwards to lift one of Caro's hands and place it firmly in the crook of his arm so that the two of them now stood side by side as they faced Brown.

The gesture was so obviously one of possession that Caro could not help but be aware of it. Just as she was aware of the warning of Dominic's fingers firmly gripping her own as he kept her hand anchored in the crook of his arm. 'Dominic—'

'It is time to say goodbye to Mr Brown and Drew now, Caro,' he instructed her tautly.

Just as if she were a child who needed reminding of her manners! Or as if Dominic meant to silence her before she had the chance to do or say something that would totally strip away even this tense veneer of social politeness. Her mouth firmed determinedly. 'Perhaps before he leaves, I might ask Mr Brown——'

'I am sure, Caro, that whatever queries you might have for Mr Brown, they can surely wait until another day.' Those long fingers again pressed down on Caro's.

'Perhaps tomorrow at Ben's funeral?' she persevered.

Silver eyes glittered down at her in warning. 'Perhaps.'

Caro's cheeks flushed in temper. 'This is utterly ridiculous——'

'Ah, Denby.' Dominic turned to the butler as he quietly entered the room. 'Mr Brown and Mr Butler are leaving.'

'But——'

'Say goodbye to our guests, Caro.' The dangerous glitter in Dominic's eyes dared her to do anything more than that.

Much as she longed to accuse Nicholas Brown, Caro had enough wisdom to know when Dominic had been pushed to the limit of his patience. And the hard tension of his body as he stood next to her informed her that he had reached that limit some time ago.

Her parting comments to the other two men were made distractedly, her agitation now such that she could barely restrain herself.

It was a lack of restraint that Dominic clearly echoed, as he waited only long enough for Denby to close the door firmly behind himself, his wife and their departing visitors, before releasing Caro's hand and rounding on her furiously. 'What did you think you were doing by calmly inviting Brown in here? No, do not tell me, I know exactly what your intentions were!'

'Someone must confront Mr Brown—'

'And someone will,' Dominic assured her fiercely. 'But not you, Caro. *Never* you! And if you dare—so much as *dare*,' he grated, 'accuse me of behaving in a cowardly manner by not confronting him myself just now, then I must warn you, Caro, that I really will have no recourse but to administer the beating someone should have given you long ago!'

Her cheeks were pale. 'I had no intention of accusing you of being cowardly!'

'That is something, I suppose,' Dominic muttered darkly.

Caro knew him well enough now to know that he could be every bit as dangerous as Nicholas Brown if he chose to be. Nor had she missed the lethal purpose in the gaze Dominic had directed at Brown when he entered the salon a few minutes ago.

The difference between the two men was, of course, that Dominic was undoubtedly a man of honour. Of integrity. A gentleman. A gentleman who had caused her to behave as less than the lady she was from the moment they had first met!

Which thought had absolutely no place in their present conversation! 'That is not to say I understand why neither you nor Mr Butler did not challenge Mr Brown, both over the attack on Lord Thorne, and the setting of the fire that resulted in Ben's death.' A frown creased the creaminess of her brow.

'Perhaps because we were both endeavouring to protect *you*?'

'Me?'

Dominic gave a rueful shake of his head at the surprise in Caro's expression. Despite the week she had spent singing in a gentlemen's gambling club, and after all that had happened these past few days—including their lovemaking—she remained an innocent. She could not conceive, it seemed, that Nicholas Brown was more than capable of killing her where she stood, and to hell with the consequences.

Yet Dominic now feared that Brown's visit here today meant that he had decided, by implication, if not yet deed, to now turn the focus of his malevolent attentions upon Caro herself...

Chapter Seventeen

It was a threat Dominic intended taking very seriously indeed. 'I have decided, now that Brown has made it so obvious he knows of your whereabouts, that for your own safety it would be a good idea if I were to remove you immediately from London and place you at my estate in Berkshire.'

Caro's eyes widened, initially in shock, quickly followed by indignation. She had already spent a night at Blackstone House, followed by another in Brockle House, both properties owned by the Earl of Blackstone; for her to now be seen to move into his estate in Berkshire was unacceptable. Besides which, there was the added insult that Dominic had not even bothered to consult her before making this decision.

She gave a firm shake of her head. 'No.'

He became very still, his eyes narrowed to silver slits. *'No?'*

Caro shrugged her slender shoulders. 'No, Dominic. I must have a say in where I go and what I do—and this makes me feel like an unwanted relative you must needs move from house to house in order to avoid their company.'

If Caro really were a relative of his then Dominic would have put her over his knee and spanked her pretty bottom days ago. For the sheer stupidity, her complete lack of caution, in coming alone to London at all, and therefore placing herself firmly in the midst of this highly volatile situation. As it was, Dominic was currently perceived—by Brown, if by no other—as being Caro's protector. 'When it comes to the subject of your safety, Caro, I feel you must do as I ask.'

'No, Dominic, I must not.' Her unblinking gaze challenged him, her chin raised in haughty disdain. 'I have not had opportunity to tell you before this, but it is already my intention to leave London once I have attended Ben's funeral tomorrow.'

'To go where, may I ask?' Dominic glowered down at her.

'No, you may not ask—Dominic!' She protested as he reached out and took a tight grip of her wrist. 'You will not be able to force my compliance simply by the use of brute strength.' She spoke calmly and clearly, her gaze reproachful as she looked up at him.

Dominic had no wish to force her compliance or hurt her in any way. But just the thought of the likes of a man like Brown ever being in a position to cause her harm caused a painful tightening in his chest.

As did the thought of Caro leaving London. Leaving *him*…

He also wondered, if not for their present heated conversation, whether she would have even bothered to inform him of her intention to leave London, let alone confide where he might be able to find her if he wished to see her again.

If he wished to see her again?

Dominic released his grip on Caro's arm to step sharply away from her, a frown darkening his brow as he studied her between guarded lids. There was no doubting that she was a breathtakingly beautiful young woman. Or that just looking at her now in that green gown, and imagining the naked curves beneath, filled him with the need to once again make love to her. But surely that was all she was, or ever could be, to him? Just a beautiful young woman who—for the moment—he felt a need to protect? To imagine she might mean any more to him than that was unacceptable to a man who had long ago decided he did not want or need one particular woman in his life. Especially if that woman was one he might care for enough that her death would drive him to the same brink of madness his father had suffered after the death of Dominic's mother.

He shook his head. 'You know I cannot allow it, Caro.'

'Why not?' For Caro to dare to hope that he might feel some of her own regret at the thought of them parting would, she knew, be too much to ask.

He looked irritated now. 'Because Brown is still a threat.'

'To me?'

'Caro, how do you imagine Brown even knew to visit you here at Brockle House?'

Her eyes slowly widened. 'He had us followed yesterday?'

'Exactly,' Dominic bit out curtly. 'And until he is…dealt with, I must insist, if you will not agree to go to my estate in Berkshire, that you at least agree to remain at Brockle House for now.'

Caro looked at him searchingly, noting the grim determination of his expression, the light of battle in his eyes. 'You intend to deal with Mr Brown yourself, do you not?'

Dominic drew in a harsh breath, wishing not for the first time that Caro were not as astute as she was beautiful. Or so forward in voicing her shrewd opinions and observations. 'It is for the law—'

'Dominic, I have asked several times that you not treat me as a child or an imbecile!'

He sighed deeply at her obvious irritation. 'Very well, then. Yes, if the law is not enough to bring Brown to justice, then I will feel no hesitation in dealing with him myself.'

'How?'

'I think it best if you do not know the details.'

'Dominic.'

'Caro!' he exclaimed in exasperation. 'Is it not enough to know that I respect you, admire you, even like you?' he added ruefully. 'And that it is because I feel all of those things for you that I do not wish to involve you any further in this mess than you already are.'

Caro knew from the implacability of his tone that Dominic really would tell her no more on that subject. Just as she knew that having his respect, admiration and liking, whilst being secretly cherished, could never be enough for her. She wanted him to feel so much more than that. Needed him to love her in the same way she had realised she loved him. Completely. Irrevocably.

Who could have ever known that, in coming to London in this way, she would meet the man she was to fall so deeply in love with? Certainly not Caro. She had thought only to avoid being coerced into a marriage she did not want. Instead she had met the man whom she would love for the rest of her life and *he* didn't want to marry *her*…

Caro stepped away from him, her trembling hands clasped tightly together in front of her, knowing that her pride would never allow her to let him see how deeply she had fallen in love with him. 'I accept that for the moment it is best that I remain here. But I do wish to leave as soon as you feel it is safe for me to do so,' she added firmly.

Dominic looked at her between narrowed lids. 'With the intention of returning to your family?'

'Yes. And please do not ask me where or who that family is,' she said ruefully as she could see that was exactly what Dominic was about to do. 'As with your own actions concerning Mr Brown, it serves no purpose for you to know the details of my destination.'

He straightened abruptly. 'And if you need to talk to me at some point in the future?'

If she found herself with child, he meant… 'Then I will know where to find you,' Caro dismissed evenly.

Dominic sighed. 'You know, Caro, I do not have so many people I consider friends that I can simply allow one of them to just up and leave London and for ever disappear.'

Dominic thought of them as being friends?

Knowing how and why, after hearing the sad tale of his parents' deaths, Dominic shunned emotional attachments of any kind, she could not help but feel flattered that he should think of her as a friend. Unfortunately, she wanted to be so much more to him than just a friend!

'I am sure that you have many more friends than Lord Thorne, Drew Butler and myself,' she said lightly.

'Perhaps,' Dominic conceded drily. 'Osbourne and I have

just spent the past month in Venice with one of our oldest and closest friends.'

Venice?

Caro stiffened, barely daring to breathe as she looked searchingly at Dominic now. He had recently spent a month in Venice? Where Lord Gabriel Faulkner, Earl of Westbourne since the death of Caro's father, and now the guardian of all three sisters—the very same man who had sent his lawyer with the offer of marriage to one of the three Copeland sisters, without so much as having met any of them—had resided for the past two years, at least?

Caro was well aware that Venice was a large city with an even larger population, Venetians as well as other people simply visiting. Nevertheless, she could not help her feelings of disquiet at the knowledge that Dominic had just spent a month there. Where he had no doubt met and socialised with both the Venetian aristocracy and those members of English society currently residing there. Possibly including Lord Faulkner?

'Perhaps you will have the chance to meet him,' Dominic continued. 'Westbourne is due to arrive back in England himself in the next few days,' he explained at Caro's questioning glance.

Westbourne!

Caro's fears had just been realised!

Not only did Dominic know Lord Faulkner, but the two of them had obviously been close friends for a number of years. Worst of all, Dominic was expecting Westbourne to arrive back in England any day! No doubt one of the first things he would do was pay a visit to his friend, Lord

Vaughn—and Dominic had just told her that he would introduce the two of them!

Caro moved carefully over to a chair and sat down, knowing her legs were in danger of no longer supporting her. What was she to do? If, as Dominic said, he was expecting the Earl of Westbourne to arrive in England within days—possibly even today—then Caro could not afford to linger in London any longer if she wished to avoid detection, no matter what she might have assured Dominic earlier.

Not that Lord Faulkner would recognise her as anyone other than Caro Morton here in London. But she had never intended her absence from Shoreley Hall, and the separation from her beloved sisters, to be a permanent one, which meant that Westbourne must one day be introduced to his ward, Lady Caroline Copeland. If he had already been introduced to Caro Morton, the repercussions to all of them when that happened would be great indeed!

Caro had dearly wanted to attend Ben's funeral before returning to Shoreley Hall, and the thought of leaving Dominic so soon was worse than painful, but the knowledge of her guardian's imminent arrival in England meant that she had no choice but to leave immediately.

Caro Morton must cease to exist forthwith.

'Caro?'

She straightened, schooling her features into the polite social mask recognisable as Lady Caroline Copeland as she looked up and saw the concern in Dominic's expression. 'Yes?'

'Will you promise me not to leave the house unaccompanied until this matter is settled?'

She could not give such a promise and mean it. Not now. 'I trust I am not so foolish as to even attempt it now that you have alerted me to the fact that Nicholas Brown is watching my every move,' she answered.

Dominic nodded, apparently sensing none of the evasion in her reply. 'I will be out for the rest of the day, but should hopefully be back in time for us to dine together this evening.'

'I will look forward to it.' They had become almost like strangers in these past few minutes, Caro recognised heavily, Dominic's friendship with Lord Faulkner, and her knowledge of her own imminent departure from London, seeming to have severed the tenuous bonds of their own friendship.

Caro could feel the hot burn of tears in her eyes. 'I believe I will go upstairs to rest.' Dominic must be made to leave. Now. Before those threatening tears started to fall and he demanded an explanation as to the reason for them. She doubted he would appreciate hearing that it was because her heart was breaking at the very thought of being parted from him.

Now that the time had come, Dominic felt an uncharacteristic reluctance to part from Caro, even for a few hours.

Damn it, apart from the friendship he had long held with Osbourne and Westbourne, he had never been a man who allowed himself to become entangled in emotional attachments. And yet he was aware he had formed a friendship of sorts these past few days with both Drew Butler and Ben Jackson.

And he had formed a friendship with Caro, too...

A friendship that Dominic knew had come into being because he had ultimately been unable to deny the respect and admiration he felt for the courage and determination she had shown him from their very first meeting. He would feel Caro's loss all the more keenly once she was allowed to return to her home and family. But it was a friendship Dominic could not, would not, allow to control either his actions or his judgement.

He drew himself up stiffly. 'Until this evening, then.' He nodded to her before turning on his heel to stride determinedly from the room.

Caro waited only long enough to be sure that he had truly gone before she allowed the tears to fall. Hot and remorseless tears that almost brought her to her knees. At the thought of never seeing Dominic again. At the knowledge that she would never again know the warmth of being held in his arms. Kissed by him. Never again know the wonder, the beauty, of their lovemaking.

Caro cried until there were no more tears inside her to be shed. Until all that was left was the knowledge that she must leave this house immediately.

Must leave London.

And Dominic...

Once outside Dominic dismissed the carriage he and Butler had arrived in earlier, deciding that the walk to Mrs Wilson's to check on Osbourne one last time before his aunt whisked him off to the country to recover from his injuries would be far more beneficial in helping to clear his head of the disturbed thoughts that had been plaguing him ever since he had realised how deeply he would feel it when Caro left London for good.

Except Dominic's thoughts remained distracted, for the duration of his walk, and whilst he chatted with the disgruntled but resigned Osbourne. And they continued to plague him after he had taken his leave and stood outside on the pavement outside Mrs Wilson's home.

He had intended lunching at his club, before returning to Blackstone House for the afternoon to deal with estate business, leaving him free to once again spend the night at Brockle House.

Yet he did none of those things, as instead, his feet took him back in the direction of Brockle House. Back to Caro.

His behaviour was totally illogical. Totally unprecedented. He felt a longing to be with her that he knew he should strongly resist. But could not...

Just as he could not believe his own eyes as he neared Brockle House and saw Caro hurrying towards him. Alone. Dressed in her dark cloak and that unbecoming brown bonnet, which should have been consigned to the incinerator along with those unbecoming gowns, but somehow had not. And carrying the bag in which her few belongings had been packed to transport them to Brockle House.

Caro came to an abrupt halt, her eyes widening in alarm, as she saw a furiously angry Dominic striding forcefully towards her. It could not be! Dominic had gone off for the day to see to other business. He was not really here at all, was a figment of her imagination, brought about by the chasm of misery Caro had fallen into at the thought of being parted from him.

'Where do you think you are going?' The grip of his

hands on the tops of her arms felt real enough, as did the fierceness of his scowl as he glowered down at her. 'Answer me this instant, Caro!'

Dominic was real! He was really here!

Caro could not breathe. Could not think. Could only stare up into Dominic's face and know that she loved him past all bearing...

'You little fool!' He shook her, eyes glittering in the harsh handsomeness of his face as he glared down at her. 'Do you not realise the danger you have put yourself in by venturing out alone like this?'

'Why are you here?' She gave a dazed shake of her head. 'You told me you had other business to attend to for the rest of the day. You said—'

'I am well aware of what I said, Caro,' he grated. 'Just as I am aware that you *lied* to me when you said you would be resting in your rooms for the rest of the morning. You have obviously taken advantage of my absence to pack your bag and make your escape without so much as a word of goodbye!'

'I—' Caro moistened her dry lips.

'Where were you going?' Dominic demanded harshly as he shook her slightly again. 'What—?' He broke off abruptly, his eyes suddenly wide and staring.

'Dominic?' Caro could only look up at him uncomprehendingly as those silver-grey eyes turned up into his head before glazing over completely, his mouth becoming lax, and his hands losing their grip upon her arms as he began to sink slowly to the ground.

Revealing to her frightened gaze the hefty and brutish-looking man who stood behind him, some sort of cudgel raised in his hand, before something was thrown over her head to cut off all sight and she felt herself being lifted and carried away...

Chapter Eighteen

Caro had no idea how long she had been held a prisoner in this opulently furnished bedchamber. It had seemed like hours, and yet it could equally have been only minutes. Time had become unimportant to her since she had seen Dominic fall to the ground after receiving that blow to the back of his head.

None of her anguished thoughts since that time had been for herself; she was far too worried whether that blow to Dominic's head had been heavy and hard enough to kill him.

A world without Dominic was unthinkable. Unimaginable. Making a complete nonsense of any concerns Caro might have for her own welfare. She had become the prisoner of Nicholas Brown, of course. There could be no other possible explanation for what had occurred. But none of it mattered to Caro in the slightest if Dominic were now dead.

She stood up and moved restlessly around the room to end up standing in front of the window. It was barred on the outside and looked out over a walled and secluded garden, with a sheltering of surrounding trees that made it impossible for anyone in any of the neighbouring houses to see either into the garden or the house.

It was a seclusion she was already aware of, because the window had been the first place she had checked for escape, once she had managed to untangle herself from the blanket that had been kept about her as she was bundled inside a coach and transported to this house.

There had been two men inside the coach with her, and although the blanket did not allow her to see their faces, she could easily guess that one of them had struck Dominic, and the second was the man who had stood behind Caro and thrown the blanket over her head. Neither of them had deigned to answer her repeated demands during the journey to know whether or not they had killed Dominic.

So far she had seen nothing of Nicholas Brown…

Caro knew that she should be afraid of the man. That the men he employed were responsible for Ben's death and the severity of the injuries Lord Thorne had received several nights ago. That those same men might also have now slain Dominic…

And yet Caro felt too contemptuous and angry towards Brown to be in the least afraid of him. Contempt, because all of those acts had been cowardly, administered in such a way that neither Brown nor any of his men were ever in any real danger of injury themselves. Anger, because if Dominic did indeed lie dead somewhere, then Caro felt fully capable of administering that same fate to Brown, if she were given the slightest opportunity.

A choking sob rose in her throat. Dominic could not be dead! It was a possibility too horrific to even contemplate—

Caro turned sharply as she heard the key turning in the lock of the door, her chin raised proudly high, sea-green eyes full of the contempt she felt as Nicholas Brown stepped into the room.

'Mrs Morton,' he greeted with his usual relaxed charm—for all the world as if they were exchanging pleasantries in a drawing room! 'You're comfortable, I hope?' he added courteously as he remained standing in the doorway of the bedchamber.

Her chin lifted disdainfully. 'I have witnessed a man being…felled before my eyes.' Caro gathered her courage after that slight falter as she talked of the attack on Dominic, determined to show this man no weakness whatsoever. 'I have suffered being covered in a rough and smelly blanket, abducted in a coach, and held a prisoner in this bedchamber for some time. Yes, Mr Brown, I am perfectly comfortable, thank you.'

Grudging admiration entered that calculating brown gaze. 'I understand now why Blackstone became so besotted with you,' he murmured.

It was an admiration Caro did not value in the slightest. Any more than she believed Dominic had ever been besotted with her. But the thought of it was enough to give her the courage to continue in the same vein. 'Unfortunately I consider you so far beneath contempt that you do not even have the right to breathe Lord Vaughn's name.'

A tightness appeared around those brown eyes as his gaze narrowed. 'We will see how wonderful you still consider him to be when he fails to rescue you in time from my "contemptuous" clutches.'

The only part of that statement that mattered to Caro was the indication it gave that Dominic was still alive! She sagged inside. If that could only be true, if Dominic could still but live, then whether or not he succeeded in rescuing her did not matter; Caro just wanted him to be safe.

She raised scornful brows. 'Dominic is worth a hundred—no, a thousand!—of you.'

Brown scowled darkly. 'Perhaps you should wait to make comparisons as to who is the better man until after I have bedded you?'

Caro's eyes had widened before she had a chance to control her reaction to this shocking statement. 'You will not find me a willing bed partner, Mr Brown,' she assured cuttingly, her chin still raised defiantly high.

His mouth twisted derisively. 'I am counting on it, Mrs Morton,' he drawled mockingly. 'Blackstone took my prized possession from me and now I am very much enjoying the anticipation of availing myself of his,' he jeered before stepping out of the room, and relocking the door behind him.

Caro sank weakly down on to the bed, wondering how she could ever have been deceived into thinking Nicholas Brown was anything other than what he was: a low, despicable man, with no honour, or, indeed, any virtues to recommend him.

She could only hope that, if Dominic truly were still alive, he would look for her—as he surely must?—and find her, before Brown decided to carry out his threat.

'Everyone is in position, my lord.' Drew Butler spoke softly at Dominic's side as the two men stood hidden in a doorway further down the road from the house in Cheapside belonging to Nicholas Brown.

The house where Dominic hoped and prayed that he

would find Caro. Alive. And unharmed. Anything else was unacceptable to him.

What he would say and do to Caro once he had delivered her safely back at Brockle House, Dominic had not dared think of as yet. He had still not got over the shock of regaining consciousness earlier only to find Caro was nowhere to be found.

'Are you sure you are up to this, my lord?' Drew voiced his concern. 'The blow to your head was severe, and—'

'Let's get this over with, Drew,' he said grimly as he raised the two pistols in his hands ready for breaching Brown's front door. 'There will be time enough to worry about the blow I received to my head once we have found Caro and I am assured she has come to no harm at Brown's hands.' The expression on his face was enough to show what would happen to said man if Caro had been harmed in any way...

Dominic had downed a single glass of brandy earlier in order to put him back into his right senses, after which he had sent for Drew Butler, and then taken him and the men who had formerly been under his command into the study at Brockle House, in order that they might devise a plan to effect a rescue without injury to Caro.

Spending over two hours observing the comings and goings of Brown's men to his house in Cheapside, so that they might count the number of adversaries they would have to deal with once they were inside, had stretched Dominic's patience to breaking point. Enough so that now he could not wait to get inside the house and have this thing between himself and Brown over and done with once and for all.

And, far more importantly, to know that Caro was indeed safe and unharmed...

* * *

Caro felt both thirsty and hungry as she lay upon the bed, several more hours having passed without anyone offering her refreshment of any kind. Something she did not feel inclined to bring to anyone's attention when she had not seen Nicholas Brown again for that same length of time.

It was—

Caro sat up abruptly as she heard the sound of several unnaturally loud bangs, taking several seconds—and a few more of those loud bangs—before she realised that what she was hearing was gunfire.

Dominic!

She rose hastily from the bed to run across to the locked door, pressing her ear against it to see if she could hear anything of what was taking place on the other side. Men shouting. Feet running. More shots. And then an unnatural and eerie silence…

Caro stepped back from the door, unsure as to whether Dominic and the men who had accompanied him were the victors of the battle or whether it was the despicable Nicholas Brown and his men. If it was the latter—

The key was being turned in the lock!

The handle was turning.

The door being pushed open—

'Dominic!' Caro cried gladly as he stood so tall and in command in the doorway, that gladness turning to horror, and her face paling, as Caro saw the blood staining the front of his jacket and shirt. She ran across the room. 'You are hurt!'

'It is not my blood, Caro,' he had time to reassure her before his arms wrapped about her and he held her tightly against his chest.

She leant back slightly to look up at him with wide, haunted eyes. 'Is it Nicholas Brown's?'

Dominic's jaw tightened. 'We struggled, and the gun between us went off. He is dead, Caro,' he added hoarsely.

'I am glad!' she assured him fiercely. 'He meant to—he threatened to—'

'Do not think of it again, my dear.' Dominic could not bear just now to know what Brown had threatened to do to Caro if she had not been rescued. Any more than he wanted to think of the battle, the deaths, that had just occurred.

All talk, explanations, could come later. It was enough for now that he held her safely in his arms...

'The physician would not approve of you imbibing brandy so soon after receiving that severe blow to your head!' Caro stood in the doorway of the study at Brockle House as she glowered at Dominic disapprovingly.

In truth, his head was pounding worse than it had this morning. But whether the physician who had been called would have approved of his actions or not, Dominic knew that a glass of best brandy, his first since returning Caro back to Brockle House two hours earlier, was necessary if he was to get through the necessary conversation with her. Indeed, that he might need more of it before the evening was through...

It had been a difficult afternoon for all of them—explanations to be made to the representatives of the law, arrangements made for the removal of Brown's body and those of his men.

With so many witnesses to what had taken place, and Caro's own testimony of her abduction and Brown's intentions towards her, it had not been too difficult to persuade the authorities that Brown and his men were the guilty parties, and Dominic and his men merely effecting a rescue. In truth, he had a suspicion that certain members of the law were pleased to be relieved of the presence of the troublesome Nicholas Brown, once and for all.

Caro, as Dominic might have expected, had stood up wonderfully well under all the strain!

'Come in and close the door, Caro,' Dominic requested softly now as he leant back against the front of the leather-topped desk.

She stepped lightly into the study and closed the door behind her, disturbed by how ill Dominic now looked; there was a grey cast to his skin, his eyes sunken in the dark shadows above the high blades of his cheekbones. His mouth was a grimly thinned line and his jaw was clenched tensely.

'Did…the events of this afternoon disgust you?' he asked huskily.

She raised startled eyes to look at him searchingly, but was unable to read anything of his mood from his expression. 'How could I possibly feel disgust when I know that if you had not succeeded in killing Brown then it would be you and I who now lay dead?'

His mouth quirked. 'There have been several occasions when you have given me the impression you would not consider my own death to be such a bad thing.'

'I was young and silly—'

'And now you are mature and so much wiser?' he teased.

Caro felt the warmth of the colour that entered her cheeks. 'I feel…older than I was this morning, certainly.'

Dominic's frown was pained. 'I am sorry for that.'

'Why should *you* be sorry?' She looked at him quizzically. 'It is Nicholas Brown who is responsible for my new maturity, Dominic, and not you. He—if you had not rescued me, he told me that he intended to—'

Dominic stepped forwards and took her firmly into his arms. 'I have already told you that it will do you no good to think of that any more,' he urged. 'Bad enough that I have to think of it, imagine it, without knowing it hurts you, too.' His arms tightened almost painfully about her.

Caro raised her head to once again look up at him. 'Does the thought of it hurt you so badly, Dominic?'

His eyes glittered a pale silver. 'Almost as much as the knowledge that you were leaving me.'

'I was not leaving you, Dominic.' She sighed. 'I merely thought it best that I return home—'

'Without so much as a goodbye? Giving me no idea how I would ever find you again?' His expression had become fierce, those silver eyes glowing with repressed emotion as he looked down at her.

Caro swept the tip of her tongue lightly over the dryness of her lips, a hope, a dream, starting to build and grow inside her. 'Would you ever have wanted to find me again?'

'How can you even ask me that?' Dominic shook her slightly in exasperation. 'Do you not know—have you not guessed yet how much I love you?'

'What did you say?' Caro hardly dared to believe the emotions she could now read in those glowing silver eyes. Warmth. Admiration. Love!

'I love you, Caro,' he repeated huskily. 'Do you think, after all that has happened, that if I were to get down on my knees and beg, you might one day be able to love me in return and consider becoming my wife?'

Her cheeks warmed as she remembered the occasion

upon which she had said those words to him. 'As I recall, you had just finished telling me that our lovemaking was a mistake—'

'Then it was a most wonderful, glorious mistake!' he assured her fiercely as he cupped the sides of her face between gentle hands. 'I have been a fool, Caro. An arrogant fool. My only excuse—if there can ever be one!—is that I have never met a woman like you before. Never known any woman with your courage, your generosity of spirit, your honesty. I love you truly, Caro, and if you could one day learn to love me in return, I promise you I will love you for the rest of our lives together. Will you, Caro? Will you give me the chance to show you how much I love you? A chance to persuade you into learning to love me?' he added less certainly.

It was that uncharacteristic uncertainty that convinced Caro she could not be dreaming, after all; even in a dream she would not have bestowed uncertainty upon a man she knew to be always confident and sure, of both his own emotions and those around him!

And yet Dominic was not sure of her and seemed to have no idea that she had fallen in love with him, too. 'My dear...' her voice was gentle, tentative '... I am already in love with you—'

'My darling girl!' Dominic swept her ecstatically up into his arms before claiming her mouth with his.

Caro was still so overwhelmed by his declaration of love and his proposal of marriage, that for several long and pleasurable minutes all she could do was return the passion of his kisses.

It was some time later before her sanity returned. 'I realise that the Earl of Blackstone could not possibly marry a woman such as Caro Morton—'

'I can marry whom I damned well please,' he told her with a return of his usual arrogance. 'And I choose to marry you, if you will have me,' he added determinedly. 'I do not care who or what you are, Caro. Or what you are running away from. I love you. And it is my dearest wish—my only wish—to make you my wife.'

This, more than anything else, finally convinced Caro of the depth of Dominic's love for her. He was a lord, an Earl, and yet he was proposing marriage to a woman he had only known as a singer in a gambling club. A woman he had already made love to. Twice!

She chewed briefly on her bottom lip. 'I should tell you that my mother ran away with her lover when I was a child, and was later shot and killed by him when he caught her in the arms of yet another lover.'

Dominic's thumb moved lightly across her bottom lip, his eyes ablaze with the love he claimed to feel for her. 'I have said I do not care about your past, my love, and I truly do not,' he vowed. 'Besides, you are not responsible for your mother's actions.'

'Any more than you are to blame for the death of your own mother.'

Dominic released his breath in a deep sigh. 'I have always felt responsible…'

Caro gently touched his cheek with her fingertips. 'Tell me what really happened.'

He gave a pained wince. 'I do not believe I could bear it if, once I have done so, you decided you did not love me, after all.'

'It will not happen,' she vowed with certainty. 'Dominic,

I know you to be a man who is honest and true. A man who cares deeply for others in spite of himself—Lord Thorne, Drew, Ben, myself, to name only four. I absolutely refuse to believe that you would ever have harmed your own mother.'

'I hope you still think that once I have told you what happened.' Dominic kissed her slowly and lingeringly before speaking again. 'I went away to school when I was twelve years old. I was not a good pupil. I resented being sent away, and got into all manner of scrapes in an attempt to be sent home again. I do not even remember what the last one was.' He grimaced. 'Only that it resulted in my mother having to travel to the school shortly after the Christmas holidays in order to stop the headmaster from expelling me.'

Caro could hear his heart beating rapidly in his chest, the harshness of his breathing as he was obviously beset by the memories that had haunted him into adulthood. 'I love you, Dominic,' she encouraged gently.

His arms tightened about her as he continued. 'Her coach slipped on the icy roads and into an even icier river. The doors became stuck fast and she could not get out as the water—'

'Do not say any more!' Caro sat up and placed her fingertips over his lips as she gazed down at him. 'You were a child, Dominic. A child who felt hurt and rebellious because he felt he had been sent away from those he loved. You were no more responsible for the death of your mother or your father than—than I am.'

Strangely, as Dominic looked up into Caro's compassionate and love-filled eyes, all of the guilt, the feeling that he was unworthy of being loved, quietly and for ever slipped away.

She shook her head. 'It is sad that your father felt he could not go on living without her but—loving you as I do, I believe I know something of how he must have felt,' she added shyly; if Dominic really had been killed earlier today, then Caro knew she would have found it difficult to go on living, too...

He gave a choked groan as he pulled her tightly against him and buried his face in her hair. 'How was I ever lucky enough to find you, Caro? How?'

Caro did not want him to be sad any more; he had already suffered enough, believed himself unworthy of love for long enough. 'But you do not know yet whom you have found,' she reminded him teasingly.

He raised his head to smile at her. 'First tell me that you will marry me, whoever you are.'

'I will.'

'Caro...' Dominic kissed her for several more love-filled minutes, the happiness on his face when he at last raised his head, making him look almost boyish as he grinned down at her.

'But before that can happen,' Caro murmured ruefully, 'you will have to obtain the approval of my guardian.'

Dominic's smile faded slightly. 'Your guardian?'

'I am afraid so.'

He frowned. 'Tell me who this guardian is and I will go to him immediately, assure him that I am a reformed character since meeting you and solicit him for his permission to marry you.'

'It is not necessary for you to go to him.' Caro's eyes glowed with laughter. 'I believe that he is coming to you.'

'To me?' Dominic frowned his confusion. 'But how—?'

His eyes widened as he became still. *'Westbourne?'* he breathed in disbelief.

'I am afraid so,' Caro admitted.

Dominic stared down at her, absolutely dumbstruck for several long seconds, and then he began to smile, and then finally to laugh. 'Westbourne!' He sobered suddenly. 'It is because I had told you I was expecting him to arrive in England any day that you were leaving London so hurriedly earlier,' he realised incredulously.

'Yes.'

'What I should have added is that Gabriel does not intend to remain in London, but travel almost immediately to Shoreley Hall.'

'Oh dear!' Caro cringed now at the thought of what her sister Diana would have to say to Dominic's friend when he arrived.

Dominic seemed to suffer no such worries as he chuckled, once more diverted by the thought that he had stolen a march on his friend and whipped one of his possible choices of bride out from under his nose. 'And which Lady Copeland will I have the pleasure of making my wife?'

'Caroline—I am the second daughter.'

'And you decided to run away to London after refusing to even contemplate becoming Westbourne's bride?'

She gave a delicate shudder. 'I could not possibly marry a man I do not love.'

'And your sisters? Have they run away, too?'

'Oh, no, I am sure they have not.' Caro shook her head, firmly pushing away the flicker of doubt in her mind about that girl in the park who had looked so like Elizabeth. 'I am the rebellious one, I am afraid.'

'Something I will be grateful for until the day I die,' Dominic assured her lovingly.

Dominic loved her just as much as Caro loved him—and she was blissfully certain that he would obtain his friend's permission for the two of them to marry as soon as it could be arranged.

She wound her arms about his neck as she arched up into him. 'Would you care to show me how much you are grateful, Dominic?'

'Gladly!' he groaned as his head lowered and his mouth once again captured hers, the two of them quickly forgetting everything and everyone else but the love they felt for one other, now and for always.

* * * * *

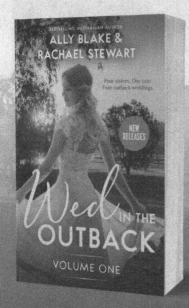
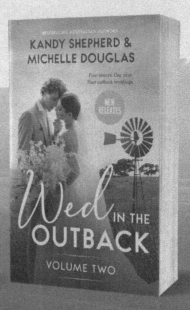

Subscribe and fall in love with a Mills & Boon series today!

You'll be among the first to read stories delivered to your door monthly and enjoy great savings.

WE SIMPLY LOVE ROMANCE

MILLS & BOON